WHITE MAN'S COTTON

R. W. SOMERTON

WHITE MAN'S COTTON

jesperson publishing

100 Water Street
PO Box 2188
St. John's, NL
A1C 6E6
www.jespersonpublishing.nf.net

National Library of Canada Cataloguing in Publication

Somerton, Randy
White man's cotton / by Randy Somerton.

ISBN 1-894377-06-0
I. Title.

PS8637.O45W43 2004 C813'.6 C2004-902464-7

Interior Design & Layout: Rhonda Molloy

Cover Design: Freak Design

Editors: Tamara Reynish, Jocelyne Thomas

This is a work of fiction. The views and opinions expressed therein represent the fictitious nature of the work and do not necessarily represent the views and opinions of the Copyright Holder, Publisher or any of their respective affiliates or employees. Any resemblance of real people and events to the characters and incidents depicted in this work is coincidental.

This novel contains explicit language and is not recommended for younger readers.

Printed in Canada.

This book is dedicated with love in memory
of our foster son,
Leo.

His was the genuine heart, the essence of good in all mankind.

CONTENTS

THE TABLES HAVE TURNED

chapter one

FOR the most part, Lance Forrest was an average Joe. Several years ago, however, Lance's life took on a new direction. It was a direction he had no control over, a direction that to this day still gives him nightmares. Lance Forrest had unwillingly become, as did many before him, a white slave to an elite and powerful group of African Americans; black men and women who were seeking revenge on members of the white race who openly displayed hatred and discrimination towards blacks.

To a large degree, this is his story, and the facts recounted here are based on his recollection of the events as they unfolded. Some of the details provided are based strictly on his personal observation. However, much of the information comes from others who were also captured and enslaved. The final pieces of this story came together as a result of the police investigation and the court proceedings that marked the closing of this chapter in his life. To fully understand this tragic, life altering experience, we must start at the center of it all, "White Man's Cotton."

. . .

As he bent over to complete the last few pickings of the White Man's Cotton, the pain in his hands suddenly grew more intense. Lance had vowed from day one that he would never allow them to see him cry. Looking at the first two fingers on his right hand, he could see tiny portions of bone fragments, bones that were protruding from his aching knuckles.

The colors on his hand were a mixture of brown, greenish-blue, white, and red. The brown was the dirt that, over the course of several months, had grained deeply into his skin. The greenish-blue was a spotted mixture of bruises that disappeared and reappeared, as one wound healed and another began. The white was bone, showing right through the broken skin, mixed in with the dried red blood.

He wanted the pain to go away. He only wished that things could be as they once were, before he was brought to this place. The pain was a combination of mental fatigue and physical hurt, but at that moment the physical part far outweighed the mental anguish that was increasing with each passing moment of each passing day.

He looked at the ground directly between his soiled shoes. Even with partially blurred vision, he could see insects crawling and sliding through the soil. He'd learned not to be squeamish. Whether they crawled over his feet or scurried down his back, this had become the least of his worries. He slowly looked at the remaining buckets to be filled. His eyes returned to his blood stained hands. He knew that before he could rest, or tend to his damaged hands, he had to finish filling two more ten-gallon buckets with the mushrooms that the slaves were cultivating in the underground. While his body was weak and his mind demanded rest, he was not allowed to stop until this task was finished.

He found himself, on many a day, looking around these pitiful surroundings; checking out his enclosure, staring up at the ceiling or at the walls. He often let his mind wander aimlessly and imagined that it was a cool evening. The sky was dark. It was beautiful, with a few stars glimmering. These daydreams were always short-lived. Suddenly, reality would set back in. He would once again realize that he was entombed several hundred feet underground. He was back in the cavern that contained tunnels and passages more complex than any maze.

From what his fellow slaves told him, this structure used to be a fully operational mining facility. Years ago, miners worked in these tunnels, digging for iron ore, which was no longer as popular a commodity as it had been thirty years earlier. The mines were eventually sold and had since become a prison for the white slaves.

The cavern was under an island, a tropical paradise, somewhere in the middle of the Indian Ocean and was completely isolated from the rest of the world. Each white slave who arrived had a different story on how they came to be there. They knew the island was isolated because they couldn't see land anywhere. No one had ever heard or seen another boat, plane or sign of life apart from themselves or those who held them captive. There were only two ways to gain access to the island, by boat or by plane. Of course, leaving was another story.

There was a state of the art, scientific research laboratory in the basement of the main house. The laboratory was used to research the organic compounds found in mushrooms and to create supplementary health care products using these natural raw materials. This elaborate business venture was called, "Salvation's Chemical and Research Facility." This company, however, was a decoy to mask its real purpose, so as not to attract attention.

The house, or more appropriately, the mansion, was two stories high and contained over sixty elegant rooms. It was a magnificently constructed building of such grandeur and size that royalty would be envious of its detail. The entire mansion was crafted in white marble and gleaming polished brass, and contained rooms full of art; paintings and statues that were brought, stolen or commissioned from the who's who of the art world.

There were also several rows of townhouses on the island, each one built and equipped with the best of everything, both inside and out. All of the structures had beautifully landscaped gardens that a select few slaves tended to with great care. When the masters, as they demanded to be called, lost a gardener, another slave would replace him. All of the slaves who were selected to maintain the gardens were given the necessary training and had to adhere to strict guidelines. Because of the captor's strive for perfection, the gardens were immaculate at all times.

New arrivals to the island were either dropped off at the landing strip or at the wharf. Every one arrived in chains and was usually decorated with red stripes, a result of having been beaten repeatedly with a half-inch rubber hose. Although, it only hurt after one lash, during the whipping, the slaves had a tendency to pass out.

There were many rules on the island. White slaves only spoke when spoken to and they always addressed and answered their black masters with respect. These white slaves were the chosen ones—chosen to pay for the sins of their forefathers, chosen to suffer because of actions taken years ago, chosen to atone for the crimes of those who enslaved and profited from blacks.

The tables had turned. This group of vengeful blacks had done the unthinkable: They forced white men, women and even children into slavery. Whites were isolated, trapped and now experiencing the same pain, torture and suffering as black people had endured decades ago. The masters populated White Man's Cotton with white people from modern day society who openly displayed hatred towards any member of the black race. It was here that the life they had known ended and the reconditioning process began.

Once a month, a person who wished to leave the island was given that chance. The slaves quickly discovered that this was not an option worth taking. One day, the slave population got an opportunity to see an escape attempt on a closed circuit monitor in one of the caves. However, their captors normally shut off the monitor just seconds before the escapee was caught. In the past, the slaves never got the opportunity to see what fate had in store for these individuals, but because none of them ever returned, they'd assumed it wasn't good.

The only potential escapee that had ever sparked hope in the slaves of the underground was a young man by the name of Frank Power. He was a natural born athlete at twenty-nine years of age, who was ranked second in the world in the five-hundred meter dash prior to his arrival on the island. He was also the tenth slave to take up the offer of a chance at freedom.

On the morning of April 14, 2017, the slaves awoke to the ringing of the alarm. This meant one of three things: someone had taken the challenge, someone had disobeyed the rules, or someone had actually attempted to escape. Either way, all slaves had to assemble in one of the main caverns at the sounding of the alarm.

Once Frank had been removed from his sleeping quarters, two of his captors guided him to the surface. On the surface, the monitor was turned on for all to see. Frank was given the usual five-minute head start. The rule was that if he could make it either to the landing or to the wharf, or if he could get off the island alive, he would not be shot, beaten, attacked, or harmed in any way.

The daylight, as beautiful as it was in these tropical surroundings, cut your eyes in two as they tried to adjust to the sun's rays. An escapee could lose about one minute of his head start while his eyes adjusted to the bright sun. When trapped underground, the beautiful outdoors actually proved to be a hindrance to any escape attempt.

Finally, Frank's pupils adjusted to the bright sun and he headed towards the thickest portion of woods. He continued to outmaneuver all of the captors sent after him. With each bullet fired, the slaves' hearts beat much faster. At the same time, their breathing slowed to a snail's pace. They couldn't help but continue to watch in total amazement. Each of the slaves hoped that, in their hearts, Frank would be the one to make it. None of the slaves were sure if the masters would keep their word, but his progress instilled hope, and in that place any amount of hope was better than none at all.

The gathered slaves were puzzled as to why Frank was not going in the direction of either the landing or the wharf. He had backtracked and was heading deeper into the woods. They presumed that Frank didn't trust what the masters had told him, and that hiding in the woods would be the only effective way for him to escape. For quite some time, Frank was out of camera range. While there were security cameras surrounding the perimeter and all open areas on the island, there were no cameras in the thick of the woods. The only objects currently visible on any of the monitors were scenery and several captors. Some were holding guns, some had whips and others had steel pipes.

Finally, after what seemed like forever, Frank appeared on the screen running for all he was worth through a clearing in the woods. Those who were charged with catching Frank received regular updates on their two-way radios. Frank was unknowingly heading right towards one of these men. Just ahead of him was a huge tree. It was about seven feet in diameter and about thirty-five feet high. As he was about to take a turn past this tree, out jumped a guard named Jeromy. He had taken Frank totally by surprise.

Jeromy and Frank were equally matched at about five-foot nine and around one hundred and ninety pounds. Jeromy was dressed in army pants and a bright red strap shirt, and was holding a leather whip, which he flicked about skillfully. He was just as talented with a whip as a magician or clown was in making balloon animals.

Both men looked directly at each other with a combination of hatred and determination. Frank seemed the most determined of the two, for he had the most to lose. Frank knew that he didn't have much time. Soon other guards would show up and he would be outnumbered. Jeromy raised his whip over his head and lashed out at Frank. It hit its mark, right over the left shoulder and half way down Frank's back. Frank clenched his teeth, while trying to dodge the repeated lashes.

Jeromy was starting to show signs of severe frustration with the determination and guts that Frank displayed during the confrontation. While Jeromy continued with his onslaught against Frank, he didn't really notice how close he had moved towards the gigantic tree. To both men's surprise, the whip struck a branch and curled around it several times. Jeromy was momentarily distracted, which was all Frank needed. Frank immediately dove into Jeromy's stomach, using his head and right shoulder as a battering ram. He knocked Jeromy down and the two rolled around on the ground, hitting each other. Jeromy then got Frank in a headlock and tried to cut off his air supply. Frank, using all the strength he could muster, lifted his opponent up. He had wrapped his arms around his aggressor's legs and in one forceful thrusting motion, managed to throw Jeromy directly overhead, slamming him to the ground. Jeromy landed on the flat of his back and had the wind knocked out of him. As he tried to regain his composure and get up, Frank jumped him from behind. He then wrapped both of his arms under Jeromy's neck and straddled his legs around his enemy's waist to secure his leverage. Frank clung to Jeromy's body like a wart to a finger. Jeromy struggled for several minutes, stumbled backwards, and slammed Frank into a tree. He tried to loosen his grip, but to no avail. He then dropped to the ground, trying once more to unlock himself from Frank's grip. Frank would not let go, for he knew what would happen to him if he did. He continued to squeeze as hard as he could.

Moments prior to taking Jeromy's life, Frank whispered into his ear, "I'm sorry, man. It has to be you or me. May God forgive the both of us for the sins we have committed."

With that, Jeromy's head slumped to one side. Frank looked at the blank frozen stare that had now covered the man's eyes. Hastily, he pushed himself away, sending his aggressor's face to the ground.

Frank heard voices moving closer to him. They were gaining ground. The slaves still watching Frank on the monitor saw a look of deep sadness on his face before he continued his escape.

Two guards came across the lifeless body of their comrade. One of the men radioed headquarters to inform them about Jeromy's death. Filled with anger, the remaining hunters were now out for revenge. Each of them split up to extend the search. Headquarters had announced that whoever caught Frank would receive a bounty of one hundred thousand dollars. Frank made it to a small river that lead into a swimming hole. He was hot, sore, hungry, and thirsty. He dipped his head into the swimming hole and felt instant relief. The cool water that ran down his straight black hair and bounced off his back restored Frank's worn-out body and sent cold shivers up his neck. It gave him the energy to continue onwards.

Suddenly, a guard jumped Frank from behind and landed with his knees to the small of Frank's back. The force of the hit was crushing. The man grabbed Frank by the back of his hair and pushed his head below the cool water. Pain and fear replaced the soothing feelings the water had provided him only moments earlier.

The guard was huge. Not particularly in good shape, as he carried nearly three hundred pounds of flab. As Frank was struggling for air, he knew just how Jeromy felt when he struggled to take his last few breaths. Frank used the guard's weight and the muddy ground surrounding the swimming hole to his advantage. The fat brute had lost his grip while struggling to hold Frank down and subsequently slid off Frank's back, landing directly in the water. Frank was practically standing upright before the big boy even had the chance to react.

He managed to reach out and grab Frank's left leg. Frank knew that he would never be able to handle someone so big. This was even more apparent to him when the kicks he landed to the big man's face with his free leg had no effect. All it accomplished was to enrage the three hundred pound man to his boiling point. The big brute was now on one knee, about to retaliate against Frank. Frank's only line of defense was to bring this tub of lard down fast and run like hell. Kicks to the face and chest were completely ineffective, so Frank lifted his free leg and landed a perfect shot to the groin. The man fell back into the water like a cannon ball. He flailed and moaned in agony, giving Frank a second opportunity to run.

The slaves who were still watching all wondered how much more Frank could endure. By this time, two additional men wielding guns were in hot pursuit. Each man was determined to capture Frank. The latest orders were to shoot him in the leg to slow him down so they could then beat him for killing their friend.

Frank's journey was coming to an end. He suddenly found that he had nowhere to run. Just slightly ahead of him were jagged cliffs. With no time to turn back or find an alternate route, the only option remaining was to plummet over the cliffs to the waters below. Frank blessed himself and without hesitation, he jumped. His descent to the waters below was magnificent! He drifted gracefully, not like someone falling, but like an Olympian, diving for the gold in perfect formation. It only took him seconds to hit the water but to the slaves watching, it seemed like forever. From the closed circuit monitors, they all watched the water, waiting for him to emerge from the ocean's grasp. Suddenly, two hands, then two arms, quickly followed by a head rose from the water. Frank began to swim out to sea the very second his body broke the surface. If the masters kept their word as they'd originally promised there would be a glimmer of hope for those remaining. Secretly, the underground slaves applauded Frank. Slight smiles swept over their faces.

However, their smiles quickly turned to frowns. On the monitor, the slaves watched as a boat moved slowly in Frank's direction. The men on the boat had no guns, nor did they touch Frank. They merely pulled along side him, cheering and clapping as he continued to swim.

Frank had accomplished the impossible task of getting off of the island, the task his captors were so sure could never be done. It seemed their secure little island was not as tight as they had bragged it was on many different occasions.

The men on the boat followed Frank for several minutes. They didn't interfere with his progress. Maybe this was because they were overcome with the fact he had gotten so far, or didn't figure he would make the distance. They probably assumed he would drown.

Their intentions soon became clear. The boat increased in speed and moved two-hundred feet ahead of Frank. The individuals on the boat were acting strangely. Much to the confusion of the slaves watching the episode unfold, some of the guards on board were dancing and singing.

A couple of men on the boat were cutting up fish from an earlier catch. They placed the heads, bodies and guts of the fish into coolers. One of the fish gutters then picked up a full cooler and dumped its contents over the side of the boat. A second cooler, then a third followed. Several huge red spots tainted the radiant greenish blue waters. Within minutes fins approached from various directions. To the horror of the slaves, the waters were swarming with sharks.

Frank, while startled, didn't panic. Rather, he stopped swimming and looked about. He then swam slowly towards the closest predator. The slaves all guessed that he knew the end was near and he couldn't or wouldn't struggle any longer. Frank could hold his own in a fight with any man, but he must have known he was clearly out of his element against a shark.

It took only about twenty seconds or so before Frank's body actually went under the water.

Their captors had kept their word. They had promised to not lay a hand on Frank if he made it off the island, and they didn't. Sea creatures had finished off Frank instead.

The slaves were ordered to the mess hall for their morning slop, which they had to cook themselves. Food was limited in both quantity and variety. They ate rice four to five days a week. Some days, they were given bits of leftover fish. Occasionally, they got to eat mushrooms and stale bread, if they were really lucky.

Following the first meal of each day, which was often their last, the slaves were herded out to start the day's work. Each one had to check the roster for their daily assigned workload.

The lucky ones went up top and worked around the main house or the surrounding townhouses. Some worked inside the main house, including a few of the white female slaves who were in charge of domestic duties. These assignments provided plenty of fresh air for the slaves, who also got to pick from the scattered crop of wild berries growing in different patches throughout the island. Those that worked on the surface were much healthier looking than those who didn't.

Lance was among the group of slaves who were assigned to pick mushrooms; he had never been sent up top to work. The mushroom pickers worked in what was referred to as, "the Cotton Fields," picking the White Man's Cotton. The emotional blow of Frank's death coupled with a disgusting breakfast left Lance feeling very weak. His hands hurt from being ripped apart each time they got caught in the barbed wire that covered the tops of the bedded mushrooms; beds that were lined up for what seemed like an infinity. He wanted to ignore the pain, but didn't have the will power to do so.

Avery Hawkins, the headmaster, was "the Man;" the one most captives didn't cherish meeting. He was the son of Thomas J. Hawkins, the warden and founder of White Man's Cotton.

Avery was one mean bastard who was in charge of Section 34, Lance's designated section. He was in his mid twenties, and stood at six-foot, ten inches. He weighed in at a massive two hundred and ninety five pounds, all of it muscle. His entire body was as firm as the steel pipe he was so overly fond of using. He always wore skintight clothes to show off his muscles and to compliment his awesome physical presence. He was ultimately the most vicious and feared of all the masters who guarded the island.

The last man who confronted Avery received a blow across the mouth with a steel pipe. Following the smack, the crunching noise made from the smashing of his victim's pearly white teeth was heard throughout the entire cavern. Screams of agonizing pain echoed loudly for hours. Everyone felt the pain as the screams continued.

It occurred as a slave who had just finished picking mushrooms, slipped while carrying his load and spilled his mushrooms all over the cavern floor. The man became fed up and kicked the fallen bucket with all of his might. The bucket drifted through the air and came down, bouncing directly in Avery's path.

Avery kicked the bucket back towards the foolish man who had snapped. As the bucket landed next to him, he picked it up and threw it back at Avery with as much force as he could muster, while cursing at his section master.

Avery raised his forearms and blocked the bucket as it flew towards him. He wasted no time in making his way over to where the poor soul was standing. The next thing they knew, Avery hit the man in the face with a steel pipe.

No one was allowed to comfort or help the injured man. He had committed sins against the master, which were forbidden in the underground. He had stood up against Avery and swore at him. But moreover, he had the foolhardiness to challenge the authority of one of the master's sons. He would have to suffer alone.

Trying to ignore the injured man's moans, Lance looked at his own full buckets. His fingers were numb. He had to bring his completed daily allotment over to Avery for final inspection. Slowly, he moved towards him with his head hanging low. Master Avery always looked at Lance with pure hatred in his eyes and Lance couldn't bear that look today.

Lance saw Avery as an alien. He was evil and destructive, similar to the vicious alien forces he had seen so often in movies. Lance felt that no human being could possess that much evil or hatred. To him, Avery's soul was the same color as his skin, black ebony, blacker than the ace of spades, and deeper than that of a black hole.

Avery watched Lance's approach and through a dirty grin he roared, "Head back to your hole now, little white trash. Tomorrow will be here shortly and dumb white fucks like you need rest. You got to be the weakest, most pathetic stinking white boy I've ever come across. I expect twice the effort from you tomorrow. Do you understand what I'm saying, fool?"

Lance responded respectfully, "Yes sir."

He understood his place and role all too well. He did whatever was requested of him without question, without expression.

His living quarters was a twelve by sixteen room that he shared with six other men. It used to be seven, but after this morning, Frank Power wasn't coming back.

Lance's roommates were Larry Howard, a college professor, Robert Lawlor, a police officer, his partner George Williams, Don Snow, a Ku Klux Klan leader from South Carolina, Harry Barbour, a professional wrestler, and Jean-Luc LeClaire, a lawyer from the New York City law firm of Bracket, Grant and Craft.

The last occupant of this cell was Lance Forrest himself. He had been a professional and lifetime student. He was never sure what to do with his life, but he'd never dreamed of anything like this. After eight years of university, studying everything from Physical Education to the Arts to Physics, he ended up a slave, forced to pick mushrooms.

Lance and his roommates all had their own story about why they had been chosen to live in White Man's Cotton, and of their capture, transport and subsequent arrival. Lance was not really one of the chosen ones. His capture was a mistake. He understood from the stories his roommates told why they were chosen, and to a certain degree, he understood why they might have been selected. His enslavement was the result of an error on someone's part for which he was now paying the consequences.

Lance often thought to himself during the quiet times of his ordeal. He had lots of time to think about such things as discrimination, diversity, indifferences, and hatred in general. He was also an individual who sought to understand why people acted they way they did.

Many times during the wee hours of the morning, his roommates overheard him whispering softly to himself, "Hatred is a horrible thing. The world seems to revolve around it. Very few individuals are without some form of hatred in their souls. I wish I understood why some people act as they do, and why they are unable to accept others of a different race, creed or belief."

Often times, he would stop whispering in mid-stream and fall back asleep. His roommates concluded that he was losing his mind, and for the most part, they totally ignored him. It wouldn't be until much later in their lives that the surviving slaves of the underground came to understand that this was Lance's way of dealing with his environment. He may have been weak physically, and at times he may have appeared even weaker mentally, but in effect he was a contemplator. And it was this trait that helped him survive his years in captivity.

Lance also thought about what his roommates had told him over the years, the stories about their lives in the real world. In their twelve by sixteen room, they revealed almost everything; stories, hopes and aspirations, but especially that which contributed to their captivity. They also provided similar accounts about the colossal black man involved with each of their abductions.

THE CATCHER

chapter two

IT was one God-awfully hot day outside! The only escape from the heat was to seek shelter inside. Air conditioning was something no one could live without. Only if you were lucky enough to work in a tightly sealed structure, could you escape the heat.

Henry's Café was set in the middle of one of the busiest business districts in the city of New York. It was three city blocks from the Page University School of Law and two blocks from the United States Court of Appeals for the Federal Circuit.

The clientele who frequented the joint consisted mainly of lawyers, their clients, students, and various others who worked or went to school within walking distance. The food was good and cheap. It was a great place for lawyers to treat their clients and students to hang out in for hours on end, sipping coffees and tasting many different types of espressos and cappuccinos.

It was probably one of very few eateries left in the city of New York, where five dollars could buy you a sandwich, your choice of a drink and a slice of homemade pie. Henry's was the best. It looked like a place from an earlier era. There were no tables, no salad bars, no stereo systems or speakers. Booths lined both sides of the café, each with a mini jukebox set on continuous play. At three o'clock in the afternoon on this particular day, business had slowed down; only five patrons and three staff remained.

Henry was the short order cook and owner. He was a grumpy fellow somewhere in his mid to late fifties. The two waitresses, Shirley and Anne, had worked with Henry for many years. Both women were from the old school, very set in their ways and used to doing things as they had been done for most of their adult life. They were lower middle class, probably two of the hardest working ladies in New York City.

Two of the patrons were young female university students. They came here on a regular basis to study and chat about professors, course loads, peers, and life in general. The tee shirts they each wore proudly displayed their school's crest. They were having a blast, laughing at the elderly gentleman who was sitting in the corner booth. He must have been extremely tired. He was doing everything he could to stay awake. His head was bobbing up and down and it looked to them like he was going to land face first in his cherry pie any minute. Every now and then, he would regain his composure and look at the girls with a silly wide grin on his face. This, in turn, only made the girls laugh louder.

The only other customers left in the café were lawyers. Jean-Luc LeClaire and his partner, Joseph Morgan, of the law firm of Bracket, Grant and Craft, specialized in harassment cases. Their firm had the best reputation for clearing clients, which often surrounded them in controversy. Their cases were usually against huge corporate managers and always involved large settlements. Regardless of their client's guilt, or how much evidence there was against them, the firm was very proud of their eighty-five percent success rate. As a result, the harassment victim suffered twice: once from the criminal actions they had endured at the hands of the perpetrator, and again from seeing the guilty party get off.

Joseph Morgan was running late. He was due back in court in less than twenty minutes. He paid his bill, included a generous tip, and proceeded to leave the café and his friend behind. On his way out, he came face to face with one of the biggest black men he had ever seen. The stranger shoved him aside as he entered. Joseph glanced backwards and hesitated for a split second. He was deciding whether he would comment on the man's rudeness. Running late for court, he continued on, avoiding confrontation.

Once inside the café, the huge stranger sat in the booth closest to the entrance. His abnormally huge oval-shaped head was clean-shaven, and in perfect proportion to the rest of his body. Due to the fluorescent lighting, his head seemed to glisten. His blue jeans were brand new, judging from their apparent stiffness and dark shade. A long black coat covered the remainder of his body. He stood out because of his immense size and the fact that he was wearing a long black coat on such a hot, muggy day.

The man acted nonchalantly, just sitting in his booth. He was quiet and alert, glancing on occasion around the room with a completely blank stare on his face. He didn't even blink. Nor did he show any visible signs of tension or nervousness.

Shirley and Anne were looking at one another, motioning silently. Each was trying to force the other to serve this jewel. Under normal circumstances, strange customers weren't a problem, however, both ladies were experiencing cold shivers that began from the moment this man walked through the front door.

The two young students lost interest in the old man. Their attention was drawn to the café's latest patron. They were in awe at the power and presence the black stranger demanded. The two behaved flirtatiously, grinning and making eye contact each time he glanced their way.

Anne had lost the face off with her co-worker. She moved slowly in the black man's direction.

Once she got to his booth, she looked directly at him and with a slightly nervous smile said, "What's your preference, sir?"

He looked at her and in a very deep monotone voice, he muttered, "Coffee."

Anne responded, "Would you like sugar, milk or cream with your coffee, sir?"

He shouted, "I like nothing with white in it lady!"

Anne just looked at him with her eyebrows squeezed slightly together. She pretended not to notice his rudeness and headed back towards the main counter. Under her breath, Anne whispered to Shirley what he said. Shirley listened attentively as she poured up the coffee.

She passed it to Anne and whispered, "What a pig!'"

Shirley chuckled to herself as she went about cleaning off the countertop. She imagined herself spitting in his coffee. But, despite the surroundings they worked in and the assholes they had to serve over the years, they considered themselves professionals. Usually they classed dorks in suits in this category, those men and women who often came in from the numerous law offices that surrounded the café. One of the main reasons they had put up with and treated those individuals with respect for all those long years was the tips. More often than not, the tips some of these jerks left were high, and at week's end, they far outweighed their weekly salaries. Both women needed every cent they could get. Anne needed the money to raise her three teenage girls. Shirley was a widow with no children to support, but more medical bills then one cared to imagine.

These waitresses put up with a lot of shit from a variety of people over the years and rarely complained. When they encountered a difficult situation, they were well equipped to deal with it. Both women had no problem dishing out twice as much as they took in.

Anne often thought about her girls when she was having a bad day or when she was dealing with overbearing customers. Her girls were her reason for living and the only reason she came to work each day.

As Anne returned to the booth, she placed the coffee cup down in the middle of the table. Some of the coffee spilled over the rim of the cup and splattered on the table. She went to move the cup to wipe up the spill, but was stopped.

Her patron placed his hand over the top of the coffee and said abruptly, "Leave it be."

Anne did as he commanded and headed back towards the counter. She had an uneasy feeling.

She looked at Shirley and in a very faint voice, she whispered, "I think you better tell Henry that we have a big weirdo out here. I wouldn't doubt it if he plans to rob the joint."

Shirley went towards the kitchen. It was situated behind the counter through a set of double swinging doors. She was but a few feet from the kitchen when all hell broke loose.

The stranger in the long black coat stood up and threw his coffee at Shirley. She felt the breeze as the cup drifted past her head. Hot steaming coffee splattered everywhere, but Shirley received the brunt of the hot liquid across her left arm.

In the same instant, the large man looked at Shirley with his eyes aglow.

He yelled viciously, "Do you folks actually think all black people are weirdoes and thieves?"

The manner in which he spoke and the pitch of his voice sent chills down the spines of everyone in the café. No one moved or spoke. Everyone in the café was breathing heavily except Henry, who at that moment was completely unaware of what was happening.

The loud music generating from a radio in the kitchen prevented Henry from hearing what had transpired in the café. Henry was too busy peeling potatoes and bobbing his head to the beat to be aware of anything going on around him.

Despite the music bellowing throughout the entire café, an eerie, gloomy feeling enveloped the place. All eyes were focused on each move the dark stranger made. No one dared answer the black man's question.

Slowly, he looked around the entire room, sizing up everyone in his path. He was enjoying the fear that filled the room. For the patrons, the fear had formed a vaccuum that seemed to be draining the air from the room. It looked like the devil was now standing directly before them. The man's mouth widened into a fierce smile, showing off two perfect rows of white glistening teeth. If his monstrous size and piercing personality were not enough to stop a man in his tracks, the Remington Military Rolling Block Rifle he pulled from under his long black coat would do the trick.

With his rifle aimed, he looked at the waitresses and said gently, "Say goodnight ladies!"

The blast from the firearm struck Shirley right in the throat. She fell to the floor and landed on her back, inches from the kitchen doors. Her death was instant and painless, but she was full of fear.

Anne opened her mouth wide. The adhesive cream that normally held her upper dentures in place lost its grip. Her smoked-stained false teeth made contact with their bottom counterparts. Anne tried not to panic. All she could think about was her girls. She knew she needed to keep her wits about her for their sake. She ducked below the countertop, hoping the aggressor's attention would be drawn to the others in the café long enough for her to make a quick exit.

Anne heard the song, "Billy Don't Be A Hero" coming from one of the jukeboxes. "How fitting," she thought. The song's main character, Billy, was going to war as he held the love of his life close to his heart. Anne was caught in her own type of war. The only thing going through her mind was the love she had for her girls.

She needed to see what was happening, to determine if the coast was clear. Still on her knees, she edged her way slowly around the corner of the counter. She poked her head out, half way between the floor and rustic looking aluminum counter top. Greeting her was the barrel of the Remington Rifle. There was no time to react, no time to beg, no time to cry, and nowhere to run. She didn't even have time to bless herself, or ask God for forgiveness. The force from the blast to her head was instantaneous. Millions of tiny pieces flew in all directions. The splatter covered a ten-foot radius. Anne's daughters were left to spend the rest of their lives fending for themselves.

The shooter promptly turned about, and sized up the remaining individuals in the café. He picked up a napkin from the counter and wiped the blood from the barrel of his rifle. As he walked about the café, the old man in the corner booth wet his pants. The intruder then veered towards the exit.

The remaining patrons took a collective sigh of relief. But rather than leave, the man snapped the bolt in place. The café's main entrance was locked. The man then turned the sign in the window around to say, "Closed." The door to freedom was officially closed.

The homicidal male moved back and forth along the front entrance, pulling down each blind as he passed. As he hit the last of the twelve mini blinds, darkness shrouded the quaint café.

All the remaining people could do was sit and wait to see what would happen next. An emotional battle was being waged in their minds. Some people were hanging on, while others were bordering on insanity. Silence overtook the room.

The two young college students wondered what he would do next and how they would be spending the next few moments of their lives.

He looked at each of them, one at a time. The more fear he saw on their innocent faces, the wider his ghoulish grin became. He held their lives in his hands.

He turned his attention to the old man sitting in the corner booth. As he approached the table, the frail man's body began to shake rapidly. He was no longer sleepy. The old man had a solid appreciation for the life he lived. He considered himself lucky to have reached such a ripe old age. However, he never, in his wildest dreams, thought that this was how he would be spending his last few minutes.

The murderer's large shadow slowly increased in length and width the closer it drew to him. The old man was shaking and his entire body was covered in sweat. The nervousness he felt began to vanish. The old man's eyes rolled upwards and his pupils gradually disappeared into his head. Only the whites of his eyes were visible. A feeling of peace overtook him. His wrinkled skin took on a darkened tinge of grayish blue. In seconds, his fragile body collapsed in a lifeless heap, slumping forward in slow motion, until it stopped on the table. The old man's face landed directly into his cold meal. The poor soul was spared the horrifying agony of further suffering at the hands of the devil before him.

For the first time since he entered the café, the black stranger showed an emotion other than anger. He was utterly astonished. He couldn't believe what had transpired before his very eyes.

Standing next to the old man, he grabbed a handful of fine gray silky hair, and returned the body to a natural sitting position.

Anger again replaced astonishment. In the black man's mind, he had been made a fool of. The old man had gotten the last laugh. Still clutching that clump of fine hair, he tilted the old man's tiny head backwards. With all his might, he slammed the old man's face directly against the flat of the table. Instantly you could hear glass breaking followed by the sound of brittle bones crunching against the wooden table. The force from the blow drove the old man's nose back into his head.

The two students were now huddled together, crying hysterically in each other's arms. Henry was still busy in the kitchen, listening to the tunes that flooded from his radio. He was completely unaware of the havoc going on.

Jean-Luc LeClaire, the lawyer, had gathered up some courage. He was attempting to display a hint of bravery in the presence of the others, but the damp stain on his eight hundred dollar suit pants belied his true character.

As the violent stranger moved towards him, Jean-Luc pulled his wallet from his jacket pocket and said, "Take what you want. I'm rich. I'm very rich. I can give you whatever amount you want. Just leave us be."

This infuriated his aggressor who lifted his rifle and aimed it at Jean-Luc. The lawyer placed his head on the table and begged for his life. A bang rang through the café, but no shot was fired. Jean-Luc had been struck in the back of the head. He was out cold.

The attacker kicked the chair out from under the unconscious man, sending him to the floor. Blood poured from Jean-Luc's ears and nose. His chest rising up and down confirmed that he was still breathing, but dead to the world around him.

The girls were sure they would be the next victims. Little did they know at the time, the black color of their skin would save their lives. The sinister giant now presented them with a stern, but gentle face. He told the young girls to proceed to the ladies washroom where he opened the door and escorted them inside. The windows inside the washroom were set high above the stalls, too small to fit through. The young students were advised to stay put, not to make any noise, and when he was finished his business, he would ensure someone came to let them out. He then left the ladies washroom and braced a stool from the front counter against the bathroom door.

The large man needed a cool glass of water. He reached over the counter and grabbed a glass pitcher filled with ice-cold water. He lifted the pitcher and gulped several mouthfuls. He then dumped the remaining liquid over his head. Instantly, he felt refreshed. He was now ready to finish the job.

He headed towards the swinging doors that led into the kitchen. As he moved inside, he caught sight of the owner, Henry, who was moving steadily to the beat of the music. His headset was muffling any outside sound. Standing over the bubbling fat, dropping one piece of chicken at a time into the fryer, Henry continued to move to the beat of the music. Henry's chicken was famous in this city. It was the tastiest and greasiest chicken around.

Henry's doctor had told him that he needed to relax and enjoy life. His business was his life, and it kept him extremely busy. He figured listening to music at work would lower his stress level and help him to relax more.

Unfortunately, it made Henry totally unaware of what was coming next. Like a panther stalking his prey, the stranger moved closer to him. Coming within arm's reach of Henry, he placed his rifle on the floor right next to the prep table. As supper hour was fast approaching, Henry's concentration was focused on preparing enough food for the next rush.

The panther grabbed a large utility fork. With a swift stab, the fork sank about two inches into Henry's upper back. Henry couldn't move. Before he knew what hit him, his face was pushed into the boiling chicken fat that had served as his livelihood for all these years. When the aggressor let go, Henry's face slipped from the boiling fat and his body slumped to the floor. He started shaking rapidly. Death was slow and very painful.

The stranger returned to the dining area. Reaching inside his coat, he removed a silver case and placed it on the counter. The case contained a set of playing darts. Each of the matching black flights had an inscription in a bold Roman font, which read:

THE CATCHER

The Catcher, as the man was known by his professional acquaintances associated with White Man's Cotton, attached flights to four of the darts. He walked to each of his victims, one by one, starting with the old man, and then moving on to Shirley, Anne, and finally returning to Henry, who by this time was dead. As he reached each of the corpses, he placed a dart through the middle finger of all his victims.

With this task completed, he picked up a second pitcher of icy cold water and walked over to Jean-Luc LeClaire. Standing directly over the young lawyer, he threw the pitcher's contents into his face.

Jean-Luc sat up abruptly, gasping for breath. He shook his head, looked about, not knowing what to expect next. Standing before him was the massive bulk of the violent stranger.

The Catcher looked at Jean-Luc with one of his eerie smiles and said, "You have been chosen to work the White Man's Cotton by a jury of my peers. I have been sent here to carry out sentencing and deliver you to your new destination. Your crime is your job and the white trash you serve."

"I don't understand?" Jean-Luc responded.

"I will provide you with one explanation. Seven months ago, you defended an oil tycoon by the name of Robert Mitchell. It was in relation to a harassment suit filed by Elvira Mossy. He abused this woman for years: sexually, emotionally and physically. You were solely responsible for getting this man off on a technicality. Elvira Mossy hanged herself three weeks following the trial. She died because of you."

"I was only doing my job, for God's sake! I'm sorry for what happened. But it's my job."

"And this is my job, white trash. The difference is that I'm not sorry for what I do, and there's one thing I hate even more than scum like yourself, and that's whining white scum."

Then the Catcher slammed the butt of his rifle into the back of Jean-Luc's head, knocking him out once again. He then bent over, picked up his victim by the waist and threw him over his shoulders. With Jean-Luc straddled over his shoulders, hanging freely like an old sack of potatoes, the Catcher walked towards the kitchen, treading over broken glass and butting his victim's body into chairs, tables and the café's counter as he went.

The Catcher headed straight for the back exit, which led into an alleyway behind the café. On the way, he reached down and picked up a donut from one of the food trays, stuffing the whole thing into his mouth.

The Catcher scanned the alleyway. No one appeared to be lingering about. The Catcher walked towards his old, light green van. When he arrived at it, he opened the back door and threw the unconscious Jean-Luc inside. He landed next to a second badly beaten individual, the oil tycoon, Robert Mitchell, whose hands had been tied up with heavy nylon rope, and his mouth covered with gray duct tape. The Catcher bound Jean-Luc in the same way.

Once secured, the Catcher locked the van's door and went back into the café. Heading for the nearest phone, he placed a brief call. The New York City Police Department was advised of the two black students who were locked in the washroom of Henry's Café. Without answering any questions, the Catcher ended the conversation by telling the 911 operator that these ladies were in desperate need of immediate assistance. With that, he hung up the receiver and returned to the van.

As he pulled the vehicle from the alley onto the main road, the screeching sirens rang loudly nearby. In the thirty seconds he was on the road, four police vehicles had passed him. The café had come alive with law enforcement officers streaming in from all directions.

The Catcher continued driving through several streets, over bridges, and down highways for hours. He passed through several major cities and many other smaller communities. To the human packages loaded in the back the drive seemed to take days.

Both Robert Mitchell and Jean-Luc LeClaire were experiencing an agonizing journey. They suffered each time the van struck a pothole or deliberately ran over the many bumps in the road. Their driver was playing cat and mouse with every vehicle on the road. He also passed everything that got in his way. Each time he swerved in or out of traffic, both captives rolled from side to side, holding their breaths, trying to avoid more pain.

Their journey suddenly took on a different feel. Regardless of how rough the previously encountered bumps and dips were, at least the driving surface had been paved. The van had now hit a dirt road. No longer did they experience pain or discomfort in intervals. The van was rumbling constantly. It was as if the potholes and dips had come alive and begun displaying aggression. The bruises and scrapes Jean-Luc and Robert had endured previously now multiplied drastically.

In an effort to dismiss his current agony, Jean-Luc began to reminisce about a time when he was only thirteen years of age. He had been riding his mountain bike through the woods and down a regularly traveled biker's path when he noticed a small opening in the trees ahead. A separate pathway veered just off the regular trail. An adventurous youth, he decided to explore the new, overgrown path. It was more suited to walking or hiking, as opposed to biking.

The young lad was having difficulty. He dispersed more energy fighting his way through the rigid terrain than he had throughout his entire ride. He had been riding for no more than ten minutes when he came across a steep decline. At first it looked like a good challenge. In no time, his run turned hazardous. He hit the root of an old birch tree sticking out of the ground and flew through the air. Next came a thump as his body made contact with the ground, rotating downwards at an amazing speed, with no control. All he could remember following the spill was that he was unable to move any part of his body. He was alone in the wilderness. He spent the rest of that day and night, up until early the next evening, lame and in horrific pain.

A group of some seventy volunteers had joined in the search for young Jean-Luc. He was found, unconscious but still alive, and was airlifted to the local county hospital. Upon arrival, he immediately underwent seven hours in surgery. He had suffered a broken leg, a broken arm, a severe concussion, and over fifty scrapes, cuts and bruises.

Jean-Luc LeClaire replayed those two days years ago, over and over in his mind as he lay there tied up, on the cold floor of the van. The thoughts and emotions that went through his mind as a young adolescent trapped and injured in the woods had resurfaced. The only other time he had ever felt this alone was when he lay helpless at the bottom of that hill, deep in those woods, as a scared little boy.

The van suddenly began to slow. They had reached their final destination. The emotional state of the captured men was about to be tested. They were very frightened yet also curious, for they were entering the unknown. Both men took one last roll in the back of the van and a violent spill towards the front seat, as their driver slammed on the brakes.

A voice rang out from the front of the van, "Welcome to the beginning of the rest of your pathetic lives."

The driver's door opened, followed shortly by the sounds of additional voices. They couldn't actually pick out what was being said, but heard three separate people now speaking.

After several minutes, the back doors to the van swung open and two strangers stood looking at the captives. Both of these men looked terrible. Their clothing was absolutely filthy and neither man appeared to have brushed his teeth or washed in months.

The strangers reached into the back of the van and each grabbed a different set of legs. In one swift jerking motion, both Jean-Luc and Robert ended up outside the van, on their backs. They were at an airstrip in the middle of nowhere. The only building visible was a hangar for small aircraft. Several small planes were scattered about. A Lear 55 Charter Aircraft was sitting just outside the bay doors at the front entrance to the hangar.

The man who had pulled Jean-Luc from the van looked at his buddy and said, "This one pissed his pants!"

They burst into laughter. The man standing over Jean-Luc laughed so hard that a long stream of saliva fell from his lips and landed right in the middle of Jean-Luc's face. The drool was brown and judging from the stench, it was a mixture of spit and chewing tobacco.

The Catcher closed the van doors and picked up a briefcase that was sitting on the ground next to the vehicle. He left Jean-Luc and Robert behind in the capable hands of the two strangers. He then climbed back into the driver's seat. As the van drove off, Mozart's *Don Giovanni* was booming from within.

He continued driving down the dirt road for several miles until he came to a small lake. It was a beautiful lake, situated in the middle of private property that belonged to Thomas J. Hawkins. The glorious sounds of nature enveloped the lake, frogs croaked, crickets and birds chirped, and fish splashed as they jumped for the flies that skimmed the water's surface. This was a magnificent place that was just as tranquil and relaxing to the Catcher as the opera music he was so fond of.

A fifty-foot ramp led out into the water. No fishing or recreational boats were out on the lake. The Catcher drove the van slowly onto the ramp, and kept driving until he reached the edge. He stepped out, placed the gears in neutral, and gave the van a little shove. It splashed into the lake. He stood there watching as it sank. The bubbles that soon followed marked the old green van's final resting place.

With briefcase in tow, the Catcher made his way back to dry dock. He walked towards a heavily wooded area to the left of the lake. When he reached the spot, he grabbed a series of branches that hung down from a gigantic weeping willow, and walked through a concealed doorway.

Seconds later, the roaring of an engine revealed the most expensive and awesome black convertible ever built. The Catcher sped off into the evening moonlight. His services would not be required again until he received an official communiqué from his current employer. The time would soon come for the next gathering of those ultimately responsible for replenishing the slave population at White Man's Cotton. The Board of Directors was preparing for their next meeting.

THE BOARD OF DIRECTORS

chapter three

IT was nine-fifteen p.m. The temperature outside was still at the twenty degree mark. The wind blew violently across the front entrance to the warehouse, at more than ninety knots per hour.

Tonight was the night for the monthly meeting of the Board of Directors of White Man's Cotton. The seven were due to congregate here this evening, as they had on the thirteenth of every month, for the last five years. All seven would once again replenish the personnel required to keep White Man's Cotton up and running. These individuals were rich and powerful. They demanded the best of everything that life had to offer, including retribution for crimes against their race.

The Gate Keeper, although not a Board Member, was charged with preparing for each meeting. He was also the organization's ultimate mouthpiece, a computer genius, who used the Internet to dispatch all communications. He ensured every person associated with or considered of importance within the organization, especially his employer, had full access to the unique service he alone provided.

The room in which the Board's meetings occurred measured thirty square feet. The cherry oak table situated in the middle of the room was oval and was just over twelve feet in diameter. The shimmering glare from the wax finish was eye-catching.

Seven black calfskin leather armchairs were positioned evenly around the table. Placed directly in front of each chair was a stack of file folders, twenty-five in total. Each file contained detailed reports that the Board would review and choose from on this warm windy evening.

A beautiful white diamond chandelier in all its brilliance was suspended directly over the center of the table. The base of this breath-taking fixture was trimmed in twenty-four-carat gold. A single emerald green candle was situated on the table next to each stack of file folders.

The Keeper walked slowly around the table and lit each of the candles. He then opened his laptop and carried it towards the only window in the room. He placed the laptop on the windowsill and turned it on. Once full access to the system was granted, he downloaded the main communication website, Merlin's Poetic Website, and uploaded the following message:

> "THE CANDLES ARE LIT, THE TIME IS HERE,
> GATHER YOUR THOUGHTS, PLEASE COME NEAR,
> DECISIONS TO BE MADE, TIME'S RUNNING LOW,
> TWENTY-FIVE TO PICK FROM, ONLY SIX WILL GO."

He noticed a separate message had been added earlier that day. The message was from the Catcher, or the big "C," as he was known on the board. It read:

> "THE DELIVERY VAN HAS COMPLETED ITS RUN,
> PARCELS HAVE ARRIVED, NOW COMES THE FUN,

I WAIT FOR INSTRUCTIONS, LATER TONIGHT,
HOW MANY MORE ARE NEEDED FOR FLIGHT?"

At nine-thirty p.m., the Keeper left his laptop on the windowsill and headed towards a set of sliding electronic doors. These doors contained no handles or locks. They served as a hidden entrance to a room that concealed highly sensitive and confidential information. The doors separated the secret boardroom from the remainder of the warehouse. A security monitor had been installed in the corner next to the sliding doors. It flashed pictures of the warehouse at different intervals. After finishing a second check of the interior, the Keeper removed a small remote starter from his shirt pocket and with one click, the doors leading from the boardroom opened.

Leaving the confines of the hidden room, he proceeded to the fire exit located at the side of the warehouse. He headed out through the fire exit, lighting a cigarette on his way. Once outside, he saw the headlights of several vehicles heading towards the warehouse. The tip of his cigarette flared with a bright orange tinge from the gusting wind. It was a miniature scale lighthouse, guiding those travelling in the dark night.

The first car to arrive at the side entrance contained Thomas J. Hawkins. Hawkins was the founder and owner of a multi-billion dollar conglomerate, Salvation's Chemical and Research Facility. He was an African American in his late fifties. He was also the Founder and Executive Director of the Board of Directors for White Man's Cotton. The other Board Members of Salvation's Chemical and Research Facility all arrived within minutes of each other. They were Daren Yohance, Shebelle Jones, Skekwan Farrakhan, Gamba Kenya, Oprah Truvile, and Larsen Black; each one a multi-millionaire.

These individuals all had, what they considered, valid reasons for becoming members of the Board. They demanded confidentiality from and ensured honor was maintained towards each of their peers. After the pain they'd suffered at the hands of whites, they all joined this elite group willingly.

Thomas J. Hawkins was raised in foster care. Both his parents were gunned down in a gang-related incident when he was just four years old. He went through seven different foster homes by the time he was sixteen. Each set of foster parents was white, and sadly enough he was brutally abused by all of them. To this day, Thomas J. Hawkins can't stand the sight of any white person.

Daren Yohance, in his youth, made history by being the first black man permitted to attend a completely white men's university. While the law had changed in Daren's favor, nothing else had. For the full five years he attended the University of Mount Edison, he was taunted, spit at, beaten, or otherwise ignored by his white classmates. He repeatedly had nightmares and spent several years after he graduated seeing various psychologists.

Shebelle Jones moved to the United States from South Africa. His parents, both of whom were doctors, moved to a small township some thirty miles north of Johannesburg to assist an underdeveloped village in one of the poorer regions of South Africa. He watched the attack on their village, while hiding among the palms of several large date trees nearby. Ninety-five percent of the villagers were slaughtered during that military raid, including Shebelle's parents. The killers were white males.

Skekwan Farrakhan was another survivor from the same massacre. He was an agriculturist who happened to be out in the fields that day doing research. Upon hearing gunfire in the distance, he ran back to the village only to discover the mass killings that had taken place. He found the terrified Shebelle alone, hiding in the brush under a date tree, and eventually became his legal guardian.

Gamba Kenya was a businessman. He owned and operated over two hundred textile factories around the world. He was considered a fair and reasonable man, who treated all others as his equal. One day as he and his family were dining out in a local restaurant, three white youths entered the restaurant with the intent of robbing the place. After removing the money from the cash register, one of the young men demanded that the customers empty their wallets and pass over their jewelry. His ten-year old daughter, who ran from the table in fear, was shot. When his wife moved towards the little girl, she too was shot and killed. The young man walked towards the table where Gamba was sitting and grabbed his young son.

He looked at the textile giant and said, "Black people deserve to die!"

He then pulled the trigger, splattering the white linen tablecloth with his son's blood. Gamba cradled the lifeless body tightly to his chest. The white male then turned the gun on Gamba, leaving him for dead. Gamba survived the shooting, but never forgot the day three white teens slaughtered his entire immediate family.

Oprah Turvile was the lone female of the group. In her younger days, she was a very beautiful black woman. Even at the ripe age of fifty-three, she was still beautiful. Her only flaws were her scars, not just the physical ones, but the emotional ones as well. She had character, charm, personality, and grace, attributes which over shadowed her imperfections.

When Oprah was twenty-four, she and her boyfriend were parked at a favorite lookout for young lovers. While embraced in a passionate kiss, the doors to the Chevy were yanked open and Oprah and her lover were dragged from the vehicle.

While two white men held Oprah down, she watched in horror as three other white attackers viciously beat her lover unconscious. All five men then ganged raped her.

After the assault, the five men stood around Oprah and warned her to never say a word about what had happened. To emphasis their threat, four of the men held her still while the fifth poured battery acid over the right side of her face. Oprah lost her lover that day: he died shortly after the beating. Oprah also lost her innocence and her self-esteem in that brutal violation.

A day never passed when Oprah wasn't reminded of that tragedy. Every time she looked in the mirror and lifted the hair back from her face, she remembered the incident as if it were yesterday. She could afford plastic surgery, but chose to keep her scars as a constant reminder, a tool to ease any guilt she might feel for her actions against certain members of the white race. Her current role on the Board of Directors was easily justified. In her opinion, she had earned the right to retribution for her suffering and loss.

Larsen Black was a professional jewel thief who earned his fortune by stealing from the rich and famous. But, he only stole from white people. He could never really explain why he hated white people. He just felt it was his duty, as a black male, to look after the interests of his own race. Stealing from white folks made him feel good; it gave him a purpose in life, something challenging to accomplish.

The Gate Keeper and the Board Members all took a few moments to welcome each other back. The Keeper then cordially ushered the group inside out of the raging winds.

When the door closed behind them, the Keeper said, "It's going to be a long evening. We have to recoup six losses tonight and time is of the essence. The good news is, the Catcher has delivered, as usual, and the plane is now in flight."

With that came a big round of applause. Wide grins covered their faces.

Thomas Hawkins looked at the others and said with a smirk, "Isn't it wonderful what one can do with money?"

The group nodded their heads in agreement. The Keeper led them towards the back of the boardroom and proceeded to open a door. Inside was a splendid bar with every type of liquor or beer imaginable.

Standing back on, the Keeper said with a smile, "The usual, my friends, or do we have any special preferences this evening?"

Oprah spoke up first, and said forcefully, "We should definitely celebrate this evening with champagne. The Catcher delivered two very special packages today. Let us enjoy the moment."

All agreed with her. The Keeper broke out the champagne glasses and a magnum of Dom Pérignon, 1993. He poured up a glass of champagne for everyone at the table and placed the crystal flutes in front of each of them.

Thomas Hawkins then took the floor and said, "Fellow associates, it is with pleasure that I see all of you here in such great spirits this evening. Before we proceed, I must remind you of why we're all here. Put simply, and as you all know, slavery is an institution in which one person owns another. The slave is required to perform a variety of functions and services for which they receive no compensation. Sound straightforward? Well folks, our forefathers suffered greatly at the hands of our white enemies. To this very day, we witness regular events where the white race still harbor feelings of hatred, anger and ill will towards our brothers and sisters. Our place and our pledge to each other is to take affirmative action against those who continue to make our people suffer, just as we all have suffered. It gives me great pride to have placed before you this evening the files of twenty-five of the latest white sinners known to our organization. Your role and our function here have not changed. We have a task before us on this eve, to select six individuals from the case studies in front of you. You all have an individual choice to make. The rules haven't changed. The Catcher will only call on those individuals you select. If seven of us choose the same file, only one person will meet the Catcher. If all seven choose different files, the last one to make his decision will lose out because we will only be taking a maximum of six this round. In closing, I wish you all the best of luck as you review the files before you. Once your final decision has been reached, you are to place your seal of approval on the front cover of the file in question as you do each meeting. Following this, you are bid a fond farewell until the same time next month."

The Board Members each picked up a file and began reading. Adhering to the rule of silence in place during the process of selection, each person focused on the task at hand. Silence was enforced to allow decisions based on individuality, not influence.

There were very powerful and influential people sitting around the table. Others could easily be swayed or even delayed from making their decision. Conversation could prove to be very distracting.

The only time the rule of silence was broken was when the assistance of the Keeper was required. Normally, this was only to provide a refill to a person's beverage.

The files included a strange array of characters. The members read the biographies of a farmer, a wrestler and various Ku Klux Klan members. Other files featured several high-ranking government officials. Some decisions would be easy, others would require much thought.

Larsen Black was usually one of the first to make his selection. He always looked for something different, someone who stood out from the other candidates. He normally reexamined the files of the two or three serious contenders he chose, while the rest were put aside. He allowed himself a few seconds to reread the files and allowed instinct to take over. The file he wanted would jump out at him, his final decision would be made.

Larsen chose file number 727, belonging to an individual named Harry Barbour. Harry Barbour was a professional wrestler who went by the alias, "The White Knight." Throughout his professional wrestling career, he boasted that there wasn't a black man alive who could beat him. In the sixteen years he spent in the ring, he had never been beaten.

The White Knight stood six-feet seven inches tall and weighed in at just over three-hundred and sixty-five pounds. He wore white tights and always sported a long white robe as he walked towards the ring. The fans, regardless of color, roared each time he entered the arena.

Black people cursed as he passed. Many carried placards plastered with derogatory comments. The majority of white fans had mixed emotions about him. Some would side against the prejudice he invoked. Others would cheer him, their hero, on. Despite the pretence professional wrestling involves, it takes tremendous strength and agility to perform the aerial feats and moves that make fans sigh in disbelief and awe, while bringing others to their feet, and the federation that sponsored the White Knight knew this.

They continued to capitalize on the concept of a white man being able to overpower and beat all black challengers. The fans loved it, and as long as the money continued to roll in, the federation wasn't about to change a thing.

White Knight matches commonly caused near riots between fans of both races. Fighting in the stands usually resulted in broken noses, severe bruising, black eyes, and broken bones.

The more this occurred, the more famous the White Knight became. To ensure his popularity, matches, especially those against blacks, were often fixed. As long as his matches kept bringing out fans and as long as he kept the fan's adrenalin pumping, the promoters were happy.

Larsen Black took the White Knight's folder, number 727, and placed it to one side. He then picked up the remaining twenty-four folders and passed them over to the Keeper. In turn, the Keeper fed each file, one at a time, into an electric shredder.

Larsen returned to his place at the table. He leaned forward and reached for the emerald green candle, which had already burned half away. Larsen picked up the candle and tilted it over file folder number 727. The wax dripped freely as Larsen carefully formed an "X" across the cover of the folder.

He moved back from the table, and nodded to each of his acquaintances before leaving the boardroom.

Outside the warehouse, Larsen stood by the side of his car and smoked a cigarette. The wind and temperature had both died down. It had turned into a beautiful evening. He flicked his cigarette on the ground and stood for a second, watching the glowing ash flickering. He jumped into his car and drove away, leaving the five others to make their decisions.

Shebelle Jones was the next person to make his choice. He selected file number 622, which belonged to George Williams, a police officer from Detroit, Michigan. George had been suspended from the police force on twelve separate occasions. Each time disciplinary action was taken against Sergeant Williams it involved charges of police brutality. Ninety five percent of the charges filed came from young black American men. The remaining five percent was a mixture of other ethnic minorities residing in Detroit.

George Williams, who was paid to serve and protect, believed in providing clients of non-white origins with "the royal treatment." However, his version of this treatment was somewhat like that of a jousting match in the days of King Arthur and the Knights of the Round Table.

Even with twelve incident reports on file, Sergeant Williams had received numerous medals for his actions in the line of duty, which far surpassed his questionable policing tactics. His superiors normally covered up the serious charges brought against Williams. When actually suspended from active duty, it was only for a period of one week up to two months. His suspensions always came with full pay.

Shebelle Jones put twenty-four files in the Keeper's care. He then repeated the same process on file number 622 as Larsen Black had. Immediately upon completion of this action, he too left.

Daren Yohance chuckled aloud as he read file number 183. The more he read, the louder his chuckles became, until they eventually turned to laughter. The others, still contemplating their choices, looked at him with annoyance.

Daren was reading the file of a student. The man in question spent his youth and adulthood as a full-time professional student. The file belonged to Evan Roberts, founder and lifetime member of Alpha Beta Roman Fraternity. Evan entered the University of Washington at the age of seventeen. He was now thirty-two, and still attending classes on campus part-time, while maintaining the title of President, Alpha Beta Roman Fraternity.

When Roberts first began university, he was not happy. Basically, he hated everyone and everything. Because of his sullen nature, he spent his early days on campus being mocked by his classmates. He felt dread the moment he awoke. He had an eerie look about him, and his cruel nature contributed greatly to the discrimination he felt and the abuse he endured as a result.

Evan had two things going for him: his intelligence and his endless supply of money. He came from absolute wealth, and when his attempt to fit in failed, he put his intelligence and money to work for him.

His problems originated with a group of black students who consistently harassed him during his first two years at university. He needed to get away from his dorm where most of the trouble took place, so he applied to the Dean of Admissions for permission to open a fraternity house off campus. Approval was granted after a three million dollar donation was made to the School's Board of Trustees. Evan strived to make his fraternity one of the best in the country. He purchased a monstrous building, previously used by several local theatre companies. He invested hundreds of thousands of dollars into equipping the structure with all the latest conveniences, turning it into a top-notch housing and social structure for students of his choosing.

Making friends was not easy for Evan because of his personality. Wooing people with his money and illustrious surroundings, however, made friendships much easier to achieve. Evan adopted a new philosophy. He was intent to make his sorority a place where he was respected, where individuals would kill to become a fraternity brother.

Because of the abuse he'd suffered at their hands, he ensured that no black students ever entered the doors of his fraternity. He would play on their emotions and weaknesses, while leading them on. Just when they felt close to making membership to Alpha Beta Roman Fraternity, he rejected them, as he himself had been rejected so many times in the past.

Daren rose from the table grinning and mumbled, "The lucky bastard."

He reached for the candle, drawing the ceremonial "X" with the melting green wax on the top of file number 183. He passed the remaining files over to the Keeper and left the warehouse. Only three selections remained.

Oprah Turvile held two files, one in each hand. She was having a hard time making a decision between file number 83 and file number 176.

File number 83 belonged to Larry Howard, a college professor from Dalhousie University in Halifax, Nova Scotia, Canada. He taught Sociology using controversial methods.

He preached and instilled in the minds of his students the belief that the nation's economy was in such a sorry state because of the effects of the women's movement, and the abuse of social programs by the ever increasing ethnic minorities. In his lectures, he often discussed nations whose economies flourished due to the fact that women held posts of lesser importance, in comparison to their male counterparts. He was a very successful and knowledgeable debater, and counterattacked differences in opinion with his wit and above average intelligence.

File number 176 concerned an accused rapist by the name of Joseph Flynn. While Oprah leaned towards this particular file, the white man was completely cleared from any wrong doings. She also noted he did not have a criminal history. Oprah normally leaned towards files that reminded her of her tragic past, but in this case she was unsure.

Each time she considered Larry Howard's file and the ignorant beliefs he force-fed his students her anger intensified. Knowing that the gap in the selection process was closing, Oprah placed file number 176 on top of the others. She then marked file number 83 with an "X" as the others had. As she was leaving, she waved goodbye.

Both Skekwan Farrakhan and Gamba Kenya had spent an enormous amount of time reviewing each of the files. They were having difficulty making their final selection. Approximately six hours had passed, and finally, within minutes of each other, the men had made their choices. Skekwan chose file number 622, belonging to police Sergeant George Williams, while Gamba had selected file number 83, which belonged to Professor Larry Howard.

The Gate Keeper immediately advised Skekwan and Gamba that duplication in the selection process had occurred. Skekwan duplicated Shebelle's earlier choice, while Gamba chose the same file that Oprah had. Both of these men would leave slightly poorer. Those who selected duplicate files or those that never completed their selection, as the rule went, paid the Catcher's bounty. Sullen, both individuals got up from the table and left quietly.

Thomas Hawkins was the final board member left. He had made his selection an hour before anyone else did, but liked to watch the others at work. Mind games were a specialty of his. He played them with friends and enemies alike.

From the moment he opened it he knew file number 799 was his choice. The file belonged to Don Snow from South Carolina. Don was the current Imperial Grand Wizard of the Ku Klux Klan, responsible for all territories in the Southern United States.

He opened the file and began to read aloud a selection of excerpts to the Gate Keeper. "This is not a hate group, we only wish to express our pride in our white heritage. There are many different political groups out there who are free to voice their own opinions—black groups, communist groups, government groups, etc."

"The Klan is starting to increase in size. It no longer believes in ruling by intimidation, as was the way of our great forefathers. Instead, we believe we can change things by popular opinion."

"We wish to recruit new members. We look for white Christian men and women who want to preserve the future of their children. If our country proceeds on the path it is currently taking, there will be no future for our children."

"I had originally set up a site on the Internet for all of my white brothers and sisters to send comments. I had to remove it due to the fact that the web host bans any form of profanity. It seems that the blacks could not make a statement or comment on this site without every other word being profane. I apologize to all those who refrained from using profanity that others couldn't read your comments simply because of these black upstarts."

"Ten reasons why you should support the Klan:

1. We are a Christian organization.
2. We work for our children's future.
3. We are governed and run by our members.
4. It's a secret organization.
5. We are a legal organization.
6. We are politically independent.
7. We oppose anyone who is not white.
8. We uphold what is written by our founding fathers.
9. We are comprised of men and women of sound minds.
10. We need your help today to secure the future of our race."

Thomas Hawkins threw the file back on the table. His lips quivered. He looked over to the Keeper and said, "Don Snow is a lonely man. I intend to make sure he receives plenty of company and attention at White Man's Cotton. I've always hated members of the Klan, but I despise their leaders a hundred times more! Let's make of an example of this redneck. Make sure the Catcher extends a special invitation to his entire family."

With that, Thomas Hawkins stood up and marked his file with the ritual "X." He walked from the boardroom, ending the Board of Director's responsibilities for the night.

The Gate Keeper shred all files not chosen this time round. He gathered the four files that remained each bearing the letter "X." He then posted the following message on Merlin's Poetic Website:

"CATCHER BEWARE, FOUR MORE ARE HERE,
HOW YOU GET THEM, WE DON'T REALLY CARE,
LOOK IN THE HAMPER, DOWN AT THE LAKE,
THE GREEN X WILL SHOW, WHO YOU CAN TAKE.

CHALLENGE IS ON, ONE WEEK PER MALE,
BOUNTY IS PAID, ON EACH ONE THAT'S PALE,
PLEASE DELIVER WITHIN THE TIME FRAME,
YOUR SERVICE IS NEEDED AGAIN IN THIS GAME."

The Keeper wiped off the boardroom table. He washed the glasses and put them away. Once he had returned the room to its original state, he packed up his laptop and headed through the door.

Finally outside the warehouse, he lit a cigarette and took several deep drags. He savored the scent of freshly cut grass before dropping his cigarette and crushing it with the toe of his boot. He opened the door to his pickup truck and placed his laptop behind the front seat. He walked around to the rear of the truck, unlocked the hatch and removed a black and white hamper. The four marked files were placed inside and the lid was shut, locking the contents inside.

The Gate Keeper had one task remaining that evening which required his personal attention. He had to deliver the hamper to the lake. Once the hamper was deposited next to the wharf, he departed immediately. This clandestine procedure was necessary to ensure the Catcher's safety.

Before the Catcher would get the opportunity to begin his next assignments, other slaves were already in transit to White Man's Cotton.

ISLAND RETREAT

chapter four

THE sun reflected off the nose of the Lear 55 Charter Aircraft, making visibility extremely difficult for the pilot. After seven hours of flying he was about to make his final descent. During the night flight, he had encountered heavy turbulence and an unforeseen thunderstorm of severe proportion. The stormy weather lasted almost two hours and had eaten away at the pilot's energy level.

Apart from the usual crates of flour, butter, meat, eggs, milk, dry goods, and liquids that normally accompanied him on each of these journeys, he was also carrying additional cargo. Two unwilling human passengers had endured the same turbulence, as did the pilot and the supplies he carried.

The pilot radioed in his position and advised the makeshift ground control tower that he was ready to land. He received the all-clear signal and immediately began his descent.

The pilot looked upon the exquisiteness of the island below. It was almost completely covered with tropical growth. Plant life bloomed in all different shapes, sizes and color. A few scattered patches of cleared land, a couple of waterholes and a lake completed the picturesque setting.

A gigantic building and several rows of smaller wooden structures were barely visible to the pilot for their roofs were completely covered in dark green vines. Some of the vines even flowed down over the buildings. Luckily, the pilot knew where the buildings were.

The lake was centered in the middle of the island and had its very own waterfall. Branching out from the lake were several streams of clear running water.

The outskirts of the island contained long stretches of glistening white, sandy beaches. It was the closest thing to the perfect island retreat, ideal for a vacation. Some of the roughest and steepest cliffs imaginable outlined this enchanting landscape.

The plane's descent was exceptionally rough due to a strong cross-wind coming from the ocean. The pilot fought to maintain a smooth descent. Shortly after he lowered the landing gears, the wheels of the plane struck the runway with a thump. He maneuvered the aircraft towards the end of the runway finally coming to a full stop. He completed a check of the control panels and then exited the plane.

Directly in front of him on the runway were several onlookers, who walked towards him shouting greetings as they drew closer. Each person was dressed in military attire. Once official greetings were exchanged with the pilot, they circled around to the plane's loading doors. They began to unload the supplies from inside the cargo hole, one crate at a time. The whole process was undertaken with drill-team precision, with no wasted time or motion.

Once the final crate was unloaded, the two human passengers, Jean-Luc LeClaire and Robert Mitchell, were made to stand up. A hunter's knife was used to remove the rope binding their hands and feet and the tape that covered their mouths was ripped off.

The barrel of a rifle appeared pointed towards both captives. Without words, a guard directed them in slow motion using his rifle towards the exit of the plane. They were led from the confinement of the cargo hold to the fresh air outside.

Once outside, the men were led towards the horse-drawn wagon that contained the supplies removed from the plane. One of the guards, dressed in a dark red strap shirt and green army fatigues and carrying a black sack, walked up to the weakened captives. Jean-Luc and Robert were bound in chains and shackles that the guard removed from the black bag. The captives were ordered not to speak. Their captors climbed aboard the horse-drawn wagon and yelled back at their captives to follow. The men tried walking without stumbling but after only a few minutes, the shackles began digging into their ankles. They would soon learn to tolerate this pain as a regular part of their world.

The wagon left the open runway and headed towards a more densely wooded portion of the island. Huge trees overhung man-made paths. The trails were rugged and uneven in several places. The captives had difficulty maintaining their footing. The horse-drawn wagon swayed back and forth as it continued onward. The constant buzzing of mosquitoes was nerve-racking. The hot, sultry temperatures and the itchiness of the bites from the blood-sucking parasites that penetrating the flesh of the injured captives, assured them that this tropical island would provide no comfort.

In the near distance, Jean-Luc noticed another group of white men heading down a separate path in the opposite direction. These men were also bound in chains and shackles. They were carrying shovels, hoes and rakes. Others were carrying wheelbarrows over their heads. You could tell from the expressions on their worn-out faces that these men had suffered hard times.

Jean-Luc and Robert continued walking along, struggling with fatigue and pain. They were nearing the danger point of possible sunstroke and acute dehydration. Much to their relief, the wagon began to slow its pace. The black captors jumped off the wagon and stood directly in front of them.

One of the men shouted, "Place your lily white ass on the ground. In just a minute, you will get to meet your owner, Master Avery."

Jean-Luc and Robert did as they were told. They lifted the shackles up a few inches from their ankles. Rust from the shackles had chafed their skin. Infection was very likely. Avery Hawkins had come into view. His immense size, body language and facial expressions said it all—this was one individual you didn't want to piss off.

Staring down at both men, he roared, "Stand up, white trash. From this moment on, you will refer to me as Master Hawkins. You are only permitted to speak when spoken to. You have both been assigned to my work detail and will do exactly what I say, when I say. I guess you have gathered by now why you are here? Let me tell you. You have been chosen for reprogramming to learn that black men and women are now your superiors. You will no longer have the opportunity to say or even think otherwise. If you listen, obey and stay in line, you will be afforded the luxury of living. Right now, you will be taken underground for processing. Anything else you need to know, you will find out from actual hands-on experience."

Inhaling deeply, he continued, "Normally at this point I give each new arrival an opportunity to express any paltry concerns they may have. However, I have reviewed each of the qualifications that landed you here in the first place. In my opinion, and here, my opinion is gospel, neither of you deserve the right to speak. Follow me and ensure no words cross your lips or I'll have the skin peeled from them, one layer at a time."

Avery turned around and began to walk towards a rocky embankment a couple of hundred feet away. Sticking out from the base of this formation was an oval shaped, man-made concrete entrance. The top of the entrance was completely shrouded over with green vines, providing an almost perfect camouflage from above. Avery glanced back on several occasions to ensure his newly acquired slaves were keeping pace. His evil aura chilled their hearts.

They arrived at the main entrance, where a guard was posted on either side of the door. Avery, assisted by one of these guards, forced his captives into the concrete shelter. Once inside, the guard walked towards a hidden doorway and unlocked a brown panel box situated at the left side of the door. He opened the box to reveal a numeric keypad and input a series of numbers. When he finished, a faint clicking sound was heard coming from the steel door. The bottom of the door opened outwards towards the waiting men. Like a garage door, the door rose upward and disappeared into the ceiling. Avery motioned with his index finger for the white men to enter. Once inside, the door slammed shut.

Darkness overtook them. The captives followed Avery as he proceeded down a very steep and narrow passage. The walls surrounding them were solid rock. Both men stumbled several times while following Avery further underground. They promptly discovered that the rock hard walls were very smooth to the touch.

Robert could see a glimmering light ahead, which brightened the closer they came to it. Entering an opening, they had arrived in a massive underground cavern, which branched out to several rooms.

The smaller rooms, constructed mostly of wood and red brick, were visible through thick panes of glass. Bolted to the floors, directly in front of each window was a series of black wrought iron benches.

Avery motioned for the men to be seated on the first bench. The adjoining room contained a row of showers and a grotesquely ugly, fat, black man, wearing a green lab coat, sitting behind a desk.

Avery tapped on the glass to gain his attention. The fat man approached the door and opened it.

He looked at Avery and said, "Take off those chains and shackles and when you are done, have them remove all their clothing. Make sure you discard everything. I want nothing of theirs to remain."

Avery bent down and unlocked the shackles from the men's legs. He stood back, and in the demanding tone they had already grown accustomed to Avery said, "Take off all your clothes and remove all of your jewelry."

Robert Mitchell responded, "What are you planning to do with us?"

Avery walked towards him and with all his strength, punched him in the stomach. Robert fell to the floor, gasping for breath. Avery stood over him and grinned.

He then told the gasping Robert, "I have already told you not to speak until I have granted permission. You need to be taught a lesson, little man."

He picked Robert Mitchell up off the floor by the hair and threw the man into the nearest wall. Robert fell to the floor once again. Avery walked to him and grasped hold of Robert's left index finger. In one swift motion, he bent it backwards, breaking it. Robert screamed wildly.

Avery repeated, "Take off all your clothes and remove all of your jewelry."

It only took the men a few seconds to comply with Avery's request. Once Robert had removed his clothes, he clenched his finger in an attempt to ease the pain. He had stopped screaming, but the pain was killing him. He never spoke a word.

The fat man shimmied into the room and shooed Avery to the exit. It didn't take long for the captives to realize this man was gay. The man turned his attention back to Jean-Luc and Robert. He instructed them to follow him into the shower room and to bring their belongings with them. Once inside, they saw a row of lockers, several storage cabinets, a series of open showers, and a furnace.

Both men were instructed to throw all of their possessions into the furnace. They hesitated, but their host was quick to inform them that he would have Avery return if they failed to cooperate.

He opened the furnace door and motioned for the two white men to comply. Huge flames were visible and the heat that came from the open hatch was intense. Jean-Luc and Robert did as instructed. Once the last article was thrown in, their host shut the hatch. The two men were now left standing totally naked in a room with a fat, ugly and gay, black man who grinned as he eyed their naked bodies.

The pear-shaped man waddled back to his desk and sat down. Slowly, he allowed his eyes to drift up and down over both men, sizing up every inch of their bodies. Jean-Luc and Robert could tell from the movement of his hands under the desk that the sick bastard was masturbating. His body continued to shake and they could see the jerking motion from his right arm increase in speed, faster and faster with each passing second. The faster his arm moved, the heavier his breathing became. The smile from his fat jowls further distorted his already ugly features. His arm stopped moving and he let out a loud moan.

Once he regained his composure, he looked at them and said, "My name is Harvey. Master Harvey to you. Take note of your humble surroundings. I assume you can comprehend simple English and are capable of following even simpler instructions?"

He directed the men to be seated in barber's chairs. Both men were still totally naked, still suffering from injuries they had incurred over the past few days. The fake leather material covering the chairs felt cool to the touch as it made contact with their skin.

The men heard the sound of clippers buzzing. The fat man took the clippers to the men's heads, one at a time, until all their hair had been mowed off and lay in scattered clumps on the floor. As the clippers glided over each head, the men felt pinching sensations. A few of the nicks that penetrated the skin began to bleed.

Once the last blade of hair landed on the floor, the fat barber came around to face them and said, "Well, don't stand around being totally useless assholes. Hop into the showers and cleanse your filthy bodies."

The water began to flow freely. Both men were aware that the man was still watching them. However, the icy cold water pouring down over their bodies captivated their attention. The men caught as much water as possible in their mouths, to relieve their parched throats.

The fat man was drooling as he watched the water trickling down the full length of their bodies. He threw the men some soap and a scrub brush. The sound of teeth chattering could be heard over the noise from the force of icy cold water.

Robert Mitchell whispered to Jean-Luc, "The cold water would be more practical if poured over the fat bastard. At least it might cleanse the stench that hangs over the hefty pervert like an invisible vapor, and cool his sick sexual urges."

Once Master Harvey determined they were clean enough, he turned off the water. He then herded them towards a neighboring room where the smell of a strong cleaning product filled the air.

The men were ushered towards a second set of shower stalls. Master Harvey walked towards another desk and pulled a switch. This time a pale blue colored powder shot at them from various angles. In addition to taking their breath away, the smell was horrible. Master Harvey stood before them wearing a surgeon's mask. He obviously did not want to breathe in any of the toxic chemicals. Once the men were sufficiently disinfected, he stopped the flow.

He then said to the now chalky blue males, "Nothing like sterilizing a filthy body. Got to make sure we rid you of any little creatures that may be lurking about. Can never be too safe these days."

Master Harvey opened a third set of doors, looked at Jean-Luc and Robert sadistically and said, "Last but not least, scum, proceed to the next room. I am required to conduct a physical examination on both of you. Apart from the dirty little creatures that could be scurrying about on your body, we can't afford to have white residents bring items with them that are hidden from view, can we?"

The men thought that having a confrontation with Avery would probably be more pleasant than what was in store for them next. The idea of receiving a full physical examination from the fat gay man disturbed them greatly. Master Harvey could sense their apprehension and quickly reminded them that resisting him meant a face-off with Avery, and once he finished with them, they would still have to undergo the physical. It was a no-win situation.

The last room they entered contained four surgical tables covered with white paper. The men were told to pick a table and lie face down with their knees up under their stomachs. They heard Master Harvey snapping on a pair of rubber gloves. The next few minutes were humiliating and extremely uncomfortable for both Jean-Luc and Robert. Their fat assailant took great pleasure in shoving his hand into each man's ass. He deliberately forced his hand up as far as it would go, causing severe pain and bleeding.

Once he finished the task, both men were directed towards a counter in the corner of the room. Both men were given pants that were two sizes smaller than they usually wore. The pants were bright yellow stretch pants that outlined every ridge and muscle of their bodies. The men were also given a light green, fluorescent strap shirt, purple socks and a pair of pink running sneakers. All of which was too small. Once dressed, they were instructed to take a seat on the wrought-iron bench and wait for Master Avery's return in silence.

They waited for what felt like hours. Without their watches or any clocks in sight, it was almost impossible to know for certain. All they could do to pass the time was to look at each other in bewilderment and think about what was happening to them.

Suddenly, they heard the sound of heavy footsteps. As Avery came within view he yelled, "To your feet, little women. I am giving you a quick tour of your new home. Once the tour is finished, you'll be put to work. Your vacation has come to an end. You are being assigned active duty in the fields. You will work in this function until I decide otherwise. You may be reassigned to other duties later, if it is determined that either of you idiots has a hidden talent we require. In case you are stupid and haven't realized it yet, your stay with us from this date forward is permanent. I trust you will find your accommodations up to standard. Oh wait, you don't have any standards, so adjusting shouldn't be a problem."

He was huge, threatening and sarcastic. He was wickedness personified. Regardless of what Robert and Jean-Luc may have felt about this situation, challenging Avery's authority was not an option. The only thing to do was to follow his instructions and keep quiet.

The two new slaves followed Avery deeper and deeper into the cavern. The lighting was exceptionally poor. Every now and then they came upon a passageway that branched off the main tunnel. They heard voices in the distance off some of the paths. They were so faint it was virtually impossible to tell whether the voices were male or female.

Lagging behind Avery, the weak men entered into an open space where six tunnels converged. Avery took the second tunnel to his left, but to the newcomers they all looked the same. Oil lanterns that hung every thirty feet or so provided minimal vision.

The rock flooring turned damp and cold. Every once in a while rats scurried by. They heard voices once again, this time coming in more clearly. It sounded like men singing or chanting. The closer they got, the clearer the sound became. The words themselves didn't change much at all. It was a chant Jean-Luc and Robert would soon be singing themselves in the days to come. It went:

"PICKIN' COTTON, PICKIN' COTTON,
PICKIN' ALL DAY LONG.
TIRED AND SORE, FINGERS NOW WORN,
FROM PICKIN' ALL DAY LONG.

THE WORK GETS DONE, IT'S SO MUCH FUN,
WHEN HANDS ARE GLOWING RED,
BLOODY REDNESS, BLOODY REDNESS,
FROM PICKIN' ALL DAY LONG."

The men entered a room the size of a football field. It was amazing that a room this huge could be found three-hundred feet below the surface.

The entire room was set up with rows upon rows of wooden bins. The bins all contained millions of mushrooms sprouting up from rich dark farm soil. Robert and Jean-Luc noticed that the bins were covered with latticed barbed wiring, which explained the bloody hands of the men standing before them. When one of the men tried to get his hands between the wiring to pluck out a mushroom, his skin would get caught in the barbed wire. The bigger the man, the more noticeable the injuries. These bins had been purposely set up this way. The masters of the underground wanted to create a substitute for the thorny cotton bushes that pricked and scratched members of their race years ago.

Two feet directly above each bin were fluorescent lights that fostered the mushrooms' growth. Because of the position of the fixtures, the bins were the only area in the entire room that was lit well. Empty white buckets surrounded the bins. Eight separate ledges had been carved out halfway up each wall around the room, each with its own entrance. Black men with rifles stood or sat on each ledge guarding those below.

Thirty to thirty-five white workers were in the massive cavern positioned at various stations throughout the room. The fluorescent lighting system above each bin made their clothes glow in the poorly lit room. Each of them wore the same vividly colored clothing as Jean-Luc and Robert.

Avery lifted up his arms and shouted for all to hear, "I have with me two of your brothers to help you, you lazy bastards."

He then looked at Jean-Luc and Robert and said, "Welcome to the cotton fields. This is where you will spend the bulk of your time. Follow me, and pay close attention. I will be introducing you to the pit where you will meet Tiny, and from there we will proceed to Rachel's swimming hole."

The men followed Avery through the fields. Not one of the workers stopped or looked at Avery. Robert, Jean-Luc and Avery passed the last row of wooden bins and left the cavern, entering yet another passage. Robert and Jean-Luc followed without hesitation. The threesome entered a circular room with a lower level, also circular in shape. On the main level, seating had been angled to allow for perfect viewing of the area below. Railing separated the seating area from the pit below, which was accessed via an elevator that was situated opposite the entrance.

Avery looked over the railing and shouted, "Tiny. Come out and see what I've got."

A man emerged, walking slowly towards the center of the spherical opening below. Tiny was a three-hundred pound black man shaped much like a professional weightlifter. He stood there, arms folded, wearing a bright red singlet.

Avery gave him the thumbs up and smiled. He looked at Robert and Jean-Luc and said, "Take a good look at him. Tiny is a scrapper, you might say. He enjoys wrestling, boxing, bone crunching, and an occasional killing. When any of our residents get out of control or disobey the rules, we set up an entertainment session for friends and special guests. They come and watch Tiny here beat the crap out of white shits like you. Something you might want to keep in mind, should you ever wish to challenge one of your masters. Would either of you like to go down and give him a try? I can assure you he won't kill you today. As a matter of fact, why don't the both of you go down? He hasn't had any real practice in weeks."

Avery, sensing their fear, laughed. He looked back down at Tiny and said, "No takers today, I'm afraid. Not to worry though, someone usually fucks up once or twice in a good month. To make sure you don't get rusty, I'll send over a few white boys for you to practice on later. Right now, I have to finish showing this trash the sights. Take care, friend."

Avery and Tiny nodded good day to one other, and then Avery motioned for the white boys to follow him. He chuckled as he walked along.

The next stop found them at Rachel's swimming hole. They had reached another open area with a small ledge that overlooked a large pool of water. The pool was about one-hundred feet below and looked man-made. It was edged three quarters of the way around with gray bricks. The remaining quarter was muddy and provided access to the water. A pressure-treated wooden bridge extended across the full length of the pond. Water fountains and statues encircled the makeshift shoreline. It was impressive.

The only way down was a narrow path descending from the cliffs. In certain places, this path was only a foot or so in width. Avery was the first to head down the cliff, making his way towards the pool. He indicated to Jean-Luc and Robert to follow him. The white men found their travel down the jagged cliffs harrowing. Occasionally, one of them would slip or stumble as they continued down this narrow pathway.

At the bottom, their black master stood very still. He glanced around slowly, taking note of his surroundings. His behavior seemed very odd. He then motioned for the two white men to follow him to the bridge. Avery's pace increased to twice its previous speed. Once they arrived on the bridge, he seemed more at ease. He stopped as he made his way to the middle of the bridge, where they came upon several white covered buckets and the biggest fishing pole they'd ever laid eyes on.

Avery opened one of the buckets. The smell of rotten fish filled the air instantly. He pulled from the bucket a large gutted fish, three feet in length. He positioned the fish on the end of the fishing pole and turned towards the white men saying, "I want one of you to take this pole and lower the fish to about two feet over the water's edge."

Jean-Luc took the pole from Avery's grip and flicked the fish over the railing, lowering it to where he had been instructed. No sooner had he placed it over the water than it disappeared into the mouth of a mammoth crocodile, which sent water in every direction. Its mouth opened wide enough to swallow a grown man whole. After it snapped the fish from the pole, it went back under the water just as quickly as it had first appeared. The force from the reptile emerging from the water sent a breeze across his face followed by a cool splash. The reptile appeared to be well over twenty-five feet long with a set of jaws that took up at least eight feet of its body length. Jean-Luc froze in fear.

Avery snapped the pole from Jean-Luc's hands and said, "Boys, I want you to meet Rachel. She provides another valuable service to us here in the underground. She serves as a constant reminder that if you step out of line or break any rules, you could be pitted against this gorgeous creature in a swimming contest. No one has ever beaten her. She tends to get bored with the fish and likes a good challenge. Here are the rules: Rule number one: you must obey each of your masters at all times. Rule number two: you will never attempt to escape. The only time an escape attempt is permitted is when we give you the opportunity. This is usually once a month. Your co-workers, I'm sure, will explain this one in much more detail. Rule number three: there will be no interaction with any females. Anyone caught engaging with a female in any way will be punished severely. If you are caught having sex with a woman, you will automatically be sent for a swim with Rachel. Rule number four: you were brought here solely to serve your masters. You will work until you drop, if it is requested of you. Every once in a while you may be called upon to perform duties you may not be totally comfortable with. Never, and I mean never, refuse to accommodate your masters regardless of what they request. Failure to do so will also result in severe punishment. Rule number five: keep your space clean. Rule number six: do not cause problems or start a fight with any of your peers. And finally, always smile, for a happy worker is a good worker."

He sighed deeply and added, "Now that the formalities are out of the way, follow me to your quarters where the schedule for work, food and sleep are posted. Head count is performed on a regular basis. Do not be late for anything that's required of you. Do I make myself clear?"

The men nodded and then followed him to the end of the bridge, back towards the trail leading up over the cliffs. Along the way, each man, including Avery, felt they were being watched. As Jean-Luc glanced back, he could see the eyes and a portion of the crocodile's head skimming along the top of the pond. She was watching them move from sight.

The trip back took them from the top of the cliff, past the pit, back through the cotton fields, and finally to a narrow pathway. At the end of the path were ten separate very small rooms, the sleeping quarters. The walls and floors were rock and dirt and the only light came from a lantern hung on the walls outside each room. The men were given candles on occasion, but these were prized and used sparingly.

The room that Robert Mitchell and Jean-Luc LeClaire were directed into was very small indeed at only twelve by sixteen feet. It seemed cluttered with just the three of them standing there. Old blankets and worn out supplies were underfoot. From the entrance, they had a partial view of two other identical rooms. The men learned that a room this size normally housed anywhere from six to twelve men at one time.

Avery advised the men to enjoy the space for now because within a few weeks they would receive additional guests. He then took the worn-out men on the last leg of their tour, the dining hall. It was another cluttered and dark space. Apart from a few rows of wobbly tables, a couple of hot plates, some cooking appliances, some pots and pans, and a selection of hard plastic dishes and utensils, nothing of any interest stood out.

Jean-Luc and Robert had thought their day was over, but instead Avery led them back to the cotton fields. The two men entered Section 34 to begin their first day picking mushrooms for their black masters. Once they entered the fields, Avery positioned them at different bins. None of the other men spoke a word to them. Within a few minutes, the chant began:

"PICKIN' COTTON, PICKIN' COTTON,
PICKIN' ALL DAY LONG.
TIRED AND SORE, FINGERS NOW WORN,
FROM PICKIN' ALL DAY LONG.

THE WORK GETS DONE, IT'S SO MUCH FUN,
WHEN HANDS ARE GLOWING RED,
BLOODY REDNESS, BLOODY REDNESS,
FROM PICKIN' ALL DAY LONG."

Jean-Luc and Robert would soon be receiving other roommates. Normally, new slaves arrived on a monthly basis. Once the new slaves arrived, the slaves knew that another month had passed and the count down for the next group would begin.

IN THE LINE OF DUTY

chapter five

GEORGE Williams and his partner, Robert Lawlor, were sitting in the locker room of Police Station 84. They were having a chat while getting ready for their seven-thirty p.m. to seven-thirty a.m. shift. Both men enjoyed working the evening shift.

George, the older of the two, had sixteen years more experience than his partner did. Although he was in his mid-fifties, he was as fit as any man in his twenties thanks to his daily five-mile jog and work out at the officer's gym two or three times a week.

His partner, Robert, on the other hand, relied exclusively on his youth. He worked on the theory that as he was still in his thirties, he didn't need to work out to achieve good health. Like most men, he believed health deteriorated with age. He figured that he had another ten years or so before he needed to start exercising.

The door of the locker room opened and in walked Joseph Donnel, a rookie who worked the front desk. Joseph was a tall, thin, black male who tipped the scales at about one-hundred and sixty pounds and was just over six feet, four inches.

George looked at his partner and whispered, "Just look at that skinny black fuck. What do you suppose he would do if a real man gave him a poke? You know what he'd do? He'd shit his pants just like all the other black fucks around here."

Robert looked back at his partner and said, "Listen George, keep it down! Mayor Long has made it quite clear this precinct is understaffed as far as visible minorities are concerned. Whether you like it or not, you are going to see a hell of a lot more minorities assigned to the station."

"Whether they are assigned here or not doesn't mean I have to like it. Black welfare scum commits ninety percent of the crime in this city. Having cops of the same color only means they'll get off with twice as much."

"Just watch what you say. We don't need any more trouble. One of these days we'll get fucked ourselves and then what?"

"Then we'll take it upon ourselves to rid this stinking city of all the black scum that sits out there, soaking up our welfare system, shooting innocent citizens, robbing our corner stores, and selling all that dope to our young. At least they put the dumb bastard behind a desk where he can't do any harm."

Joseph heard most of what George had whispered. He also knew not to say anything in retaliation. His fellow black officers had advised him to keep a record of what flowed from George's mouth. He was also told to take care of himself, for George was the type of man who would sit back and watch a black man choke on a peanut rather than offer his assistance. The only time he would wrap his arms around a black person would be to throw the individual to the ground while making an arrest.

Joseph removed his belongings from his locker and walked past the two white officers without so much as a word. From the locker room, he headed down the hallway towards the front desk. Once seated, he removed a journal from his back pocket and began to write down exactly what the officers had said.

Williams and Lawlor continued getting dressed. They were tremendously proud of themselves and their profession. Both men loved their jobs and enjoyed coming to work. They also loved the empowerment and respect that came with it.

Robert turned to his partner and said, "Let's go partner. Another day, another dollar, or should I say another bill paid?"

They left the locker room and headed down the hall towards the front desk. As they came within view, Donnel looked towards his white peers, making direct eye contact. He then nodded to both men without showing any expression. Williams and Lawlor kept on walking. As they passed the black officer, Williams saw Donnel's journal.

He looked at his partner and said, "I didn't know blacks could read or write, did you?"

Robert made no response. As soon as Williams and Lawlor were out of sight, Officer Donnel picked up the phone and called dispatch. A newly hired recruit, named Marla, answered the phone. Marla was an acquaintance of Officer Donnel's, and was black. She was a strikingly beautiful woman with a voice to match.

She said, "You have reached the dispatch of Station 84 and have the pleasure of speaking with Marla. How can I assist you?"

"It's Donnel. I just wanted to let you know that Williams and Lawlor have left the station. They have been assigned to car 82 and will be working the east side of the city tonight."

"Thanks, sweetie. I'll take it from here. If you have no plans later this evening, we should go for a drink and take in a show. I hear there's a really good action show playing later tonight."

"Call me, Marla, once it's time."

Inside the elevator, Robert pushed the button for lower level two. George continued muttering condescending remarks about Joseph as the elevator descended. Robert allowed his partner to rant on. He had a special knack for tuning him out. While Robert agreed in part with several of his comments, he believed they were also true of members of the white community.

The elevator continued downwards until it came to a full stop. The doors screeched open. As Williams and his partner exited, they were surprised to find seven other officers waiting to enter. All of them were black and wore a strange smile. Williams wasn't stupid. He knew when to make comments and when to keep quiet, especially when outnumbered. Robert looked back at the officers who were getting into the elevator. They were staring at the white officers with huge smiles still plastered on their faces. Finally the elevator doors closed.

Lawlor nudged his partner on the arm and said, "Did you find that as creepy as I did?"

"Just a bunch of stupid black idiots. They wouldn't know an appropriate facial expression if you showed them pictures first. Did you ever hear the joke about how many blacks it takes to operate an elevator?"

"No, can't say I have."

"The answer just entered the elevator. I bet, if you went over and pressed the button they'd all still be there at the lower level, with the same simple smile planted on their faces!"

Hundreds of police cars were parked in the lower level garage. The officers continued walking towards their assigned vehicle, finally reaching car 82. As they approached, the men noticed a poster, which had been taped to the trunk of their vehicle. It was a picture of a black woman dressed in a police uniform. She was standing over an elderly white male, holding a pistol in her hand. The slogan at the top of the poster read:

"I CAN BANG HARDER THAN YOU CAN!"

Williams walked to the back of the vehicle, ripped the poster off and crushed it into a ball. He said to his partner, "Do you see what those black motherfuckers did to our car? Just take a look at this garbage. Can you imagine the nerve they got? They have no idea who they are dealing with. Get in Lawlor. We will see who has the bigger bang when it comes down to it. I have one more joke for you friend. How many blacks can we fit into our squad car in a given night?"

Lawlor shrugged his shoulders. He knew all too well that when his partner got this mad words meant nothing, not a damn thing. George Williams was completely pissed that someone had disgraced his police car. George routinely dished out trouble, but couldn't bear to be on the receiving end.

He sputtered, "The answer is unlimited. I intend to fill this car, refill it again and again until I've had my fill. Let's see how smart the licorice is tonight."

■ ■ ■

Patrol car 82 drove around for hours. Strange, they thought, that no calls had come through for the east side of the city. Even on a slow night, the officers took a steady influx of calls for assistance and back-up. This was highly unusual.

Lawlor picked up the radio and called into the station, "Dispatch, this is car 82. Traffic seems light this evening. Calling for spot check and verification due to low lying traffic over the air waves."

Within seconds, an extremely beautiful sounding voice responded, "Car 82, this is dispatch. Things are very quiet this evening on our end too. All communication lines are up and running. There are no problems. We'll keep you posted."

"Ten-four dispatch."

Lawlor looked at his partner and said, "Have you ever heard a voice like that on dispatch before? It sounds like she should be working on one of those nine hundred lines. Jesus, I'd call in to her anytime."

"Must be someone new. I haven't heard that voice before. What she needs is a long hard stiff one from an old fellow like myself. Just something to keep her honest."

The officers cruised for well over an hour. Most side roads were empty. Every once in a while, they saw a person hop into their cars, hail a cab or walk to the nearest bus stop to await the next scheduled run.

That sexy voice they'd heard earlier interrupted the quiet, "Car 82, car 82, please respond."

"This is car 82. Go ahead dispatch."

"We have a report of a disturbance at the old Abraham High School on Michelan Avenue. Please investigate."

"Ten-four dispatch. We are en route. Estimated time of arrival is seven minutes. Over and out."

The old Abraham High School was an abandoned school located in the far, east end of the city. The school was a gigantic concrete structure. In its day, it held upwards of eleven-hundred high school students.

Taking a right turn off Maple Drive, the police cruiser drove onto Michelan Avenue. About four-hundred feet ahead, the school's main entrance led into a parking lot. The grounds themselves looked empty and were dark, as the lights that previously glowed from overhead the school's foyer had all been broken. A touch of misty rain and fog gathered in clumps added to the eeriness that shrouded the school grounds. The school, closed six years earlier because of health hazards and unsafe conditions, was now home to several street people and drug dealers.

Williams drove the squad car around the school several times while his partner scanned for any signs of life. Everything was quiet and still. After the third circuit, Williams drove the squad car back to the front entrance and brought the car to a halt.

Robert Lawlor picked up the car radio. "Dispatch, this is car 82. Please come in dispatch."

"Go ahead car 82."

"Dispatch, we are now in the schoolyard of the old Abraham High School. There are currently no visible signs of a disturbance. Please advise."

The gorgeous voice replied, "Car 82, we have received several complaints regarding violence and a disturbance inside the old school. Please investigate."

"Ten-four dispatch."

Both men were clutching their sidearm as they left the safety of their police vehicle. Nothing seemed out of the ordinary at the stairs leading to the main entrance, except the silence that surrounded them. Even the wind had died down to a mere breeze.

Both men began walking up the steps, moving slowly and cautiously. At the top of the steps was a concrete landing. The entrance to the school contained three separate pairs of doors. Although the Department of Education had chained the doors shut several years earlier, only a few rusted links remained.

Lawlor reached for one of the door handles. His fingers felt something sticky. He shook his hand to get the substance off. When that failed, he wiped his hand down the face of the door. He then slowly pried the door open. Williams looked at his partner, shaking his head at the younger man's actions. Standing firm and slightly to the left of the opened door, George Williams listened for any sounds. When all appeared clear, Williams entered the school briskly, maintaining his awareness.

He was carrying his gun in perfect alignment with his upper chest. Once inside he did another quick but thorough scan of the school's vestibule. Satisfied, the senior officer motioned for his partner to enter. Enough moonlight shone through the windows to provide them with some visibility. Both men reached for the flashlights they had strapped to their belts. They held their flashlights in their left hands while their weapons remained steady in their right. Very slowly the beams from the two flashlights began moving up and down, from left to right, towards the other connecting doors, up over the stairwell leading to the second floor and towards the stairs that led to the basement and furnace area. They couldn't see anything other than mounds of garbage and old wood scattered throughout the main foyer.

Williams said to his partner, "We'll cover more ground if you take these stairs. I'll go around to the west side of the school and take the other set of stairs leading to the second floor. We can do a clean sweep of the second floor first to see what we come across. If anyone tries to flee from you, I will be on the other end waiting. Clip the radio to your breast pocket, where you'll be able to speak freely if need be. We'll check in every couple of minutes."

Robert responded, "I don't think it's such a good idea separating just yet. It's too quiet for my liking. Something doesn't seem right. Any other time we've been here, its been hopping with activity. It was always noisy. I don't like how quiet it is!"

"Listen bud. The station knows we're here. They're well aware we'll be doing a sweep of the building to check things out. If we don't call in with an update within twenty minutes, they'll send a second squad car. You have your gun. If we go upstairs, anyone wrecked out of their trees won't move an inch. It's the drug pushers who'll run. I'm not interested in the users. We can get them any time."

Lawlor looked Williams in the eyes and said, "Whatever you do, don't go fucking around. If you come across anyone, let me know right away. Don't go playing hero on me. Do you understand?"

"No prob. Come on, let's move out."

Williams knew all to well what his young partner meant when he said, "Don't go playing hero on me." He had spent his entire cop life doing what he pleased. He liked to break the rules. He took more chances and played more odds than he could remember. But, Williams kept his partner's words in the back of his mind as they parted ways.

Williams moved cautiously towards a set of double doors that led towards the west side stairwell. Before entering, he put his flashlight through a hole in the broken glass. Not detecting anything, he slipped through the entrance and entered a long dark hallway.

A series of tin lockers lined both walls. Very few of the lockers still had doors attached to them. The ones that weren't hanging on by only a hinge were either dented or busted entirely apart. Every twenty feet or so, there were classrooms, washrooms or storage and utility rooms on each side of the hallway.

Williams continued to walk up the center of the hallway. As he passed the rooms, he stood in their entrance and sized them up with his flashlight. All the rooms were littered with garbage. It was still tremendously quiet. The only noise Williams heard was the sound of his own footsteps.

He came across a section of hallway where several beaten-up lockers had been piled. While attempting to maneuver the rubble, the leg of his pants snagged on a piece of tin. Williams stumbled, face first, to the floor. Several lockers came tumbling behind him. The piece that he tripped over was still stuck in his pants. In the fall, Williams dropped his flashlight and gun.

His partner heard the commotion over the radio. Lawlor, totally out of breath, yelled into his radio, "George! Come in George! What's going on? Do you need assistance?"

Williams responded in a cocky and condescending tone, "Just tripped over some fucking lockers. I'm fine. Getting back on my feet as we speak. How about you? All okay on your end?"

"Nothing's happening here. I've reached the top of the stairs and I'm ready to do a sweep of the second floor. I had to climb over a bunch of beat up wooden desks. Some assholes had a party since our last visit and threw hundreds of old desks down the stairs. They're piled up everywhere along the steps creating one hell of an obstacle course. The only contact I've made is with some splinters. Trying to get my breath back as we speak."

"I told you you're out of shape. You're wheezing like an old man. Calm down and watch your step. I'll check back with you later."

Williams wasn't actually on his feet. He had successfully retrieved his flashlight but was still crawling around the floor searching for his gun. What with all the garbage lying around, he knew it couldn't have gone too far. He began looking under mounds of garbage, to locate his gun.

After several minutes, he spotted the gun's handle sticking out from under an old poster. While balancing himself, George reached under the poster to recover his gun.

"Bang!"

The officer's heart nearly burst from his chest. One of the locker doors that had been hanging by a hinge fell to the floor with a crash. He leaned back against a pile of garbage and inhaled deeply. He started to laugh.

After a few seconds, the older cop looked in the place where he'd last seen his gun. He couldn't find it. Did it get moved when he was startled and jumped back? He continued to search for it and found the gun directly under a set of lockers still fastened to the wall. Although this gave Williams an uneasy feeling, he shook it off. He figured he must have kicked it by mistake during the scare he had minutes earlier.

He leaned over to grab for the gun, which was barely visible. As he made contact with his pistol, a rustling noise came from behind, only inches from his body. As he turned, he saw a pair of size fifteen, brilliantly shined black army boots. With no time to react, the right boot made direct contact with his face. He was out cold.

. . .

The Catcher had come to play. He reached down and grabbed Williams by the back collar of his police jacket. He picked the cop up off the floor like a rag doll and dragged him down the hallway to the teacher's lounge. He took his playmate into the lounge and pitched his unconscious body on the table. He then sat at the head of the table and wrote the following note:

> "POLICE SCUM. TONIGHT WE PLAY A GAME. YOUR FRIEND LAWLOR IS ALONE ON THE SECOND FLOOR AND I HAVE A SURPRISE IN STORE FOR HIM. BEING THE GREAT SPORTSMAN I AM, I WILL ALLOW YOU TO PLAY IF YOU WISH AND IF YOU HAVE THE BALLS REQUIRED. IF YOU CAN FIND LAWLOR IN ONE PIECE, WHICH HE WILL REMAIN IN UNTIL 12:00 A.M., HE WILL LIVE. THE GRAND PRIZE IS A FULLY PAID, ALL EXCLUSIVE VACATION PACKAGE TO AN EXOTIC ISLAND, AN ISLAND WHERE LIFE STANDS STILL: A TROPICAL PARADISE. IF YOU FAIL, YOUR PARTNER WILL DIE A VERY SLOW AND AGONIZING DEATH. TO EVEN THE ODDS AND GIVE YOU A FIGHTING CHANCE, I HAVE TAKEN YOUR RADIO. HOWEVER, YOU WILL FIND YOUR GUN, FULLY LOADED, EXACTLY WHERE YOU LEFT IT. YOUR CAR IS GONE AND I HAVE PERSONALLY NOTIFIED DISPATCH, ON YOUR BEHALF, OF YOUR CURRENT PREDICAMENT. SOME MEMBERS FROM YOUR PRECINCT WILL BE ALONG SHORTLY. IT'S NOW 11:00 P.M., AND I NOTICED THAT CHEAP WATCH OF YOURS STILL WORKS, SO I'VE TAKEN THE LIBERTY OF SYNCHRONIZING IT WITH MINE."

Williams awoke to the sensation of icy cold liquid making contact with his body. For a brief moment he was unaware of his immediate surroundings. His body was covered in rotten cherries. Williams saw the note. As he read it to himself, he wondered if he was imagining this. After all, he did take a hard kick to the head. He read the note once more, cursing out loud.

He looked around the room. He had no radio and no flashlight, but if the note was correct, he could retrieve his gun. He left the teacher's lounge and returned to the hallway. In the distance, he could see a beam of light from his flashlight, left on the floor. He walked rapidly but carefully towards the light, making sure he didn't trip or stumble on the way.

Lawlor spoke into his radio: "George, come in! George, come in! You better not be jerking my chain! Come in Williams! Pick up the radio and speak to me now, Goddamn it!"

He repeated this message a few times to no response. Robert Lawlor was enormously nervous, as he had made his way thirty feet down the hallway. There were no signs of life. The silence, however, was still pure and alive. As on the first floor, there was garbage everywhere.

With his gun balanced in one hand and the flashlight in the other, Lawlor headed straight to the first floor as quickly as he could. He avoided the same route he came from, as the stairs were too cluttered. He was hoping the other stairwell would provide easier access. He walked fast, trying to stay alert but watching where he went at all times.

He held his gun two feet in front of him. He was walking past a door that said, "Janitor's Room" when a colossal black man appeared from the doorway, reached out and snatched the weapon right from the police officer's hand. It happened so fast that Lawlor didn't even feel the gun leave his grasp. Standing in front of him was the biggest and scariest looking black man he'd ever seen. All Lawlor could do was stare up at him in total amazement.

Controlling his fright, Lawlor looked into the giant's eyes and said, "I am a police officer, and if you know what's best for you, you will drop that gun immediately."

Lawlor showed his badge to substantiate his claim. The Catcher reached out and grabbed the silver badge from the terrified Lawlor, taking material and all as he tore the badge from the cop's jacket. Lawlor reached for his belt and removed a can of mace, spraying the huge guy right in the eyes. He tried to grab Lawlor by the jacket, but Lawlor had already started to back away at this point. He slipped his body from the jacket and left it in the big mitts of his attacker. Doing an about face, he fled towards the stairs from which he came. Running, he called out frantically to his partner for assistance. His calls were in vain.

Robert Lawlor was successful in catching the black giant off guard. The Catcher was actually dumbfounded. Never in his years of carrying out contracts for the Board of Directors had anyone ever gotten away from him that easily. He had never been sprayed with mace before, but now knew firsthand how it felt. His eyes were burning up and his vision blurred. He walked as fast as he could in Lawlor's direction, using the lockers and walls as his guide.

Lawlor was only ten feet from the top of the stairs when he received a smack right across the shins. As he fell forward, he noticed a young black teenager holding a piece of board in his hands. The boy mysteriously disappeared as quickly as he had appeared. Lawlor stumbled back to his feet and started running towards the top of the stairs. His legs hurting and his heart racing, the officer feared for his life. In the background, all he could hear was the sound of locker doors slamming shut or falling to the floor. The vibrations were growing louder and moving closer.

When he reached the stairs, he noticed additional desks had been thrown down the steps, making his escape that much more difficult. He walked down five steps before encountering a blockade of wooden desks sculptured to form a mountain. The ones he had fought his way through on the way up had doubled.

He knew the giant was coming nearer with each passing second. He jumped into the desks and started climbing upwards as fast as he could. He felt a hand wrap firmly around his left ankle. He was dragged back down over the desks receiving bruises and scrapes from every desk in his path.

As the Catcher tried to pick the young man up, Lawlor aimed the mace at him a second time. The Catcher ripped the spray from his victim's hand and sprayed it in Lawlor's eyes. He then sat back on the steps, watching the young man suffer the same burning agony. Once his thirst for revenge was satisfied, he grabbed the officer by the back of the head and pulled him down the hallway. His victim kicked and screamed foul obscenities at the giant as he was dragged away.

. . .

Williams reached down to pick up his flashlight. He looked along the bottom of the lockers, trying to locate his gun. After a few minutes, he found the weapon. As he reached down to pick up the gun, he felt a sharp pain in the index finger on his right hand. A large rat scurried out from underneath the lockers and ran right between his legs. Its bite had left a deep gouge in Williams' finger. The pain was constant and increasing in intensity each time he moved the finger. Blood dripped from it at a slow, steady pace. He pulled his shirttail free of his pants and ripped a piece of the fabric away. He then wrapped it around his index finger, secured a knot in the fabric, endeavoring to hold the makeshift bandage in place. Once he had patched himself up, he used his left foot to kick the gun away from beneath the locker. The gun slid outwards, hitting his right foot. He picked it up off the floor. His finger was still throbbing with pain, and the makeshift bandage made holding the gun awkward.

. . .

The Catcher pulled the struggling Lawlor into a classroom on the second floor. The Catcher threw the officer down a large hole in the floor of the far corner of the classroom. Lawlor landed with such a crash it winded him. While he struggled to catch his breath, the Catcher took his time climbing down. They were in the foyer at the back of the school. Without giving his victim a chance to recover, he grabbed Lawlor and began to drag him once more. Inside the gymnasium, an assembly of young black teenage men greeted him with cheers.

The Catcher dropped Lawlor to the floor and placed his foot in the middle of the man's back. Robert moaned, trying to squirm his way free, but he was unable to move because of the Catcher's weight. The black man removed an envelope from his pocket and passed it over to one of the young teens.

He then said, "Ten thousand dollars, just like I promised. It's time to get lost. Thanks for covering my back. Make sure the building is empty and no brothers are left."

The teenagers left promptly. They knew never to return to this place and never to speak a word about the night's events.

The Catcher removed his foot from Lawlor's back and stood him up. He threw a couple of playful smacks at each side of Lawlor's head. Oddly, he had gained respect for the young man; Lawlor was the first white man ever to get one up on him. That impressed him, but only enough that he wouldn't kill him instantly.

He continued mocking the officer, taking multiple smacks and making lunges towards him, forcing the man to travel around the gym in an effort to escape the torture. Robert Lawlor demanded to know what was going on. The Catcher just grinned and continued to push Lawlor around. At one point Lawlor lost all patience and kicked the Catcher right in the stomach. The impact had no effect. The large man didn't even blink. He laughed it off, and in a taunting fashion, held out his massive chest inviting Lawlor to take a few free smacks.

He quickly took advantage of his aggressor's offer and punched his chest and head. The more hits he landed, the wider the black fellow's grin became. He was actually enjoying the pain Lawlor was inflicting upon him. The Catcher liked a good fight every now and then and often allowed his opponents to get in several punches. Normally, his sparring partners were one of his black brothers he fought at the gym. Very rarely did anyone from the white race have this honor. He was a big man who could endure much pain. Pain was a sign of his power. The more he endured, the stronger he felt.

The Catcher wiped the blood from his lower lip. He looked down at Lawlor and said, "Alright boy. We've had our fun, but I have work to do and you're my bait for the catch of the month. I can make this easy for you or we can play it hard. See that rope hanging from the rafters? The noose on the end will be placed around your legs. I plan to pull you about fifty feet in the air. You will hang from there until…"

"Until what?" Lawlor interrupted.

"See this little box I hold in my hand? This is a special remote with a built in timer. It's connected to a little bomb at the other end of the rope. Not to worry though. The bomb is only powerful enough to blow the strands of rope apart that will be holding you securely in the air."

"Are you completely mad?"

"Mad is a three letter word. It stands for Man Against Dog. I am man and you are dog. I wouldn't worry too much if I were you. Your partner is running around the school looking for you right now. If he gets here by the stroke of midnight, you'll be fine. I've invited him to play a very special game with me, and you just happen to come along. Works for me, you know? Getting two birds with one stone always makes my day."

The Catcher was standing only a few yards from Lawlor. With the Catcher's back to him, Lawlor charged. As he came to within a foot of the black man, he jumped into the air and landed with both feet in the lower half of the Catcher's back. The contact had little impact, as the bulky male only moved slightly.

Trying to catch himself, the force of Lawlor's body ricocheting to the floor caused both of his wrists to bend backward. Lawlor howled and tried to get to his feet without the assistance of his arms. The Catcher walked over to Lawlor, reached down, and clamped on to the injured man's left wrist. Once again, he pulled the white man to his feet and with one swift yank threw the cop over his shoulder. He then walked over to where the line had been secured and untied the knot. The noose fell in a swirling motion from the rafters above. Within seconds, the Catcher had secured his victim by the legs.

Once the line was secured, the Catcher dropped his shoulder, sending his victim to the floor. Lawlor's head struck the hardwood surface and rendered him unconscious.

The Catcher headed back towards the winch and began to lift his bait up into the air. As the body rose upwards it started to swing back and forth. The higher the elevation, the faster the body swayed. Once the bait was high enough and positioned nicely, the Catcher secured the line and then headed up into the balcony, which surrounded the entire gymnasium.

When he reached the balcony, he used a grappling hook to pull his bait towards him. When he felt this would create sufficient momentum, he unleashed the rope. This, in turn, sent the younger police officer swinging wildly, high above the gymnasium floor.

Lawlor woke from unconsciousness. His whole body felt as if it was being torn apart. His heart was racing, his legs and head ached and he thought he would die. He was nauseous and queasy. He felt completely alone. The blood rushing to his head didn't help; the more the rope swung, the tighter the rope around his legs became. Lawlor began to vomit. The noise echoed throughout the entire room.

Williams had just entered the hallway that would lead him to the school's gymnasium. With flashlight and weapon in hand, he continued down this passage searching for his partner. From the other end of the hallway he could see lights. Signs on the wall indicated that the gymnasium was directly ahead.

As he approached the gym, he could pick out a series of floodlights moving about inside. They appeared to be stationed up in the balcony area, and were in constant rotation. He peered through the window, but was unable to make out anything inside. One of the floodlights was now aimed directly at the entrance. Cautiously, Williams opened the gym door and walked in.

Officer Williams was sickened at the sight of his partner swinging upside down from the rafters. He saw the vomit on the hardwood flooring beneath Lawlor. The constant movement of the floodlights impaired his vision. As he moved towards the center of the gym, his feet slipped out from under him and he fell to the floor. A woman's voice rung out from the balcony. It was the same sexy voice Williams had drooled over earlier that evening.

She said, "Officer Williams, darling. Welcome to the game. I wish to congratulate you on being selected for attendance at the penal institute known as White Man's Cotton. My superiors have selected you to pay for your criminal actions over the years against the black race. I leave you now in the capable hands of your host. Have a good evening, officer."

"Who are you and what do you mean?"

Officer Donnel's voice echoed throughout the entire gym: "You're awful pale this evening, even for a white man. You also have no authority here, so your questions will not be answered. All you need to know will be told to you in due course. I have put up with your shit long enough. I now take great pride in watching you sweat as the night's entertainment continues."

Williams shouted, "Donnel, you black bastard!"

The Catcher laughed loudly as he moved the floodlights from Robert Lawlor to his partner George Williams. He then slowly moved the light away and followed the rope until he rested at the site of the bomb.

The Catcher then said, "In order for you to finish the game the way you would want to, you have seven minutes remaining before your partner takes a swan dive onto the floor. I kind of like the little punk. He's got balls, like a real man. Not like one of those cops who hides behind his badge, making life miserable for my black brothers and sisters. What you have to do is try and find a way to get your partner down before he falls and makes a really unpleasant splash. Hitting hardwood from that height would not be a pretty sight. If you get him down safely, he lives. If you fail, he dies. As for you, once the entertainment ends, you will be taken to a new life and a new home. This is where you will get to spend the remainder of your life, paying for your sins. Good luck. Let the games begin!"

Williams ran towards the bomb. He was not a bomb expert, and the tension he felt quickly turned to panic. He was totally confused as to what to do. He knew his partner would die if he didn't do something quickly. He also knew that with his damaged hand, he wouldn't be able to control the rope long enough to lower his partner to the floor.

Laughs and jeers erupted from the balcony. Williams wanted to run up there and shoot everyone in sight, but that wouldn't accomplish anything. Wasting time would only end in the demise of his friend and partner, Robert Lawlor. He looked at the timer connected to the bomb. Only four minutes and fifteen seconds remained. He decided to muster up whatever strength he had and try to lower his partner to the ground.

It took him over two minutes to undo each of the knots that kept the young officer dangling in the air. Prior to releasing the final knot, Williams wrapped the excess rope around his waist to allow extra leverage. He then carefully pulled the rope free. His hands ached immediately as he tried to lower the rope slowly. He began to lose his grip. Williams felt the rope slipping through his fingers. It started to burn both his fingers and his side. He knew he was unable to hold on any longer. Lawlor was just ten feet from the floor when Williams lost his grip.

The young cop's moans converted to frantic screams as he began to fall. His partner ran towards him as fast as he could. George Williams failed to catch his friend, however, he did break his fall. Both men went crashing to the floor, fully unconscious.

Marla and Joseph prepared to leave. Their job was done and the money it paid was well worth their time and effort. Going undercover at the precinct was a risk that had really paid off. On their way out, the Catcher handed them their money and bid them both good night.

The Catcher reached over the balcony and turned the timer off with just seconds remaining. He then walked down the flight of stairs leading to the gym floor to check on the cops. Williams and Lawlor were out cold. The younger officer had survived the fall, thanks to the cushioning effect his partner's body had provided. They would be in pain for several days.

After the Catcher tied them up, he picked up Lawlor's limp body and threw it over his shoulders. He then left through the back entrance where a black hearse was waiting. The driver jumped out and unlocked the back of the hearse. Inside were two white coffins lined with the finest white satin money could buy. The driver lifted the lid of one of the coffins and the Catcher placed Lawlor inside. The lid was then closed and a portable oxygen tank was hooked up to the side of the coffin. The Catcher then returned to the gym and repeated the process with the second officer.

The driver passed the keys over to the Catcher, who then shot him in the chest. The driver was a sly white man who would sell his own mother, if the price were right. The Catcher couldn't afford to take chances, and since this was a white male, killing him was the only option. He picked the body off the ground and pitched it through one of the few glass windows of the school still intact. He then returned to the hearse and drove from the parking lot. Once he was about a mile down the road, he pulled a second remote from his jacket pocket and pushed firmly on the bright yellow button located at the top right hand corner of the device.

The explosion leveled the old concrete school and shook the ground for miles. Fire and smoke filled the early morning skies with the flames lighting three city blocks. Within minutes, fire trucks, ambulances, police cars, and several other emergency response vehicles headed towards the school. The peacefulness of the early morning hours turned into chaos.

The Catcher switched on the hearse's radio and drove on, listening to a variety of soft rock. He had completed yet another job and provided a valuable service to the Board of Directors. In this instance, he would give them a "two for one" special. The Catcher regularly had flexibility in this regard. With few stops, the drive to the airstrip would take a day and a half. He decided to stop once every eight hours to take a break. He sat back and enjoyed the drive.

THE MAIN HOUSE

chapter six

MARSHA Grenning was the cook for the main house. She was a middle-aged white woman whose husband had murdered two black children and their mother, seven years earlier. Marsha was at home with her husband on the night the Catcher came to call. When things went astray in his original plan, she, a victim of circumstance, was selected to replace her husband, Patrick Grenning, at White Man's Cotton.

Patrick Grenning had been waiting several years to go on trial for his crimes. The proceedings, however, were regularly postponed for reasons unknown. Many assumed it was due to the Grenning's net worth. It was estimated that Patrick and Marsha were worth in the vicinity of seventy million dollars. It was rumored that the Grennings were in the process of making arrangements to skip the country. As a result, their file was referred to the Board of Directors.

As was documented in her husband's file, Marsha was a gourmet cook. Well-known and respected, she often threw lavish dinner parties for the richer members of society. Because of this, she was immediately stationed in the kitchen of the main house when she arrived on the island.

The night the Catcher arrived at the Grenning residence, all was quiet and very peaceful. Both Marsha and her husband, Patrick, were sitting in their living room reading and listening to an early recording and special collector's version of the opera, *Turandot*. Marsha found opera very soothing and had an extensive collection.

Patrick rose from his chair and told his wife he was going to the washroom. As he reached the bottom step, he looked at his wife and asked, "Would you like me to pour you a nightcap, honey?"

"That would be fine, sweetheart."

Patrick headed up the staircase towards the second floor. Once he reached the top landing, he felt a draft coming from the master bedroom. He walked into the bedroom and saw that the window had been left open. It was a very unusual thing for his wife to do, he thought. She was very compulsive about keeping windows and doors locked at all times. She was also in the habit of double-checking everything in the house to make sure it was secure. Patrick walked over to the window and pulled it shut. As he closed the window, he heard someone behind him. Patrick turned around and facing him was the Catcher.

Patrick looked at him and said sternly, "Who are you? I don't care what you're looking for, I just don't want any trouble. Tell me what you want and you can have it. Let's not get excited or anything."

"I don't want your money, boy. I want you. Besides, no amount of money can save you now. You have been selected to become a permanent resident of White Man's Cotton. You thought you'd escape your crimes, but I'm here to ensure that justice is served."

Patrick Grenning was unsure of what the black man was talking about, but he wasn't too interested in finding out. Patrick grabbed a gun from off of the nightstand. Before he could point it, the Catcher clasped his hand. With very little effort, he bent Patrick's hand completely backwards. Suddenly the gun went off and Patrick fell to the floor. The bullet killed him as it pierced his heart.

Within seconds, the door to the bedroom opened and in ran Marsha. She started to scream, but the Catcher knocked her out with one swipe from the back of his arm. He grabbed her just before she fell to the floor, picked her up and threw her on the bed.

The Catcher saw electronic plane tickets to Novosibirsk, Russia sitting on the top of the night table. His timing was perfect. The Grennings were planning to depart in just three days. Patrick's wife, Marsha, had made all of the arrangements for their departure. The Catcher gathered up the tickets, picked Marsha up from the bed and flung her over his shoulders like a chunky rag doll. Once again, the Catcher decided to use his discretion. He substituted Marsha for Patrick: after all, she was guilty in assisting her husband in his attempt to flee the country.

▪ ▪ ▪

Marsha's situation had changed forever. She became a permanent resident of White Man's Cotton and spent her days cooking for the masters. French onion soup and Caesar salad were the two appetizers for today. This would be served with steaming hot sourdough bread. The main course consisted of prime rib roast still sizzling in its own juices, creamy mashed potatoes, green peas, turnip, and carrots freshly picked from the garden that very morning. A full gravy boat was placed in the middle of the table to accompany the mouthwatering meal.

This type of meal was a daily occurrence at the main house. As much as the Hawkins family disliked the entire white race on principal, they each took a liking to Marsha for the mastery she displayed in the kitchen and the obedience she showed them.

As the family continued their meal, Marsha returned to the kitchen to prepare crêpes and Irish coffee. The homemade crêpes were filled with vanilla ice cream and topped with a special strawberry purée.

Marsha was one of the better fed slaves on the island, tasting as she cooked. She was a bit of a bulky woman and only stood four feet, nine inches tall. The back door to the kitchen opened and in walked Oral Davis. Oral was one of the gardeners for the main house. He was a subdued man and loved gardening. He supervised all the white folks who worked in the gardens. He was also a very short man with a shape quite similar to that of Marsha's. Each day, Oral would drop in for a visit. He would stroll into the kitchen, sit down at the island in the middle of the kitchen and sample Marsha's cooking. He enjoyed just sitting and talking with Marsha. Oral knew all too well what he was getting into when he first came to the island. What he didn't know was how hard it would be for him to adjust to the cruelty he witnessed daily.

"Smells great, Marsha. Dropping by for one of your feeds is the highlight of my day!"

"Wash your hands now, before you touch one of Master Hawkins' China dishes. You know just you being here every day upsets him. At least let's not give him any other reason to get mad."

"I smell sourdough bread and it's making me drool. Can I get a slab of it to dip in your gravy Marsha?"

"You can eat whatever you want. I've got one of your favorites tonight. Prime rib roast with all of the fixings. For dessert, you can have some crêpes. Would you like salad or soup?"

"Soup, please."

"Just give me a second or two. I have to check if the Hawkins are ready for dessert yet."

Marsha walked over to the door, opened it and peeked out. The family was still eating the main dishes and chatting about the day's activities. Marsha returned to the stove and took up a bowl of French onion soup.

At the dining room table, Thomas J. Hawkins, his wife Rita, and his two sons, Eddie and Randle, were listening to Avery talk. Everyone shook their heads in repugnance as Avery elaborated on the idiotic activities of some of the slaves from Section 34.

Oral was nearly finished removing the ground-in dirt from his hands. He took great pride in what he did and ensured that all of the gardening was completed to perfection. He was often found planting and weeding in what he thought of as his gardens. The white slaves who worked along side Oral respected him the most of all of the black men who ran the island and treated him accordingly.

As Marsha placed the soup in front of Oral, Mrs. Hawkins rang the dinner bell. She wanted Marsha to know it was time for her to clear the table and serve dessert.

Marsha hastily left the kitchen and went to collect the dishes in the dining room. As she entered, she said, "How was your dinner this evening, Mrs. Hawkins?"

"It was all fine, Marsha. You've done a wonderful job, as always."

"Will you be wanting your dessert now, Mrs. Hawkins? I've made Master Avery's favorite."

"That will be fine, Marsha."

She finished clearing the table and returned to the kitchen. Oral had finished his soup and was now started on a big plate of dinner. He had served himself and was already halfway through eating it.

"Are we hungry, Master Davis?"

"What did I tell you about calling me 'Master?' You know my name. Please use it."

"And you well know that if the master heard me calling you by your first name, I would get whipped. I won't take that chance."

Marsha collected the dessert and left the kitchen. She had already completed the bulk of her work and would only have to clear away the dessert dishes before retiring for the night. Marsha was one of three women who had the privilege of staying in the servant's chambers located in the back of the main house. Each of these women was on twenty-four hour call, ready to serve any of the family's needs. When Rita Hawkins determined that additional domestic help was required at the main house, she made arrangements to have extra women brought up from the underground. The two ladies that shared the servant's quarters with Marsha were responsible for cleaning the entire main house. Isabel Snow was charged with the second floor. Her identical twin, Irene Snow, cleaned the main floor.

Once Marsha finished clearing the table for the evening, she saw Oral to the door. She then returned to the center of the kitchen where she proceeded to stuff her apron pockets with slices of prime rib and mashed potatoes she had wrapped in waxed paper. She then headed back to the servant's quarters and gave her two roommates the spoils from the evening.

. . .

Isabel and Irene had only been on the island for two weeks. Both girls said a sad goodbye to their long black hair when they arrived on the island. Actually none of the female slaves were permitted to have hair any longer than shoulder length. Once a month, everyone received a haircut, whether it was needed or not. The girls' skin was extremely pale and without their usual makeup or facials, they appeared sickly.

Marsha's return from dinner was Isabel's cue to begin her nightly task. Every night prior to the Hawkins' family retiring, Isabel was required to go to each bedroom, turn down the sheets and fluff the pillows. She did this very quickly and always attempted to do Eddie's room first. Otherwise, he would often corner her in his room and proposition her, causing her tremendous stress and disgust.

Once she entered Eddie's room, she walked briskly towards his bed. Suddenly, she heard a noise behind her. She turned around to see Eddie closing the door. He walked slowly toward her. Although he was the smaller of the Hawkins' boys, he stood at exactly six feet. As with his siblings, he too had the body of a Roman god. He beckoned Isabel to untie his shoes. She always did as she was told, regardless of how nervous or revolted she felt. The first night she and her sister arrived on the island, Avery broke two of her sister's fingers because Irene slapped him across the face for being ignorant with her. Isabel knew that each of the Hawkins' boys were violent and depraved. Isabel attended to Eddie's shoes.

He began to pat her on the head while whispering, "Good little girl. Good little girl."

His tone made her extremely uneasy. Eddie was acting strangely. She was more nervous this evening than she had ever been before. Once his shoes were removed, Eddie took her by the arm and walked her over to his bed. He sat on the edge of the bed and ordered her to remove his socks and massage his tired feet. She did as he requested and increased the pressure she was applying to his feet gradually. His feet were damp with sweat and it was turning her stomach, but she did not react.

"You can stop with the feet now, bitch. I want you to assist me in getting ready for bed. I feel tight all over and need to unwind. Start removing my clothes, woman. Do it slowly and act as if you're really enjoying it."

Isabel's eyes filled with tears, but she wouldn't give Eddie the pleasure of seeing her cry. She first unbuttoned his shirt. He pulled himself backwards and lay down on the bed.

"Climb up on my waist and continue removing my shirt."

She crawled slowly over his legs. She tried to balance herself, upright over his waist, while still on her knees. As she looked at his face, she pictured herself cutting his smiling lips right off.

She tugged at the bottom of the shirt, trying to remove his shirttails from his pants. After a couple of forceful tugs, she was successful.

"Now remove my pants, and be gentle, girl. There's precious cargo stored in there."

She unbuttoned his pants and then pulled down his zipper. Her hands were shaking the whole time. She then moved backwards, while still on her knees, pulling the pants with her as she went. Eddie had developed a full erection. He pulled off his shirt and threw it at her while laughing. He lay there, on the bed, wearing only his underwear.

"Now bitch, take that oil from off my dresser and give me a complete rub down. By the time I am ready to sleep, I don't want a tense muscle anywhere on my entire body. Make sure you put your full body into it."

Isabel did as she was told. First she massaged the entire front of his body, avoiding his groin. He then turned over and she repeated the process to the back. When she'd done this for him in the past, he would normally tell her to get out at this point, however, tonight his routine changed.

"Girl! I want you to light all of the candles in my room and be quick about it. When you're finished, come back over here for your last duty of the evening."

Isabel could barely hold the matches steady as she continued to light the candles in the room. With each one she lit, Isabel tried to think of some way to escape.

"Turn the lights out and close my curtains like a good girl."

When Isabel finished, Eddie motioned for her to return to bed next to him. "Pull off my underpants, Snowflake. I want you to become more useful to me, even if you're only a lesser white woman. I want you to blow me like you've never blown anyone before."

Isabel knew this night would eventually come, but she was still not prepared. Eddie grabbed her by the back of the head with both his hands, and guided her mouth down over his erection. He wrapped his legs over the top of her back and held her firmly over his midsection. He jerked her head up and down with his hands. Isabel gasped and choked while Eddie moaned and groaned until he eventually exploded. He then pushed her over the side of his bed.

"Blow out the candles, bitch, and get out."

When the last candle was extinguished, she closed the bedroom door behind her and ran to her quarters. By the time she had reached the door to her room, she had burst into tears, unable to speak. She entered the room and fell into her sister's arms. Both Irene and Marsha knew what had just happened. Each woman knew it was only a matter of time before one of them would fall victim to one of the Hawkins' boys.

Marsha looked at Irene and said, "Finish up your sister's chores. I will look after her until you get back."

Irene gave her sister a big hug and left Marsha to comfort her. As she was walking down the hallway approaching Eddie's room, his door opened. He looked at Irene and smirked. She did not respond. She was not going to encourage him or exacerbate the situation. She knew her time would come when she too would eventually fall victim to one of the depraved Hawkins boys.

. . .

Isabel and Irene were the identical twin daughters of Ku Klux Klan leader Don Snow, from South Carolina. When the Board of Directors selected file number 799, they requested the entire family be taken as a package deal. Thomas Hawkins had made the decision that one member of the Snow family was just as bad as the other ones, when it came to their beliefs. From the father, to the mother, to the twin daughters, each had the same faith and convictions. They were all racists and openly displayed their hatred for black people on numerous occasions.

After they reached the Island, the girls never saw their parents together again. Their father became a permanent resident of Section 34. Their mother died from a massive heart attack and her body was fed to Rachel.

Helen Snow, the twin's mother, had worked in Section 32. Her role was to clean and package mushrooms. Eddie Hawkins inspected all manual work processed in this section on a regular basis. Any women who submitted boxes of poor quality were whipped ten times. He would tie the perpetrator to a makeshift cross and pull her top down. He would then give her the lashes across the back.

Helen was a fifty-eight year old woman with a history of high blood pressure and cholesterol. She packed twenty-two boxes of mushrooms and stacked them on the table for inspection. Eddie walked over to the table and opened the first box. He was furious when he looked inside. He took the box and threw it on the ground, spilling the contents all over the dirt below.

He yelled, "Do you call this clean, you stupid old hag?"

He continued to open more of the boxes. With each one he opened, his anger increased. Seven more boxes ended up on the floor.

He turned around to Helen and said, "Over to the cross you stupid, stupid bitch!"

Helen resisted and attempted to walk away from Eddie, but he grabbed her by the hair and dragged her to the wooden cross. He took her arms, one at a time, and secured them to the wooden structure. He then ripped the cloth from her back, revealing her aging white skin.

Helen turned her head as far around as she could and shouted, "Fuck you, you stupid nigger!"

All of the women were shocked.

He turned towards the other women and shouted, "I want every single one of you to come over here and take a good look at what I'm about to do. If any of you ever decide to answer back to me in the future, this is what you're in for."

No one moved. Eddie looked at them once more and said, "You have exactly ten seconds to get over here or you'll all get it!"

The women reacted quickly for they knew he meant business. They didn't realize the extent of what was about to happen. Eddie reached back and came down with his whip across her back with all his might.

She screamed out in retaliation, "Fuck you, you stupid nigger!"

She repeated this phrase over and over. Each time the words sounded from her lips, Eddie came down harder across her back until her words were a whisper. He continued to bring the whip down across her back until finally her head fell to one side.

Eddie turned to the other females and said, "I never want to hear one of you low lives utter that word again. I want you all to take a good look at this old piece of worn-out trash. If I ever hear that word again from anyone, you will each get ten times what this old bitch just got. Is that clear?"

They responded in unison, "Yes, Master Hawkins."

"Now go over and tend to the bitch. Take her back to your quarters and clean her up. You have all fallen behind because of this piece of garbage. I want an extra two hours work from the lot of you. Consider this a lesson in insubordination."

The women took Helen down from the cross. Eddie could tell by the looks on their faces that something was wrong. Helen was dead. Eddie picked up his radio and called for two of his comrades to come to Section 32 immediately.

He then turned to the women and said, "Back to work now."

The women took extra care with their work. They kept their heads down and cleaned like they had never cleaned before. They worked in silence, as if nothing had happened. They were very frightened, but were left with no choice except to act as if things were normal.

Eddie's handymen entered Section 32. He instructed them to feed the body to Rachel. They picked up Helen Snow's lifeless body and headed away.

. . .

It was ironic how the Catcher managed to infiltrate this Ku Klux Klan family in the first place. It was also the first official time he was assigned to apprehend an entire family and he was delighted. It was an even bigger delight for him when he realized the head of the family in question was the leader of the Ku Klux Klan for South Carolina.

For weeks on end, all the local and national news stations provided coverage of various chapters of the Ku Klux Klan, which were demonstrating outside a small courthouse in Charleston, South Carolina. They concentrated heavily on the Klan's high-ranking members, including Don Snow. Klan members had gathered in droves because of a case currently being tried. A group of young black teenagers killed the lone occupant of a Honda Civic during a carjacking. The woman was an elderly white lady named Sadie Kelland. The accused teenagers were fighting to have their case tried in youth court.

Each time Don Snow spoke, his wife Helen and two daughters, Irene and Isabel, were with him. They cheered him on and encouraged the crowds. Thousands had gathered. However, there were just as many blacks as there were whites. The blacks jeered and tried to out-shout the white hooded racists.

Many of the Klansmen carried placards and passed out brochures to all of the white citizens present. This was a tightly knit community and most of the residents either knew or knew of Sadie Kelland. She had been working at the town's public library for over thirty years. The public outrage regarding her murder provided a soapbox for the Klan.

Isabel and Irene were moving around the crowd, passing out leaflets, which outlined the crime and the attempts of the accused to have their cases tried as youths. They also spoke to those who listened, and elaborated on how citizens could not allow these young blacks to be treated as children due to the brutal nature of their crime. While Irene was standing at the edge of the crowd, two black men started throwing eggs at her.

Suddenly, from out of the crowd came one of the biggest Klansmen ever to fill a white hood and robe. He knocked both men to the ground. Five or six other black men tried to take on this huge Klansman, but each of them was also knocked to the ground. Police officers stepped in and dispersed the crowd. Irene walked up to the white-robed giant and thanked him for stepping in.

He replied, "You're welcome! Anytime. The name is Jonathon Walker and I'm from Alberta, Canada. You?"

"I'm Irene Snow. It's nice to meet you. What brings you to these parts?"

"Not much work in Canada these days. I was hoping to hook up with something down here. I was a nightclub bouncer back home, but needed a change of scenery. Got myself fired for beating up too many blacks. Nothing but troublemakers and dirtbags, if you ask me."

"I want you to meet daddy. I'm sure he can use a big fellow like you. We are swarming with black trash everywhere in these here parts. Follow me and I'll introduce you to daddy."

The white-robed giant followed Irene back to the stage where her father had been speaking. As they approached the bottom step, three Klansmen blocked their path.

Irene said, "He's a fine boy, fellas. He just beat up seven or eight niggers for me."

They moved aside and let them through. Irene instructed her newfound friend to follow her.

"Daddy, this is Jonathon Walker from Alberta, Canada. He's down in these parts looking for work and he's a good old boy, a real nigger hater. He just took care of a bunch of them that tried to attack me!"

"You're a big fellow, that's for sure. Big ones like you are a prize package around here. Why don't you stick around and enjoy yourself? We'll be heading back to the ranch in a few hours. You can hitch a ride in the back of my truck with the rest of the boys. You'll come for supper and we'll talk about future employment opportunities. But first, you must join us in the parade—we always end our rallies with all Klansman in full dress, parading through the city."

The man, who referred to himself as Jonathon, left the platform and continued to walk about the crowd. The rally had started to wind down and crowds diminished. Today's court proceedings were over and the press had gotten its share of coverage: The Klansmen could go home. The police stayed to ensure no riots broke out.

Don Snow announced that the parade was about to begin.

When Jonathon reached the pick-up, Don looked at him and said, "I'd like you to meet my protectors, so to speak. Can never be too careful around here. This is Joseph Warren, Gerald Whittle and Harry Strong."

"Jonathon Walker. Pleased to meet you."

The men all jumped into the back of the pick-up truck still wearing the traditional Ku Klux Klan garb, however, Jonathon was also wearing white skintight gloves. The parade through the town took approximately fifty minutes. Crowds either cheered and waved, or jeered and threw objects.

Isabel opened the window and shouted to the men, "Daddy says we're heading home now boys. So hold on, it won't be long."

The men sat back to enjoy the ride. The town was far from sight when the truck's tires hit an old country road that led to the Snow's residence.

Joseph Warren removed his hood, using it to wipe the sweat from his brow. He was a heavyset man in his mid-fifties. Gerald and Harry also removed their hoods.

Harry looked at Jonathon and said, "For Christ's sake man, take your hood off before you perish in this heat."

"Yeah, it is kind of hot out. I think I'll take off the whole thing."

He reached behind his head, grabbed the back of his robe and slowly pulled it off. The men were stunned. Jonathon had to be the biggest black man they'd ever seen. From under his robe, the Catcher proudly displayed two handguns. He pulled the weapons out and before anyone knew what had happened, he shot Joseph and Gerald right in the middle of their foreheads. Before Harry could react, Jonathon threw him from the back of the speeding truck. The Catcher quickly pulled his robe and hood back over his head.

Hearing the sounds of gunfire, Don Snow slammed on the brakes. The Catcher gripped the side of the pick-up to steady himself. When the vehicle came to a halt, Don flung the driver's door open and jumped out, rifle in hand.

Standing alert, he shouted, "What in the fuck is going on?"

The Catcher angrily replied, "Someone starting shooting at us from the side of the road and then hightailed it back into the woods. Let's go get the bastard!"

"Take the truck and the girls home, Helen, and call in the boys. Who's hurt?"

"They got Joseph and Frank. Harry lost his balance when you jammed on the brakes. We got to go back and check on him. Wait. You stay here and I'll check. You can't go out in the open. Keep your eyes peeled and cover me. You're much too important to take any chances getting shot."

"I'll watch your back, Jonathon."

The Catcher headed in Harry's direction. He dodged back and forth on the old country road, pretending to be watching for possible snipers in the woods. Don positioned himself in the ditch, looking around while Helen drove off with the girls.

The Catcher finally reached the spot where Harry had landed. To his surprise, the man was still breathing. Don could see Harry and Jonathon in the near distance, but Jonathan's mammoth size blocked a full view of his injured friend. Harry tried calling out, but was barely able to speak. The false Klansman leaned over the vulnerable man and gently placed his hands on the man's neck. He promptly squeezed his fingers as hard as he could, kneeling on the man's side to keep him from moving. Within seconds the helpless man was dead.

Jonathan turned his head back, shouting, "I can't get a pulse. I think he's dead."

Jonathan hung his head low and shouted with a vengeance, "Come on. Let's go get those motherfuckers!"

Don came running. He too moved back and forth along the road, alert and scanning all activity near the woods itself.

Once he reached the place where his deceased friend lay, he said to Jonathon, "Did you see where they went?"

"Yes, I did. They went directly into the woods, right between those two oak trees. Come on, you stay close to me. We can't afford for anyone else to get hurt."

Don cautiously followed the big man into the woods staying very close. He was confident and secure in the big man's ability, judging from his size, speed and the loyalty this fellow had shown to his daughter earlier that day.

The deeper they headed into the woods, the tenser Don became. Don stayed within feet of his companion the entire time. Every time a branch snapped under their feet or a bird flew out from the trees above, the head Klansman's tension soared. After more than twenty minutes, his traveling companion stopped dead in his tracks and ordered Don to drop to the ground. He told the Klansman he thought he could hear voices up ahead in the near distance.

The Catcher then said, "Quick, give me your gun. I'll sneak around to cut them off."

Without reservation, he swiftly passed his rifle to the stranger. Jonathon took the rifle and slipped quietly into the woods.

The little Klansman lay in the moss and wooded growth with insects crawling over his arms and flies buzzing around his head. His ears were cocked, listening for shots or voices.

Ten minutes passed when a voice coming towards him said, "I've got the dirty black bastard. He's a big boy at that, but I've got him covered."

A large black man emerged from the trees and walked towards the waiting Klansman.

Don Snow immediately stood and roared, "You stupid black bastard. You will pay for what you've done to my comrades."

Don stood there staring at the black man with pure hatred in his eyes. He waited and watched. He then shouted, "Jonathon?"

No one else came out from the trees. There was no response.

The man looked at Don with a quirky smile and said, "I've come across a lot of tough white folks in my day. Those who think they are better than anyone else in the world. Do you know what's so funny? You have got to be one of the stupidest white men on this planet. I'd like you to meet the Catcher. You might say he's Jonathan's alter ego. Well, it's time to get back to reality. You've been selected as a permanent resident of White Man's Cotton."

Don Snow interrupted his black foe shouting at the top of his lungs, "Fuck you, nigger. You don't scare me. Do you really think you can get away with this shit? It's only a matter of time before reinforcements arrive. You'll never get out of here alive."

"I won't, hey? Well maybe it would be somewhat difficult for a man of my color and stature to just walk out of here without being noticed. However, I think that Jonathon would probably find it much easier."

The Catcher then put on his white robe and hood. He went towards Don and punched the white man in the face, knocking him out. He picked him up and slung him over his shoulders. The walk back to the road was fast and steady. Don's body weight didn't slow him down. Reaching the main road, he turned right and began walking along the curb towards the Snow's ranch. It was still very hot outside but the Catcher made good time.

The Catcher heard a truck off in the distance. Its spinning tires shot rocks and dirt as it maintained its high speed and moved closer. The Catcher removed a grenade from his pocket using his free hand. As the truck came nearer, it slowed.

The Catcher, still carrying his prey, pulled the pin from the grenade, looked at the ten Klansmen in the truck and said, "Don't worry. Our illustrious leader is fine. Justice has been served. Those bastards that have made life miserable for the rest of us this day are dead. Those that follow in the same footsteps will die shortly."

His statement puzzled a couple of men in the truck. Most of them had seen Jonathon at the rally and didn't pay much heed to his words. The Catcher whipped the grenade into the back of the pick-up. Seconds later, there was a huge explosion and all of the men in the truck were dead. Body and truck parts flew off in all directions.

The Catcher looked at the burning debris that now littered the road and said, "Another day, another dollar and a hell of a lot less assholes roaming the streets. All gone and soon forgotten!"

He continued walking down the old country road. The sun was setting, lighting the horizon brilliantly. It was beautiful and peaceful—the perfect time for a stroll. Crickets were chirping in the woods and a gentle breeze was blowing. The Catcher finally stopped in front of a roadside mailbox. Painted on the mailbox were the words:

"The Snows, as white as the name implies."

The Catcher's boot made contact with the mailbox with such force it broke its post completely in half. He proceeded up the driveway to the farmhouse's front entrance. The front door flew open and out ran Helen, followed by her two daughters.

Helen said, "What's going on? My God, what's happened to him?"

"There's a Goddamned revolution taking place! There must be at least thirty niggers out there with guns. The reinforcements are doing what they can to hold them off, but it doesn't look promising. Half of our men are down and the others aren't doing so well. Don got hit in the head with the butt of one of the bastard's rifles. I think they want him alive, for they didn't hesitate in killing anyone else. I managed to get him away, but there's no way our men can hold off the black fuckers much longer. We've got to get out of here while we still have a chance. Who owns the mini van in the driveway? We need a place for Don to lie down so you can attend to him when we leave."

Irene said, "It belongs to Gerald Whittle. He always leaves his keys in the van. No one would touch the van out here."

Irene opened the back doors to the van and she and her sister jumped in. The Catcher placed Don in the backseat directing his daughters to pull him further in. He then told Helen to help the girls look after their father. Helen joined her family in the back of the vehicle. The Catcher proceeded to close the doors behind them. Just before he shut the second door, he pitched a small canister into the van. The canister immediately released a sleeping gas, which quickly engulfed the van's interior. Within a matter of seconds, the entire family was unconscious.

After removing the white hood, cloak and gloves, the Catcher opened the doors of the mini van and allowed it to completely air out. He bound and gagged all of them and then drove off.

The ride to the docks took approximately eight hours. The Captain and crew of the ship, *The Dark Side*, was awaiting their arrival. It wasn't exactly a pleasure craft, but the vessel contained sufficient sleeping quarters for its crew of six and a very spacious cargo hold, which was more than enough to accommodate the family of four.

When the Catcher pulled into the dockyard of Pier 20, all was quiet. He drove down to the end of the pier, stopped in front of the docked vessel.

After the Snows were on board, the ship's Captain, Oliver Wallace, disembarked. His glass eye was forest green and glistened in the dark.

"Good evening, my big friend. You are early, but not to worry. Must have been an easy day's work for you, then?"

"Rather enjoyable, old friend."

"It must be precious cargo. This time they are paying six times the bounty. Here you go, friend. Don't spend it all in one place."

"Take care and make sure you give the van a real good washing."

"As always my friend, my crew and I aim to please. You'll find your car in its usual place. It's fueled up and ready to go."

The Captain returned on deck and gave the orders to hoist anchor and prepare for the journey that lay ahead.

Sitting in his black convertible on a hillside overlooking the pier, the Catcher watched *The Dark Side* through a set of binoculars as it headed out through the harbour. He could make out the silhouettes of several figures on the main deck. He also noted the crane held the van sixty feet in the air, suspended directly over the water. Within seconds, the vehicle hit the water. He stayed there on the hillside until the van had disappeared completely under water. He then placed his binoculars on the passenger's seat and put the convertible in reverse.

. . .

Irene Snow woke from her deep sleep. She was shaken and disoriented. Her surroundings were dim and a strong scent of fish filled the stale air. After a few moments, her eyes adjusted somewhat. She was in a huge storage area. Because of the rocking motion, it only took seconds for her to realize she was on a boat. She heard noises near her. She crawled towards them, calling out, "Mom, is that you?"

"Yes, Irene. Where are we? Where are your sister and father?"

Don and Isabel soon spoke. The family gathered in a group huddle and tried to clear their heads.

Don said, "I'm not sure what's happening here, but I do know it has everything to do with that big black motherfucker we met at the rally. He pulled the wool right over my eyes. Are you all okay? Is anyone hurt?"

The entire family was fine, except for their bruised egos. Of all the things that could happen to a member of the Klan, this was the worst. The Snow family huddled tightly together as they began to piece together the events that transpired since the rally. They were trying to determine where they went wrong and whether they could have prevented the mess they were in.

Suddenly, a series of loud noises interrupted their conversation. Several individuals were walking about directly overhead. After a few minutes, the hatch opened and beams of sunshine flooded the dim cargo hold. The figure of a man appeared, blocking some of the glare that came from the sun.

He leaned his head through the hatch and said, "Nice to see you have all survived the first leg of your journey. I'm Captain Oliver Wallace and you have won an all expenses paid vacation to White Man's

Cotton. Your cruise will take approximately another thirty hours, weather permitting. I wanted to welcome you personally to my ship. It's not every day I have the pleasure of entertaining members of the KKK."

"Listen here, asshole. You won't get away with this. I have friends in high places and it won't take long before you're fucked."

"Little white man, you have no friends where you're going. It is, however, a beautiful tropical paradise, owned by the most influential man you'll ever meet. He was the one who personally selected your entire family for White Man's Cotton. Anyway, once we arrive, you will be brought up to speed."

Don Snow looked up at the Captain and said, "I don't know what this is about, but if it's money you're after, maybe we can work something out."

"I'll say this once and once only. No amount of money can get you out of this. It's useless to try, and the sooner you get that through your empty head, the easier it'll be for you."

The Captain shut the hatch, leaving the family to wonder what the hell was going on. They had no idea what was in store for them: not that knowing would make it any easier on them.

The Captain instructed a few crewmembers to supply water and food for those below. One of the deckhands, referred to as Little Lou, enjoyed this part of the job tremendously and was quick to volunteer his services. He prepared a vile, rancid fish stew and proceeded to deliver it to their captives. He then summoned two of his mates to accompany him down into the cargo hold. When the hatch opened, Little Lou's friends lowered a ladder down. His mates entered first and Lou followed. Soup splattered everywhere as the cook descended. When the men reached the bottom, Lou instructed his mates to force the Snows toward the back of the cargo hold. Little Lou placed the pot of fish stew on top of an empty wooden crate.

He said to his guests, "I've prepared some fish chowder just for you.

I apologize for not having bowls or spoons to give you, but get used to it. I'm just helping you get practice."

Don shouted, "We're not eating that shit, you stupid nigger."

Lou's mates held Don's head into the pot until he inhaled, which only took a minute. His wife and daughters were in a panic, but all they could do was watch. The men pulled Don's head out of the pot. He was choking, spitting and gasping for breath.

Lou looked at the defeated Klansman and said, "Listen here, you weak, pathetic excuse for a white man, you and your family have exactly one hour to finish this. If you don't finish the entire pot within the hour, I will have no choice, but to send your two daughters up on deck. My friends would like nothing more than to get their hands on those milky white bodies. Being out to sea brings out the bulges, so to speak. If you care anything for those brats, I suggest you start eating now. We'll be back in exactly one hour."

With that, Lou and his buddies climbed out of the cargo hold. The family stood around looking at one another. Helen said to her family, "I suggest we start eating. Time is wasting."

The family dug in with their hands and started eating the broth. It turned their stomachs.

The men returned exactly one hour later, as promised. The pot was empty. Lou inspected the cargo hold to see if he could locate any remnants of the fish, but he could not.

. . .

Roughly thirty hours later, the ship pulled into dock and the Captain instructed his men to bring the Snows on deck. As they walked towards the end of the wharf, the Snow family came face to face with Thomas Hawkins and his sons, Avery, Eddie and Randle.

Avery looked at the Snows, and in a condescending tone said, "You should feel privileged. This is the first time in the history of White Man's Cotton that an entire family has been selected to visit. I assume you're all only half as stupid as you look, so I'll make this brief. We hate Klansmen. But getting an entire family of them on the island makes our day. You can say your goodbyes now. It's the last time you will see each other again as a family unit."

Irene looked at Avery and shouted, "What's the meaning of this? Have you all gone mad?"

Avery walked slowly towards Irene and grabbed her breasts.

He then said to Eddie, "Look brother. A feisty one."

Irene raised her hand and smacked Avery across the face. He immediately grabbed her hand and broke two of her fingers with just one snapping motion. His brothers pointed rifles at the remaining family members. Irene dropped to the ground in agony.

Thomas J. Hawkins interceded saying, "Eddie, take the mother to Section 32. Avery, you can take the main asshole to Section 28 for temporary assignment to help those lazy cops. When the cleanup is finished, integrate them all back into Section 34. As for the girls, Eddie, you're out of luck. These two will not be going to your work section to join the other women on the island. Randle, take them to the main house. We need cleaners. Bring them to Marsha for orientation. They can each have their own floor to clean."

After Thomas finished speaking, Avery motioned for his brothers to move out with their respective Snow.

He then shouted for all to hear, "There's lots of work to be done. Let's get moving boys."

STANDING AT WATER'S EDGE

chapter seven

ONE particular morning, Jean-Luc LeClaire awoke with a huge beetle crawling over his face. The beetle had just passed over the middle of his cheek and was approaching his ear. Still half asleep, he lifted up his hand to wipe the beetle away and squashed it against his skin. The beetle's shell crunched and its guts spewed outwards.

Jean-Luc's stomach growled. He picked up the flattened remains of the beetle and placed it in his mouth. He had grown accustomed to eating bugs, so he didn't even cringe. It tasted rather bland. Only the feeling of the bug in his mouth disturbed him.

He sat up and looked at his roommate, Robert Mitchell, who was still sound asleep. A half-inch mat separated this man from the rock hard floor. He snored something awful. Several others, who slept in rooms close by often complained, as sleep was valuable here. It was the one time they were able to forget their troubles.

As a wealthy lawyer, Jean-Luc had indirectly helped to destroy many lives. Since his capture, he often reflected back upon his life and wondered if he would ever get another opportunity to start over. He also learned the power of prayer, which gave him some peace when all seemed lost.

Mitchell, on the other hand, had little time for prayer. He was a wealthy and miserable old man who was used to everything being handed to him on a silver platter. He was accustomed to treating others like dirt. When charged with sexual harassment, LeClaire got him acquitted. It was assumed that this made LeClaire just as guilty as Mitchell was known to be.

Rumor had it that several new men had just arrived and they were soon to become LeClaire and Mitchell's new roommates. LeClaire hoped selfishly that they would never arrive. Apparently both the plane and the boat had arrived weeks earlier with human cargo. For the interim, the men were being housed and working just outside Section 28, due to a recent cave-in. No one knew anything about these men, except that one of them was a member of the Ku Klux Klan and that he was going to become one of LeClaire's new roomies.

Jean-Luc woke his roommate and reminded him that it was time to get moving. As Mitchell got up from the floor, Jean-Luc could tell from his stiff movements that the older man wasn't meant for hard labor and missed his soft, comfortable bed.

The men headed out to the dining area. When they arrived, they were surprised to smell rolled oats cooking. Apparently, the masters had determined that too many men were dying due to starvation and dehydration, and very little work was getting done. In order to combat this, Thomas decided to provide extra food to the men in the underground. Food that contained a little more substance would increase their energy levels and result in more productive workers. The aroma of the morning meal had filtered through several of the nearby caverns and intertwining passageways. It didn't take very long before the eating area filled. LeClaire and Mitchell each collected a large bowl of the precious oatmeal and sat on the floor by the far eastern wall. They immediately gorged themselves.

. . .

The day Don Snow, Robert Lawlor and George Williams arrived on the island was probably the most alarming day they had ever endured. In Section 28, work was continuing around the clock. Time was of the essence. Fifteen days earlier, a cave-in had blocked off the entrance to the section. Twenty-five men, including their black master and twenty-four white slaves, were trapped inside. Approximately ten yards of fallen rock blocked the opening to this section. As the entrance itself was just five feet wide, only a few men could work side by side at any given time to pull the fallen rock away. Hope for any survivors inside had dwindled. Radio contact with the head master trapped inside had stopped after the third day.

The men inside knew there was little to no hope of anyone getting out alive. As a result, they decided to do away with their black boss. Presumably, knowing the end was near made it easier for the white slaves to satisfy their thirst for revenge.

The last words the head of Section 28 spoke over the radio to the main house were, "Get me out quickly. These white bastards are going fucking nuts!"

Only two more feet of rock separated the workers from an opening to Section 28. Avery, who had been on temporary assignment for the recovery mission, demanded that the men move faster. Don Snow, Robert Lawlor and George Williams had arrived on the island fifteen days earlier and were immediately assigned to clear the fallen rocks. Each of them was completely worn out. Their once colorful clothing was now covered in dust and dirt. Most of the fluorescent colors were no longer visible.

Avery stood behind the men and shouted, "Get a move on. I want this done today. Young children would have this cleared up a week ago, you lazy bums. Move it!"

The men continued, trying to shift and break free the tightly packed rocks. Each rock they shifted chipped away at their strength. Robert Lawlor was the first one in the cluster to actually notice light coming from the top right hand corner from inside the rock pile. He looked at Avery and pointed to the light that was barely beaming through. Avery was delighted that they'd finally made some real progress. Avery walked closer to the pile and pushed his head towards the opening to see if he could see through. He couldn't. He demanded that the three men continue.

Just the notion of possibly finding someone alive gave each of the men a renewed strength. A sudden burst of energy had overtaken them. After all this time, the end was in sight.

It took an hour for them to finally break through. The opening was big enough for one man to crawl through. George Williams was the first one to enter. He vomited immediately once he was inside. Don Snow, Robert Lawlor and then Avery himself promptly followed him. They too were deeply disturbed with what they found.

The entire structure had caved in to some degree. The fallen rocks had destroyed most of the mushroom bins. Several of the lighting fixtures that hung over the bins were completely crushed or hanging by their wires. Most distressing was the various body parts scattered throughout. Legs, arms, heads, hands, and more could be seen everywhere, poking out amongst the rocks.

Avery instructed the men to ignore everyone else and to locate Foster first. He was the lone black man who ruled Section 28. The three captives climbed through the rubble looking for signs of life. They didn't particularly look for Foster, but wouldn't give Avery that impression. The sight they eventually stumbled upon was sickening.

They called Avery over. The head of Section 28 was found on a wooden table that stood upright. His body had been nailed to the table with at least twenty steel spikes. Avery walked up to his dead friend and tipped the table back on its legs.

He then roared, "Check all the bodies. See if anyone is still alive. Someone will pay for this."

The three men continued the search. They had checked the pulse of more than a dozen mangled bodies before coming across a pile of ten men gathered in the one area in the room that appeared clear. These men seemed to have escaped the fallen rocks. Apart from the dust that cloaked them, not one of their bodies looked damaged in any way. Robert felt for a pulse as he moved from one man to another. He finally got a pulse, on the sixth man he checked. Robert lifted up the head of the sixth man very slowly and slapped his face gently. He was barely breathing. He then called out to Avery to let him know one of the men was still alive. The remaining men in the pile were also dead.

Avery called the main house on his radio. "Foster is dead. It appears some of the workers had a field day before they killed him. We have one survivor. Send a medic down right away. I want this one alive so I can find out exactly what happened. Then I'll take care of the little bastard."

Avery looked at the others and said, "Leave him be. Help's on the way."

Lawlor laid the injured man's head back on the ground and stood up. He backed away and took his place next to the others. Within minutes, several black men squeezed through the small opening in Section 28. While they tended to the lone survivor, Avery ordered Lawlor and the others to follow him to their new quarters, Section 34.

Each man in Section 34 was busily picking mushrooms. When Avery entered the section with the three newest captives close behind, they broke out in song:

> "PICKIN' COTTON, PICKIN COTTON…"

Avery looked back at his new recruits and said, "This is where you'll be stationed. Learn to follow the rules and tune your vocal cords. The men in my section are required to sing while they work. If they're not singing, I take it they're not working. If you don't work, then you'll be punished."

It wasn't long before all three were initiated into the way things were done. Blood soon began to pour from their knuckles. They had to pick mushrooms until they completed their assigned daily quota.

As the day ended, Robert Mitchell was the only one not finished filling his quota. Even the new men who had been digging rock several hours earlier managed to catch up to and surpass the inexperienced Robert.

Avery said to the dismal man, "You're a poor excuse for a man, even a white one. Finish up now, and I may give you a chance to make up for lost time tomorrow."

Mitchell complied and headed back to his sleeping quarters with the others. When he arrived, he was introduced to Snow, Williams and Lawlor, the new roommates. All five men then sat around and discussed their current predicament and the new arrivals were briefed on how things worked in the underground. After they had become acquainted, they cleaned up as best they could, and headed out for the evening meal.

. . .

In the main house, Marsha Grenning was called to assist the island's medic with the lone survivor of the cave-in. Once the medic bandaged his minor wounds and stabilized his vitals, Marsha was ordered to sit with him. She sat there wiping his forehead with warm water and any time he opened his mouth, she tried to get some nourishment into his worn out body. It would be a long night.

The medic briefed the Hawkins' family on the man's condition. He advised them that with plenty of rest, food and water, he would be up and around in no time. Avery was delighted to hear the medic's prognosis.

The young man spent the majority of the night tossing about in an unconscious state. Every now and then, he opened his eyes and looked at Marsha. He was delirious and didn't realize he was in a warm bed with a friendly white woman beside him who tended to his every need. Little did he know that it was only a matter of time before this would end. Marsha was sitting quietly, wiping down her patient's forehead when his eyes opened wide. At first she was startled.

He looked at her with tired, watering eyes and asked, "Who are you?"

"Marsha Grenning is my name. You should relax and take it easy. You must have had a rough time?"

With tears now beginning to stream down his face, he looked up at her and said, "Did anyone else make it?"

Marsha reached her hands down and gently rubbed the sides of the man's cheeks. She then replied, "Just you son. Just you."

"Where am I?"

"You're in the main house. They brought you here after your rescue. I don't know what's going on, but the entire family is in a rage over what happened in the cave-in."

"I wish now that I had died."

"Shhhhhhhhhh!"

"You don't understand. After the cave-in, there was about ten of us that survived. Master Foster was one of them. We were all fine for the first few days, but then we realized our chances of getting out alive were next to nil. People started dying one by one. We all thought it was the end. We went mad. Pure hatred took over. We decided to make that black bastard's last moments the worst a man could ever experience."

"What do you mean?"

"We tortured him to death. The men all started going crazy. We were convinced we would die, so we attacked him. We first beat him to a pulp and then we took him and…you really don't want to know exactly what we did."

"You don't have to say anything if you don't want to."

The man looked at Marsha. At first he hesitated, but he needed to tell someone. "After he died, there were only six of us left. Every day someone died. We had practically no air left. We were breathing dust. When a man died he was placed in the center of the section. I was the last one left. When I ran out of energy, I laid down in the middle of my dead friends to die. I was waiting to die! Insects were the only things that kept me going for the first week. I ate whatever I could find. I also found a small container of water that once belonged to Foster and I drank it sparingly. It didn't last too long."

"Why don't you sleep now? Try and get some rest, lad."

The young man closed his eyes and fell back to sleep. Marsha felt a presence behind her: Avery Hawkins had heard every word.

He looked at Marsha and said, "You can go back to your room now. That'll be all for this evening. There will be no need for you to return. The family will take care of things from here on."

Marsha got up from the chair and left the room. Avery followed her out and closed the door behind him.

The next morning, a flood of sunbeams flowed through the window of the servant's quarters. It was 6:30 a.m. and Marsha was running late. She usually woke earlier than this to begin preparations for the morning's meal. She jumped from her bed and threw on her clothes. When she entered the hallway, she noticed the bedroom door where the young man had been staying was open. As she walked past the room, she noticed the empty bed. Shrugging it off, she proceeded to the kitchen to attend to her morning routine.

When she entered, she could hear voices coming from just outside the back door of the kitchen. She peeked out through the window to see Avery standing next to two other black men. The two men were helping the young man from the night before to walk. They were heading towards the underground. Marsha put her head down and said a silent prayer for the young man. After she had finished, she began preparing breakfast.

. . .

In the underground, Snow, LeClaire, Williams, Mitchell, and Lawlor were all fast asleep. They had stayed up late the night before discussing the grisly tales of the cave-in. Avery, his two black assistants and the young man who was basically being carried at this point, woke them.

Avery shouted to the sleeping men, "Get up you lazy bastards. I have some temporary company for you. I am making each of you personally responsible for keeping this little shit alive."

With that, they dropped the young man to the floor. He moaned aloud as his body impacted with the rock surface. Robert Lawlor picked him up and moved him onto his bed.

He then said to the young man, "What is your name?"

The young man looked up at Lawlor and said, "It won't make a difference soon. It's probably better if you never know."

"What do you mean?"

The young man looked at the others in the room. Fighting back tears, he repeated the story he had told to Marsha the night before. This time, however, he didn't leave out any details. The men listening couldn't believe their ears.

"Master Foster for the first few days treated all of the men trapped with him like dirt. No different than usual. There was no compassion for any of the hurt or dead men lying on the floor underneath all that rubble. We just couldn't take it any more. The more he commanded us, the more our anger grew. The time came when we couldn't take it anymore."

Robert Mitchell interrupted him. "What did you do to the black bastard?"

"We all took turns beating and kicking him until he was near unconsciousness. Then, we picked him up and carried him over to one of the packing tables. We originally planned to pin him up against the table and throw stones at him, but one of the other men came up with a better idea. He picked up a handful of spikes, the ones we normally used to fasten down the mushroom bins to the rocks. He then shouted for us to go and look for a maul. I was the one who found the maul and brought it to him. He instructed us to put the table up on its side and hold the master up against the table. We did it. He then took one of the spikes and, using the maul, drove the spike through the black fuck's right hand. He screamed in agony and begged us to stop. We all took turns driving the spikes in through different parts of his body. We all made sure not to damage any vital organs, for we wanted him to suffer. This continued for the longest time until we figured there were no spots left on his body to puncture without killing him right away. When we were finished, we all sat back and watched him bleed to death. The most frightening thing about it is that we enjoyed it! I don't believe there was one man there who had any remorse. Not one of us thought we would get out. We just wanted some satisfaction before we died."

Robert Mitchell tried to comfort the young man. "Don't worry son. That bastard got what he deserved and if I had it my way, the rest of the black bastards here would get the same."

Mitchell didn't know that Avery Hawkins and his henchmen had been waiting just outside the door. When Mitchell finished, Avery entered the room and came down across the defiant man's back with a piece of lead pipe. Mitchell collapsed to the floor, his head and back throbbing in agonizing pain.

Avery sneered at the group and said, "This makes my job a little easier. I have imported a new attraction to the island. It's a miniature man-made pool. I have filled it with some of my favorite pets. Little furry creatures not commonly known for their swimming ability, but they are very special indeed. They're the sweetest little creatures ever created, in fact. I was planning on putting the young man in a cage and filling it to his chest with water. I was going to keep him there for three days, and if he didn't pass out or drown, I was going to let him live. The thing is, he is still too weak to undertake such a test. I came here seeking a volunteer to help the young idiot. Well, Mr. Mitchell, thanks for volunteering."

When Avery and his men reached the doorway, Avery turned and said, "I'll be back after breakfast. Ham, eggs, toast, bacon, hash browns, and a nice hot cup of fresh coffee. I'm not much into performing recreational activities on an empty stomach. I offer each of you a personal invitation to see my latest creation. It's outside, but who gives a damn. A bit of sunshine every once in a while never hurt anyone."

They left. You could hear their footsteps as they proceeded through the passageway. The guards' laughter faded as their distance increased.

Don Snow asked, "What furry creatures is he talking about?"

The young man responded, "Rats. Water rats. Big, gigantic, nasty water rats."

LeClaire went to get some food for the young fellow. Everyone else just stared at the floor. They were all trying to block out the images of what was in store for both Robert Mitchell and the young man.

. . .

Marsha Grenning had prepared a breakfast plentiful enough to feed all the residents in Section 34. Unfortunately, the men in Section 34 wouldn't get to experience this feast. She rolled the cart out into the dining area where the Hawkins family had already taken their places. Avery was telling them about what had just transpired in Section 34. He finished with an overview of his plans for the midday break. While Rita Hawkins stood firmly by her family's convictions, she didn't wish to hear the details. She requested Marsha to bring her breakfast into the parlor.

Marsha followed Rita and placed her meal on the coffee table. She then returned to the main dining area to finish waiting on the others. After the male members of the family had finished gorging themselves on the buffet-sized breakfast, Marsha cleared the table and returned to the kitchen. As she entered, Oral Davis was sampling food from one of the heating trays Marsha used. He turned around long enough to bid her a good morning. She acknowledged him with a nod.

As Oral continued to eat the delicious food before him, she stood next to him and asked, "Are you aware of what's to take place shortly?"

"Some things are better left not discussed. This just happens to be one of them."

Oral finished eating his breakfast as Marsha started cleaning up the dishes. She couldn't help but think about the young man and what Avery had said of his eventual demise. It was going to be a low day for Marsha. She continued her duties, deep in thought.

The kitchen door opened and Avery appeared, followed shortly by his two assistants. He headed towards the back exit. He veered in disgust at Oral as he passed.

The three men were heading towards Section 34. When they entered the cramped room, all five white occupants were sitting together, conversing on the hard, uncomfortable floor. Avery ordered, "Assist the younger one to his feet, and the rest of you follow me."

Everyone did as they had been instructed. Under normal circumstances, the walk to the surface might have been somewhat refreshing. The fresh air and a chance to look around could have been welcomed. This particular trip, however, was very quiet. Not one of the men, black or white, spoke a word. As they reached the surface, the black men put on sunglasses. The white men stumbled about, each of them waiting for their eyes to adjust to the sun's rays.

The walk to the homemade pool took them twenty minutes. As they arrived, the captives looked mystified. The calm water looked like a regular fish farm. The structure was formed with concrete blocks. Not a rodent was visible anywhere. A platform was situated on the far side of the pool. Several cages, hooked up to heavy metal cables, running concurrently up through several steel beams, were lined up at the end of the platform. The beams all connected back to a small shed, thirty-two feet from the pool.

Avery instructed Snow, LeClaire, Williams, and Lawlor to take a seat at the edge of the pool. He then instructed his own men to escort the two remaining white men to the platform.

Robert Mitchell was the first one placed in a cage. The men bolted the door. Then the younger man was placed in a separate cage. After both of the cages were tested to ensure they were indeed locked, Avery and his assistants proceeded to the shed.

The luckier white men who had avoided this destiny were suffering in the unbearable heat. Williams placed his legs into the pool's cool water to seek some relief. His three buddies followed suit.

The sound of a motor soon emerged from the shed. The tightening cables then lifted both steel traps off the platform and extended them about six feet in the air above the water. The cages were lowered into the water, just inches apart.

Snow felt a jerking motion on his pant leg. Looking down, he saw two huge rats swimming around his legs. They all pulled their legs from the water just as a plague of huge water rats poured into the pool from a trap door. These were the biggest rats any of the men had ever seen. Judging from the rips in Don Snow's pants, at least two of these creatures had tried to bite him.

The men inside the cages were now immersed in water up to their chests. Robert Mitchell noticed that the young man was having great difficulty staying above the water. He was still very weak. Robert reached through the bars of both cages and managed to grab the younger man's left arm. He struggled to hold him from slipping under the water. The young man didn't have the strength or energy to hold himself up. After a few seconds, screams erupted from the cages, the bulk of them coming from the weakened man. Robert Mitchell was horrified. Over twenty water rats attacked the young man, biting and crawling all over him. At first, Robert didn't realize that just as many of these creatures were preparing to attack him. He was bit on the hand he was using to hold his neighbor above the water. His released his grip and fell backwards, hitting the wall of his own cage.

All of the men who had been watching from poolside turned their heads. LeClaire started throwing up.

Robert Mitchell saw that the bubbles in the neighboring cage were vanishing slowly. He watched in fear as the last bubble popped. Robert fought off the rats, trying to kill as many of them as he could. He figured that each one he killed meant that there was that many less to attack him. He died thirty minutes later.

Avery and his two acquaintances came out of the shed and headed towards the pool. When Avery came to within a few feet, he said, "I want you all to make sure you spread the word about what just happened. If anyone else even gets the idea that they can harm another black person on this island, they will meet with the same fate. For every crime, for every sign of disrespect, this is one of the punishments to follow!"

Don Snow had been looking away from Avery as he spoke. Avery grabbed him by the back of his head and threw him into the pool. The minute he hit the water, rats swarmed him from all angles. The Klansman swam hard but it didn't take long for the rats to get close to him. Don was only feet from the edge and within a few seconds of climbing out when at least six of them latched onto his clothing and flesh. Don hurled himself onto the deck.

One of the rats was still biting Don's left shoulder. He reached over his shoulder and brutally grabbed the rat by its neck. Using all his strength, he pulled it free, tearing with it his own flesh. He then threw it directly at the concrete blocks below. Unharmed, the rat scurried off, back into the water and straight back to the cages.

Avery took a deep breath and spit on the white men's feet. He walked around them for several minutes, not speaking. He eventually said, "I'm going to show you dogs another site I take personal pride in. It's the new mud bath behind the main house. You'll all get the privilege of being the first to test it for me. But, I'll only afford each of you one minute of this luxury, for a longer period would affect your complexions."

Avery directed the white men to leave. Their last glimpse of the makeshift pool, which would be forever etched in their minds, was that of little dark objects crawling around the metal frames of the cages.

The sun continued to thrust forth its brilliant rays. The temperature became increasingly hotter. Sweat covered every inch of the men's bodies. It was the first time some of these men had seen sunshine and breathed fresh air in a long time.

They reached the end of the wooded trail. The men stepped out onto a concrete walkway, which led them directly past a series of townhouses. Several other white folks were tending to the gardens along the fronts of these homes. Not one white gardener raised his head. After they passed the last townhouse, they ventured upon another path. This one was extremely rugged, overgrown with tree branches. The men had to fight their way through it.

When they reached the end, they entered into a clearing. It was only a few hundred yards from the edge of a cliff. Several holes had been dug dead center in the middle of the clearing. As they drew closer, they realized that these were holes from backed up septic tanks that were connected to both the main house and its fleet of town houses.

Avery stopped the men a few feet from the first hole. The smell was nauseating. He barked, "Strip down. This is your mud bath."

The men stood there looking at him in disbelief. However, the minute he began to move closer to them, they ripped off their clothing. One by one, his white captives were directed into the raw sewage where they promptly threw up.

After one minute, Avery instructed the men to climb out and get dressed. The men were then led back to their underground world. They were not permitted to shower or clean themselves. They were to stay as they had arrived for the remainder of the night.

The adults who lived in the underground weren't the only ones to endure much pain and suffering.

SUFFER LITTLE CHILDREN

chapter eight

ONE of the biggest tragedies of White Man's Cotton, was that it punished white children, along with adults. Many innocent children suffered at the hands of their black captors.

After the cave-in at Section 28, a team of engineers was brought in to investigate exactly what went wrong in the underground complex. They spent several weeks examining the ruins as well as all of the passages and caverns that made up the underground mines.

Everyday, many of the slaves watched the team of engineers going from one section to the next. Extra precautions were taken to ensure the safety of all the masters in the underground. Only one heavily armed master now guarded those sections that previously had several men with rifles standing on the overhead ledges. Fewer blacks were permitted in the underground until the engineers completed their investigation and ensured the Hawkins family that there was no further risk of cave-ins.

Mr. Bellows, the head engineer had just finished putting together his report on the underground dwellings. He dismissed his staff and proceeded to the main house for a meeting with Thomas J. Hawkins. Oral Davis greeted him as he walked up the pathway towards the main house. They chatted for a minute then Mr. Bellows walked up the steps to the main entrance.

He was just about to knock on the door when Rita Hawkins pulled it open. She grabbed the man's arm and said, "So nice to see you again, Mr. Bellows. You're looking good, as always."

"Thank you, Rita. Please, call me Bert."

"Okay Bert. I assume you're here to speak to Mr. Hawkins. Please come this way. Have a seat in the parlor and I'll have Marsha make you some cold lemonade."

"Thanks, that would be great."

Rita left him and headed to the kitchen. When she entered, she called out to Marsha, "Could you whip up some lemonade for me Marsha, and bring it into the parlor with three glasses?"

"No problem, Mrs. Hawkins."

Rita Hawkins left the kitchen and walked towards the library. She opened the door and poked her head in, "Thomas, Mr. Bellows is here to see you. He's in the parlor. I have Marsha making some cold lemonade right now. Come along dear, let's not keep the man waiting."

"I'll be right with you. Keep him company for me, I'll need a minute or two."

Rita headed back to sit with her guest. As she entered the room Bert stood up from his chair. She said, "No need to be that formal, Bert. Thomas will be with us directly."

The two continued to speak for a few minutes until finally Thomas Hawkins entered the room. Bert stood up and shook his hand. The three then made a few more minutes of small talk until Bert was ready to provide specifics on his investigation.

He started by saying, "Before I go on with the report, I just want you to know this is based on my personal expertise and should you wish to seek a second opinion, by all means, do so. I won't be offended in any way."

Mr. Hawkins replied, "Don't be so foolish, Bert. I have always valued your opinion and see no reason to start doubting it now."

"Well, after reviewing the structures in Sections 20 through 36, I find it very disturbing to note that Sections 24, 25, 26, 27, and of course, Section 28 are all disasters waiting to happen. With the sizes of the rooms, the tonnage of rock and dirt that are directly above these structures, and the amount of water that is slowly leaking through, we could very well be looking at more cave-ins or maybe even serious flooding. It appears that several underground freshwater springs have formed throughout these sections. Over the years, a lot of erosion has occurred and what happened in Section 28 could easily repeat itself in the other sections if we don't take measures now."

"What are you suggesting we do?"

"What we should be looking at doing is setting up a series of retaining walls and beams in those sections I've mentioned. This will involve rewiring each of the sections completely. Beams should be set up at least twenty feet apart throughout each room. The beams and walls will need to be reinforced with steel. A rough estimate on the cost will set you back between three to three and a half million dollars."

"When and how long would it take for such an upgrading?"

"I can have my men ready to go in about two weeks. We can use several of the white men to assist in the reconstruction. The only other delay would be having the materials shipped in."

Thomas said confidently, "Overall it doesn't seem too bad a situation to correct. I'm not overly concerned about the costs. However, judging from the expression on your face, there's something else, isn't there?"

"If we are to reconstruct all of these sections, we have to make sure that no one, apart from the workers on this project, is near the work site. It would mean we have to move or rearrange much of the living and working spaces underground."

"That does pose a problem. As it stands now, most of the folks underground already live and work within inches of each other. We were planning on digging out three new sections prior to year-end to accommodate future arrivals. Well, not to worry Bert. This is my problem, not yours and like everything else that goes on around here, there's never been a problem I couldn't solve."

"Alright then, it's in your hands now. I'll make the necessary arrangements regarding my men and provide you with a complete listing of all the materials we will require for this job. Good day to both of you and good luck."

With that, Bert Bellows got up from his chair and shook Thomas' hand. He left the room and headed out the front door. On the way, he stopped to say goodbye to Oral Davis, who was still hard at work in the gardens.

. . .

Seven months ago, Section 26 had been turned into a room similar to that of a cadet's barracks. It was used to house sixteen women and five children: two were nine years of age, one was eleven, and the remaining two were fourteen. The two fourteen-year-old girls worked in Section 32 every day with the adult women. The eleven-year-old boy was left to look after the remaining two nine-year-old kids, a girl and a boy.

The youngest girl's name was Melanie and the boy's name was Joseph. Their unwilling babysitter was Adam. His job was to keep the younger kids within the confines of Section 26 and to ensure they didn't cause any disruptions. The black bosses of these caverns didn't really care how old a child was when their skin color was white. Their main concern was that they obeyed the rules and respected the masters at all times.

Adam had to poop, so he headed in to where the pails were kept for that purpose. He told the other children he would be back in a minute. Joseph and Melanie were totally bored with their surroundings and each other. They had wandered over towards the exit to Section 26 and poked their heads out. They could hear singing in the distance and decided to sneak down and take a quick peek.

As they walked along the corridor, they became very confused and distracted. They had wandered into an open area where four tunnels intersected. After they had entered and walked around the open area, both children became disoriented.

Joseph and Melanie heard men coming in their direction, which made them nervous and scared. They had been warned on several occasions about the black men running these sections and the horrors they were capable of. In an attempt to hide, Joseph and Melanie ran into one of the passages. They ran for several minutes until they couldn't hear voices anymore. They were lost.

Adam came from around the corner and looked for the children. He called their names repeatedly to no avail. He was becoming irate, but his mood switched from anger to panic. He looked everywhere in Section 26, but the children were nowhere to be found. He knew the rules of the underground all too well. He was not allowed to wander outside the section. He wondered, *what am I going to do about those kids?* He had been whipped before for leaving Section 26, so all he could do was sit and wait. He huddled up against the wall just inside the main entrance and began to cry.

Melanie and Joseph were also upset. They had run in so many different directions that they were lost and very frightened. Joseph took Melanie by the hand and told her to follow him. He tried to reassure the little girl that he would find their way back. She held on tightly, but continued to cry as they walked along the dirt and rock corridors. The children became even more frightened when they noticed several rats running about.

They hurried along, trying to avoid the creatures that lurked beneath their feet. Up ahead in the darkened tunnel, they could hear the sound of water running. They followed the sound until they came upon a large cavern. It was extremely damp and cold as they stepped through the entrance.

. . .

Section 32 had finished their day's shift and all of the women were being escorted back to their barracks. As Eddie led the women into the section, Adam was still huddled by the main entrance, sobbing aloud. Alana Normore and Grace Kieley asked frantically where their two children were.

Adam, through steadily streaming tears, sputtered, "I only went to the bathroom and when I came out they were gone."

He took a couple of deep breaths and continued explaining what had happened; "I called out their names, but they didn't answer me and I was told never to go outside of here, so I couldn't go look for them."

Adam's cries increased in volume and frequency. The missing children's mothers were also in a mad panic. Eddie told them to shut up and calm down or the children would stay missing. This only heightened the women's pain.

They all stood back as Eddie picked up his radio and called the main house, "I'm going to need a few men down here. Two of the white brats have gone missing from Section 26."

The main switchboard responded, "We'll put the word out and have some extra bodies sent down."

Eddie advised the women to remain where they were, and that he would send his men to look for the kids. He swore that when they were found, he would teach them a lesson they'd never forget. The women pleaded with Eddie not to harm their children. The harder they begged, the more rapid and intense their crying became. These ladies were as afraid of what Eddie would do to their children, as they were upset about them being lost.

. . .

Joseph and Melanie slid down a very steep bank, only feet from the main entrance of the room they had entered. It led them six feet down to a second landing. When they hit the flat surface of the lower landing, they were knee-deep in icy cold water. They both turned around and tried to climb back up the slope. With each attempt, they slid back down, as the foundation of the slope became softer and muddier. Finally, the kids gave up trying to get back up the slope. Joseph and Melanie were now wet, upset, cold, scared, and hungry.

All they could do was wade through the water. Icy cold liquid was splashed over their bodies with each step they took. Nearing the middle of the room, they could hear running water. They proceeded towards the area where they thought the water was flowing from. As they came closer, Joseph noticed a giant hole in the top portion of the far wall. Water was pouring through like a miniature waterfall. Both children instantly noticed that the hole expanded with every gush of water.

. . .

Six men finally arrived to assist in finding the missing children. Eddie informed the men that a thorough search would be required and when they were found, he wanted to be notified immediately. He further advised the men he could be reached at the main house.

The men broke off in groups of two and each group took a different direction to begin their search. They had figured it wouldn't take that long to find the children and that in all likelihood, they would come across them in one of the other passages. Unfortunately, the search continued for hours. Although the search parties discovered the kid's footprints in various places, the many groups of slaves and their masters moving about in the underground had trampled them.

. . .

Joseph knew they needed to get out of the water because it was starting to get deeper and neither of the children could swim. He tried to reassure the frightened girl that she would be much warmer if they were out of the water. The children splashed along the rock walls looking for an area they could climb up on. Melanie spotted several indents on the wall that looked like worn-out stairs. She and Joseph headed for them and climbed up the rock wall. The makeshift stairs ended about ten feet from the water. The ledge was only a foot of flat rock that stuck out from the top step. It was just wide enough for both kids to sit side by side and balance their feet on the lower rocks.

They had been sitting in that same position for close to four hours. Every now and then, one or both of them would call out for help, but no one responded. Causing increased panic, the once miniature waterfall expanded an additional five feet in diameter. A huge chunk of weakened rock around the hole had given way. Water began to surge into the pool.

Melanie screamed, startling Joseph who fell from the ledge into the waters below. At first Joseph thought he was drowning as he fought to gain his footing. It wasn't until he stood that he realized it didn't go over his head.

Melanie continued screaming. He shouted for her to shut up. He slowly tried to climb back up towards the small ledge. Melanie had begun to aggravate the boy. Although he repeatedly told her to shut up and that everything would be fine, she wouldn't listen.

The water level was rising fast. It was now only five feet below where they sat. Suddenly, the entire wall with the waterfall collapsed. Another two feet of water filled the cavern. Joseph was lucky, for a few minutes earlier and he would have surely drowned. The wall that had fallen was built as a retaining wall to secure Rachel. The ugly reptile emerged, slithering over the collapsed rocks. She and the two terrified children now shared the same part of the cavern.

Just then, two black men entered the cavern. Melanie's screams had drawn their attention. One of the men shined his flashlight around the water-filled enclosure. Within seconds, he spotted the two children sitting on the ledge. They were both shivering and the girl was still crying hysterically. He shouted to the children to remain calm and stay put while he called for additional help. He tried to reassure them that it wouldn't take long. He then picked up his radio and called into the main house to let Eddie know that he had found the children and that Section 16 was severely flooded.

The second black man left to get assistance. The remaining man called Eddie a second time to inform him that he was going to swim over to the kids and try to get them down from the unstable ledge.

He then lowered himself into the water, and started to swim towards the kids. Joseph shouted for the man to watch out for the alligator. Unfortunately, Melanie's screams were of a much higher pitch and the man didn't hear the warning.

. . .

At the main house, Eddie advised his family of the flooding and the man's attempt to aid the children. Thomas Hawkins said hurriedly to Eddie, "Section 16 was reconstructed to enable the insertion of a retainer wall. It was needed to help secure the crocodile's underwater lake. If the section's flooded, there's a good possibility we've sprung a major leak. Call your man and make sure he checks things out thoroughly before he attempts to do anything else. If there's any damage to the retaining wall big enough for the crocodile to squeeze through, she will."

Eddie quickly repeated his father's words on the radio for the man to hear. However, he would never hear this message for his radio was far from reach, still resting back on dry land.

Other black men soon entered the cavern. To their horror, the large reptile's head was gliding slightly above the water, swimming towards their friend. Melanie, although nearly hoarse, was still screaming at the top of her lungs. The other black men on the bank were shouting warnings at their friend. Joseph just sat there and pointed in the direction of the creature. He was too dumbfounded to shout anymore and in all likelihood knew he wouldn't have been heard above the others.

The swimmer finally reached the children. He stretched out his arms, motioning for the little girl to jump. He intended to take one child at a time and swim back. Melanie froze. The look of horror on the child's face frightened the would-be rescuer. He immediately knew something drastic was afoot. When the man turned around to see what startled the girl, he heard his friends' calls.

Then he saw her. Without time to scream, the crocodile grabbed him solidly between her jaws from his waist to his feet. The reptile turned around and pulled him back out into the water, where she began thrashing him about. She tore his body to shreds. Within seconds, his eyes bulged from their sockets and his body went lifeless.

Those remaining on shore had no intentions of assisting the kids at this point. They were all too familiar with Rachel's strength. There wasn't a man or beast on the entire island considered a match for her.

One of the men on shore picked up his radio and called the main house. When he had finished talking with Eddie, he told the others to go get the children's mothers. If they wanted to get their kids back, they would have to do it themselves. Eddie wasn't about to lose any more of his men.

Rita Hawkins overheard Eddie's conversation and was livid. She moved towards him and stood inches from his face. She told him that these kids were innocent and must be helped. She then shouted to her husband that if no rescuers were to be sent, the slaves should be given the option to help. Rita then stormed from the room. Thomas took the radio from Eddie and informed the rescue team they were to proceed through all the sections and look for volunteers to assist the two young children. He agreed with his wife, white men would be more eager to help one of their own. Besides, he thought, they're much easier to replace should the need arise.

. . .

Another hour had passed and the children's energy levels were fading. Their legs were extremely tired and their body temperatures had slowly dropped. Their attention and concentration was focused solely on the ferocious crocodile that swam beneath them. Every now and then, she would stop directly in front of the children and stare at them.

The mothers arrived and were taking turns shouting words of encouragement to their kids, telling them to stay alert and to be strong and brave. Grace told them that help was on the way, and to keep calm and that everything would be all right. Even though the kids were scared out of their wits, those words of comfort went a long way to console them.

. . .

Three black men entered the sleeping quarters of Section 34 and explained to the occupants what had happened. None of the men currently inside would volunteer their assistance. Shortly following this, two other white men walked in with their black masters leading. They had come from two other sections to seek volunteers for the rescue mission. They volunteered because each of them had arrived on the island with a child. As the black masters did not mention the trapped children's names up front, the men who volunteered were not about to take the risk of losing their child.

Robert Lawlor couldn't believe what he was witnessing. Not one of his roommates had offered to volunteer in the children's rescue. He said to Don Snow, "Don't you have two girls, Snow?"

"Both my girls are in the main house. I saw them yesterday when we passed by. They waved to me from the upstairs window."

"Lucky you! I wonder, would you be so quick to sit back if you didn't see your girls yesterday?"

Robert Lawlor stood up and said, "I'll go. I'd rather spend my time trying to outsmart the beast in the water, than sitting here with a bunch of yellow-bellied snakes."

LeClaire stood up and joined Lawlor. As the rescue party left, the rest of the men just bowed their heads.

Finally reaching their destination, they piled inside the cavern and stopped on the bank away from the water's edge. The two men who accompanied LeClaire and Lawlor sighed deeply with relief. Neither of the children on the ledge was theirs. One of the men had a fourteen-year-old daughter, while the other was Adam's father.

One of the guards addressed the four white men, "Here's the situation. Separating you from the children over there on the ledge is the croc. I don't see her now, but believe me she's there. You'll have to decide how you'll get to them. Some of my men, on their way as we speak, will be bringing a raft. I don't think it will help much, for I'm sure the beast can eat that too."

The youngsters' mothers, still standing on the bank, pleaded for the newcomers to hurry and do something to help Melanie and Joseph. Lawlor reached down and picked up a fair-sized rock that was on the ground near where he stood. He then walked to the edge of the water and threw the rock out as far as he could. It landed fairly close to the opposite rock wall where the children were trapped.

Rachel's scaly body emerged from the water's surface. She began to swim in the direction that the rock had been thrown. She returned her focus to the children the minute she realized nothing was there. Every few minutes, she would rise slowly from the water just below the frightened kids and thrash. Their time was running out. Both children were showing signs of weakness. No one knew it better than their mothers, who were growing more frantic by the minute.

Lawlor pointing to the crumbled wall on the opposite side of the room said to one of the black men, "How far away is it from here to the other side of that wall?"

He responded, "A four-or five-minute walk."

"What we need to do is go over there and distract the crocodile away from the children. Two people can swim for the children while the other two can work on getting the beast's attention. If we can keep the creature distracted long enough, it may buy us enough time to get the kids off the ledge and back to this side."

None of the men relished the idea of having to get into the water to help the children, but it had to be done soon. Lawlor volunteered to attempt the water rescue. Adam's father, Randolph, had agreed to be the second man. LeClaire and Jeff Hanlon, who was the second volunteer of the day, headed off with their black escort, around to the other side.

Shortly after the three men left, two guards carrying the rubber raft arrived. The men immediately began the difficult task of inflating it. Just as the raft was full, LeClaire and Hanlon had reached the other side. LeClaire ran to the bridge and picked up a bucket of fish. He then joined Hanlon and walked to the crumbled wall.

Once they arrived, LeClaire shouted across to the men on the other side, "We're here. Any signs of the ugly bitch?"

Lawlor responded, "She's still lurking around the children. Maybe if you start making some noise on your side, she'll head in your direction."

LeClaire and Hanlon each found a solid footing along the wall approximately four to five feet above water level. LeClaire threw fish into the water, while Hanlon threw rocks and shouted.

The plan appeared to be working. The crocodile's eyes appeared along the top of the water and were headed straight toward the two men. Ferociously, she attacked the fish as they were hurled at her. Thrashing violently, she would compress a fish between her jaws and swallow it instantly.

Lawlor and his partner lowered the rubber raft into the water. They were extremely quiet, keeping a close watch on the other side of the flooded cavern. Rachel appeared preoccupied. With only one paddle, the men made their way over to the children, keeping a close watch on Rachel the entire time. They were within a few feet of the children, when Rachel's scaly body withdrew from LeClaire and his partner's sight.

Hanlon shouted frantically to the men in the raft, "Rachel's disappeared. Can't see her anywhere. You better get out fast."

Lawlor was too close to the children to turn back now. He shouted to the kids to jump into the raft and he would catch them. They could hear their mothers in the background encouraging them to listen to the man. Both children leaped from the ledge at the same time and landed in his outreached arms. Lawlor fell backwards into the raft. He pushed the small ones aside and grabbed for the paddle. Adam's father had already beaten him to it.

Lawlor shouted, "Get this raft moving now!"

Randolph paddled with all his might. With only one paddle and more weight in the boat, movement was slow and awkward. The raft moved mostly side to side, rather than heading in its intended direction. Adam's father was unable to switch the paddle to the opposite side fast enough to gain the momentum needed to move the raft.

Hanlon roared at the men in the raft to move faster. In all the excitement, he lost his footing on the rocks and fell into the water. Right away, LeClaire headed over to help his friend out. Rachel, sensing that something had entered the water, swiftly headed straight for her intended prey. Just as LeClaire grabbed Hanlon's hand, Rachel was upon him. She yanked Hanlon into the water pulling Jean-Luc LeClaire in too.

As Rachel was busy mangling her latest victim, LeClaire swam speedily back to safety. He was just pulling himself up out of the water when her jaws closed only inches from his body with one tremendous snapping motion. She had barely missed, as he scrambled further away from her. It was the fastest he had moved in his life.

Lawlor looked at the activity that was taking place across the way and without a word he picked up the girl and jumped into the water. Holding the girl in one arm, he swam towards the bank where both mothers stood waiting anxiously. Lawlor made it to safety with the young girl, who by this time had slipped into a complete state of shock. He lifted Melanie out of the water and into her mother's arms. She grabbed her daughter and hugged her tightly.

Rachel was heading directly to the raft. With only twenty feet separating the rubber craft from safety, Rachel pierced it and the raft exploded. This sent both Randolph and the young boy flying into the water. The man began swimming towards the left of where the others now stood. LeClaire tried frantically to regain the crocodile's attention. He dumped the remains of the fish, bucket and all into the water. When that didn't get her attention, LeClaire even jumped into the water himself and started to splash around next to the shore. Rachel was stalking easier prey and totally ignored his futile actions.

Adam's father continued swimming. He was less than ten feet from the edge of the pool when the scaled body of the big crocodile came to within inches of his head. He began treading water, trying to determine his next move. He was nervous and unsure which direction he should move in. His main concern was to avoid Rachel's deadly grasp.

Young Joseph had gone under twice and came up splashing and gasping for air each time. He grabbed onto the already deflated rubber raft, which provided a perfect camouflage. Rachel totally ignored the little boy and his slowly sinking raft.

Lawlor and the others watched from the shore, as Rachel moved in on her latest prey. She didn't charge him though; she may have been full from her previous eats. LeClaire was still kicking and screaming, trying to attract her to him, but it was to no avail. Joseph's mother fainted from all the excitement. Melanie's mom, unable to withstand the tension, had already returned the child to the safe confinements of their barracks.

Rachel continued to glide back and forth in front of the frightened man. She appeared to be forcing him closer to the middle of the pool. With each sweep, the space narrowed. Rachel was now in the middle, between Joseph, who was struggling for his life, and

Randolph. LeClaire's attempts to distract the deadly female had failed repeatedly. The reptile's attention was now on Joseph one hundred percent.

Lawlor felt that if he didn't act soon, the young boy would certainly die. He began swimming towards the sinking raft, keeping his eyes focused on Rachel. Just as the boy went under, Lawlor grabbed him by the head and pulled the tiny lad up for air. The little boy gasped while he desperately tried to fill his lungs with air. Lawlor immediately commenced his swim back to shore, holding the tiny figure firmly against his chest. He scanned the water, keeping his eye on Rachel as he swam.

To Lawlor's horror, Rachel appeared at water level, staring at him. Randolph took full advantage of the situation and got himself to the safety of the opposite shore. Lawlor was successful in getting himself and Joseph to safety with no time to spare. He was barely away from the water's edge when Rachel emerged from the water, slashing out in defeat.

Joseph's mother had slowly regained consciousness. She was confused and started to cry. Joseph looked at his mom and said, "Don't cry mommy. It's okay now."

She picked her boy up in her arms and headed back to their sleeping barracks. On the way out, she thanked the others.

Adam's father was slowly moving along the base of the rock wall. He was taking his time to ensure he wouldn't slip. He was getting closer to safety with each move he made. Lawlor stood by, quietly encouraging the man to continue moving carefully towards him.

The two black masters that remained appeared bored.

Rachel's eyes were visible at the surface of the water, keeping track of every movement the man made. She stayed focused on him as he continued to edge his way along. Every now and then, she would leap up from the water and come back down with a huge splash. He tried to ignore her, for he knew that one false move would mean his demise.

He came upon a section of rock wall where he was unable to locate a secure footing. He called out to Lawlor and LeClaire, "I can't go any further. It's too dangerous to try and go back. I'm right-handed, and totally useless when I use my left. I think I'll have to make a jump for it. Is there anyway you can distract that ugly beast for me?"

LeClaire shouted back, "I'll throw some rocks into the water and see if that helps."

He picked up a handful of rocks and started throwing them out towards the middle. After a few minutes had passed, Rachel's eyes disappeared. A long time elapsed and still there was no sign of her.

The two black men who remained were persuaded to move their flashlights back and forth over the top of the water looking for signs of movement. Rachel was nowhere to be seen.

The man called out once again, "I can't hold on much longer. The walls are very damp. Some of the dirt and rocks are coming loose. I'll have to make a jump for it. Try to reach out and get a grip on me. I don't want to fall back into the water."

Lawlor and LeClaire positioned themselves where they would be able to grab hold once he leapt. The man took one last look for signs of life below. The water was completely still. He pushed himself, using all his strength, out from the wall in their direction, seeking a solid landing. He was but inches from his friend's grasp when the water below him stirred. At the same instant Lawlor and LeClaire made contact, the crocodile hooked him by his left leg and with one mighty snap, the leg disappeared. Rachel retreated back into the water, splashing the three men.

Immediately, Adam's father went into shock. Blood poured rapidly from his left leg. His body went into convulsions. Lawlor and LeClaire pulled him from the water. They looked at the two black men hovering over them and said, "Call in some help, quick before he bleeds to death."

One of the men replied, "Follow me back to your quarters. My friend will take care of it from here."

Lawlor replied, "We'll stay and help."

With that he received a smack across the side of his head with the butt of a wooden club from his black master. "I said, you go back to your quarters now and he'll be taken care of."

LeClaire assisted Lawlor off the ground and out of the cavern. He had received a sharp gash to the back of his head. Adam's father remained on the ground. His convulsions increased rapidly with each second. LeClaire and Lawlor were left with no choice, but to obey their masters and leave the man behind.

A shot rang out. Adam's father, Randolph, was no longer shaking or convulsing. His black master had shown pity towards a white man. Rachel watched as the dead body was dumped in the water and devoured swiftly.

Lawlor and LeClaire had heard the gun shot as they walked back to Section 34. LeClaire patted his friend's back and whispered in his ear, "We both know he's much better off. He's gone to a better place now. A much happier and peaceful place where he's finally safe."

When they arrived back at Section 34, the others were fast asleep, or at least pretending to be. The rescuers were still visibly upset with their sleeping friends for not offering to help. They had endured enough pain and torment for one evening and were glad not to have to talk about it.

. . .

Melanie and Joseph were both lying in bed with their mothers. Melanie was wide-eyed and staring off into space. Her mother ran her fingers through her daughter's hair, singing softly, but the little girl made no response. Joseph was clinging tightly to his mother with both arms. He had fallen into a soft sleep. Every few minutes, his body would twitch. His mother looked down at him with tears streaming down her face.

Adam had left his bed and was leaning against the far wall. He was watching his two little friends and their moms with tears in his eyes.

He overheard the women talking about how his father died.

The children endured more than their fair share of suffering while they were residents at White Man's Cotton. For the most part though, they were often shielded from the hard work and torture. After this episode, replenishment of the slaves in the underground was required and very few of those who followed were children.

THE WHITE KNIGHT

chapter nine

IT was a Monday night in May. A sellout crowd had gathered at Madison Square Gardens in New York City. Tonight, the White Knight was to make another appearance as the "slayer of the black race." This special event for the New World Wrestling Resistance Federation brought people out in droves. Tickets for this event were two-hundred and fifty-two dollars per person. Many wrestling superstars had top billing this evening.

The main event for the evening featured the White Knight taking on two opponents at once. They were two black men known as the brutal tag team, Skull and Bones. These individuals stood at a combined weight of four-hundred and seventy-two pounds. While neither was overly muscular, they were large and extremely solid.

The original White Knight, Harry Barbour, was no longer active on the wrestling scene. Unofficially, he had been retired for just over three years. Since his last match, three other individuals had assumed the role of the White Knight. However, due to his flamboyant portrayal of the White Knight, he was still used for special guest appearances and interviews. Both loved and hated, of all the White Knights, he was the one crowds still reacted to the most. Each time the White Knight made an appearance, security in the auditorium was tripled to stop the fans from fighting rather than to keep them away from the professional fighters.

There were seven feature matches prior to the match between the White Knight and the tag team of Skull and Bones. Everyone wondered, *would this be the night that the White Knight finally faced defeat?*

The Catcher sat patiently in the audience and watched the match in progress. He knew the strength and endurance it took to put off such a show and had a special appreciation for wrestlers.

Two fat white dudes sitting behind the Catcher had become very annoying. Every few minutes, one of them would make a derogatory crack.

The one on the left quipped, "You would think they would be able to find a few blacks who could make the White Knight break a sweat."

The Catcher could take no more. He turned around and said angrily, "Listen here, you fat fucks. If you don't shut up shouting that crap in my ears, I will reach inside your throats and remove your innards. Got that?"

"Fuck you!"

The Catcher turned around and grabbed both men by the balls. He then squeezed tightly. The men fell back in their seats, dropping their food and struggling to breathe. After the Catcher let go, the men picked up their belongings and quickly moved from their seats. They headed as far away from the man as they could, cursing their assailant under their breath.

Suddenly over the loudspeaker the announcer said, "Ladies and gentlemen, friends and foes, and people of all ages, the moment you have all been waiting for. Coming down the aisle in the blue trunks, weighing in at a combined weight of four-hundred and seventy-two pounds, the everlasting, the ever-powerful, Skulllllllll and Bonesssssss!"

The crowd erupted into a mad screaming frenzy. Skull and Bones slapped the fans' hands and waved wildly as they walked towards the ring. They jumped up on the apron and hopped over the ropes, landing inside the ring.

The announcer raised the microphone and said, "And now, the moment of truth! The moment we have all been waiting for! Coming down the aisle…"

The announcer stopped. On the many closed circuit television monitors that surrounded the entire auditorium, the impressive physique of the White Knight suddenly appeared. This projection made him look twelve feet tall and well over four-hundred pounds of solid muscle. He wore white trunks that complimented his perfectly tanned body. His face was covered with a white mask.

A hush spread over the audience, and the White Knight shouted to the ring announcer, "Shut up you little shrimp. I have something to say. Tonight, as usual, I come here to waste my time and energy to pulverize another two useless fat black boys. I call them boys because it'll be like kicking the shit out of kids. I only trust the next time this Federation seeks someone black to take me on in the ring, they come up with someone, some two or even some three opponents, who are worth fighting. I hate wasting my time on weak pathetic crap like these two."

The crowd erupted. Some roared while others jeered; Harry Barbour had a way of inciting the fans to madness. Harry himself would not be going into the ring. White Knight number three was already positioned to take the walk to the squared circle. Harry just stirred up the fans prior to the start of the match, and then headed for one of the private spectator's booths. These booths were reserved explicitly for clientele who were willing to pay five-hundred dollars for them. They offered privacy, each booth had its own entrance, spacing, five seats per booth, and free customary beverages and other refreshments.

The Catcher headed towards the Micto Tech Booth, which was only accessible by elevator and pre-reservation. He flashed his ticket to one of the ushers who monitored the area, stepped inside the elevator and within seconds had reached the private booth. Inside sat Harry Barbour.

Harry had an uncommon interest that only those closest to him knew about. He enjoyed erotic wrestling with other men. He especially loved having private bouts with other men his size. Harry kept his homosexuality a secret. Apart from his manager, the promoters and some close friends and associates, no one else knew of his sexual orientation or this extracurricular activity, let alone the fact he was the original White Knight. Although in the ring Harry portrayed a character who despised blacks, that was not how he truly felt.

Harry struck up a conversation with the large black man sitting behind him. "How are you this evening?"

The Catcher responded, "Just fine, and hopefully a great deal finer before the evening ends."

"How so?"

"Love to watch men wrestling. The White Knight is an awesome individual. I think he'll have his hands full this evening, though."

Harry sized him up. He thought to himself how great it would be to take him on in a private match. He would love to see what this man had to offer.

The Catcher moved so that only one seat separated him from the wrestler. He removed his long black coat, displaying his truly unique physique, which was evident through his skintight jeans and white strap shirt. The Catcher then stood up and headed to the complementary bar. As he turned around to ask Harry if he was interested in a drink, the Catcher noticed Harry had been sizing him up.

He said, "My friend. Would you care for a drink?"

"That would be nice. A White Russian would do fine."

The Catcher replied with a grin, "How about settling for a Black Russian?"

Harry smiled back. The Catcher passed a drink to the White Knight, who smiled, thanked him and sat back to watch the main match already in progress.

White Knight three was in the ring doing battle with Skull. He had picked the black man up, lifted him over his head and slammed him to the mat. He then grabbed him by the back of his head and pulled the man to his feet. He pushed him towards the corner, generously allowing him to tag out with his partner, Bones.

Bones entered the ring and kicked the White Knight in the stomach, sending the champion to the mat on one knee. He then took a run into the ropes, bounced off them and charged the White Knight. The White Knight was struck from behind with an elbow to his shoulder blades, which sent him face first to the mat.

The fans were going wild. Bones pulled the White Knight to his feet. Holding him by the back of his mask, he forced the white wrestler towards Skull. His partner tagged in and both Skull and Bones sent the White Knight into the ropes. He bounced back and was greeted with a double flying backdrop. The White Knight landed on the mat with a crash. His two opponents then came down across his chest with a double elbow drop. The referee finally jumped in and pushed Bones back into the corner who jumped over the ropes and stood proudly on the ring's apron, watching his partner continue the assault on the White Knight. The fans were still going wild.

The Catcher looked at Harry and said, "Great routine they have going in this match. The fans are eating it up."

"You got that right, but keep watching. It's going to change pretty soon."

With that, the White Knight rebounded. He moved just as Skull was about to deliver a high-risk maneuver from the top ropes. Skull landed on the bare mat and rolled around the ring displaying agonizing pain.

The White Knight was on his feet and the crowd roared. He ran towards Bones and landed an elbow in the man's face. Bones flew from the outside apron onto the concrete floor. The White Knight then rammed himself back into the ropes, gaining additional momentum, and flew into the air, coming down across Skull's chest with a heavy leg drop. He jumped up and repeated this move three more times. Each time his leg made contact, Skull would bounce around the ring as if he was trembling with convulsions.

Harry asked, "You look like you may have done a bit of wrestling in your time. Have you?"

"Well, I'm what you'd call an amateur. Always looking for anyone interested in going a few rounds, just for the fun of it. I really don't know a lot about the holds and special moves, but I'm eager to learn. Tried a few times, you know, but there's not too many big men out there I can wrestle with to keep it on an even keel. Most of the fellows I've wrestled are much smaller. My size doesn't exactly help me when I'm looking for fun and practice at the same time."

"Know what you mean, friend. Don't mind if I call you, 'friend'?"

"Not at all."

The Catcher stood up and returned to the bar. He didn't ask this time. He just went ahead and poured Harry a drink. He continued to do this several times over the course of the next half hour. The drinks were going down like water. The Catcher continued to charm Harry.

The wrestling match had been going on for almost an hour, and it was steady back and forth between the White Knight and his tag team opponents. Harry had developed a glow from all the triples the Catcher had been mixing him. The White Knight dropped his glass to the carpet and looked over at his companion, laughing.

The Catcher looked back at him saying, "I think you're cut off. I was hoping you could hold your liquor. Maybe we could set up a match between us down the road. I don't think you'd be in a state to try your hand against me tonight."

"I've been involved as a wrestler both inside and outside the ring all my life. I can wrestle sober or drunk and give any man a run for his money."

The Catcher said with a smile, "I have a ring set up at my house. I wouldn't mind taking a few lessons now if you're up for it. Don't let my size fool you. It's only the little fellows that find wrestling me awkward. They have trouble throwing me about or bringing me down to the mat. We could have a few more drinks back at my place and maybe have some fun in the process."

Harry was interested, but was also very cautious. He said to the Catcher, "Why don't you give me your address and I'll see?"

The Catcher pulled a pen and paper from his coat pocket and wrote down the information.

As Harry reached for the paper, the Catcher grabbed his hand playfully and said, "Let's just have a little arm wrestle before I go. Just want you to see what you'd be up against, should you ever decide you'd like to give me a try."

Harry returned the squeeze and both men stood up and walked to a small table in the corner. Harry removed the lamp from the table and placed it on the floor. Following this, they began their arm wrestling match. The Catcher let the White Knight totally destroy him. After which he reached over and wrapped his massive arms around the White Knight's neck, pulling him from his chair onto the carpeted floor below. The two men wrestled with each other on the floor of the private booth.

Harry was extremely impressed with the size and strength his black opponent displayed. He wrapped his arms around his opponent's waist, flipping the black man onto his stomach. The White Knight made his way behind the Catcher and secured a sleeper hold.

The Catcher pretended to weaken from the hold, and raised his arm in defeat pleading, "I give. I give."

The White Knight broke the hold on his man and said, "You're a solid contender. Could be a good challenge. I say we'd have a great time going a few rounds on the mat. I tell you what. I know the outcome of this match. As a matter of fact, it will be all over in exactly ten minutes. The White Knight wins, of course. Why don't we get out of here before the crowd starts to disperse and we're stuck here for another hour? I have your address. I'll swing by my place and get my gear. I have an extra singlet if you need one."

"Not to worry. I have my own wrestling gear. Just take your time. You know where I am and if you're interested in trying your luck on my turf, then I'll see you when you get there."

The White Knight helped his partner to his feet. The men grabbed their jackets and headed towards the elevator. After a few more minutes of joking around with each other, the elevator doors opened to the main concourse. The Catcher was the first to exit, with Barbour following.

On his way out, an usher and former wrestling partner commented: "Looks like you found a match close to your own size, Harry?"

"He's just a pussycat, Tom."

Harry Barbour stood on the front steps of the stadium and watched as the muscle-bound black man walked towards his convertible. He thought, *this was definitely a man with class. It could very well turn out to be an interesting night after all.*

The convertible drove off. The completion of file number 727 was close. He drove down Route 62, taking Exit 74, which eventually led him to Harper Subdivision. He pulled onto Lipton Avenue and proceeded down the street until he came to number 33. He pulled into the driveway and turned off the ignition. Stepping from the convertible, he gazed around the brand new subdivision. Only five houses were completed. All looked calm and quiet. He walked up the driveway towards the side entrance to the house. When he entered, it was in complete darkness.

He threw the light switch and headed for the living room. To the right of the living room was a set of stairs, which led to the second floor. He jogged to the top and proceeded down the hallway. He came to the only closed door on the second landing. Inside the room, lay his previous encounter still tied up on the bed. This middle-aged man was new to the city and even newer to the wrestling scene. His ad on the Internet read:

> "LOOKING FOR SOME HONEST CLEAN FUN. I AM IN MY LATE FORTIES AND HAVE JUST MOVED TO THE NEW YORK AREA. IF YOU LIKE IT GENTLE OR LIKE IT ROUGH, SEND ME AN EMAIL AND WE'LL SET SOMETHING UP. I HAVE MY OWN RING AND WRESTLING GEAR. SUBMISSION, AMATEUR AND EROTIC WRESTLERS ARE ALL WELCOME."

When the Catcher searched the Internet for potential prospects to assist him in his abduction of Harry Barbour, there weren't many erotic wrestlers in the general area. When he read this posting, he knew he'd found the person he was looking for. He had intended to get rid of the man as soon as the Barbour file was closed. The only thing that saved this man's life was his skin color: he was a middle-aged black man.

The Catcher left the room, closing the door behind him. He headed back to the garage, which had been converted into a makeshift wrestling room. The ring was of regulation size, taking up much of the floor space. The Catcher left the door open and walked towards the liquor cabinet in the kitchen, which overlooked the wrestling ring. He pulled from it the necessary bottles and glasses for their Black Russians. After he was satisfied that the house presented a warm, inviting atmosphere, he sat on the sofa by the front window and made himself comfortable. It was now a waiting game.

Headlights came towards the driveway from the near distance. Harry emerged from the taxicab carrying a gym bag in his right hand. He paid the driver and then looked at the house. He asked the driver to wait a moment while he confirmed the address. He walked up to the side door and knocked three times.

The Catcher, who was already waiting at the side door when he arrived, opened the door. Harry stepped back from the side entrance and waved the cabby off. As he stepped inside, the Catcher teasingly placed him in a headlock and led Harry through the kitchen towards the living room. As the two men passed the entrance to the garage, he released his grip.

Harry looked inside saying, "Now that's what I call a setup. Most people just have mats placed on the basement or garage floors."

"Just as well to be comfortable when you're having fun. This makes it as close to the real thing as you're going to get. Why don't we have a few more drinks to loosen up before we go at it?"

"Sounds good to me."

They went into the living room where Harry took a seat. The Catcher picked up two glasses and began to pour his drink. Before pouring Harry's, he reached into his pocket and removed a clear plastic pouch containing a white chalky substance. He poured the powder into Harry's glass. The narcotic would take at least an hour to kick in. It was meant to weaken an individual, not knock them out. It also contained no flavor and therefore would not be detected. He stirred the drinks and returned to the living room where he discovered the White Knight had already gotten quite comfortable. Harry had changed into his wrestling gear. He was wearing a white mask and white trunks, and had draped a large white cape over his shoulders.

The Catcher said, "Impressive. You almost look like the White Knight in that outfit. However, let's just sit back and relax for a few minutes before we head out to the garage."

"Sounds good to me. I like getting into character before my matches. Hope you have no problem with the White Knight routine?"

"No problem for me, as long as it's not a problem for you?"

"Why don't you go ahead and get changed yourself? I like a heads-up on how my opponent presents himself."

The Catcher hesitated at first, and looked at the White Knight. After a short pause he said, "Alright. You go ahead and enjoy your drink. I'll go get changed."

He strolled over to the garage and went inside. He was extremely meticulous during each recovery mission he undertook. This one was no exception. Prior to traveling to the stadium that evening, he had performed a comprehensive search of the house. Everything he needed was piled neatly upon a shelf inside the garage. The owner had singlets of all shapes, colors and sizes. He even had a size XXL dark green singlet that fit the Catcher perfectly. His colossal build stretched the cloth to its maximum, revealing each ripple.

Harry stood up as the man entered the room and declared, "You're bigger than you look, much bigger indeed. Your clothes hide your true essence. How about another drink before we rumble?"

"Sit down my friend, and relax. I'll fix you another drink. After we finish this one we'll head to the ring and have a go at it!"

"I can hardly wait!"

The eager man watched the Catcher as he walked to the kitchen. He thought to himself, *could this be the night? Could this be the start of a brand new relationship with someone to share future pursuits with?*

After another drink and more casual conversation, the White Knight stood and said, "Well I don't know about you, but I'm ready to get it on."

The Catcher replied, "Well, what are we waiting for?"

The two men headed to the garage. The White Knight followed his host. As the wrestler in green set foot on the bottom step, the White Knight jumped onto his back.

Jokingly he said, "Sometimes I like to cheat in getting one up on my opponent. Thought you'd like to work off some extra energy by giving me a ride to the ring."

The Catcher ran towards the ring as fast as he could with the masked man still on his back. At the ring's apron, he flipped his opponent over the ropes and into the ring. His strength astonished the White Knight. Harry was by no means a small man, and even though he was slightly bigger than his foe, he wouldn't have been able to duplicate that move with such ease.

The White Knight stood up and shouted to the man still standing outside the ring, "I like to go by the White Knight when I'm wrestling. I also like getting into character. What do you call yourself, little man?"

"Simply refer to me as the Black Avenger: Nemesis to all who are white."

"Well, hop on up, Black Avenger, and let's see what you've got."

The Catcher entered the ring and stood, facing the White Knight. He said, "Now, White Knight. I'm not what you would call a professional, but I do know how to scrap. You're quite big for a white boy, you know? You're probably the biggest white boy I've ever tangled with."

"You're not so small yourself, for a black boy."

Harry figured that this fellow playing the role of Black Avenger was going to make an exciting sparring partner. He looked forward to a good work out that was also arousing at the same time. They started their bout, encircling each other. The White Knight lunged forward and got the Black Avenger in an arm bar, taking him down to the mat on one knee. He then forced the arm backwards, applying pressure on his hold. It was at this point the Catcher realized exactly what he was up against. This was one powerful wrestler. He may have been retired professionally for some years, but Harry fought with the same conviction as he had years earlier. When he applied pressure, he brought it on strong.

The White Knight continued his onslaught. He forced his opponent to his feet and threw him into the ropes. When the man bounced back, the White Knight body slammed him to the canvas. He then stood over the Catcher and asked, "This isn't too rough for you, is it?"

"Don't worry about me. The fun is just getting started. I'll need a few minutes to get my feet wet and then I'll offer you a challenge you won't forget."

The White Knight accelerated towards the ropes to gain momentum. Rebounding, he dove into the air and landed across his opponent's chest with a crashing elbow blow. The Catcher knew his partner wasn't going all out. He also knew that he would only be required to play this game just a while longer. His foe was a big man and could definitely pose a challenge under normal circumstances. Luckily for him, the drugs would take affect soon.

The White Knight covered his opponent's body, trying to make the first pin. The Catcher gathered his strength and picked up the White Knight in a bench press. He managed to toss him to the floor. He tried to stand on his feet, but Harry grabbed him again and threw him back into the ropes a second time. This time they collided in a double body check. Each of them stopped and looked at each other.

At this point the wrestlers began to really get into it. The Catcher knocked his opponent to the mat and they started Greco-Roman wrestling. The White Knight climbed onto the Catcher's back and wrapped his legs around the man's waist. He tried once again to place a second sleeper hold on his man, but it was broken. The Catcher struggled to his feet with the White Knight still clinging to his back, and forced himself backwards into the corner turnbuckle. This maneuver freed him from the White Knight's grip.

The Catcher was weary. The medication should have kicked in by now. This was indeed a tough individual and he was getting tired. He was a consummate professional and would do many things to close a file, but his limits were being tested.

The White Knight liked it rough, and was getting his wish. Reaching down, he pulled the White Knight to his feet. He then flung him into the opposite corner. He struck the turnbuckle at the broad of his back. His shoulders tensed up from the force of the hit. Harry shook off this latest plunge and headed back towards his opponent. As he approached, he kicked the black man in the stomach. The Catcher buckled over in pain, as the White Knight smashed a heavy elbow across his shoulder blades, sending him back to the mat.

The Catcher had met his equal. He was momentarily stunned. The White Knight proved to be more difficult than he had anticipated. Once again, the Catcher tried in vain to knock the wrestler off his feet. He was proving to be a royal pain in the ass. The masked wrestler attempted another sleeper hold, sticking to the Catcher's back. The Avenger struggled to his knees, carrying Harry with him. Something was happening. The white man's grip was suddenly beginning to weaken. The drugs were finally taking effect.

Using his arms to release his foe's grip from around his neck, he bent over and sent the White Knight flying to the mat. He reached down and dragged him to his feet. Taking a grand run off, he sent him reeling towards the ropes. As the White Knight bounced back, he met with a clothesline. Once again, the Catcher picked him up and body slammed the white man to the canvas floor.

The White Knight was not sure what was happening to him. He yelled out to the Catcher, "Let's take a break, man. I feel light-headed."

The Catcher replied, "I was hoping we could have a little more fun, white boy! If you get me to submit, you can do with me what you please!"

The Catcher dropped to the mat, next to the White Knight shouting, "Come on man. I'm all yours."

The White Knight attempted to get upright. He struggled as he stumbled towards the Catcher. His knees weakened, inches from him.

He collapsed across the chest of the Catcher, who looked at the drugged male declaring, "Now that you've settled down some, I wish to apologize. You see, I'm not really into the wrestling scene and certainly not a perverted fuck like you. I'm here to collect you for transport to White Man's Cotton. All along, we knew you were the brain, so to speak, behind the White Knight. You continue, to this very day, promoting violence against blacks with your alter ego. You've been chosen, and I always deliver."

The Catcher held the White Knight's head up high and landed a few smacks to his ears. The Catcher continued to taunt him. "So come on, let's have whatever you've got left. I was actually having some fun here before you started getting freaky on me. It's not every day a white man can bang me around quite like you have. Good thing I put a little sedative in your drink to slow you down."

The White Knight was flabbergasted. He pushed the Catcher away and tried to get to his feet. Both of his legs were extremely weak, but he managed to get upright. The Catcher immediately stood up next to the sluggish man and mocked him. He walked around the White Knight and pretended to be receiving jabs from him.

The White Knight tried desperately to escape from the ring, but failed. With each attempt, his opponent would pull him back in and continue play fighting. The Catcher's final move was to pick up his opponent and throw him over his shoulders. He walked over the ropes and jumped to the concrete floor below. Three large storage bins containing floor mats were in the corner of the garage. The Catcher dropped the White Knight's body, head first, into the center bin. His massive legs stuck out and his knees bent slightly over the sides. The Catcher removed his wrestling gear and redressed into his street clothes. He took the used green singlet and threw it in the bin over the White Knight's head.

The medication proved to be very potent. The liquor the White Knight drank didn't help his paralysis. He was weak and dizzy and unable to lift himself from the bin.

The Catcher left the garage and proceeded upstairs to the bedroom to check on the homeowner. He was still where the Catcher had left him, struggling to free himself. The Catcher untied the man and dragged him from the bedroom. He escorted the man down stairs and into the living room.

Looking directly at the frightened man he said, "Sorry for this pal, but you gotta do what you gotta do."

With that, he punched the man in the face, immediately knocking him out. Turning around, he walked into the garage where he had left the White Knight. He reached into the bin and hauled him out. He threw the man back over his shoulders and departed.

As he headed towards his vehicle, he said gently, "Tonight you go out in class, white man. It's the last time you'll enjoy such a ride."

He opened the car door and placed the dazed man in the passenger seat. He strapped his seat belt and then got into the driver's seat. Once his car soared onto the highway, he opened it up for all it was worth. He passed every car on the highway for miles.

As the black convertible powered down the road, the Catcher removed a bottle of clear liquid from his inside jacket. Using one hand, he popped the stopper and poured the contents onto a handkerchief. He then reached over and covered the White Knight's mouth and nose. Within seconds, his passenger went from being numb to deep sleep. The Catcher's work was still not done. He would soon move onto his next assignment.

BACK TO SCHOOL

chapter ten

LANCE Forrest's parents had always told him that school was of the utmost importance and everyone should have a quality education. Lance and his cousin, Evan, both attended Mount Batten Memorial University in New Jersey. Lance and Evan were complete opposites.

Evan was the radical one. He evoked trouble everywhere he went. He had also inherited a mean streak from his father and was extremely prejudicial when it came to ethnic minorities. These traits went entirely unchecked, which caused many people to hate him. But he was also liked for his honesty. He had character and a contagious personality. He was a lifetime professional student with more degrees under his belt than most of his professors. Evan was also filthy rich. His wealth assisted him on countless occasions in getting away with his many injustices.

Some would say that because Lance Forrest stood by his first cousin, he was just as guilty of Evan's innumerable injustices. Lance, however, would strongly disagree. Lance was guilty of taking his first cousin's money. Evan always looked after his younger cousin. He ensured Lance was kept in money. He insisted he wore the best clothes, frequented the right establishments and more importantly, he insisted Lance stay with him at his fraternity house. Lance was ten years younger than Evan, but most said they looked more like twin brothers than first cousins.

Lance's final exam for this semester was today and he was very nervous. Much to his parents' chagrin, he wasn't an overly bright student, but managed to pass most of his subjects. He tried to study hard and would only stop when Evan and his other fraternity brothers interrupted him. They drove him crazy whenever possible and were always on his back to relax more and have fun.

This past week was no exception. Six nights in a row, his fraternity brothers' partying had distracted him to no end. He felt these latest nightly disruptions would hurt his grades, and probably cause him to flunk his Physics exam that morning as well.

Lance opened his bedroom door and entered into the hallway. From the railing, which overlooked the main floor, he could see empty liquor bottles and pizza boxes and a couple of people still passed out on the floor. The party the night before continued into the wee hours of the morning. As Lance looked down, he remembered all too well why he felt so excessively tired. Forcing one foot ahead of the other, he walked to the stairs. Evan bolted from his room, dressed in only his underwear. His hair stood straight up and his eyes were only partially open.

He rushed towards the washroom and mumbled, "Good luck on the test, Lance."

"Thanks."

Lance walked down the steps, kicking the litter as he went. It was a good thing Evan had hired a couple of women to come by everyday to clean up. They always arrived by noon and usually spent four to five hours clearing away the chaos. Evan wouldn't permit them to arrive any earlier, for the majority of the residents stayed in bed until at least noon.

Most of his fraternity brothers had either late afternoon or early evening classes. Only Lance and Frank Hussy ever rose from their beds before nine each morning. Frank always ran an average of ten miles every morning. After his run, he would come back into the house, beat it up the stairs and shower quickly, before both men left together for campus. Not overly athletic, Lance usually slept while Frank was out for his jog.

Every morning without fail, as he reached the bottom of the stairs and walked past the front entrance, Frank would sprint through the front door, shouting, "Be with you in just a minute."

They were in half the same classes. Lance believed that Evan arranged it that way so Frank could help him with his studies. Frank had as much brains as he had strength and endurance. As Frank bolted in, Lance would walk out the front door and head down the ten stairs that lead to the parking lot. Frank's vehicle was a seven-year old, four-door Honda Civic that still worked like a charm. Lance would sit inside the car and wait. He often left the door open to feel the gentle morning breeze, something he would never experience inside the frat house. The smell of stale beer and leftover pizza never did sit well with his stomach.

After sitting for a moment enjoying the scenery, he opened his notebook and began reviewing his notes for the morning's final. Each morning, he would study like this for twenty minutes or so while waiting for Frank. Frank was usually prompt, and today was no exception. As the twenty-minute mark drew nearer, he came running over to the car. He was still buttoning his shirt as he reached the driver's door. When he jumped in, his hair was dripping with water and wet patches were visible all over his shirt. Lance assumed he jumped from the shower and threw his clothes on without even drying himself off, relying on his cotton shirts to do the trick.

As he turned the ignition, he said, "So are you ready for the big exam today, champ?"

"Let's just say I didn't have much of a chance to do any studying last night."

"Know what you mean. Rowdy bunch, weren't they?"

"You got that right."

The tires flicked tiny rocks as Frank sped from the parking lot. As he drove the Honda into traffic, he began pumping Physics questions at Lance. Any time he gave a wrong answer or insufficient information, Frank would explain the problem to him in the simplest terms possible. He always thought that twenty-percent of the overall mark he received on any test was thanks to this question and answer period.

It was only when they arrived on campus and parked the car in front of the science building that Lance's stomach began to churn. He knew this test would make the difference in whether or not he passed the term. His parents would be devastated if he failed a semester. They were very strict when it came to his education and he didn't want to let them down.

They entered the school and walked to the auditorium. Desks had been set up to accommodate the two-hundred and ten students who were supposed to be writing today. Frank took a seat at the back of the gym. Lance walked to the nearest empty desk and sat down.

Ten minutes had passed before their Physics professor arrived. He stood at the head of the gym, facing everyone. When the room was silent, he explained the structure and procedures for the exam. Once the professor had finished speaking, moans escaped from the crowd. When the students were finally quieted, the professor handed out bundles of exam papers to those sitting in the front of each row.

As the exams were handed backwards, the professor said, "Ladies and gentlemen, do not turn over the test papers until I give the word.

You have two hours to complete this test. If you finish ahead of time and wish to leave, please raise your hand and I will have one of my assistants gather your papers. I trust as young adults you will not require reminders regarding the confidentiality of the papers before you. And don't cheat! Good luck and please begin."

When Lance turned over the paper, he felt relieved. He could answer the first three questions with ease. There were ten long answer questions in total, so if he were right, he would have already achieved a thirty-percent grade. As he began to write out the answer to the first question, his nerves started to settle.

Throughout the process, he felt like he was being watched. He began to feel very uneasy. Once in a while, he would glance over his shoulders. A young black man in his early twenties was sitting to his right. Each time his eyes landed on Lance, he would smile and quickly turn his head away.

Lance only had four questions remaining and was feeling very good about the exam. Physics was one of his harder subjects but he was convinced a "B" or "B+" was forthcoming. He picked up the test and started reading over the last answer he had written when he noticed the black student had leaned in to read his answers.

He ordered, "Keep your eyes on your own paper."

He responded, "Fuck you."

This took him completely by surprise. Every few seconds or so, the young man continued to lean towards his paper. When Lance looked back in annoyance, the man would glare back in retaliation. This went on for well over fifteen minutes. All of a sudden, the Physics professor stood between them. He reached down and picked up the young man's test. He then walked towards Lance's desk and collected his.

Before Lance could speak, he pointed towards the exit and demanded, "Follow me!"

They followed the professor, passed their gawking peers. Once they stepped into the unoccupied hallway, the professor exploded. "One thing I do not tolerate here is cheating. You both fail automatically!"

Interrupting the professor, Lance declared, "I didn't cheat, sir. I was writing my own answers. He was the one copying off me!"

The professor looked at him and said, "The point of the matter, Mr. Forrest, is that specific instructions were given that if there were questions or problems during testing, they were to be addressed to me, or to one of my assistants. You said nothing. Therefore, I can only assume you were cheating, or equally as guilty for allowing it to happen."

With that, the professor returned to the auditorium causing the double doors to click briskly back and forth against one another. Lance felt as if they were slapping him in the face and taunting him for the current entanglement he found himself in. He looked at the offender who was solely responsible for his recent troubles standing just feet from him.

Snapping at him, Lance said, "Why didn't you say anything?"

He responded, "Evan likes to play games. So do several of my acquaintances!"

He turned and walked away without another word. Lance was screwed. This was the first time in his university life he actually knew most of the questions in such a complicated subject, only to get shafted. He left the science building and started walking back to the fraternity house. The walk would take him an hour but he needed the time to consider the events of that terrible morning. As he walked along, he came across the town's only park. He decided a leisurely walk would help him clear his head. He entered the park and strolled amongst the trees and plants. It was a beautifully warm day outside.

Nearby was an empty swimming pool. It had been closed for much needed repairs due to vandalism that had occurred over the course of the last few weeks. As he came closer to the pool, he noticed a small group of black men standing around. Only a few yards from them, Lance realized that one of them was the young fellow who cheated off him during that morning's exam.

While his buddies surrounded Lance, the young man approached him, and in a cocky manner said, "Here comes Evan Roberts' little cousin. He's the one who cheated off me during my Physics exam this morning and got me an instant fail."

Not really thinking, he said, "You little fucker! That's a lie. You cheated off me and got us both 'Fs'."

The words were no sooner out of his mouth than all five of them started punching and kicking him. They took his sneakers, his coat and his wallet.

After they had virtually beat him unconscious, the black man, whom the others had referred to as Eddie, while egging him on, said, "You tell that bastard Evan Roberts that if he ever lays a hand on another brother again, we'll get revenge, ten times over. Do you understand, you stupid shit?"

There was a slight pause. Not that Lance was being rebellious, but his mouth couldn't say what his brain wanted it to say.

Eddie repeated himself a second time, only this time he kicked Lance with every word he spoke, "Do you understand, you stupid shit?"

Struggling frantically to speak, he replied, "Yes."

After they had finished beating him some more, the black men took off running into a wooded area. As the last of them slipped through the trees, he struggled to his feet. Once he felt stable enough to walk, he continued through the park. Several people stared at him as he walked along. However, no one stopped to see if he needed assistance or to ask him if anything was wrong.

The final phase of his walk was long and painful. Each time he inhaled the fresh air his stomach would erupt in a steady throbbing ache. What was normally a twenty-five minute walk seemed to take him hours to reach the edge of the park. As he left the imaginary boundary line that separated the tranquility and peacefulness of the park from the city, he knew it was only moments before he would reach the security of the fraternity house.

As he approached the parking lot, he saw Frank's car parked in its usual space. He had arrived back before Lance did. With each movement up the front steps, he thought he would pass out from the pain. As he reached the top step, Evan, Frank and several others greeted him in the doorway.

Evan blurted out, "Frank told me what happened at school. What in the fuck happened to you?"

Mustering together what strength he could, he pushed past them without saying a word. He felt numb and his hands were shaking. As he headed for the couch, he felt himself stumble. Frank ran into the kitchen to grab some ice and a cloth, while Evan guided Lance to the couch. Once he regained his breath and managed to gather together enough energy, he told Evan and the others the full story.

Evan was absolutely livid. He stood up in the middle of the living room cursing with words that even Lance had never heard before. He then vowed to get even with this fellow, Eddie, and the rest of his gang. Frank sat next to Lance on the couch. He took a damp cloth and wiped dried blood from his face. He insisted Lance hold an ice pack to his eyes, even when he complained that it was too cold. His left eye had swollen to twice its normal size and shades of black and blue had developed around the swelling.

Lance's head was throbbing. He asked Frank and Evan to help him up to his room. He was so weak, he thought he would pass out. Frank and Evan started plotting their revenge. They placed Lance in his bed and within a few seconds, he had fallen into a deep sleep.

He awoke several hours later, his head still beating violently. When he opened his eyes, Evan and Frank were still at his side. Lance tried to raise his head from the pillow, but couldn't. Evan was standing over him, still talking to Frank about getting his revenge.

When he finally managed to get Evan's attention, he said, "Listen, Evan. I think we should let this rest. I don't want any more trouble."

"You have nothing to worry about. All you have to do is get your strength back. There's no way in hell that I'm going to allow a bunch of niggers get away with this. Me and the boys will take care of this and I assure you, it'll never happen again."

Lance tried to argue, but knew it was useless. Evan's mind was made up; he was going after Eddie and his buddies. The only problem was that no one knew who Eddie and his buddies were. Neither Frank nor Lance had ever seen him in any of their Physics classes before. It was as if he appeared from out of nowhere.

. . .

Several days passed and while Lance's bruises and cuts were starting to heal, Evan's attitude had not. He was frustrated and angry all the time. He wanted nothing more than to seek revenge for what had happened to his cousin, and to save face with his fraternity brothers. It was late Friday morning, when doors slamming bolted Lance awake. The sounds of roaring car engines followed immediately. He left his bedroom and walked out into the hallway. He called out to see if anyone was around, but no one responded. It was the first time since he had been living here that the house was completely empty. He figured the boys had headed out to get supplies for the weekly Friday night poker game.

As he reached the landing at the bottom of the stairs, the front door flew open, startling him. In walked the two cleaning ladies to begin their day's work. They were older women who complained constantly about the mess and how hard it was to clean the place. Most of the boys living here found it amusing when they complained, so nothing was ever said to them. As they entered the living room Lance was forced to flee from their paths. They almost knocked him over with their cleaning gear. He headed towards the kitchen while they, in turn, acted as if he wasn't even there.

A pot of perked coffee was sitting on the kitchen countertop. It was still hot and looked to be made recently. He took down a mug from the cupboard and helped himself. The burnt taste told him it must have been made the day before. As he sipped the stale coffee, he spotted a pack of cigarettes lying on the table. He removed one and lighted it. He hadn't had a cigarette in over two years. After the first few inhales, he became extremely woozy. He sat back trying to clear his head and wondered what the boys were up to. It never took the entire household to prepare for poker night before.

. . .

Evan and five of his fraternity brothers had pulled away from the parking lot in his red pickup truck. Frank and three other men took his Civic. They were headed to the park to take a spin around and check things out. In the days that followed Lance's attack, Evan had sent out feelers to all his connections. He wanted his contacts to keep their ears and eyes open for any signs of this man, Eddie, or his associates. Earlier that morning, a call came into the fraternity house informing Evan that they had been spotted in the park.

The two vehicles drove in different directions along the outskirts of the park. Finally, Frank pulled in off the road and parked. He told his friends they were better off scouting around inside the park to see if they could spot the culprits. Once outside the car, he called Evan on his cell phone to divulge this plan. Evan's wanted to maintain contact and promised he would call if he spotted them.

Frank scaled the cast iron fence that surrounded the park. Joe, Scott, and Bob followed. Frank told them he would walk ahead to scout out the park. He asked them to follow, but at a distance. As Frank was walking past a copse of enormous maple trees, he noticed a cluster of young black men standing around. They were chatting and carrying on with each other. He reached behind him and signaled for his friends to stop. He wanted to check out the situation first. Frank was now crawling along the wet grass, through the copse. The ground was so damp from the morning's dew that the dark green grass instantly stained his tan colored shirt. It took him roughly ten minutes to drag his body close enough to the youths to hear what they were saying.

For the longest time, the young men talked about nothing in particular. One of them looked somewhat like the person who had gotten Lance in trouble during his exam, but he wasn't a hundred-percent sure. Suddenly, when no more than ten-feet from the five black youths, Frank's cell phone rang.

One of them came running over to Frank and shouted, "Get your butt out here, boy."

Frank walked over to the group. His buddies, who watched from nearby, had decided amongst themselves to see what happened before they took any action. Scott, however, called Evan on his cell phone with an update and directions.

As Frank neared the group, he said, "I'm looking for Eddie. Do you know him?"

"Who's asking, honky?"

"The name's Frank. I have an issue to resolve with Eddie and it's only him I'm interested in. Do any of you know a guy named Eddie?"

"What do you think, that there's only one black person in this city named Eddie?"

"I'm looking for the Eddie that beat the crap out of my good friend, Lance. He and his flunkies did the job on Lance and it's payback time."

"First of all, what makes you think that you can come into our park and start looking for a brother? You could end up in the same situation as Evan's cousin."

"And how do you know he's Evan's cousin?"

"Because I'm Eddie, and you're dead meat asshole."

With that, the entire group charged Frank. He turned and started to run towards his friends, who were still waiting in the trees only a few yards away. As he entered into a clearing, Frank turned and stood his ground. Joe, Scott and Bob stood behind him. At first, this took Eddie and his gang totally off guard, but Eddie recovered quickly.

He looked at the four white boys standing before him and said, "We've beaten up twice as many assholes as you before breakfast, while still half asleep and completely hung over. You'll be sorry you even showed your faces on our turf. Get'em boys!"

With that, a gang fight erupted on the park grounds. Surrounded by huge maple trees and thick brush, blacks and white were now fighting in what resembled a private arena. Frank and his buddies were slightly outnumbered and were taking a beating. The gang of black youths used sticks, rocks and anything else they could find to pummel their white opponents. They were intent on teaching these white boys a lesson in territorial rights and aggression. Screams of agonizing pain echoed through the air.

The group of black men was handing out more in the damage department than Frank and his friends could handle. The white fraternity brothers were tough and no strangers to a good fight. Knowing their friends were not too far behind gave them the extra courage they needed. Once their reinforcements arrived, the odds would be more in their favor.

Eddie punched Frank repeatedly in the stomach and face while a second black man held Frank in a Full Nelson. Eddie was intent on causing enough damage to his athletic foe to slow the man down. Frank had taken enough. Using leverage from the youth holding him, he kicked out, making direct contact with Eddie's midsection. This winded Eddie and sent him falling to the ground. Frank struggled desperately to free himself from his lone aggressor's grip, but to no avail.

Two men came crashing through the brush. Finally, their fellow fraternity brothers had come to the rescue. Evan and five others emerged from the surrounding maples. They had arrived to end the battle, just in the nick of time. The new arrivals branched out to help those most in need of their assistance. By this time, Frank and the original men on the scene had endured a severe beating at the hands of their black enemies.

Evan tackled the guy who had Frank secured from behind. All three men landed on the ground. Frank's aggressor had let go but Frank was winded. When he fell, he struck a rock and hurt his lower back. Evan was now sitting on the black man's chest, punching him repeatedly in the face. He was suddenly smacked in the back of the head with a piece of wood. Eddie had regained his composure and was now striking out at Evan. The more Evan tried to get up, the more Eddie hit him. Within seconds, however, several of Evan's friends jumped Eddie and began pummeling him.

What started out as a beating for Frank and his friends, changed. Eddie and his gang of thugs were now on the receiving end of the brutal thrashing. The fighting didn't stop until Evan was certain Eddie and his gang endured more of a beating than they'd given Lance. As they regrouped, Evan instructed the boys to remove each of the black men's sneakers, jackets and wallets. He wanted these things taken and burnt in one of the metal garbage bins located throughout the park, like they had done to Lance. Evan, Frank, Scott, and Bob headed out, while the others finished the job.

Before heading back to the fraternity house, Evan stopped to pick up beer and other supplies they required for a perfect night of poker and camaraderie. The shop keeper looked at Evan and his buddies and said, "My God, what happened to the lot of you?"

Evan replied, "All in a day's work, boss. All in a day's work."

. . .

Lance was sitting in the living room relaxing and watching television. The house sparkled. The cleaning ladies had long gone, and not a thing was out of place. When Evan entered, he ordered the boys to place the beer on ice and set up the card table in the middle of the living room. Evan strolled proudly over in his cousin's direction. Without even asking, Lance already knew. The only comment he made was, "You couldn't leave well enough alone?"

"You know me, Lance. A tooth for a tooth or should I say, a whole set of teeth for a tooth."

Evan looked just as bad as Lance had when he was beaten up. His eye was black and he had multiple cuts and bruises all over his upper body.

As if reading Lance's mind, he said, "It's not as bad as it looks. A quick shower and most of it will disappear. Anyway, I hope you're up for a good game of cards tonight. We're celebrating. The boys and me are planning on having a blast. As it stands now, there will be six of us playing. It'll be you, Frank, Scott, Bob, Tony, and me. The rest of the boys are all going home for the long weekend."

"Let's hope things are more relaxed. You look like you could use a stiff drink or two."

"Sounds good to me. But I'm gonna get a shower first."

Evan headed upstairs. A truck pulled into the parking lot. Tony entered the house looking just as battered as the other guys did. He declared proudly, "All done Lance. I don't think that bunch will bother you again."

Lance shook his head and turned his attention back towards the television set. Before he knew it, he had drifted off into a deep sleep.

. . .

Evening moved in quickly, as Lance woke to the sound of Evan singing at the top of his lungs. He jumped up from the couch and looked at his watch. He needed to get to the drugstore before it closed. None of the boys were fit to walk, let alone drive by the look of the empty bottles everywhere. He grabbed his jacket and told Evan he'd be back in a few minutes. Evan insisted on going with him, but Lance told him not to bother.

He added, "The drugstore is only a ten-minute walk from here. The fresh air will do me a world of good. Beside, cousin, I don't need a bodyguard every time I leave the house."

During the entire walk to the drugstore, Lance felt as if someone was watching him. He chalked it up to paranoia. Once he reached the drugstore his mind was more at ease. He walked inside to pick up the items. After paying the clerk, he headed back home. The presence he felt previously had returned. The nervous tension he had experienced these past few days must have been getting to him.

The weather outside had changed suddenly. He had only been walking a few minutes when it began to pour. In seconds, he was soaked. He began running clumsily, dodging the small puddles that had already formed on the ground. By the time he reached the house, water poured from every inch of his body. When he pulled his sneakers off, he tipped the water out into an old plant, which stood dead in the corner. The water from his socks was also rung out into the plant. His jacket, he flung on the closet floor.

The boys were already sitting around the card table when Lance entered the room. He looked at them and said, "I have to go upstairs and change. My clothes are soaking wet."

"Take your time." "Fuck it." "As long as your money is dry." "Bring back a few beers when you return." The comments went on.

Lance walked into the bedroom, removing his wet clothes, as he headed towards the hamper. He stood in front of his dresser and put on clean underwear, socks and a shirt. He then proceeded to the closet, reaching inside for a pair of dry jeans. Suddenly, the room went dark. He lost his bearings and fell directly into the closet.

As he picked himself up, he could hear the boys downstairs shouting at one another to find matches and candles. He used his hands to feel around the pitch-black room. After stubbing his toes a few times, he finally managed to locate an old candleholder that had been on the top of his dresser. His dad had given it to him several years before but it was even older than he was. He normally kept a tea light candle inside. It was a funny old thing, designed so that once the candle was lit, stars would glimmer across the walls and onto the ceiling above.

He knew he had a box of matches in the room, but wasn't quite sure where. After feeling about for several minutes, he came across a small carton. He opened the box and took out a single wooden match. Fumbling about in the dark, he struck the match against the flint. Once the candle was lit, the flame shed sufficient light for him to finish getting dressed. The darkness made him edgy. As he headed back downstairs, he could see several candles flickering throughout the living room. His housemates scouting around for additional candles cast shadows throughout the first floor.

When he reached the bottom step and asked what had happened, Evan laughed, and said patronizingly, "The power went!"

"No!"

Evan stopped laughing long enough to say, "We called the power company and they're not sure what's going on. The power's gone on several blocks. They're working on it now and hopefully will have it restored shortly."

That's just great, Lance thought. He was in a room with several drunken friends who, in their current state, had enough trouble functioning in the light, let alone in the dark. He thought it was amazing that they managed to light the candles without causing an inferno.

He went into the kitchen to get a beer. The kitchen sink had been packed full of ice and several beer were jammed in between the ice shavings. He plucked one out and opened it. He guzzled the cool liquid until the bottle was empty. Then he reached back into the sink and took a second.

He found the setting eerie. It was raining heavily outside and flashes of light reflected through the windows each time lightning struck. Candles were burning all over the living room. The guys with their slurred speech, poor coordination and inane laughter, all added to the discomfort that was building in Lance. No sooner had he reached the card table and taken his seat when he began to sneeze violently.

The downpour he was caught in earlier had gotten to him; he began shivering in the chair.

Evan looked at him still chuckling and said, "Are you shaking or have I had too much to drink?"

"Shaking, Evan. I think I'm coming down with the flu."

"Here, put my jacket on before you end up with pneumonia."

It fit perfectly. Not only did they look alike and wear the same sizes, even their bruises and bumps matched tonight.

It wasn't long before Lance started raking in the money. They were playing a five dollar ante per hand with raises limited to a maximum of twenty dollars per round. None of the boys at the table could play, as they were seriously drunk. Lance didn't really have time to catch up, as the others had been drinking for most of the day while he slept.

They had been playing for well over an hour and Lance had already won almost enough money to pay for his next semester's tuition. This was one time when it pays to drink, at least from his perspective. The laughing and taunting during play continued until suddenly, there was a crash in the kitchen. Tony and Scott got up from the table and went to investigate. The remaining frat brothers continued to play.

Shortly afterwards, several additional noises came from the kitchen. Those around the table looked at each other puzzled. Evan was about to get up from his seat when Tony and Scott returned. They had been shoved through the kitchen doors and stumbled back into the living room. Everyone at the table stood up knocking their chairs over, only to come face to face with one of the biggest black men they'd ever seen.

The man looked at the group and said, "Nothing like a good game of cards to relax the soul. Take a seat, boys, and deal the cards."

Evan looked at the man and said, "Who the fuck are you and what are you doing here?"

"I'm called, 'the Catcher' and I'm here to play cards and what happens to each of you shits will depend on how well you play my game."

Evan looked at his fraternity brothers and shouted, "Take him, boys!"

They all jumped on him, but it was like hitting a brick wall. Scott was sent flying about ten feet. Frank and Bob were knocked out cold with one retaliatory smack. Tony hung from his neck, having no effect, while Evan was kicked in the guts and crashed to the floor.

He then reached out and grabbed Lance by the jacket, lifted him straight in to the air and said, "You're the one piece of merchandise I plan to keep intact."

He then dropped Lance to the floor and held him down with his left foot firmly on his back. Lance's first thought was that this must be Eddie's older brother out to seek revenge for what they did. They were in deep shit. His brother must have been a set of triplets amalgamated together at birth to produce this colossal brute. He was not a happy camper.

Balancing himself on one foot and using the other to hold Lance in place, he reached behind his head and grabbed Tony by the neck. He then flicked Tony over his head to the floor, much further than he had thrown Scott. The black stranger pulled a gun from beneath his coat and held it up for all to see.

He said, "Enough fun for now, boys. Take your seats. We're going to have a friendly game of cards."

He walked backwards towards the front door and opened it up. In walked Eddie and two of his groupies. The Catcher said to Eddie, "You can take the two asleep on the floor and do what you want with them. Take them upstairs, I don't want to be disturbed."

Eddie and his accomplices picked up an unconscious Frank and Bob and carried them upstairs. All kinds of noise soon came from the upstairs rooms. It sounded like a portion of the house was being ripped to shreds. Once the Catcher had forced Lance, Evan, Scott, and Tony to their seats, he pulled a chair up to the table. He looked over at Tony and demanded that he deal the cards.

Tony looked back at the Catcher and said in a hostile tone, "What game?"

The Catcher glared at him. He picked up his gun, aimed it at Tony's head and pulled the trigger. The force of the blast sent Tony and his chair toppling over. Blood splattered all over the table and the men sitting around it.

The Catcher said to the three traumatized individuals, "No one else is permitted to ask questions or show attitude. You speak only when spoken to. The only time I wish to hear a peep from any of you is during the bidding process. Is that clear, idiots?"

"Yes," everyone replied simultaneously.

The Catcher then said to Lance, "Okay now Evan, you can deal the first hand. The game is straight poker and we'll play the first hand for whip lash."

No one at the table remarked on the fact that their gun-wielding guest had referred to Lance Forrest as Evan. They didn't want to end up with a bullet to the head like Tony did. Lance had been wearing Evan's jacket, which had his name embroidered on the right sleeve. They both looked enough alike to be brothers, rather than first cousins. It was clearly a case of mistaken identity on the black man's part.

The cards were dealt. When all of the cards had been finally turned over, Evan had the best hand with two pair, tens over threes.

The Catcher stood and walked around the table to where Evan had been seated. No one dared move. As he stood directly behind Evan, he raised his gun up in the air and came crashing down across the back of Evan's neck with all his might. Grasping the back of his aching neck, Evan fell from his chair and landed on the floor next to Lance. Evan had almost passed out.

The Catcher shouted with a smile, "Whip lash."

He then returned to his seat and said to Scott, "It's time we got a bit more serious. This time we'll play 'walk the plank.' By that, I mean the stairs. The winner of this hand will get the privilege of going upstairs to join his two friends."

Scott picked up the cards and started to deal. He was panicked and his hands trembled. Lance had suddenly become extremely ill and started to heave. He tried to hold it in as long as he could, but the sensation overtook him. He leaned to the side and threw up all over Evan.

Scott and the others tried to ignore Lance. Once the final card was revealed, it became apparent that the dealer was also the winner. The Catcher pointed his gun in Scott's face and motioned for him to head upstairs. Scott rose slowly from his chair. As he made his way to the bottom step, the Catcher dialed his cell phone and advised one of his assistants that another was coming in their direction. He was ordered to greet Scott upon his arrival. He no sooner had placed his foot on the top step, than Eddie and one of his associates grabbed him. Immediately, they began beating him as they dragged him towards one of the bedrooms.

The Catcher looked at Lance and said, "This time I will make it interesting for you. If you win, I will send you on a trip to a beautiful island resort. If you lose, I will shoot your friend on the floor in the legs."

This caused Lance to become sick once more. The Catcher laughed. The more Lance retched, the louder the Catcher roared. He picked up the deck of cards and began to deal them out. The first card turned over was a four. The Catcher turned over a king. The second card Lance received was a ten, while the Catcher drew a seven. When the third cards were turned over, Lance got a second four and his aggressor showed a jack. It was looking good for Lance. When he turned over the fourth card, it was a seven. His fourth was a queen. The last and final card for Lance was an ace. It was the ace of spades, cold and black. The Catcher slowly turned over his last card. It was a seven. He won the final hand with his last card and ended up with a lousy pair of sevens. Once again, he rose from his seat, knocking the chair over as he stood.

He walked towards Evan as Lance pleaded, "Please, don't shoot him. Please."

He ignored Lance's plea and shot Evan in the legs. Evan howled.

The Catcher then said to Lance, "Evan Roberts. You've won a consolation prize. An all expenses paid trip to a beautiful tropical island. We call it, 'White Man's Cotton,' and you will get to spend the rest of your pitiful little life there. Consider this your reward for the crimes you have committed against blacks during your lifetime."

Lance was speechless, totally dumbfounded. Evan was in too much pain to realize what was going on. The Catcher took his gun and before Lance had a chance to utter a single word, he struck him across the back of his head. The impact sent Lance to the floor unconscious.

Lance believed even though he was unconscious, he could vividly hear screams coming from Frank, Bob and Scott. This seemed to go on for hours until, in the back of his mind, all he could hear was fading whimpers. All kinds of noises began to erupt around him, but he was unable to focus on any of these. His vision was totally blurred and his head pounded violently.

The next thing Lance remembered was lying at the bottom of the stairs, bound and gagged. He could see Scott, Evan, Frank, Bob, and Tony, all hanging by their feet over the railing. Some of them were still alive, but had been badly beaten. Lance only recognized who was who based on the clothes they wore.

Eddie and his gang had gone. The Catcher was fiddling around the stairs with wiring of some kind. When he finished doing that, he walked down the stairs and picked Lance up, slinging him over his shoulder.

He walked to the front exit and opened the door. He was momentarily startled. Another one of Lance's fraternity brothers, Joe, was now standing in his path. His flight was cancelled due to the bad weather outside. He had just arrived back from the airport after waiting ten hours for a second flight, which was also cancelled.

He looked at the Catcher and said, "What the fuck is going on?"

The Catcher made no response. The only noise that Lance heard was a brief snap, followed by a thump. As the Catcher continued to walk out the front door, Joe's limp body lay across the threshold. His head was tilted to one side at a sixty-degree angle. He was dead. The Catcher carted Lance out into the parking lot and stopped directly in front of Frank's car. Lance couldn't remember much after that as he passed out.

With criminal activity of this magnitude happening on a recurring basis, it was only a matter of time before someone started to put the pieces together.

SHE'S GOT BRAINS

chapter eleven

IT was 6:00 a.m. as Detective Wade Leaman stepped from his vehicle to head into work. He was a veteran who'd been with the Brooklyn, New York Police Department for more than thirty-five years. He was nearing retirement, with just three months remaining. Due to his age and the fact he was so close to retirement, he had been assigned a desk position for the remainder of his term.

When he entered the Tenth Precinct on Liverpool Avenue it was very quiet. It was the only time Detective Leaman could remember the atmosphere being so calm.

Crime in the city usually didn't pick up until noon. As he walked up the middle of the steps leading to the second floor, he thought to himself just how peaceful the day had started out. Once he reached the second level, he took his usual route towards the main entrance of his work section passing at least six other officers, each of them smiling. It was a funny sort of smile, which made the seasoned detective very uneasy.

When he pushed open the double doors that led into the squad room, he was surprised to find a young woman sitting at his desk. She was using his computer and by the clicking noises her fingers were making she must have been typing over ninety words per minute.

Wade walked towards her and said, "Excuse me. Can I help you?"

"Detective Leaman, I assume. My name is Tyler Collins and I have been temporarily assigned as your new case partner. It's sort of an on-the-job training exercise for me. I am told that you're one of the best in the business, so to speak."

Wade turned around without saying a word and headed back through the double doors. His peers watched him as he headed to the Captain's office. He was in such a huff, he didn't even remember that his superior wouldn't be in at this hour in the morning until he reached the Captain's closed door.

He said to the Captain's assistant, "Do you know what's going on with that Collins woman?"

"I only know she's not much in the looks department, but we're told she's got more brains than Kellogg's got Corn Flakes. She graduated with a Criminology degree from Yale University at the top of her class last year and holds the highest marks in her league from across the country."

Tyler Collins was in her late twenties. She was an African-American woman who stood close to six feet in height, but only weighed in at one hundred and thirty pounds. She wore her hair in dreadlocks and it fell three-quarters of the way down her back. Her facial features made her appear very haggard, but her I.Q. more than made up for it. She was undoubtedly one of the smartest women in the state, and possibly the nation.

Wade walked back in the direction of his squad room. As he entered, he stood behind Collins and said, "Until I get this matter straightened out you can find another desk to work at. I'm not a people person and have little to no patience. Why don't you amuse yourself with some of our unsolved files stacked up in the gray filing cabinet in the corner."

Collins replied, "I was told you are a bit feisty. You don't like people getting in your way and may be a tad old-fashioned. I think you'll learn quickly enough that for the next three months at least, we're going to be a team."

With that she got up from his desk and headed towards the filing cabinet. She pulled out the top drawer and removed about a dozen files. She walked into one of the empty interrogation rooms and spread the files out onto a table. Wade sat at his desk, watching her through the large glass window to the right of the room's entrance. She opened the first file and glanced at it. As she finished her cursory review, she placed it to one side and started another file. With each review, she would write something down on one of those yellow Post-it notes and stick it on the file's front cover. When she finished looking at all the files before her, she revisited the filing cabinet and removed another stack. She spent approximately three hours repeating this process.

It was now 9:35 a.m. and Wade hadn't even signed on to his computer. He was still watching the new girl in action. Several other detectives had arrived, and each of them appeared fascinated with their new co-worker. The Captain suddenly appeared through the double doors and stopped directly in front of Wade's desk.

He looked at the veteran detective with a wide grin and said, "Got you a little pre-retirement present. I hear you've already met. Regardless of what you think or say, she's yours for the duration. Do you understand?"

"Is this some sort of punishment for doing a bad job or screwing up somewhere along the line that I was unaware of?"

"Listen Wade, I had to go to great lengths to obtain this woman. I had to call in all of my favors to get her here. She's in great demand. Do you remember the Bronson murders and the Lakeside Killer case? Well, this woman solved both cases. Over fifty men and women were assigned to each of those cases for months on end and nothing happened. They bring in this computer genius and wham. She solves both cases within six months. We need someone here who can help us with our backlog and she's the one. You are going to guide her along and do so with a smile. Do I make myself clear?"

"Clear as mud."

"Don't get funny with me, Detective. You only got three months left and let me tell you, crime won't stop after you walk out that door."

The Captain turned around and walked over to the interview room. He poked his head inside the entrance and said, "Hello, Collins. I trust you're getting settled in okay?"

"Yes sir. I like a good challenge."

The Captain backed away from the entrance and walked towards the double doors. Before pushing them open he turned around to face the staff and shouted, "Now folks, the show is over. Get back to work and have a great day."

Wade's phone rang; it was his daughter, Brenda. She was looking for another loan. His daughter was always looking for a handout from her father and normally only contacted him when she needed money. Four years ago, she married a man who was unemployed. Wade hated his guts. He referred to him as "his daughter's bum." After he made a few digs about her lazy husband, Wade caved in as always. He told her he would drop by with some cash later that day.

Tyler Collins had wandered over to the detective's desk during the tail end of his conversation with Brenda. When he hung up the phone, she said, "Your son-in-law sounds very similar to my late husband."

"I'm sorry about your husband."

"Don't. He was an evil bastard who took me for the ride of my life. He was a looker and I was stupid. It was the one time in my life when I didn't really care or know what was going on around me. My old man slept during the day and he partied all night."

"Sounds familiar. The parties and the sleeping part, I mean."

"Well it gets worse, Detective. One day he must have gotten sick of pretending to be 'in love' with me and decided he wanted out. He was very creative."

"How so?"

"He hatched a plan to get rich off my insurance policy."

Wade sat up straight and looked at Tyler with extreme interest as she continued, "One night as I was sound asleep, Freeman, my husband, was busy setting up the apartment to make it look as if a break-in had occurred."

Tyler lowered the turtleneck that was covering her neck. She looked back at Wade, whose mouth, by this time, was wide open and said, "See the scar on my neck? That's where he slit me with a butcher's knife, as I lay in bed sound asleep. Blood poured from me like a water fountain. Freeman left me for dead."

Tyler's eyes were swelling up, but she held back the tears. She tipped her head down and continued on with her story, "I managed to reach over the side of my bed and dial 911 with one hand, while holding back the flowing blood with the other. After I finished the call, I slid from my bed and crawled over to the bedroom door. I eventually gathered enough strength to lock it."

Wade looked at Tyler and told her to take a seat while he poured her a cup of coffee. When he returned, he told her that she didn't have to go on if she wasn't up to it.

She persevered. "When the cops finally arrived, I vividly remember the sound of guns going off both inside and outside the apartment.

He was shot in the chest several times. It ended up that we were both put in the same ambulance. On our way to the hospital, he looked over at me and called me an ugly bitch. He told me that he fucked me all those months for the money and that I ruined everything. I turned my head away from him and cried. I vowed that from that day forward I would spend my life helping the innocent. That's why I eventually became a cop. Now, after a story like that, the least you can do is spring for a good cup of coffee."

Wade got up from his chair and apologized to Tyler. She told him to forget it. She definitely had her fill of problems with men and Wade felt he didn't need to add to them. They headed out of the squad room and took the elevator to the ground level where the cafeteria was located. Another officer entered the elevator, guiding a prisoner by his shoulder. He was taking the man to the first floor for further processing. Just before the elevator's doors closed, the man broke free from the officer and tried to make a grab for Tyler.

The next thing they saw was the prisoner was lying on the floor of the elevator as Tyler looked to the officer and said, "Next time, try cuffing him."

The officer picked up the prisoner, who was visibly shaken and cuffed his hands behind his back. His neck and face turned bright red. Wade tilted his head down trying to hide his grin. After the two occupants got out on the first floor, Wade burst out laughing. Tyler soon followed suit.

Tyler looked at Wade and between laughs said, "I'll never let a man fuck me over again."

They continued walking and laughing as they made their way towards the cafeteria. Once they had paid the cranky old cashier, they headed over to enjoy their break at a little table in the back of the cafeteria. Wade commented on how ornery the old lady was and made a few sly remarks about her probably being undercover for the Russians. They both had another fine chuckle at the old lady's expense.

After regaining their composure, Wade rested his hand against his chin and asked Tyler, "What do you think about the White Files you reviewed?"

"Do you want the short or long version?"

"You choose."

"Let's see. For many years now, several white men, women and children have gone missing or turned up dead in cities all across the United States, Canada, Australia, and Europe. In all cases, it appears that at least one of the missing people in each disappearance had it in for blacks and other minorities. In all cases where there was a black witness, no harm has ever come to them. The only similarity in all of these cases is reports of a gigantic black man, who is assumed to be responsible for the murders and abductions. He also loves darts, apparently, for he leaves each of his dead victims with a dart punctured through their middle finger. Also, and probably most interesting, is the fact that not one of the individuals abducted has ever turned up anywhere, alive or dead. Another thing I find very unusual is that you would think a man the size of three professional football players would be simple to locate. But it's like he doesn't even exist."

Wade was impressed. What took others days on end to review, had taken Tyler one-tenth of the time.

Tyler finished drinking the last of her coffee and said to Wade, "If you don't mind, I am going to go over some of those old files again just to see if I can find anything that may have gotten overlooked. Sometimes, we tend to look at things and not really see them. It's something of a paradox."

"Countless people have gone over those files and each time it's the same thing. Nothing new comes to light."

Prior to getting up from the table, Wade looked at Tyler with curiosity in his eyes and said, "Not to be too inquisitive, but what ever happened to your husband?"

"The man got what he deserved. He died on his way to the hospital. He choked on his own blood. He got exactly what he had wished for me."

Tyler and Wade got up from their seats and returned to the squad room. He headed to his desk and Tyler returned to the interview room, where she began the monotonous process of reviewing the countless number of files before her. She isolated the files pertaining to the murders and abduction of white folks. Any files not fitting into this category were excluded. The bulk of her day was spent sorting and writing notes on each of these files. In total, she had come across one-hundred and eighty-eight files she felt fit into the White Files category. Not one of these cases had ever been solved. One particular file she reviewed with interest pertained to the abduction of an individual by the name of Jean-Luc LeClaire who was taken from a restaurant. Not one of the restaurant's patrons had survived, with the exception of two young black girls. She started to read their statements.

Both girls provided little information as to what had actually happened that day, but they did give a clear description of the assailant. They described him as massive, black and remorseless. Tyler pushed this file aside and placed a green sticky note on its cover. The green files would all require follow-up.

By day's end, Tyler had read most of the White Files in their entirety and had placed over twenty of these files aside for follow up. In each case where a black witness existed, she was determined to do a thorough review of the statements and facts. If this meant interviewing each witness again, then so be it.

It was now early evening. Wade decided it was time to head out and go see his daughter. As he left the office, he bid his new partner farewell. She acknowledged his gesture with a tiny grunt.

The squad room was now very quiet. Tyler continued working, placing one phone call after another in an attempt to verify each of the statements contained within the files. She was astonished to find that most of the individuals she spoke with hesitated or resisted to respond to her questions. She concluded these people were either too scared to speak or didn't have a problem with the crimes committed.

She turned to the comfort of her computer. She accessed the FBI's database and performed searches of crimes with similar or common links. Her main objective was to see if she could come across something more recent, files that the police had not yet received. Three files appeared almost immediately. The first involved the murders of several white college fraternity brothers, with one being abducted. Three days earlier, another abduction had occurred involving a retired professional wrestler known as the White Knight. The third file involved the abduction of a college professor named Larry Howard. With the last two files, several witnesses all indicated the same huge black man who was apparently involved and could be placed somewhere on the scene.

Tyler Collins was seeing double. It was time to call it a day. She had been the only one left in the squad room for several hours now, and she was overtired. She gathered the reports she printed and stuffed them into her briefcase. As she left the building, she nodded good evening to the lone officer on the front desk. It was a delightfully peaceful night.

Tyler unlocked her bright blue Dodge Mini Van. As she turned onto the main street it started to rain heavily, making driving very difficult. Being so overtired, Tyler had trouble battling the rain. She spotted a drive-through coffee shop and pulled her van into the lot to place an order.

Over the speaker, she heard, "Can I take your order please?"

"Two large coffees with one Sugar Twin in each please."

"That'll be four-thirty. Please drive through."

While waiting for her coffee, she noticed several phrases spray painted all over the walls of an adjacent concrete building. Most were derogatory and belittling to members of the white race. One verse in particular really stood out:

> "WELCOME TO OUR SHOP. PLEASE ENJOY OUR SLOP. WE GRIND IT, WE PERK IT AND WHEN IT IS DONE, WE SERVE IT TO WHITE TRASH, JUST FOR THE FUN. POWER TO BLACKS, WE'VE ALL BEEN THROUGH HELL. IF YOU NEED MORE INFO, THE INTERNET WILL TELL!"

It didn't make too much sense to her. Someone obviously didn't like the coffee served here but hated white folks even more. What were they referring to on the Internet? As she pulled up to the wicket for her order, she commented on the graffiti scribbled across the building.

Her server said, "It doesn't make a difference how many times the owners of that building paint over that crap. The neighborhood kids repaint it the very next day. They always spray paint poems and stuff that is normally down on anyone white. Anyway, have a nice evening and drive safe in this rain."

Tyler pulled her van from the drive-through and headed for home. Pulling into her driveway, she noticed the kids from next door had left their bikes in her path. She jumped out and moved the bikes on to the lawn. Kids will be kids, she thought to herself, reflecting back on the kids' graffiti next door to the coffee shop.

Her mailbox was overflowing with envelopes. She reached up and emptied it. She had a hard time balancing her mail, briefcase and the coffees in their cardboard tray. As she walked through the front door, most of the mail burst from her arms and scattered all over the floor. She walked briskly towards the kitchen table, kicking the mail as she went. After dumping everything else on the counter, she returned to the scattered mail. Reaching down to pick it up, she noticed a flyer advertising for a month's free Internet service. Walking back into her kitchen, she continued to read the advertisement. The front cover read:

"Access Millions through the Internet."

Opening the flyer, she began to read its contents aloud, "Place your advertising where it counts. You can design your own web page at no extra cost. Do you realize that by using the Internet you can advertise and sell all your products to millions of households across the world?"

Tyler, now sitting at the table, picked up one of her coffees and took a big gulp. Then it struck her. If you were involved in highly organized, worldwide criminal activity and you were mandated to set up multiple hits on others, the Internet would be the most effective means of communication.

Tomorrow was going to be a busy day. She knew there had to be some kind of set-up on the Internet used to communicate information about the abductions and the murders. There had to be a way to link the files, to find some common ground, something to help her with the investigation.

. . .

It was nearing 1:00 a.m. and Wade Leaman was sitting contentedly at home, half asleep, watching television and sipping on his fifth beer. The phone rang, startling the old veteran. The only time his phone ever rang at this hour in the morning was when something was wrong with his daughter. He grabbed for the phone and knocked his beer into his lap.

"Hello, shit!"

"That's not a very polite way to answer one's phone now is it?"

"Tyler…is that you?"

"Sorry for calling so late, Wade, but I wanted to let you know I won't be in tomorrow, or should I say later this morning. I have to follow-up on a couple of files."

"You're calling me at this hour to tell me you won't be in?"

"Actually, I'm calling you to let you know I need your assistance. I have to do some research tomorrow and I need you to get me a class five security clearance to the FBI's main computer systems. I believe you have some contacts with the Bureau and I need you to use them so I can carry out my research first thing. Can you look after that for me?"

"I'll see what I can do and get back to you in the morning. Will you be at home?"

"I will be here until 6:00 a.m., then I'll be driving down to New York City to do a follow up on one of the White Files. You can reach me by cell. Look, I know it's late and I'm sorry for calling you at this hour, but I need you to do me this favor first thing. I think I'm on to something. Can you do this for me or not?"

"It shouldn't be a problem, but I need to know what you're up to."

"I think the main reason none of the witnesses are talking or giving much information has to do with the fact that they were not interrogated by one of their own. Not just someone black either, but someone who can relate to the plight of being a black person in today's society, someone like myself, who has already gone through a traumatic experience. I think I can get a bit more information out of them."

"You're not to do anything stupid or without my knowledge. Do you understand?"

"Sure. Now don't forget to call me on my cell as soon as you get the clearance. I'll call you with updates if I find anything."

Tyler hung up and headed to bed. Wade sat up in his chair and finished the beer he had salvaged from the spill before retiring for the night.

Coffee cups littered the back seat of Tyler Collins' van. Each time she finished a coffee, the paper cup would end up back there. It was past 6:00 a.m. and Tyler was on her way to New York. She had several hours of driving ahead of her, and traffic was picking up. She would begin her search at Page University Law School. She needed information to assist her in the investigation of the White Files.

A ringing noise exploded inside the van. At first, Tyler was so distracted she didn't realize her cell was ringing. She reached over to the passenger's seat to retrieve her purse. As she began rifling inside, the van swerved slightly towards the left-hand shoulder of the highway. Several car horns erupted around her. It was awkward for her, keeping both eyes on the road while fumbling about in her purse. She finally found the phone.

Wade said, "Collins. Just calling to let you know you now have the necessary clearance you were looking for. You have been granted temporary B classification, which means you have almost full access to all of the FBI's criminal files. In addition, you will also be able to review all of the FBI's monitoring systems for suspected or intended criminal activity. Your password is Feline021. I want you to check in with me on the hour. Do I make myself clear?"

"I'll do what I can. Over and out Leaman."

The Page University Law School was built four years earlier. It was among the most prestigious law schools in the world. A total of thirty-eight buildings, varying in size, made up this institution. As she passed through the security gate on the main road leading to the university, the commissionaire handed her a map. Tyler pulled over to the side of the road to study it. She would have to locate the Admissions Office in order to find the female witnesses who provided statements pertaining to Jean-Luc LeClaire's White File. Once she found what she was looking for, she proceeded to the Admissions Office.

The rude secretary was somewhat hesitant to provide any information to the female detective. Only after a call had been placed to the Dean of the University, did the secretary's tune change. The girls' schedules revealed they were in the same class at that moment. Tyler left the Admissions Office and headed towards the Language Arts Building. It was there she would find Professor Sherman Kerr's English 2047 class.

As she entered the Language Arts Building, it brought back fond memories. She had thoroughly enjoyed attending university and had made many friends and accomplished much as a student. She looked around, sizing up the hundreds of students walking about, sitting on the floor doing last minute studying and just standing about chatting with one another. So many young, innocent faces. Tyler headed up the stairwell leading to the second floor, dodging the hordes of students coming towards her from every angle. Once she reached the top landing, she started to walk down the hallway, looking for Professor Kerr's homeroom.

After a few more minutes, Tyler found the wooden door that read:

> Room 2047
> Professor Sherman Kerr

She peered through the window and tried to get the professor's attention, but he was totally engrossed in his lecture. She decided to review the LeClaire file while waiting. The names of the two witnesses were Audrey Carrow and Geraldine Simms. Both girls were in their early twenties, and each of them had received a scholarship that enabled them to attend this first-class facility.

Their original statements were very vague and inaccurate. Notes on the file indicated that both girls were extremely nervous during their first few interviews with the police. With each new interview, slight discrepancies appeared regarding the details of the large black man responsible. The only consistent remarks were that he was big and he hated white people. The only other piece of information they both gave was the fact that they were locked in the washroom. As a result, they were not in a position to relay anything more than they had already provided to the police.

At eleven a.m., the door to room 2047 finally flew open and the students emerged. Tyler walked over towards the door and started to shout, "Audrey Carrow. Geraldine Simms. Does anyone know these girls?"

A young skinny guy shouted, "They're still in class."

Tyler fought her way into the classroom towards the professor. She held up her badge, asking him to identify the two girls. He called out for the girls to remain in their seats. Once the remaining students had left, the professor advised the detective she could use his classroom if required, as it was not needed for the remainder of the day. The two young black girls were sitting at the back of the classroom.

Tyler walked towards them, holding up her badge and said, "Hello, girls. My name is Detective Tyler Collins and I'm here on official police business. I'm looking for some more information regarding the murders and abduction that took place at Henry's Café. I know you have previously provided multiple statements to the police regarding this case, but I need clarification on a few points."

Audrey Carrow said to the detective, "We've been through this several times. We told the others before you everything we know. When are you going to leave us alone?"

"You know girls, I fully realize both of you witnessed a series of brutal murders and it must have been very traumatic for you."

After looking at their expression, she continued, "I want you to know I'm here to find out who committed the murders that day. I am interested in making sure it never happens again. The people who were murdered that day have kids, parents, brothers, and sisters. Some of them even had grandchildren. The relatives left behind have so many unanswered questions. Do you realize how much they have suffered and still continue to suffer to this day?"

The girls never said a word. They just looked at Tyler with tears in their eyes. Tyler smiled softly and said, "Both of you are extremely lucky to be alive and well. We have reason to believe the individual responsible for the massacre that day has since committed more murders. Several other innocent people have not been as lucky as the two of you, and we fear many more will follow in their footsteps if we are unable to find this man soon."

Audrey Carrow said, "I really don't think we can help you any more than we helped the others."

Tyler got down on one knee in front of the girls and responded, "Let me be the judge of that. All I need you to do is answer a few questions for me. I'll try to make them as brief as possible. What you have to keep in mind is that I really need your assistance. We have reason to believe the murderer has even taken children and God knows what has happened to those poor innocent babies."

Audrey and Geraldine exchanged agitated glances. They had thought that tragic day was finally behind them and hoped they would never have to deal with it again.

Audrey said, "Ask your questions so we can get this over with. But, I want you to keep in mind that we still have to contend with the fact that we too could become victims ourselves some day."

"I fully realize where you are coming from. Each of you should know where I'm coming from. Any light you can shed on this case by answering my questions may help you rest easier and hopefully stop others from suffering and even death."

The two girls sat up and looked alert. Tyler sensed it was time to begin her questions. Tyler had composed a long list of questions for the girls and documented each response. One thing that stood out was the fear on Geraldine's face and the trembling in her voice as she started answering Tyler's questions. Geraldine looked at the ceiling as she recalled what the huge black man said to the lawyer, Jean-Luc LeClaire. Her account was a bit muddled, but it was, however, interesting that most of the information she provided had never been documented in the original police reports.

After awhile, the students relaxed and information flowed more freely from them. Audrey remembered that the big black man had mentioned the lawyer would be delivered to a new destination, and that a jury of the black man's peers had made this decision. He had called the lawyer "scum" for representing a rich man against a black woman who eventually committed suicide. Tyler later discovered this other man's file was also among the White Files.

Another thing that really stood out was that both girls repeated the phrase, "White Man's Cotton." The detective knew these were hate crimes, but she was amazed at how much the tables had turned. Usually hate crimes of this magnitude were against members of the black race, not committed by them.

Tyler had finally finished her questions. Because of the information the girls had provided, she was able to establish a clear mental picture of the events and did not feel the need to go any further with the girls. Tyler stood up and shook hands with each girl. She thanked them for their help and wished them well.

Before she left room 2047, she passed each girl her card asking them to call if they remembered anything else, but also if they ever needed her help or just wanted to talk. The two young women escorted Tyler to her vehicle. Tyler drove from the parking lot, watching the two girls in her rearview mirror grow smaller and smaller as the distance between them increased.

Tyler picked up her cell phone and called Wade. She only managed to get his answering machine and left him a message: "You must be deep into your work. I'm assuming that's why you're not answering the phone. Things are progressing fine. Call you later."

Tyler's last stop in New York was at Precinct 7 on the corner of Snelgrove and Lacey. She had prearranged with a former acquaintance to have full access to one of their computers. Once inside the precinct, she located her reserved workstation in the congested squad room. Police officers, detectives and criminals were in constant motion around her.

Once she started working, she automatically tuned out her surroundings. She input specific key words and phrases into the FBI's criminal database. "White Man's Cotton" yielded hundreds of potential sites, but not one of them panned out. She typed in several other keywords and phrases to enhance her chances of success. These other entries resulted in thousands of hits, each with some potential. This was going to take a lot more time than she'd anticipated. As it turned out, she would have to continue her search back home.

The drive home was a long one. She drank four coffees on the way and by the time she arrived back at the precinct, she was totally wired. Inside an interview room, she emptied her briefcase on the table. She sifted through the mounds of paper she had collected that day. Each sheet was placed in a pile, based on the category of phrases and words used.

Wade and the others had all left for the day. Their work was done, but her's was just beginning. It was late in the evening and Tyler had already put in sixteen-hours. But she was eager to continue on. Once she'd reestablished access with the FBI's criminal database, she began to plug in additional phrase combinations she had come across earlier that day. Combining and changing some of the phrases helped her narrow down her hits from thousands to a more workable number. She was now in the hundreds.

Deep in concentration, she thought she heard her cell phone ringing. She paused for a moment, but heard nothing more. She continued scanning more web pages when the ringing returned. This time, however, it had startled the young detective. She dismissed her nervousness as coffee overload. Detective Leaman had called looking for an update. He also wondered why Tyler was still at work so late. He told her to pack it in for the night or she wouldn't be fit to do anything in the morning. She took his advice. She was exhausted. Once she arrived home, it wasn't long before she drifted off into a deep sleep.

The next day, she couldn't get to work quickly enough. When she arrived at the precinct, she was surprised to find Wade Leaman in the interview room going through the files she had placed on the table the night before. He had written more notes and was more alert than she or his co-workers had ever seen him before.

She said, "Did you get an eviction notice from your place or what?"

"Did I ever tell you that you're a funny lady?"

"Not lately, sport."

"I've been running through some of your notes and thought I'd run a few ideas past you. The combination of words you have been using has yielded multiple results, right?"

"I would have to say, 'yes' to that question."

"Well, why not try running your multiple phrases with some you already have? Now it's just a suggestion, but I thought I'd run it by you."

Tyler grinned at Wade and said, "Do you have any thoughts on which words I should use?"

"Now that you mention it, why don't you try using words like, 'capture,' 'bounty,' 'funds to be paid,' 'jobs to be done,' and different variations of 'white men,' 'white folks' or 'white' period? I have several others listed which you may also find useful."

"Let me take a look."

"I've even managed to get my hands on two rookies to help us in our search. You know, someone else to do the brunt of the grunt work."

"So, it's help with 'our' search now?"

"You've got it, kid."

"When do we get the extra help?"

"All we have to do is knock off a few lists of potential leads that need to be followed up and then we can pass them off to the hired help, with clear instructions, of course. I can have the rookies ready to go today if need be."

"It's nice to see you've come on board with such enthusiasm and energy. It's always nice to have good help, even from someone your age."

"Let's not get personal now, girl, or I may just get cranky all over again."

Leaman and Collins spent a few hours drafting sets of keywords and phrases they felt would yield better results. After much debate over various slang terms and expressions, and whose statements made more sense, they compiled a list of over seventy phrases. Further Internet research was now required.

Leaman divided the list in two. He sought out the two rookies, Lawrence Kelloway and Marilyn Daily, and put them to work. They were told to keep their eyes open for web pages or sites where configurations of these key phrases existed. They were to place great emphasis on sites where someone could send encoded messages.

Marilyn was a computer whiz, and her patience and work ethic would prove invaluable. Collins and Leaman took a few pages to go through themselves. Even with the new phrases, they continued to get numerous additional possibilities.

. . .

Four days had passed. Marilyn was comparing her list with Lawrence's and was pleased to discover a series of duplicate hits all referring back to the same web page. It was called, "Merlin's Poetic Website." When she further compared their data with Leaman and Collins' lists, she was certain they'd found something that could not be coincidental. Marilyn and Lawrence proceeded to the interview room with the news. As they entered, the veteran Detective saw the proud look on their faces.

Marilyn smiled and said, "It looks like we've found what we've been looking for: 'Merlin's Poetic Website.' We cross-referenced each of our lists with yours' and this website is on all four lists and had an unusually high volume of hits. Taking into consideration the different combinations of words and phrases we were checking, this particular site had hits on over thirty percent of the phrases used. There's not another site that even came close."

Marilyn took in a deep breath. In her excitement, she was speaking quickly and had run out of air. Continuing on, she said, "It actually looks like a site for those into poetry, but once you read the verses…well, check these out…"

The police officers each took a turn reading several of the poems aloud. Some of the poems had been submitted as far back as six years ago. The group's next step was to see if they could match any of the poems' upload dates to the incidents of missing people. After a bit of review, they concluded that an associated abduction or murder had been committed within a month or less of the poem's Internet publication. Several of the time frames matched perfectly with the White Files.

It appeared the group had indeed hit the jackpot, but they had also hit a stumbling block. There was no way they could trace the individual or individuals who published each poem, or the actual owners of the website itself. Each avenue they took in trying to trace the origin of the website came to a dead end because the owner's names and addresses were all fictitious. The website's host could only confirm that cash had been paid up front for the website. There was no additional information to be found anywhere.

. . .

Lawrence, Marilyn, Wade, and Tyler all arrived at the office the next morning just before 8:00 a.m. Collectively, each of the four individuals had spent much of the night contemplating the discovery of Merlin's Poetic Website. As the meeting got underway, Wade gave each of them an opportunity to summarize the situation. After everyone had spoken, they concluded that Merlin's Poetic Website was being used to send and receive messages related to the murders and abductions of hundreds of white people over the years. Normally, the first poem in a given month was used to establish a meeting. Shortly afterwards, a second poem followed, which was a request to carry out the decisions made at the first meeting. A third poem was normally added weeks later, which advised that the requests had been carried out. They all agreed that the next thing they needed to establish was the location of the meetings. This task proved impossible.

Wade stood up in the middle of the interview room and said, "Okay folks, this is what we know so far. Each month, at about the same time a group of individuals are meeting, somewhere in the United States. The purpose of these meetings is to set up the next murder or abduction. I think we all agree that the murders are not the actual intent of these meetings. It appears from the various poems that this group is interested in abducting racists only, and anyone else who gets in the way is simply collateral damage. The only thing we can conclude is that the missing victims are all racists to some degree and someone wants to kill, torture or hold these people against their will. None of the missing people have never been found and the individual grabbing these people has no problem committing murder. From this, we can draw the conclusion that the missing people may indeed still be alive, or kept alive for long periods of time and later disposed of, presumably somewhere they'll never be found again. In addition, we can conclude that the individuals responsible for these actions are black. Do we all agree?"

They all nodded in agreement. They had gone over the details of the various cases and everything appeared consistent in each of the cases: murders, the abductions, the poems posted on the website, and the overall timing of these events.

Pacing the room, Tyler said, "We know that these missing people were racists or at least known to have associated with racists, based on the evidence gathered. We also know these people are disappearing off the face of the earth. We can conclude that if their intent was to murder these racists or their known associates, then the job should have been completed with the rest of the murders at the original crime scenes. This may sound out to lunch, but hear me out. I think what we need to do is to set up someone undercover, as bait. We need to find ourselves an undercover officer and establish a fake background with a history of hate crimes. We can plant a tracking device on the person that will never be found."

Tyler looked at her peers to ensure she still had their attention and then proceeded, "We constantly monitor our undercover agent and hope he becomes selected somewhere down the road, hopefully in the near future. The only way this will work is for us to create a fictional character and feed him to the wolves, the media. We will have to ensure he receives statewide coverage. I know it sounds wacky and I can tell by the expressions on your faces that you're unsure, but think about it. As it stands now, we have come to a dead end. Unless we come up with something fairly quickly, we may lose more people and God knows how many will never be found."

The three of them looked at Tyler. No one said anything for the longest time. They just stared at her, trying to grasp what she had suggested.

Finally, Wade spoke, "I think it could work, but we'll have to be sure we do this right. We need to get us one mean-looking motherfucker and create a story line to feed to the media that would make even a rabbi want to kill him personally. This way, we could almost ensure he will get the attention of Merlin's Poetic Website."

One by one they all agreed. They needed to establish the perfect headline.

Tyler looked at the group and said, "One thing that really gets people going in the worst sort of way is when harm comes to children. What we should do is set up an undercover officer who is a mass-murderer of children. The only difference here is this particular individual only murders black children. We capitalize on the darkest and most sinister of all racial hate crimes. We create false names for each of his 'victims,' and for the undercover officer himself. Well, what do you think?"

Wade responded, "It's way out to lunch, but if we can get it approved, we may just find a way to get a publication on Merlin's Poetic Website. I will speak to the Captain and get his okay, which I'm sure he'll give because he'd like nothing more than for us to solve these cases. Then we can get the plan in motion."

Wade got up from his seat and headed to the Captain's office. He was gone for about an hour when he returned with a broad smile on his face.

He looked at his partners and said, "Well folks, we can thank Tyler for this one. If it had not been for that track record of hers, I would have been thrown right out of his office. But, we got the green light. Now all we need is to find an officer to go undercover."

Tyler responded, "That won't be a problem. Detective John Lynch has worked with me on other undercover operations in the past. He is a perfectionist and can assume any character, for any job. I will contact his superiors this afternoon and make the necessary arrangements. What we should be concentrating on now is how we will feed him to the media."

The day passed quickly, but not before the planning stage had been finalized to everyone's satisfaction. Detective John Lynch had been notified and cleared for his new assignment. Marilyn and Lawrence had contacted the department's media relations officer and had come up with the ideal story line that would be fed to the media throughout the following days:

"White Racist Child Serial Killer, Richard Pope, To Be Freed On A Technicality."

Many of the news stations and major newspapers throughout the United States and the world picked up the story within minutes of it being released. Over the next few weeks, each of the articles published and interviews with Tyler and Wade on the various networks across the country, portrayed the police department as being crushed and devastated by a criminal justice system that would allow Richard Pope to get away with these horrendous crimes.

Richard Pope was further depicted as a rich socialite who used his money and power to beat the rap for his crimes. Money and connections, this man had boasted openly in the media, were the foundation of the privileged and enabled them to get what they wanted without any consequences. The media often broadcast live from the outside of the borrowed mansion, which the undercover cop had been living in for this operation.

A day didn't pass in the next couple of weeks without some group landing outside the mansion of Richard Pope, alias John Lynch, to protest. He was detested for the crimes he was accused of committing. The African-American community especially was going crazy with hatred for him. It got to the point that "Richard" had to hire security for the mansion, as things were getting out of control. His role was to incite the public, gain media exposure, and hopefully draw the attention of those responsible for Merlin's Poetic Website. Every once in a while, a news station would show Richard Pope driving freely, to and from his mansion, each time giving a reporter the finger. He was grandstanding and playing right into the media frenzy.

Tyler and Wade were pleased. They had put together one of the wildest master plans ever in the history of their precinct. Now it was just a waiting game. Richard Pope's every move was being tracked with the help of a tracking device in the form of a miniature hearing aid. A second tracking device had been implanted under his left thumbnail.

Wade, Tyler, Lawrence, and Marilyn each took turns monitoring Richard Pope's every move. They were in constant contact, and gave one another daily updates. They also monitored Merlin's Poetic Website for any updates.

While things proceeded for Leaman and Collins in their current undercover operation, new slaves were about to arrive at White Man's Cotton.

LANCE FORREST'S ARRIVAL

chapter twelve

LANCE was suffering from a vicious migraine. The pain was so severe he didn't even notice the blood running down over his lips from chattering teeth periodically clashing against his swollen tongue. The noise inside the cargo area of the plane didn't help. The sound of the engines was deafening. It was so powerful that the cold steel flooring underneath him vibrated wildly.

Sandwiched between two other men, he was no longer wearing a gag. Only his hands and feet remained tightly secured with nylon rope. He gathered that whoever placed him here figured he would probably choke on his own vomit if they didn't free his mouth. His vision was also partially blurred, due in part to the massive headache pushing against his temples.

It helped him to know that he was not alone on this excursion. Every once in a while, a large man would roll into his back. Lance couldn't see him, but later learned that this huge man was none other than the original White Knight.

He could, however, make out the figure of the individual lying directly in front of him. Lance had hoped it was one of his friends, but immediately recalled his last few moments at the frat house. It would have been impossible for any of them to survive that gruesome ordeal. The unconscious man, Larry Howard, was older and balding. He was a college professor and very private. He never revealed the reason for his abduction and no one pressed him for it. If not for the fact his stomach arched up and down with each breath, Lance would have mistaken him for dead.

The plane ride was coming to an end. The plane hit the runway with a bang, but none of his fellow passengers stirred with the impact.

Like so many before them, the ritual was always the same. The doors to the plane opened and in walked several black men all carrying weapons. No one displayed any personality, nor did they show sympathy. One of the men pulled out a knife and used it to slit the ropes around Lance's feet. He grabbed him by the back of the hair, lifted him to his feet and pushed him towards the exit.

The guard then turned to Larry Howard who was not quite as fortunate as Lance had been. Once Larry's legs were freed, he still didn't move. They picked him up and slapped him across the face in an attempt to wake him. The professor's slow response time angered the guard so that even when his eyes had opened, he continued striking him. These people had very little tolerance, and even less patience with those who aggravated them. The men dragged the professor towards the exit and pushed him down the steps leading from the plane. The fall had knocked the older gentleman unconscious. The guard, unable to wake him up, radioed for assistance.

Within minutes an old pickup truck came speeding down the runway. Larry was picked up and placed in the back of the old truck. It was several more days before Lance saw him again.

The guard's attention had suddenly shifted to the lone man still inside the plane. Lance could hear a ruckus ensuing. Apparently, the big man wasn't eager to be moved once he awoke from sleep. While his captors took great pleasure in kicking and beating the wrestler, it was not without consequence for them either. For, even with his hands tied securely behind his back, he was still able to knock two of the guards off their feet.

The racket lasted for almost ten minutes. Finally, Harry Barbour emerged from the plane. The two black men following him tried to push Harry down over the steps, but could not match his strength. Smiling defiantly, Harry walked down each step of his own accord until finally reaching the solid ground below.

The giant man took his place next to Lance on the runway, towering over him by almost two feet. Lance was very quick to catch on. Basically, if you didn't want any trouble, your best bet was to do as you were told without question. He knew instantly he was not in a position to dispute the guards. His companion was not as eager to please. Continuing to show attitude and resistance, he gave the men outside the same trouble as he had given those inside the plane. This was short lived; within seconds, the big man was down.

He had been poked with a stun gun to the middle of his back, which instantly brought the giant to his knees. He landed with such force he ended up skinning them both out.

The guards ordered them to unload the contents of the plane into the waiting horse and cart. Once Harry recovered from the jolt, he resisted the urge to struggle any further. He began unloading the supplies. When there was only a few crates left to unload, Avery, their new boss, approached.

He ordered the men to move quickly. He stood, watching them, shouting as they worked. After all the supplies had been removed, they were ordered to follow behind the horse-drawn cart.

It was an exceptionally hot day and on top of being exhausted, Lance was dehydrated. He could feel himself swaying from side to side and thought for a split second he would pass out. When his newfound companion sensed the state he was in, he held Lance upright as they walked. Both men were sweating from head to toe. With each step they took, their breathing became more labored. As they walked along the rugged path, lingering slightly behind the cart, Lance became weaker by the second.

He couldn't quite remember what happened next. His vision blurred, his legs gave out and he crumbled to the ground. In falling, he also knocked over his companion, who had kept him on his feet this far.

The masters did not find this amusing, nor did they show any tolerance for this weakness. Avery jumped from the cart and began striking the men across their backs with a black leather whip. To his right, Lance could see through blurred vision that the white giant was grinding his teeth together. The anger and spite that flowed through Harry's body indicated that at that moment, he could have easily snapped Avery's neck, regardless of the black man's size.

Avery had little tolerance for any person who showed even the slightest sign of resistance or attitude. He looked at the wrestler who was attempting to get back on his feet and kicked him right in his stomach. It sent the White Knight back to the ground. Avery then called for his associates to assist him in teaching the big man a further lesson.

It didn't take much coaxing. His men immediately leaped from the cart and took turns kicking, slapping, punching, and kneeing their prey. Harry Barbour was one tough bird. He took the punishment without so much as a single whimper. If Lance were the one on the receiving end of that assault, he would have surely died.

After ten minutes of continuous beating the men returned to the cart. Once they settled in, Lance heard them laughing and gasping for breath while they guzzled greedily from the water jugs they held, cruelly taunting their captives. Lance ran his tongue across his dry scaly lips as he watched each man take his turn drinking. Every now and then, one of them would break out laughing as the jug hit his lips and water spouted forth.

Harry didn't look the worse for wear, once he managed to get back on his feet. His first concern was to see if Lance was okay. If the situation was reversed and Lance had taken the beating because of something Harry had done, Lance honestly didn't know if he would have been so quick to attend to Harry's needs. In all probability, he thought he would have wanted to seek vengeance himself rather than selflessly care for him as Harry had done. Lance would soon learn a lot more about this bigger man as time went on, as well as learn more about himself.

The captives arrived at a set of enormous steel doors, which led into White Man's Cotton. One of the guards stationed at the main entrance entered the appropriate code into the keypad and the doors lifted. Lance and Harry were ushered hastily inside. As they entered the rock cavern, Avery began his speech.

He told the men why they had been selected for White Man's Cotton. He announced that as the lowest form of life, they had no rights and were never to disobey or show aggression, for they would be punished severely if they did.

It was at that moment Lance realized just how bleak his future was going to be. He tried to explain to Avery how an error had been made, how he was not who they thought he was. This sent Avery and his associates into fits of rage. Rather than remedying the case of mistaken identity, all it got Lance in the end was another beating.

Harry had tried once again to intervene, but he was struck from behind with the stun gun and knocked to his knees. One would think the big man had a little more sense. Not that Lance didn't appreciate all he was trying to do for him, but this was a rough place and the big man had already taken his fair share of abuse for one day.

Each black man there took turns drubbing Harry. Pleasure shined through on every one of their faces, as they continued to beat a man twice the size of any one of them.

After they had finished, Harry rose slowly to his feet. This time a look of pain glimmered briefly across his face, although he quickly disguised this sign of weakness.

Entering further into the underground, both men finally ended up in the cleansing area where they were left in the hands of Master Harvey, the pear-shaped pervert. Intimidated by the White Knight, Harvey requested two of the guards to remain close by.

Things had gone from bad to worse. They were hundreds of feet below the surface and were being utterly humiliated. They had been stripped of their dignity, used as objects of sexual desire for an ugly fat bastard and had an audience of two guards who took turns zapping Harry just for the fun of it.

Lance felt as if he had gone crazy. At one point while no one was looking, Harry got right up in Lance's face and demanded he snap out of it. Lance could only gawk with a fixed blank stare. Unexpectedly, Harry smacked him directly across the face.

He then whispered forcefully, "If you don't smarten up soon little man, you won't last any time. Smarten up now before you get the two of us killed."

He gave no response. Minutes later, both of them had finished being processed. From here they were escorted to Section 34, where they met the rest of their roommates. During the first night in their new quarters the others promptly brought the two men up to speed.

Their roommates were surprised to learn that neither of the new captives had been placed in shackles upon their arrival. It was the usual custom for everyone else who came. To this day, Lance or Harry didn't know the reason why. Lance only assumed it was due to the confusion that resulted from Larry Howard being taken off. Things just seemed to go astray from there.

During the course of the conversation, Harry Barbour revealed that he was waiting for the right opportunity to make his escape. The others laughed at his overly confident statement. This only seemed to make him more resolute. Don Snow suddenly mocked the wrestler. Harry lashed out at the Klansman, quickly silencing all present.

Each of the men in the room already had their fair share of problems with Avery and his men. They didn't need to compound these problems with trouble from a man of Harry's size.

It didn't seem to take very long for these men to finish their stories or to provide Lance and Harry with survival tips for White Man's Cotton. It was Lance's turn to speak. As he attempted to tell them of how he had been abducted in error, none of the men seemed to care. He felt like he was trapped in a nightmare. It would take time before any of these individuals would believe him, but time was all he had at this point.

The next morning they were kicked awake by a group of black men. It soon became obvious as to why all these men had arrived. They were going to test their newest and biggest arrival.

Harry Barbour sat up the instant he awoke. Temporarily disoriented, he tried getting to his feet. He was greeted with a stun gun to the back of his neck, which sent him involuntarily into his original position. One thing was clear, in these surroundings size and strength meant nothing.

After the guards were satisfied Harry was not going to offer resistance, they were ushered directly to Section 34 to begin the day's work. No food would be provided this day because of the resistance Harry had shown upon arrival. From here on in, the group would be held collectively responsible for each individual's actions and errors.

Inwardly, the groups' tempers flared. One day, rations were increased, the next day they were reduced, and lastly wiped out all together. Lance sympathized with Harry. Harry had acted on pure kind instinct, in Lance's defense, which got the whole group in hot water with the masters of the underground. None of the men knew what he had done for Lance, but based on what they'd been through, Lance doubted they would care.

The new arrivals were quick to learn what their assigned duties in the so-called underground cotton fields consisted of. They also later learned that Harry had been the first man in the underground to have a stun gun used on him. His size and strength intimidated the black masters, with the exception of Avery. Avery did his best to show him who the real boss was, shocking him with the stun gun at least twenty times that first day. Anytime Harry even looked at one of the black masters he was zapped.

Lance's stomach began growling incredibly loudly. Robert Lawlor, standing close by, whispered for him to stop flicking the worms to the floor. Lance knew food was scarce and he needed to keep his strength up, but wasn't willing to make that much of a compromise. Lance looked at the man as if he were nuts. Surely they would feed them something soon.

Hours passed and everyone continued working. The only time work stopped was when poor Harry would receive another shock. The men only paused for a brief second, taking a quick look at the former wrestler on the ground and then returned to work.

Blood began to steadily stream down Lance's hands. The pain was unbearable, however, the hunger pains were more prevalent. He squeezed his hands in between a small square section of barbed wiring and successfully retrieved a giant-sized white mushroom. He rubbed his hands all over the mushroom, removing the dirt. He checked to see if anyone was looking. When he thought it was safe enough, he slipped the raw fungus into his mouth.

He never knew what hit him. He had just begun to chew when he felt a hand around his throat. It was Avery. An armed guard standing on a ledge directly above the men had tipped him off. Lance struggled desperately for breath and tried to gain freedom from Avery's grasp. The black man's grip remained firm. He pried Lance's mouth open and forced his head to the ground. Mushroom and spit deflected off his chin and hit the earth below.

Lance had committed one of the cardinal sins. He had disobeyed his master's order: no food was to be eaten this day. Avery lifted him off the ground by the back of the neck and threw him into a pile of empty white buckets. No one dared move. The guards' rifles were aimed. No one would be coming to his aid. Avery reached down and righted Lance with little effort, as if he were as light as one of the empty white buckets. He then struck him across the face several times with the back of his hand. Lance tried to speak, but Avery wouldn't let him. Avery then drove his knee into the young man's stomach. He bent over in agony. Avery continued his attack.

After Avery was satisfied that Lance couldn't take any more, he relaxed his grip. Lance dropped to the rock surface with a thump. He tried desperately to regain a lungful of air. The pain was sickening.

Two of Avery's men forced Lance to his feet and returned him to his workstation. It took everything in his power just to stay on his feet. Avery barked, "Show's over folks, get back to work!"

For the next three hours, Lance used every ounce of strength he had to fill his daily quota. Most of the men had finished their work for the day, but no one was permitted to leave until everyone had finished.

Lance only had a half of a bucket left to fill as he pushed onwards, forcing his hands through the barbed wire covering the tops of each bin. His hands continued to bleed, but the pain had shifted to the rest of his body. It took him another twenty-five minutes to complete the shift. Looking around, he noticed the others had finished and all eyes were on him.

Avery walked over to inspect the buckets he had filled. He said sarcastically, "Not bad for a broken-down little bastard."

Lance wanted to respond to the rotten bastard's words, but knew better. Avery could sense that he wanted to say something and the look on his face responded, "Open your mouth and I'll kick your ass."

After being dismissed, he headed over to join the first group he saw.

Harry moved towards him to offer his assistance. Lance's eyes were filled with tears, but he wouldn't cry. Harry patted him on the head and smiled. He then said, "It's all over now little man. You took a good beating, but you'll be fine."

Lance thought things couldn't get worst, but he was wrong. Avery made an announcement that Lance didn't hear. But the way they were acting and the stunned expression on their faces told Lance that this wasn't good.

Avery told them a draw was going to take place amongst all workers in the section. There would be two winners who would be given an opportunity to fight with a man, who Avery referred to as, "Tiny." It would be a two-on-one fight and if the two white men won, they would be rewarded with a steak supper with all the trimmings. If they were unsuccessful, none of them would eat for another day.

Avery placed the names of the thirty-six men present into the tin, drinking cup. Just from their sleeping quarters alone, Robert Lawlor, George Williams, Don Snow, Harry Barbour, Jean-Luc LeClaire, and the name "Evan Roberts," who the masters of the underground had mistaken Lance Forrest for, were entered.

Only three of Avery's thick fingers could fit into the cup, but he managed to grasp onto one of the pieces of paper. "George Williams" was the first name removed. The look on George's face said it all.

Avery reached into the tin cup and said, "The lucky winner of the second draw is 'Evan Roberts'."

Lance froze at the sound of that name echoing throughout the cavern. It was useless for him to deny the name. No one believed that Evan was his cousin and that Lance arrived here because of a big mix up.

Harry stepped forward and shouted, "Let me take the young fellow's place. Someone his size and the fact he's hurt isn't fair. He will get seriously injured."

Avery motioned to one of his associates and without a word Harry was poked from behind with the stun gun. Avery looked at the fallen man and responded, "Listen here big boy. You speak when spoken to and at no other time. That young fucker will have to learn to look after himself. It's not like you'll be kept around forever if you keep interfering in our business. Do you understand? Answer me or I'll shove this stun gun down your throat. Once it makes contact with that white poisonous saliva in your big fucking mouth, your head will explode from the shock of an electric current going through that empty fucking head."

"I understand fully."

"That's, I understand fully, Master Avery."

Harry Barbour responded with a slow drawn out voice, "I understand fully, Master Avery."

From the venomous hatred in Harry's eyes the rest of the men predicted that one day, Harry would lose it and break one of these black bastard's necks. They hoped he would get this opportunity before they ended up killing him, for Harry was the only man there to pose any real threat to the guards.

Avery ordered them back to their resting quarters. He then advised Robert, Don, Harry, and Jean-Luc that they too were to attend tonight's soirée to lend moral support to the lucky lottery winners. The two fighters were permitted just three hours rest before the commencement of the evening's entertainment. From the stories George and Lance had heard about other slaves who had fought Tiny, getting the shit kicked out of them was the best-case scenario.

When the men arrived back at their sleeping quarters, George looked at Harry and said ignorantly, "I don't know why you aren't the one going anyway. You've caused nothing but trouble for the rest of us since you arrived."

The big man roared back at his attacker saying, "Listen here you little shit. I've had about all the mouth I'm willing to take from the likes of you. Keep it up and you won't even have a fighting chance this evening for I'll fracture every bone in your stinking body."

Stupidly, George made a lunge at Harry. The big man grabbed him by the shirt and lifted him off his feet. George kicked him in the stomach. Harry dropped him but before he could successfully grab him a second time, Robert, Jean-Luc and Lance managed to tackle the big man, smoothly bringing him to the floor.

Don Snow quickly moved in front of George and ordered the man to shut up. His pride at stake, George feigned moving towards Harry. He didn't want to be seen backing down. But he knew if Harry really got his hands on him, he would be dead.

Lance looked at Harry while the three of them, using great effort, tried to hold him down and pleaded, "Harry, try and calm down. This is not going to help any of us. We shouldn't fight amongst ourselves. We only have each other right now and squabbling isn't going to help. We all realize you could take any one of us, or the entire lot of us with ease. You have nothing to prove here to anyone. Just give up, okay?"

After Harry had relaxed, Robert stood up and pulled George aside. He looked at his senior partner and shouted, "Listen George. You know as well as the rest of us we're here for the long haul. Fuck off with the power trips. I'm sick and fucking tired of the whole thing. None of us are perfect. We just live with what life throws at us and take each day as it comes. But if you keep provoking Harry, you won't live another day."

George walked away, mumbling under his breath. After a few minutes, he walked back towards Harry and offered his hand. He said, "I'm sorry, Harry. Just the thought of what is about to happen to us has set my anger in motion."

Harry patted him on the back and said, "We've heard this Tiny fellow is like a brick wall. He's also a mean son of a bitch. There's not much I can tell you that is going to help. Maybe if the two of you try knocking him off his feet and then immediately go in on the offensive you may have a chance. The main thing would be to keep him down and hopefully keep him from doing any damage."

Harry began offering more suggestions to the two men. At the time, Lance wasn't sure any advice would help, but Harry's words later proved to be a great boon.

With just an hour left, two black men entered with an additional roommate. It was the college professor, Larry Howard. He had been badly beaten. He wore a makeshift cast on his left arm and could barely move his neck. The flight down the steps of the airplane had caused serious injury. Harry assisted the professor to a resting position on the floor. His new roommates could only offer words of comfort to the older man. They spent the remaining hour talking and looking after the college professor.

Like clockwork, at 7:00 p.m., they were all escorted, one after the other to Tiny's domain. The men entered the top landing overlooking the circular area below. Harry had carried the professor. Avery left instructions that no one was permitted to stay behind.

George and Lance were escorted towards the elevator. Their roommates were placed in seats overlooking the fighting arena. As both men walked past the bleachers, they were booed and taunted and spit flew at them from every direction, even from the women present. They noticed that most of the seats were filled with blacks. Judging from how they dressed, there were some high rollers in attendance this evening.

After Harry placed the professor gently in a seat, he turned around and glared at the crowd. Avery hastily commanded two men to secure Harry's arms and legs to his seat. With such a select group of colleagues and personal friends in attendance, Avery was not about to take pointless risks. Even though not pleased at being bound, the stun gun pointed at his face, prevented retaliation.

The doors to the elevator opened. George and Lance had reached the lower landing. They were then forced into yet another room, which their masters referred to as the preparation area. It was located directly outside the actual combat arena. The room was a temporary locker room. There was no time for them to relax, even less to think. They had been ordered at gunpoint to change their clothes. Looking at the clothes available to pick from, they realized the masters weren't just interested in having the two men beaten to a pulp. They were intent on inflicting as much humiliation as possible. The costumes that hung on hooks all along the wall were nothing more than a full array of women's bathing attire.

George looked at the two men who had accompanied them thus far about to protest. The taller of the two cocked his gun. They had precisely one minute to get dressed. As the guard aimed at George, and then Lance, and back again, they undressed swiftly, and put on the first thing they came across. George looked at Lance with his mouth wide open. The agony in his eyes and the fear on his face must have been the same for the many others who got trapped in this nightmare.

Both men were forced outside towards the awaiting audience. They were paraded through the arena, amid a flurry of slurs and insults. The deafening boos hurtling down upon them suddenly became cheers. Their opponent, Tiny, had entered the arena.

He looked like a professional power lifter. As he strolled slowly about the showground, the cheers amplified. Tiny pointed at his opponents and started to laugh wildly.

Suddenly silence descended. Eddie Hawkins strolled in, carrying a microphone. He raised the microphone and said, "Ladies and gentlemen, I trust you all had a safe flight. Let the fight begin!"

Tiny encircled the two men, moving in closer with each rotation. Instinctively, George decided to follow Tiny in an attempt to take him down from behind. He leaped towards Tiny, but failed to make contact. Tiny grabbed his right arm and bent it upward, sending George down on one knee. He then lifted up one of his legs and threw it over George's arm. In doing so, he was able to use the weight of his entire body to sit back on George's shoulder pressing his head outward.

Lance attempted to move in and knock Tiny off his feet, but was unsuccessful. Using his free hand, Tiny struck the young man in the neck and sent him falling to the ground in agony.

Rolling around clutching his throbbing neck, Lance could hear George's screams. The louder he roared, the greater the pressure the black fighter used. George allowed his entire body to fall limp to the floor, while holding firmly onto his aggressor's ankles. Tiny lost his balance, but fell with all his weight directly onto George.

The crowd cheered Tiny on. He jumped to his feet lifting George as he rose. He battered the smaller man in the face. He tried to fight back, but his punches had little effect on Tiny. George was backed into the wall and could do nothing to stop the black fighter's onslaught.

Once Lance managed to get back on his feet, he ran towards them. Inches away, he heard a snap. Tiny had taken George's arm, and forced it downward across his own knee. George's screams were heard above the crowd, and the anger and pain in his face flared. He tried lashing out with his one good arm. Tiny landed a punch to the center of his face sending the man to the floor. George was out cold.

Tiny turned around and looked in Lance's eyes. Spit flowed from his evil grin. Lance thought back to Harry's advice from only an hour earlier.

Tiny was still caught up in the excitement of his first win. He believed that he could quash his second opponent easier than his first. His ego was as massive as his body was.

Standing his ground, he allowed Tiny to move to within inches of him. As Tiny's fist reached out to make contact with his opponent's face, Lance tilted his head back and kneed him in the groin. The pain caused Tiny to lose his breath and he fell forward on all fours.

Instantly, Lance jumped behind him and repeatedly kicked him in the balls, over and over, showing no remorse.

The crowd grew silent. The only voices Lance could hear were his roommates encouraging him to keep it up. He continued to kick Tiny until the man started to turn blue. Tiny had tried to block the kicks using his hands and legs. Lance broke many of his fingers in the process. The fear and spite that flowed through Lance's veins kept him alive. Allowing this man to get back on his feet was not an option.

Eddie Hawkins shouted, "That's enough. The game's over."

Lance chose not to listen for two reasons. He wanted to ensure this man never got an opportunity to fight again. Secondly, the adrenalin flowing through Lance's body forced him onward. He turned into what he had never understood and never felt he could, a savage creature.

Somewhere deep in his mind he could hear the many different voices of his companions. They were trying to get his attention, get him to stop whereas moments before they were egging him on.

Eddie and Avery Hawkins had walked over to where Larry Howard had been sitting. They picked him up from his seat and suspended him over the railing. Lance was in a trance, and not only did he not see the Hawkins brothers, but he also couldn't stop himself from attacking this man.

He knew nothing until he saw the figure of a man falling into the arena directly in front of him. As Larry Howard, the college professor, hit the floor, you could hear the crunch. Blood flowed rapidly from his nose, ears and mouth. Lance stopped dead in his tracks. He couldn't tell from where he stood if the professor was still alive.

Lance walked over to the elderly professor and bent over. After looking at his lifeless body and realizing his death was his fault, he broke down and cried. He never felt that sick in his entire life. His actions caused a man to be killed.

The doors to the elevator opened and several black men emerged. One of them hit Lance on the head with a club and he lost consciousness immediately.

Later that night, Harry and Robert advised him that the professor's body had been fed to Rachel. George Williams was taken to the infirmary and Harry had helped carry him back to their quarters.

Lying next to him on the floor was a steak supper with all the trimmings. The note placed by the side of the platter read:

"Compliments of Larry Howard."

He pushed the platter to one side and turned his head to try and sleep. He wanted to sleep this nightmare away. His roommates told him to eat it, as Avery ordered. Without turning, he advised them to finish it off. There was no way on God's earth he could have eaten one mouthful of that food. But his roommates didn't have a problem with it.

Lance was totally devastated. With each passing day as a slave in captivity, he didn't think life could get any worse. But one bad thing always led to another, and each day was more catastrophic than the last.

SICKNESS SETS IN

chapter thirteen

LANCE contemplated why certain individuals are so blessed. Whether it was riches, good health or just pure luck, he often wished he and his fellow slaves could only be so lucky. Wishing for luck was a wasted wish. In his current surroundings, he learned quickly that luck had a tendency to sour. He also learned to be very careful what he wished for, for it could come true.

The day finally came when Eddie and Avery did not show up for work. Everyone thanked their lucky stars: they had a day of freedom from their masters. The Hawkins boys had come down with a virus. Apparently they were too ill to tend to their daily routine. However, the celebration didn't last, for soon the underground slaves would all feel the true strength of the virus.

During the week that the masters were ill, work was very relaxed. They'd grown accustomed to the extreme tension that Avery inspired. This was also the case in Eddie's section. Their replacements were nowhere as cruel as the Hawkins men were.

Avery's replacement in particular was a lazy bastard who spent the bulk of his day reading and eating, and little else. He might have gotten up from his chair once that entire day. He attempted a walkabout, however, it was short-lived. No sooner he had left his chair than he determined it wasn't worth the energy, and returned to his seat.

Don Snow became very flushed as the day progressed. He was performing his assigned duties, as were the rest of the slaves, but he worked very slowly and was extremely tired. It wasn't until much later in the day that several others began feeling just as bad as him. The virus had invaded their work section. Eventually, the bug spread throughout the entire underground.

Half the masters had already been infected and were receiving treatment from the island's medics. The slaves would have to fend for themselves.

Medication to inhibit the virus from establishing had been provided to each of the work sections. For those already contaminated, it offered only slight relief, with poor odds for a speedy recovery. The virus had gotten to the point where the medicine was needed to cure, not prevent.

Due to the rapid spread of the virus, the slaves were dismissed from the cotton fields and ordered back to their sleeping quarters. One by one, each person succumbed to the virus. Between the stomach cramps, the diarrhea and the vomiting, there wasn't a single well person. It had taken charge of everyone; no one could escape its grasp. One after another, men bolted to the underground garbage dump, which was located in one of the biggest caverns underground. Each sleeping quarter was allotted one roll of toilet tissue per week. Taking the five-minute trot to the dump was the only time an individual was permitted to leave their sleeping quarters outside of usual work or eating detail.

The dump was sectioned off into separate areas, each with its own entrance. One exclusively for the white men and the other was for the white women and children. Contact with the opposite sex was not permitted in the underground, even at the dump. Anyone caught breaking this rule was strapped severely with a leather whip. Women and children were no exception.

Lance suddenly took ill. Pain had overtaken his bowels and the urge to relieve them was fierce. As he ran from his sleeping quarters, he crashed into a man from across the hall who was also on his way to the dump. Lance plummeted into the rock wall, while the other fellow hit the ground. Desperate to find relief, they scrambled to their feet and ran full out to reach the dump.

The men were not the only ones who had fallen victim to the virus. Several women and at least one child occupied the other side of the dump.

The magnitude of the actual sickness was beginning to register. Things were serious. Judging from the looks of those around him, things were going to get much worse, before they got any better.

Robert Lawlor made his way to where Lance was crouched. He instantly threw up. Lance responded in kind. Robert looked at him with swollen eyes and a beet-red face and said, "Do I look as sick as you do, Lance?"

"That's an understatement!"

"Don Snow is in quite a state. He's too weak to even move. He looks really bad. I tried to see if one of the masters would get a medic for him, but was told to go fuck myself."

"What about the rest of them?"

"The others are basically the same as you and I. I don't know what's going on, but it looks like we're in the middle of a big fucking epidemic and it's not looking good for any of us."

The squalid conditions they lived in combined with the poor medical care they received made for a sorry situation for all concerned. Lance thought no person ever deserved this, no matter what they've done. He was particularly concerned for the well being of the children in Eddie's section. He knew the adult body could take much more than a child's could. He wondered how those children were making out when most of the men were fighting just to lift their heads up.

A woman from Section 32 had just entered the dump from the opposite corner of the cavern. As she walked towards her side of the trash heap, their eyes met. She looked as pitiful as Lance did. He stood up, pulled up his pants and proceeded to walk over to her.

Robert called out to him, "Lance. Get your ass back here. If you're seen heading in that direction, you'll be whipped raw."

"Not to worry. I'll make sure I'm not seen."

Cautiously, he moved slowly towards the woman, scanning as he went. Being brave was not his style, but he assumed that none of the masters would visit the dump considering the circumstances. As it stood, they were down to half their numbers in manpower. If he were in their shoes, this was one place he wouldn't venture.

Nervously reaching the forbidden grounds, he rounded the corner. Looking about, he noticed five women and one child. His sudden appearance had no affect on them whatsoever. After living in this underground environment for so long, and because of the illness, dignity was the last thing they worried about.

Lance walked over to Grace Kieley and her son, Joseph. He thought about how they must have suffered that tragic day at Rachel's pool. Lance smiled at Joseph. The little boy looked gravely ill, barely able to balance himself.

Grace updated him on the ordeals of the women in Section 32. She was just about to tell him what Robert Lawlor and Jean-Luc LeClaire had done for her and her son, when Robert appeared. When she saw him, she broke down crying. Between sobs, she looked at Robert and said, "I never did get a chance to tell you how much I appreciated what you and the other men did for me and my Joseph. You all risked your lives for us. I'm so sorry that some of the men didn't make it. I am eternally grateful to you all!"

"No need for thanks, madam. How is the little tyke doing anyway?"

"He's not doing well. The little girl you rescued is also extremely ill. She is bedridden. The poor little thing can't even move and is getting worse by the minute. Joseph has the same symptoms. It's only a matter of time before he will also be confined to bed."

"Has anyone asked one of the masters to take a look?"

"All we get is the 'fuck off' routine."

With that, another woman came rushing in their direction and hissed, "Three masters heading in this direction. Hide quickly!"

Robert and Lance looked at each other with pure panic. If they were caught it would result in severe punishment. They had to disappear from sight. The only option they had was to dive into the garbage heap and begin digging. Hastily, they hit the garbage pile and began to bury themselves underneath the foul rubbish and human excrement, using their hands like miniature shovels.

The smell was utterly unbearable. The majority of the garbage had rotted. The dump was also a haven for rats, one of Lance's biggest fears. He had nightmares of being eaten alive by the huge rats, which were seen daily throughout the underground. These rats had bitten several people, both blacks and whites. Some of the bites were so severe many individuals suffered infections, which took months to heal.

Breathing heavily, Robert and Lance were carefully concealed only a few feet from one another. They could hear the black men approach Grace and the others. One of the guards taunted the women. "Just look at those dirty stupid bitches. You're all nothing but a bunch of filthy old bags. Who'd ever want the likes of you?"

It was at times like this that Lance would have given anything to put these scoundrels in their place. However, he might as well have been hoping to get to "Never Never Land."

Lance and Robert were both breathing loudly. The only thing that kept them from being heard was the racket the masters were making while they continued torturing their female victims.

All of a sudden Lance's heart started to thump so hard he sensed his chest was rising up and down erratically. An ugly furry rat had brushed against his left leg and crept up his side. Panic had set in. All he could think about was hideously disgusting vermin eating him alive.

He wanted to flee but his whole body went numb and he was too terrified to move. He knew he would be whipped brutally if he were discovered. He also knew he couldn't excite the rat, for any sudden motion could have startled the little beast, and probably result in him being bitten.

He must have blacked out briefly. The next thing he knew, Robert reached over and pulled him into a sitting position. The women had been calling out to the men, telling them the coast was clear. Lance heard nothing. The men jumped to their feet and hurried away from the garbage pile. They had taken enough chances for one day. They quickly said their goodbyes to the ladies and little Joseph.

The men's side of the dump was still full. Robert stopped to relieve himself a second time. When he had finished, both men began the walk back to their quarters. During their walk, they conversed about the poor state of the women and children. With saddened eyes and a big heart, Robert created a mental picture of the sick little girl lying in her bed. They felt really bad for the children, but what could they do?

Another night had passed slowly. Although no light penetrated the underground to indicate that morning had arrived, the slaves who usually worked above ground had recently left for their shift. The first to depart each morning, these individuals were the unofficial timekeepers. In addition, because they spent most of their time above ground, the virus had not affected them. The rapid spread of the virus confined most workers to bed rest. Work details were at a bare minimum. Ninety-nine percent of the remaining able-bodied workers worked above ground. The remainder was on standby.

Later that morning, there was a surprise visitor in the underground. Thomas J. Hawkins himself, his son Randle and four other black men came to call. They were conducting an inspection, trying to get a grasp on the seriousness of the virus that had taken so many in the underground. They wished to see first hand exactly what damage the illness had actually caused.

Randle and the other men entered first. Shortly afterwards, Thomas himself appeared. All six were wearing surgical masks, and clear plastic gloves covered their hands. It was surreal, like a scene from the X-Files.

At first, it appeared Thomas Hawkins was somewhat concerned about what was happening to the white men who lived in the underground. After Lance and the others listened to the six men talking amongst themselves, it was apparent they were only concerned about how many workers they might lose. They were also concerned as to when they would soon be able to restart White Man's Cotton's assembly lines. One thing was certain: they needed to get things back to the way they were, and soon.

Mr. Hawkins scanned each man in the room. No one dared speak. He stared at each of them through squinted, shifty eyes for several minutes at a time. He delighted in seeing Don Snow drenched in a steady stream of sweat from head to toe. Don looked like death warmed over.

Thomas Hawkins motioned to his men. No one outside their party knew what the signal meant until two of them picked up the Klansman, body and bones, and carried him out of his sleeping quarters.

Lance made eye contact with Thomas Hawkins who responded with a glare. Lance had tried to open his mouth to speak, but the words simply froze on his tongue. Seizing the rare opportunity, he gathered enough courage to raise his arm slightly in the air. He remembered this was the only way his university professors would acknowledge any student and thought it might work on old Hawkins, regardless of how stupid he looked.

The old man's lips curled up, trying to hold back an evil laugh. It was either that, or he had developed a serious tick. After he composed himself, he looked at Lance and snapped, "What do you want, boy?"

"Master Hawkins, sir. I wish to bring up an issue regarding the young children in Section 32."

"What do you know about Section 32?"

"Well, I saw one of the children enter the dump last night from the other entrance. His mother had to carry him in. From where I was standing, he looked like he was on death's door. I was wondering if something was being done for the little ones?"

"I am in the process of checking out White Man's Cotton as we speak. You may not know this due to the fact you're white and probably as stupid as your color implies. White Man's Cotton is my responsibility, shit for brains."

"Yes sir, my apologies, sir."

"What's your name boy?"

"It's Lance Forrest, Master Hawkins."

"Ah yes. You're the error. Evan Roberts' cousin, isn't it?"

"Yes sir, that's me."

If he had not been sitting, he would have fallen down. Thomas Hawkins knew who Lance was and was aware of the circumstances surrounding his arrival.

Randle Hawkins walked towards Lance with his left arm raised high. His father motioned for his son to retreat. After Randle complied, his father, almost displaying graciousness uttered, "Due to the nature of your visit with us and due to the fact that I find myself in a position to admit error when at fault, I'll allow this insubordination on your part. In future, be very careful when choosing to speak. I wouldn't want to see your head secured in a noose that doesn't loosen."

"Yes sir. My apologies once again."

The six men then exited with Don Snow. The slaves discovered later, as they had thought, the Klansman was seriously ill. He had reached a stage where he needed much more than the medication currently provided to him. Most of the slaves in the room were in much better condition than their comrade was. They were able to fight the dreaded virus somewhat easier. Later it was discovered that many others in the underground had already died.

Once the masters left, Lance turned around and faced his remaining roommates. Angrily, he said, "No one believed me! I told you I was here by mistake. Now you've heard it from the horse's mouth."

They were all astonished. Every man in this room and all occupants of the underground, except the children, were here for a reason. They, in some way, committed a racial crime against a black person. To a minuscule degree, Lance too fit in there somewhere. The only difference was the Board of Directors had not directly chosen him. He was totally against everything racists stood for.

. . .

Don Snow was one of two men, three women and two children removed from the confinements of White Man's Cotton that day. All seven were transported to the main house where Marsha Grenning and Isabel and Irene Snow cared for them.

One by one, the unconscious men, women and children were taken upstairs to the servant's quarters and placed in separate cots. Although not exactly the most comfortable setting available, it was a big improvement from where they had been. Temporarily, they would no longer feel the cold and dampness of the underground. Dehydrated, they would soon experience the wonderful sensation of refreshing liquids pouring over their dry cracked lips.

The island's medics had examined each member of the main household, including servants and family, before the group was placed in the servant's quarters. They wanted to ensure the safety and well being of those currently living in the main house. The medics instructed Marsha and the Snow sisters on exactly what was required of them in providing this short-term care.

As Don Snow was carried into the servant's quarters, the twins were overwhelmed with both excitement and sadness. They were horrified at the poor state their father was in. Irene was heartbroken at the sight of her once powerful father, now quivering like a sick child.

Although Don was hallucinating due to a high fever, like the others who had entered with him, he still knew these girls were his daughters. That gave him the strength to carry on.

During the next few days, the condition of the children taken from the underground continued to worsen. They remained unconscious, and visits from the medics only reconfirmed what was already known. On several occasions, Rita Hawkins herself came to check on the status of the two kids. While she firmly agreed with and stood by her husband's convictions, she was still human. The lady of the household was heartbroken over the children's deteriorating health. Following several visits and even more consultations with the medical staff on hand, Rita could take no more. Accompanied by the two medics, she decided to speak with her spouse about taking the children to a medical facility before it was too late.

She had intended upon a short meeting, but it had dragged on for well over three hours. While Thomas Hawkins agreed with his wife, in principle, he strongly believed that the risk factor was just too high. A heated debate broke out between the couple regarding the well being of the bed-ridden youngsters, and the possible consequences of doing the right thing. Finally, a mutually satisfactory agreement had been reached...at least satisfactory for the female member of the Hawkins family.

Thomas begrudgingly agreed to have the children flown off the island first thing in the morning for much-needed medical treatment. Thomas and his sons would spend the better part of the night finalizing all the details. Once delivered safely to a hospital, they were to be abandoned.

Thomas contacted his pilot, advising the man to be on the island at first light for an emergency outgoing transport. The particulars of flight were that the children were to be flown directly into Melbourne, Australia, the closest major children's hospital. A black guard and the cook, Marsha Grenning, would accompany them. Thomas thought a white woman would be needed so as not to arouse suspicions once they entered the hospital.

Marsha was then briefed with precise details as to what was to happen. She was warned not to deviate from the plan in any way. She didn't speak the entire time the instructions were being relayed. The Hawkins men looked on in silence as their father talked. Throughout the remainder of the night, the brothers kept an eye on Marsha. If she displayed signs of being overly nervous or if they felt she would betray them in any way, their presence acted as reassurance of what she might expect.

Thomas Hawkins continued to provide his orders to Marsha. Once she explained the children's symptoms to a physician, she was to excuse herself. She would explain that she needed to go back to her vehicle to obtain the children's medical records. As soon as she walked out of the hospital's front doors, her mission was complete. It would be the last time she would see or hear from the children again. Thomas Hawkins and his family had determined that the children were too young to pose a real threat.

Marsha was shocked. After realizing the full impact of their request, she hesitated and sat back in her chair. Several minutes had passed. There was complete silence in the room as Marsha looked at the males around her.

Thomas said, "I'm waiting for your response! Before you answer, however, I want to tell you something else. If you do anything outside of what we have described or if you try to be a hero, there will be dire consequences. I will have your two roommates killed, along with the remaining females on the island. I trust you will have no problem in following these simple instructions?"

Dumbfounded, but now fully alert, Marsha responded in a quiet tone, "No, Master Hawkins. I'll do as you ask."

"As added security, I have instructed your traveling companion to keep close watch on you at all times. If you deviate from the plan in any way, shape or form, he has specific instructions to return with you to the island without delay. Upon your return, if you fail me, you will be shipped to Section 32 with the new recruits. When I say new recruits, I mean the women who will replace the ones you will be responsible for having killed."

Marsha didn't have anything to say. She was uneasy and wanted to throw up. Thomas instructed her to return to her quarters and move the children to one of the spare rooms for what was left of this night.

Once they arrived at the spare bedroom, Marsha opened the door for the two men, who in turn gently placed the young children in separate beds. After they left, Marsha sat in a chair between the beds. She was left alone to care for these kids until their departure.

The night felt like it took weeks to pass. She thought about a possible escape, but was unable to formulate a plan. Her mind would not allow her to come to grips with the feelings flowing through her. In the end, she kept returning to the threat of Irene, Isabel and the other women on the island being murdered, should she screw up.

Marsha was gently wiping the little girl's brow. She was so confused. She found herself in great anguish. Slowly, her mind drifted back to the horrible memory of the night her life so drastically changed. She was appalled as to how easily she had been taken that night, the night she was delivered to the island. She also had overheard similar conversations during her stay on the island. She knew all too well that the Hawkins' were true to their word. If she ever did manage to escape, the other women would die. Additionally, she knew that eventually she would be recaptured.

Other thoughts entered her head. She didn't even know where the island was located. It was completely isolated. Except for those occupying the research facility, the master's quarters and the slaves of the underground caverns, no one else lived here. A few invited guests occasionally arrived, but all were devoted to the Hawkins family and their elaborate setup. She was crushed.

. . .

Each of the workstations in the underground of White Man's Cotton had been vacated. Because of the illness, there was no longer a fit male in the entire place capable of putting in a day's work. The new medication and rest the men had gotten was finally yielding some results. Many were starting to feel much better than they had in days.

The suffering of the men underground eased as most of their masters had also come down with the same virus. Supervision was basically non-existent. The slaves were allowed to suffer in peace, without anyone around to torment them.

There was one true benefit of the virus that mysteriously appeared in their lives. They were able to converse with their female counterparts without fear of reprisal. Lack of real supervision at the dumpsite was a welcome change for all. The slaves were braver now. They had established a surveillance ring between opposite sexes. Men and women were on the lookout at all times for any masters. When a black man came within viewing distance, men and women alike broke out in song, the ritual chorus of the cotton fields.

Lance was pleased to hear that Joseph and Melanie were on their way to receiving the much-needed medical attention they so deserved. At the same time, he was deeply dismayed for their mother's loss.

Joseph's mom, Grace Kieley, was looking so much better than she had earlier in the week. She was feeling better too. Her medication finally kicked in and her son was headed to Melbourne, Australia. Joseph's medical needs would now be cared for. He would soon be in the hands of proper medical professionals and what was even more pleasing, starting a new life away from this horrible place. She would miss him tremendously and her heart would ache for the remainder of her life. However, she knew this was a sacrifice she would never regret.

Don Snow would be returning later today. Knowing his daughters were alive and well had to be an enormous relief to the man, even if this might be the last time he saw either of them. He had already lost his wife so very tragically, but at least his daughters were still alive.

Most of the island inhabitants had lost loved ones who had arrived with them. The slaves of the underground witnessed more grown men and woman cry these past few days than was witnessed during their entire stay in the hellhole known as White Man's Cotton.

Harry Barbour was now well enough to resume exercising. He started with sit-ups and then moved to push-ups. The rock hard surface beneath his bulky body didn't seem to bother him in any way. He was in an exceptionally pleasant mood, gearing up for some weight training, as he so gracefully put it. He playfully began taunting his roommates about how he was able to bench press each of them, one body at a time, without even breaking a sweat. They all had a splendid time laughing with him. George Mitchell, the heaviest among them, even joined in on the fun. He bet Harry a full day's rations that he wouldn't be able to bench press him twenty times.

The bet was on, and it seemed to work wonders for the group's spirit. They were laughing, carrying on and making bets amongst themselves as to if Harry would win. Harry lay down on his back and balanced George by placing one hand in the middle of his shoulder blades and his other hand on George's lower back. The first couple of times he lifted George in the air, he did so with ease. His roommates all started to count aloud as he bench-pressed the older cop into the air, "...three, four, five, six..."

Without warning, the spectators in the room became silent. Harry and George didn't know what was amiss. Avery was fully recuperated. The men were just about to yell number seven when Avery and two of his men entered their quarters and kicked Harry in his left side.

This, in turn, sent George flying over Harry's head to the ground below. Landing on his back, he was winded and he had taken a smack to the arm Tiny had broken.

Harry tried standing, but was greeted with his master's stun gun. That joyous feeling was no longer evident in the room. Avery had managed to ruin yet another day for them. Harry stayed very still on the floor. He managed not to move a single inch, fighting the spite flowing through his veins. He knew all too well what would happen again, if he got up.

Avery turned to leave the slave's quarters, but stopped and said, "I wanted to personally let you know I'm back and the vacation stops here. You can thank Mr. Forrest for my visit. Maybe he'll think twice before he opens his mouth to a Hawkins again."

Once Avery and his men left, Harry looked out to ensure they had gone. He returned, his mood foul. He looked at the others and said, "I'd like the opportunity to break that bastard's neck. One on one is all I would need to break him in two with ease, and much gratification!"

No one commented. Each of them would have loved to see him try. They also figured that the day would come when he would attempt such a feat. In all likelihood it would mean his death.

. . .

Marsha Grenning was busy preparing for her trip to the mainland with the children. Rita Hawkins had gathered some more appropriate clothing for her to wear. Once Rita had finished assisting Marsha, she called the woman into the living room and reminded her of the importance of this trip. She told Marsha how they were making a big sacrifice in allowing her to take the children off the island. She told her over and over the only reason the children were going was to ensure they got the best medical attention possible to ensure their survival. Rita confided in Marsha that it was she who convinced Thomas to allow her to escort the children. She also told Marsha how she considered her to be the most dedicated and loyal of all her servants.

The plane had arrived and was in the process of refueling. Two guards carried the children from the main house to the plane. Once they were settled in, Marsha was permitted to board. Lex Hangler, one of Thomas Hawkins' men, would accompany her. He would remain with Marsha and the children for the duration, staying by her side at all times until the children were safely inside the hospital's walls.

Once the flight was cleared for take-off, Marsha began strategizing in case circumstances changed during the trip. She noted the direction they were taking and watched for any promising landmarks. She did so without making it look too obvious. Her plan was soon put to rest. Minutes into the flight, Lex removed a blindfold from his pocket and secured it firmly over her eyes. He knew the stakes and would not take unnecessary risks during this trip.

The flight itself took what seemed an eternity. Marsha felt a rush over her body as the jet finally made its descent. The turbulence they encountered during landing heightened her anxiety. As the plane made contact with the runway, she gave an intense sigh of relief. Although a regular jetsetter in her time, she was a nervous flyer.

Their final destination was a privately owned, discarded airfield. Two elderly black gentlemen greeted them as they departed the plane. A black Dodge Mini Caravan awaited them. Lex unloaded one child at a time from the plane, placing them in the back seat of the minivan. Marsha was instructed to sit between them. Both the young girl and boy were sweating persistently. Marsha checked their temperature regularly. The boy's stayed around one-hundred and four degrees. The girl's fluctuated between one-hundred and two, and one-hundred and three degrees.

Marsha retrieved a shoulder bag from the floor of the back seat. It was the only piece of luggage she was permitted to take with her. She reached in and pulled from it a sealed pitcher filled with crushed ice and water. It was still cold to the touch. Removing a small hand towel from her bag, she wet the towel thoroughly. One after the other, she patted the towel over the children's faces and necks, hoping to offer some relief to their over-heated bodies.

The van's windows had been tinted from the inside and prevented the occupants in the back from seeing where they were driving. Marsha didn't really care at this point. Her priorities had shifted to ensuring the children arrived at the hospital still breathing.

Each time she enquired as to how much longer it would be before they arrived at the Children's Hospital, she was told to shut up. It was now somewhere close to noon. Marsha was attempting to persuade her little friends to drink some juice. She was startled when Lex abruptly turned around and grabbed her arm. The juice box fell to the floor.

He glared at her over the spill, but his statement demanded her full attention. "We are just about to turn into the hospital's parking lot. I will assume that you have taken your warnings well. I plan on being with you the entire time. If you so much as say or do anything out of the ordinary, you will live to regret it. Do you understand fully what I am saying to you?"

"As I have stated to you, Mr. Hawkins and his wife, I fully understand what has been requested of me. I will not jeopardize the children or anyone else. Do you understand what I'm saying?"

Glaring, he replied, "Don't get smart with me, white slut, or when we return to the island I'll give you a lesson you'll never forget!"

"My apologies, Mr. Hangler."

"That's Master Hangler to you."

"My apologies, Master Hangler!"

The van came to a dead stop directly in front of the emergency entrance. Without delay, Lex opened the door and got out. He slid open the side door, reached in and lifted the boy outside. He then told Marsha to pick up the girl and follow him inside. She did as he had requested, cradling the helpless child against her body.

Just before leaving the van he had instructed the two elderly gentlemen to park and wait for them on the other side of the parking lot. He told the men that his business would take but a few minutes to complete.

The automatic doors to the emergency entrance opened. Lex walked inside and waited for Marsha to enter with the little girl. Once they had all passed through, the doors automatically closed behind them. Both Lex and Marsha immediately headed for the admittance desk. Nurses, ward clerks and multitudes of other medical professionals were running in all directions.

Reaching the main desk, the black male nudged her forward while whispering in her ear, "Make it fast and good."

"Nurse, excuse me. My name is Eileen Williams. I don't know what's wrong with the children. I'm their nanny. Both of the children have come down with terrible fevers. Their temperatures are extremely high. I'm worried sick. They need to see a doctor right away."

The nurse on duty first looked at Marsha and then Lex. She questioned, "You folks are not from here, are you?"

Lex nudged her in the back to hurry the woman along. She, in turn, replied, “The children are vacationing with their parents. Both of them came down with colds this morning and were not up for any sightseeing with their parents. They didn’t seem too bad this morning, so their parents went on and left the children in my care. I haven’t been able to reach them. Please, can you have someone see them immediately?”

“Follow me please. Sir, you can place the young boy in examining room seven. You can follow me with the young girl to examining room three.”

Lex said to the nurse, “We prefer to keep the children together in the same examining room.”

“The examining rooms are not equipped to hold two people at once. It’s also against hospital policy to make any exceptions, sir. Both of them will be looked at right away.”

Lex glared at Marsha. She knew what the look meant.

Marsha followed the nurse to examining room three. The nurse instructed Marsha to lay the girl on the examination table. Before leaving with Lex, the nurse advised Marsha that a doctor would be with her shortly.

Lex was led away from examining room three still holding the young boy in his arms. The look he gave Marsha sent chills up and down her spine. As soon as Lex was gone from sight, a young male doctor entered.

Marsha looked at the doctor and pleaded quietly, “Please check the little girl. Her name is Melanie. I have to try and reach her parents by phone right now.”

He replied, “First I have a few questions for you with reference to the child’s condition leading up to your arrival.”

A strange look appeared across the doctor’s face as he watched Marsha walk towards the entrance and peek outside. As soon as she saw Lex entering examining room seven with the young boy, Marsha turned to the doctor and said, "Listen carefully! I don't have much time. My name is Marsha Grenning and I have been a prisoner of Thomas J. Hawkins and his family for several years now. I am being held on a deserted island, three or four hours flying time from here. I don't know where the island is located or even what direction it is in. The children I brought in are not my children and I am not their nanny. They too have been living on the island, against their will, with at least two-hundred other people."

Marsha took a deep breath. She had been speaking so fast, she had lost her ability to breathe normally. Once she managed to fill her lungs with much needed air, she continued, "We are being held on the island by a group of black men who are trying to get revenge on any and all white people they see as threats to their race. The man who took the young boy down to examining room seven is one of them and he'll kill me if he hears what I'm saying. Call security and have him stopped before we leave. It's the only chance I have. Please do as I say immediately and don't make it look obvious."

Marsha started to leave. The young doctor followed her saying, "If you're in trouble, madam, stay with me and I'll call security right away."

As Marsha exited the room with the doctor, Lex was blocking the door. He had been there, listening to the bulk of their conversation. The minute he had placed the young boy in the other room, he advised the nurse he was getting the nanny to answer any questions the doctor may have.

He removed a gun from underneath his jacket, and displayed his weapon in plain view. Nurses, patients, visitors, and other staff witnessing this event panicked. Individuals were running and screaming up and down the hallway. Lex fired several shots into the doctor's chest. Marsha tried to push the doctor to one side, and ended up taking the brunt of the shots fired. She buckled over, landing in the doctor's arms, as they both fell to the floor.

By this time, security officers were headed towards all the

commotion. Lex witnessed several of the guards now moving within plain view. He immediately turned and ran towards the nearest exit. Prior to heading through the doors, he fired off several more rounds to where Marsha and the doctor lay motionless.

Cautiously, security trailed closely behind the treacherous man. They dared not fire a shot at him for fear of hitting the hordes of innocent people still positioned throughout the hallway. Children and adults were scattering, terrified. The minute the fury of bullets erupted, most people dove to the floor in fear of being hit. Several of those who didn't drop were shot.

Lex kneeled down in between the emergency doors, facing his aggressors and fired several more rounds up into the congested hallway. Three additional people were shot in the crossfire.

The shooting stopped. Agonizing cries rung out. The young doctor lying next to Marsha took a bullet through his right ear. While bleeding and visibly shaken, he was still alive. He was placed on a stretcher and wheeled off to the emergency room. Marsha had not survived.

Security finally had made their way to the exit door where Lex once crouched. Their attempt to follow him at this point was futile. He was long gone.

The corridor suddenly turned into a chaotic swarm of bodies. Doctors, nurses and security guards administered to the wounded and covered the dead. Two women and a young male teenager had died.

Lex returned to the van. He quickly opened the door on the driver's side and got in. He told his companions the plan had backfired and Marsha was dead. They sped off. As the van was pulling away, seven police vehicles, all with emergency lights flashing, passed them in the opposite direction.

Lex placed a call on his cell phone. Once the connection was made, Lex said, "Mr. Hawkins. We have a problem. The bitch was no sooner in the hospital when she opened her mouth and started spilling her guts."

There was a brief pause as Lex continued driving with the phone plastered against his right ear. Every once in a while he would squint his eyes as he listened to the person on the other end.

After a few minutes, he replied, "Yes sir. It's been taken care of. She is dead. I emptied a full round into her. She won't be able to speak. You have nothing to worry about. We are on our way back to the airstrip as we speak."

Lex wanted to reassure Thomas Hawkins that everything was fine. At first, he provided his superior with very limited information. He led Thomas to believe that Marsha had been taken care of prior to her revealing anything relevant to the young doctor.

. . .

The police were now reviewing the surveillance tapes. They could see Lex and Marsha enter the hospital, walk to the nurse's station and then proceed to the examination rooms. The outbreak of bloodshed followed. First the gunfire, and then people running and dropping to the floor.

The tapes would have to go back to the station for further evaluation and enlarged stills. The police wanted to identify the shooter as well as the dead woman who accompanied him.

The children were moved to isolation for treatment and for their protection. A guard had been positioned outside each of their rooms. The doctors advised the police that the children were both extremely weak and still dehydrated. No one would be able to speak with them for a while.

Doctor Richard Fern was doing relatively well under the circumstances. He did endure some hearing damage, but it wasn't permanent. The police proceeded to take his statement.

The doctor repeated to the officers, in full detail, the woman's comments as he remembered them. He also gave them an overview as to her physical and mental state, essentially she looked traumatized and feared for her life. She'd told him that a group of black men were holding her and several others prisoner on some remote unknown island. The only things he really couldn't remember were the names she had told him, the name of the place or her captors. In the upheaval, it had left his mind.

Lex and his associates arrived at the airstrip. He placed a second call to Thomas Hawkins. This time, however, he provided more information as to what the doctor may or may not have known. While standing outside the examining room where Marsha and the man had been, he did overhear a few of her statements to the young doctor. Lex admitted he was unsure of exactly what information Marsha may have shared with the doctor prior to being killed, but sufficient comments he did hear caused him concern.

At the moment, Thomas Hawkins' only concern was whether the young doctor was still alive. Lex wasn't sure. Thomas was irate and screaming. Lex had screwed up. Thomas would have to get the Catcher to clean up Lex's jumbled mess.

Hawkins called the Gate Keeper and explained the situation to him. He advised him to make urgent contact with the Catcher whose services were needed to ensure the young doctor was silenced.

. . .

The young girl was lying in her bed resting peacefully when her door suddenly opened. In walked a black male orderly. Melanie screamed at the top of her lungs with what little strength she had. Within seconds, the guard who was situated outside her door burst in. The orderly was petrified. All he could say to the security guard was that he didn't do anything. The guard asked the man to leave the room. The guard knew his friend was innocent. He also knew something of the children's situation, but didn't anticipate this type of reaction from the young girl.

After having been advised of what had happened, the nurse in charge entered the room. She comforted the startled child who was weeping and trembling. The nurse was unable to get her to speak. The little girl's fever remained incredibly high and she was still very ill. She rubbed her face with a cool cloth for an hour before the child fell back to sleep.

Lex finally arrived back at the island. As he stepped from the plane, Thomas, Avery, Eddie, and Randle, greeted him. His boss was still livid. He hurled verbal abuse upon Lex who stood there and took it.

That night at the main house, the family was briefed on the events of the day. Thomas told each of them how the Catcher was being called in to clean up the mess. They were also informed that, from here on in, security measures on the island would be beefed up tremendously.

. . .

Later that evening, Lance and his roommates were in their sleeping quarters still recovering from the virus when Avery entered. He was ecstatic.

"Harry and Robert," he said, "I have a job for you. Four others have succumbed to the illness. I need your assistance in carrying the bodies to their final resting place."

Harry and Robert stood and followed Avery and his men to the dump where the bodies of all those who died were being delivered. Three hours passed before they returned. Both men were sickly pale. The only thing they said was that Rachel was well looked after this night. With that, they all turned in and attempted to sleep.

While each of them felt much better physically, they suffered mentally. The only good thing to happen this week was the evacuation of the sick children. Lance and the others wondered how they were. Tomorrow was another day, which comforted Lance somewhat. After some time had passed, he fell into a deep sleep. He dreamt that he was at the Children's Hospital, reading books to Joseph and Melanie.

CHECK-UP PLEASE

chapter fourteen

THE Gate Keeper had a huge ego when it came to his work. He knew his field of expertise was a priceless commodity, one that was frequently requested of him. He was seated in front of his laptop, singing to himself. The speed of his typing was in sync with the beat of the song he sang. After the appropriate connection had been made, he transcribed a poem onto Merlin's Poetic Website:

> "PROBLEM HAS CROPPED UP FROM THE LAND DOWN BELOW. IT REQUIRES YOUR SKILL SO NOW YOU MUST GO. A DOCTOR HAS LEARNED FROM ONE OF OUR GUESTS, TOO MUCH INFORMATION, TOO MUCH RISK. TAKE THE NEXT PLANE AND WHEN YOU ARRIVE, CHECK THE MORNING PAPER TO ENSURE WE SURVIVE. NO TIME FOR PACKAGES TO PROVIDE YOU WITH MORE. THE INFORMATION WILL APPEAR IN THE '*ADORE*'."

After the message had been uploaded, the Gate Keeper turned off his laptop. He was heading out to a fundraiser for a low-income housing project in Boston. He would be rubbing elbows with some of the richest and finest folks in the city. Each of those involved with White Man's Cotton were mandated to make special appearances at various charitable functions whenever possible. It didn't hurt them to maintain positive relationships with the right levels of society.

The Catcher walked through the airport like an individual about to embark on a secretive assignment. It was 11:30 p.m. and traffic at the airport was at a lull. The Catcher had his own special function to attend to. He was on his way to his next official engagement. He was particularly pleased with his pending job, for he was given free rein to execute it in whichever way he pleased. His flight was leaving in thirty-five minutes. It would take him an additional twelve hours before he arrived in the land down under.

. . .

Doctor Richard Fern was resting comfortably in his hospital bed. He had been moved to a private room. The head nurse who dropped by to give the doctor an update on the children's condition had recently left the room. She also discussed the staff, for since the incident, most of the staff was visibly upset.

He began to think about the events of the previous day. He was racking his brains trying to remember the name the woman had revealed to him. He tried to imagine what it must have been like for her and the others held captive, if in fact she had told the truth. That poor woman almost cost him his life. Her death and how she had died saddened him. He just couldn't understand how anyone could be so evil to stand there and start shooting at people for no apparent reason.

It was now 6:30 a.m. People were moving about in the hallway. The average person was still asleep at this hour, but in hospitals this was the norm. Staff was busy making rounds, waking patients, delivering breakfast, running baths, providing medication, and being escorts for those requiring treatments or tests.

. . .

Near the end of his flight, the Catcher heard an announcement: "Passengers, this is your Captain speaking. Once again, I apologize for the wait. Due to mechanical problems encountered earlier this morning, our departure time had to be delayed. I hope you have enjoyed your flight with us. We look forward to serving you in the future. Please have a nice day and enjoy your visit."

The plane had arrived at Melbourne Airport in Australia. It came to a full stop in front of one of the main terminals. The passengers crowded into the plane's aisle, gathering together their carry-on luggage and other personal belongings from the overhead compartments. A few of the people aboard were still sleeping. As the steward squeezed his way towards the front of the plane, he started waking them up as he passed.

Another steward repeated to the passengers as they disembarked, "Have a nice day. Thanks for joining us. Have a nice day. Thanks for joining us."

The Catcher heard the man repeat this phrase at least twenty times before he got near the exit. As he was about to disembark, he looked at the male steward and asked, "Can't you say anything else?"

The humble steward was dumbfounded at the black man's comment. It was probably the only time in his working life that he was stuck for words. Awkwardly, he regained his composure and continued his farewells to the other departing passengers.

Walking through customs was like walking in slow motion. The only item the Catcher had with him was a black leather bag draped over his shoulder. He entered the security check at Terminal A. It was the one place in the entire airport where it was mandatory for travelers entering Australia to pass through. One particular customs officer's function was to look at all passengers as they entered. He, in turn, would point individuals to continue in one of two directions, left or right. If you were cleared to move through customs, you were sent right. If their intent was to do a luggage or baggage check, you were steered to the left.

As the Catcher moved closer towards the customs official, he instantly took note that the majority of passengers had been directed to the right. When his turn came, the man directed him left. The Catcher looked at the employee remarking, "Do you have a problem with black folks? I noticed that not one of the white people who came through ahead of me have been sent to have their bags checked."

"Move along, sir. You're holding up the line."

The Catcher glared angrily at the man as he proceeded over to where his bag was to be inspected. He placed it gently on a conveyor belt and watched it move slowly through an x-ray machine. After it passed through to the other side a female customs officer said, "Please open your bag, sir."

The Catcher complied without hesitation or attitude. The officer happened to be an elderly black woman. When she spoke, it was with friendliness. She was a full-sized woman whose broad smile and pleasant mannerism were very inviting to the weary traveler.

When she was finished inspecting the contents of the leather bag, she looked up at the large black man in front of her and said, "Traveling light sir. Not planning on visiting for very long, are we?"

"Not this trip."

"What brings you to Melbourne, business or pleasure?"

"As luck would have it, business. However, I believe it's bound to bring with it some enjoyment. I plan to do some exploring while I'm here and maybe even a little hunting."

After closing up his bag and passing it back to him, she leaned towards him and whispered, "You enjoy yourself now. And just for the record, don't let that asshole over there get to you."

The Catcher smiled back at her as he took his bag and proceeded through customs. A few steps landed him directly into the main part of the airport. He never took anything with him while traveling. He always purchased what he would need when he arrived at each destination. Cash was a very powerful tool. In addition to his endless supply of it, he had many connections in each country he visited.

While heading through the main terminal, his attention was drawn towards a small magazine store. He walked inside and said to the clerk behind the counter, "Where are your daily papers?"

The lady responded, "Which one were you looking for, sir? Did you want the *Melbourne Gazette*, *Age*, *Dutch Courier*, *Geelong Advertiser*, *Herald*, *Sun*, or the *Adore*?"

"The *Adore*, please."

"Here you go, sir."

After paying for his paper, the Catcher headed through the airport in search of the nearest coffee shop. He saw a maze of small souvenir stores, a duty free shop and various rental agencies as he walked along. Finally, he spotted what he had been seeking. When he entered, he noticed that all of the tables were occupied.

The Catcher was a patient and tolerant man when this attribute was required. He stood back, scouting out his surroundings and watched the shop's clientele. He noticed two women preparing to depart and briskly walked towards their table to claim the space. Once settled, he raised his hand to draw the attention of the young Asian woman behind the counter. As she proceeded towards him, he requested a coffee. While waiting, he unfolded the newspaper and glanced through the articles on the front page. His eyes focused on one heading in particular,

"Tragic Shooting Takes Multiple Lives at Melbourne Children's Hospital."

He was so focused on the article that he completely ignored the waitress when she placed the coffee before him on the table. The Catcher continued reading the story. It revealed important news that had to be relayed to his employer. Not only had the article spoken of the tragedy that had taken place, but of a mystery woman's story, told just moments before her death. It revealed the woman's tale of being one of many held captive on a remote island in an unknown location.

Reading on, he noted that a Doctor Richard Fern was recovering from minor injuries he had sustained during the shooting. The article also stated that any well wishers could send get-well cards to the doctor at the Children's Hospital, as he was staying there during his recuperation. This was very unusual, he thought to himself. Why would they keep the doctor at the Children's Hospital, the Catcher wondered? Either he was too weak to move, or working at the hospital came with certain perks.

Draining the last sip of liquid from his mug, he paid for his beverage and then left the hectic atmosphere of the coffee shop behind. He continued walking until he passed through a set of automatic doors leading to the outside. Passing through them, he inhaled a fresh breath of air, while stepping speedily to one side to evade the hordes of travelers moving to and fro. Away from the congestion of travelers, he leaned his bulked-up body against the red brick building.

The Catcher reached into his inside coat pocket and removed a cell phone. His first call took mere seconds. Several others soon followed, with varying durations. The Catcher had spoke with multiple parties for well in excess of two hours. He was gearing himself up for the latest mission and supplies were vital. He called information to obtain the phone number and address of the nearest Internet Café in the region. Once confirmed, he hailed an airport cab.

The young native man welcomed his passenger to the city. Exercising his prerogative, the Catcher made no effort to respond to the greeting. Sitting back, he provided the driver with the destination. He'd just had a long flight and wished only for silence. By not partaking in casual conversation, he assumed his driver would get the hint. The drive itself was roughly three quarters of an hour, but to the Catcher it felt as if it was taking twice as long.

On the way, the driver would not stop talking, despite the Catcher's unresponsiveness. He talked about the weather. He talked about the economy. He talked about the United States. He talked about tourism. After talking to himself for a long period, he tried his utmost to drum up a dialogue with his fare.

By this time, his fare had lost all patience. Being driven by a white man was one thing, but having to listen to the man's bullshit was something else. Leaning in towards the front seat, the Catcher whispered aloud and firmly, "Listen here man. I've had a long flight. Take me to my destination and shut the fuck up. Do you hear me?"

"No need to get on with that, man. I know when to shut up. All you had to do was tell me you wanted a bit of peace and quiet and it was yours. I can keep quiet when requested. All you had to do was ask. I was only being hospitable."

"Now you've been asked. Not another word!"

The driver shut his mouth. At least, he turned the volume down somewhat. Under his breath, the driver went on and on about his passenger's ignorance. It finally reached the point where the Catcher ordered him to pull over, so he could get out.

The driver pulled the cab over to the shoulder of the road and came to a full stop. He then turned around to face his passenger, demanding the full fare. The Catcher removed a fistful of money from his wallet. When the driver reached back to collect, the Catcher pulled the man into the back seat.

The man was petrified, having been taken totally off guard. He moved his head ever so slightly in his assailant's direction, without actually making direct eye contact and pleaded, "Look man, I apologize if I seemed rude. Please take your hands off me. I don't want any trouble, man."

The Catcher pulled the man to within inches of his face and replied, "You drive me nuts, little man. I will give you one more opportunity to allow your head to remain on its shoulders. You are to get back in the front seat and take me to the address I gave you. If you open your mouth or even move your lips for the remainder of this ride, I promise, I will break your scrawny little neck!"

"No problem, man."

With that, he lifted the cab driver up by his armpits and threw him back into the front seat. Hurriedly, the driver got behind the wheel and drove off.

The drive had turned into a soothing experience for the Catcher. The man at the wheel of the taxi never spoke a word. Deep down inside, he really wanted to tell his fare where he could go. He knew better.

The cabbie left the highway and headed straight for Hogan's Internet Café. Upon arrival, no parking spaces were available so the driver stopped his cab in the middle of the road, directly in front of the establishment. He waited for his passenger to depart.

The Catcher looked at him and said, "Pull the car around to the next corner. I have no intention of stepping out into oncoming traffic. You are also too close to the parked vehicles to allow me to open my door."

The driver hesitated momentarily, but upon seeing his passenger's expression, he did what had been requested of him. The vehicle proceeded to the next corner where the driver made a sharp right and moved slowly down the side street. He was intent on flanking the nearest parking space he could find. He drove about thirty yards before finding a parking spot.

After the cab driver pulled into the free space, he turned his head around slightly and made eye contact with his black passenger. Courteously he said, "Is this okay, man?"

"Perfect."

Once again, the Catcher removed a wad of money from his wallet. He leaned forward, clearly displaying the cash. The driver was still extremely panicky as he extended his hand to retrieve the fare.

Grabbing the driver by his arm, the Catcher pulled him into the back seat a second time. Once again, he started to panic. Repeatedly, he told the Catcher how sorry he was and begged the man not to give him any trouble. Babbling on, he told the Catcher to forget the fare for all his troubles.

He wrapped one of his massive hands around the cabbie's chin and guided the young man's eyes to stare into his own. Tears gathered in the man's eyes and rolled down his cheeks. He pleaded with the Catcher to release his hold.

The Catcher was having too much fun. He enjoyed playing with another man's emotions. He clenched his fingers so tightly together that signs of bruising started appearing on his prey.

The cab driver was desperate. He tried punching him several times in the face. Every time he raised his fist, the large man used his free hand to block it. Not one hit landed on its intended target.

Playtime was coming to an end. The Catcher lifted the cab driver into his lap. He then smiled at the scared stiff man and said, "I hate little white bastards like you. I also pity their stupidity. Consider yourself a lucky man this day, my little friend. I grow tired of playing with you. I intend to put you out of your misery without further ado. Have a good night's sleep, little man. Maybe in your next life you'll come back as a real man. A big black son of a bitch, just like me."

The Catcher snapped his victim's neck. The lifeless body fell across the Catcher's legs. He looked down at the dead Aussie and spit in his face. He then lifted up his knees and pushed the limp carcass to the floor of the back seat.

Prior to exiting the cab, he looked out each window. The Catcher maintained his position for a few minutes waiting for two elderly ladies to pass by. Once the coast was clear, he stepped out onto the sidewalk. He slammed the door and began walking towards Hogan's Internet Café. Behind him, in the background, sat the cab with its "occupied" light glowing.

Once inside Hogan's Internet Café, he scanned his new surroundings, sizing up the occupants within. There were only two black people in the entire place, including him.

As he made his way to the center of the store, several people stopped what they were doing and looked at him. He obliged them all with a penetrating glare. The vast majority quickly turned but a couple of people continued to occasionally glance his way.

Finding an empty seat equipped with a fully operational computer was easy. There were at least fifty set up for consumer usage. He pulled back a chair and sat himself down directly in front of a Packard Bell. Removing a floppy disk from his leather bag, he inserted it in the device. The disk contained a specially designed program to inhibit anyone from tracing the whereabouts of its user. In minutes, he had accessed the Internet and was signed on to Merlin's Poetic Website. Once the site opened, the home page filled the screen. Its bright logo appeared before him. He placed his fingers over the keyboard and typed the following message:

> "THE MASTER MUST KNOW THAT THE WORD IS OUT. THE DOCTOR HAS SPOKEN AND THE COPS ARE ABOUT. I HAVE ARRIVED SAFELY TO BEGIN MY WORK. I'LL ERASE THE MOUTH AND COLLECT MY PERK. LET THIS BE A LESSON TO ALL WHO READ. IF YOU WANT THE JOB DONE RIGHT, CONTACT ME FOR SPEED."

He then signed off the site and removed the floppy disk. He stood up and strolled leisurely over to the cashier. He passed the young Asian woman a newly folded, one-hundred dollar bill and said with a smirk, "This should take care of five minutes on-line?"

She nodded, displaying a grin herself. She reached under the counter and proudly retrieved a bright blue purse. Opening it, she guardedly removed a five-dollar bill from her wallet, which she graciously placed in the till, replacing her personal endowment with that of the customer's charitable contribution.

The temperature was comparatively hot, with high humidity for this time of day. As the Catcher started moving away from the shop, he noticed three children standing on a street corner, all begging for money. They too had noticed the big man coming their way.

Two of the children were of Asian descent. The third child was a young white boy. All three ran towards him with hands out and their mouths flapping. The Catcher took out his stash and gave each of the two Asian children a one-hundred dollar bill. They both darted off screaming with delight.

He looked down at the little white boy before him and said, "Go home you little fucker and tell your white trash folks to get a job."

The boy ran off, giving the Catcher his middle finger as he went. The Catcher mimicked the boy's action. He then continued on his way up the street. He noticed as he went how several young people were set up along the sidewalk, posing as beggars. It was too well organized for him. He even witnessed several of the children successfully picking the pockets of citizens and visitors alike.

It had been twenty minutes since he left the Internet café, when he suddenly sensed something was amiss. Three men had been following him, by car, in close proximity. He noticed that the white boy was sitting in the back seat with one of the adults. He quickly picked up his pace until he ducked into the first alley he came across. He could hear car brakes screeching behind him. Over his shoulders, he noticed the three men had jumped from the car and were now following him down the alley. He made his way deep into the bowels of the lane until he finally reached the end, a dead end. He turned sideways and leaned his back against a stack of milk crates piled high alongside a dark gray brick wall.

The three men who followed were all reasonably large themselves. All three wore white strap shirts, faded blue jeans and torn sneakers. You could tell from the limpness of their potbellies that each of them enjoyed the occasional brew.

The one who appeared to be the leader of the pack started to strut about. Cautiously, he moved back and forth, several feet directly in front of the Catcher. He looked the black man over, evaluating his size and potential threat. The Catcher didn't move a muscle. He looked very relaxed and acted as if things were perfectly normal.

Suddenly, the man pointed a finger in the Catcher's face and said, "We don't take kindly to strangers insulting our kids, mister. Hand over your money peacefully or we'll cut you into little pieces and feed you to the dingoes."

"How about you take your two ugly girlfriends, turn around and leave now or I'll be forced to break each one of your arms and legs. Then, I'll leave you for the dogs to feast on. I'm sure your dingoes would enjoy eating three pear-shaped ding bats."

The men broke out in thunderous laughter. Then, their leader motioned for his buddies to move in and take the big man on. All three of them jumped the Catcher at once. They began pounding the black man. They were intent on reminding this man of the importance of territorial respect.

The Catcher stood his ground, taking several smacks from each of them. He actually started laughing as the assault escalated. At one point during the scuffle, the Catcher was knocked off balance. He fell back into the crates, knocked them over and landed on the ground. He dragged two of the men with him. Once on the ground, one of the men jumped on top of the Catcher, trying to hold him down while the others continued their attack from different angles. He responded by kneeing the man's groin. This sent him falling to the side, sniveling and gasping for breath. A second man moved in. The Catcher grabbed his arm and bent it backwards until it snapped.

The lone man left standing began kicking his opponent repeatedly. With the other men still on the ground, screaming in excruciating pain, the Catcher reached out and grabbed the fellow's feet. Twisting them sent the man crashing to the ground. The Catcher was growing tired of his would-be aggressors.

He took the man he had just knocked down and turned him over so he was lying on his back. He then sat on the man's stomach and positioned one of his gigantic feet against the fellow's left kneecap. As he began applying pressure, another of the attackers had gotten his breath back and jumped the Catcher from behind. He wrapped both of his arms tightly around the black man's neck, squeezing with all his strength. The Catcher wedged the man's arms under his chin and then jerked his body backwards, while firmly holding their leader's leg. The leg snapped outwards, looking like the letter "L."

The jumble of bodies and limbs was confusing. The man sporting a broken arm was now facing the Catcher. He, in turn, was still sitting on top of their leader, whose kneecap he had crushed. The third man was trying to squeeze the air from the Catcher's lungs. He wrapped his legs around the Catcher's waist, giving himself a tighter hold.

While still in a sitting position, the Catcher shot his arms over his shoulders with lighting speed. He punched the man behind him with both fists. This released the grip to his neck and waist. He got up from the ground and latched on to the one good arm of the man standing before him. Bringing his knee up and bringing the white man's arm down, he popped the limb painfully out of its socket. Both arms were now broken. The Catcher tossed him to the ground.

His attention quickly turned to the man who had been hanging tightly to his neck and back. He noticed a series of four-inch nails sticking out from a piece of two-by-four lumber that was lying on the ground. He turned and allowed his body to free-fall backward to the ground, landing precisely on the rusty nails. The man on his back immediately released his hold, letting out a scream of excruciating pain.

During the next few minutes the Catcher managed to complete his task. He broke the remaining arms and legs of three grown men, as promised. All three were left in the dirt crying out for mercy, screaming in pure agony. In contrast, the Catcher had only received a small number of bruises and some minor scrapes.

He then left the alley and the men behind. When he reached the main street, he noticed the little boy still in the car. He walked over and pressed his face against the window, peering at the youngster within. The boy moved to the other side of the car and pressed his body against the opposite door. The Catcher lifted his fist and smashed out the rear window. He then poked his head in and looked at the little boy who was now crying. He said to the terrified child, "Your family might want to consider other career options. There's got to be a better way to make a living."

He then turned and continued his journey up the street. Hearing the car door open, he turned around in time to witness the little boy running into the alley. He turned back grinning as he went about his business.

▪ ▪ ▪

At police headquarters, Tyler Collins and Wade Leaman were on their way to the squad room. They had just finished a meeting with the Chief of Police, in which they had provided him with an update regarding the undercover operation. Wade pushed open the swinging doors leading to their work section and they entered. Lawrence Kelloway had been waiting for their return.

The rookie's face was beet red and he was totally out of breath. He looked at his seniors and said, "We've got new updates on Merlin's Poetic Website. It looks like a request has gone in to have someone erased. In addition to this, a second poem has been uploaded, advising that the job is now being executed. The poems indicate that the next hit will be taking place somewhere in Australia."

Tyler and Wade headed towards the interrogation room with Lawrence in hot pursuit. Tyler sat at the computer and downloaded the first poem that had been posted. They all followed along as she began reading aloud. She commented on each line she read, "The land down under most certainly refers to Australia. That's a given!"

"Take the next plane and check the morning paper. That's original isn't it?"

Tyler stopped analyzing the poem. She pushed her chair back and said to Wade, "We can view most articles from any of the morning papers sold throughout the world on the Internet."

She returned her focus to the computer terminal. The frequency of clicking increased as she rapidly typed information into the computer. She brought up a search option and selected Australia. From there, she keyed in the words, "major newspapers." After a few seconds, several hits appeared on her screen. She scrolled down through the hits until her eyes made contact with the paper, *Adore*. Double clicking on the logo, the web page came up on her screen.

All three sighed loudly as their eyes made contact with the bold print before them:

"Tragic Shooting Takes Multiple Lives at Melbourne Children's Hospital."

This time Lawrence started to read the article for all in attendance. When he finished, he looked at the others and said, "I think we hit the jackpot!"

Wade replied, "What did the second poem say?"

Before Lawrence could respond, Tyler had Merlin's Poetic Website back up on her screen.

All three spoke at the same time, "The doctor's the hit."

Right away, Tyler was on the phone trying to contact the local police station in Melbourne to fill them in.

. . .

The bright green taxicab pulled up in front of the Children's Hospital. The gargantuan commuter paid his fare and exited the vehicle. He walked into the main entrance and up to the front desk. Once there, he pulled a badge from his coat pocket and told the nurse he was a detective from New York City. He informed the woman in white that he was here on official police business. He was interested in questioning Doctor Richard Fern.

The nurse looked at the black stranger, pausing for a moment and said, "Looks like you've had a rough flight, judging from the cuts and bruising."

"Police work is dangerous business, lady. Could you please direct me to Doctor Richard Fern?"

Before replying, she thought to herself, typical New York detective. Always wearing sunglasses, indoors and out and always wearing long coats, trying to look so cool.

"He's on the sixth floor, room 6648. You'll have to check in with the nurse's station on the sixth floor prior to going in. Outside normal visiting hours, you see."

"Thank you so much for your help. It's always a delight to deal with such professionalism."

The nurse blushed, waving the big man onwards. Once inside the elevator, the Catcher raised his hand and waved goodbye to the nurses. A couple of them waved back at him. When the doors closed, he pushed the button for the sixth floor. The elevator made two stops in between. The first stop saw two male doctors entering the elevator. On the second stop, a nurse entered, pushing a wheelchair that was carrying a little girl about eight years old. The little girl kept staring at the Catcher. He ignored her.

The numbered lights inside the elevator glowed as it reached each floor. The door finally opened on the sixth floor. Now standing in the corridor, he noticed a series of numbers inside a glass casing. Arrows pointed in different directions, showing visitors where the patient's rooms were located.

The Catcher looked down through the listing and said to himself very softly, "Rooms 6625 to 6650, to the right."

He turned right and started heading for room 6648. His journey was interrupted when an old fat nurse called out to him, "You! Where do you think you're going? Visiting hours are not for another two hours."

"Detective Harland Homer from New York City. I'm here on official police business to interview Doctor Richard Fern. The main desk told me I'd find him on this floor."

"The main desk also told you to check with me first. All visitors have to sign in regardless of why they're here."

The Catcher walked towards the obese female and flashed his false badge in her face. She turned her register around and pointed her pudgy finger to the space requiring his signature. He signed illegibly.

When he left, she looked down at the signature and under her breath whispered, "Damn Americans."

This was a quiet ward. All the rooms were private; most were empty. Staff in training, or those on call mostly used this section of the hospital. It was more like a fancy hostel. The Catcher finally found himself standing outside room 6648.

He pushed the door open and entered. The young doctor inside was taken off guard. He looked at the man and said, "Who are you?"

The Catcher pulled out his badge. Once again he repeated his fictitious story to the young doctor. When he finished, he asked the doctor if he would answer a few questions regarding the shooting.

The doctor nodded. The phony officer took a seat next to the man's bed. He began by asking the doctor to recount for him the events as they happened that day. Due to the gun shot wound he had taken to his ear, the doctor was speaking rather loudly. His hearing had been partially affected, but he happily told the officer it was a temporary thing.

Doctor Fern revealed everything the Catcher needed to hear. He was delighted to learn that the doctor had trouble remembering the surname of the party accused of holding the white people captive. When he was satisfied with the information he gathered, he stood up and bid the doctor farewell.

As he reached the door, about to leave the room, he turned and said, "There's one question I forgot to ask doc?"

"What's that?"

The Catcher walked over to his bedside, leaned over the man and said, "You've been a doctor for a few years now. What is the worst way for an individual to die, not including natural causes?"

Richard looked at the Catcher, totally bewildered, and replied, "All forms of death are tragic. Watching anyone die by any means is not a pleasant experience, detective. I wouldn't be able to choose one among the many."

"That's too bad. I thought you'd humor me."

The Catcher reached over and pulled a pillow out from under the man's head. He then pushed the doctor's head flat to the bed, smothering his face. The doctor struggled, but was no match for the Catcher's strength. After several more minutes, he finally stopped fighting back. He was dead.

Once his work was finished, the Catcher turned to leave the room. Before he touched the knob, the door bolted opened and in walked the overweight nurse he had encountered earlier. She was doing her rounds, checking on the doctor's status. He pulled her quickly inside. Before she had the chance to squeal, he slit her throat with a six-inch blade. She immediately fell to the floor, grabbing her throat as she struck the hard ceramic.

She tried crawling along the cold floor, towards the signaling button that was hanging off the dead patient's bed. The Catcher walked in front of her and stomped on her free hand. She couldn't even scream. He stood there with his full weight on her hand for a few minutes until she eventually passed out. Within a short period of time, she bled to death.

He reached down and picked up the woman by her uniform, but it ripped from the weight of her lifeless body. Her naked corpse then fell with a splatter to the floor. He reached back down a second time and lifted her from the floor. He dragged her body to the bed and placed the naked stiff face down on top of the young doctor.

Before he left the room, he pulled a set of darts from his pocket and placed them in his victim's middle fingers, exactly as he had done so often in the past. He quickly departed the room, headed down in the elevator until he reached the main floor.

As he passed the front desk, the nurse who had greeted him earlier called out, "I trust you found what you were looking for?"

"I was a little perturbed by the young man. He was actually carrying on with the huge nurse on the sixth floor. You know the old one with the crooked disposition? It was repulsive."

Those at the front desk were stunned. They all knew the young doctor and they definitely knew the old hag. None of them could imagine such a thing.

Once past the exit to the hospital, he headed to a taxicab near the front entrance. He boarded the first one he came across and requested to be driven downtown.

. . .

Wade Leaman, Lawrence Kelloway and Tyler Collins had all just gotten off the phone with various members of the Melbourne Police Department. As Wade hung up, Tyler was waiting for him with her coat in hand. Both of them were heading for the airport, about to take a flight to the land down under.

They were well over halfway between the station and the airport when their cell phones rang simultaneously. Both individuals answered their phones. Silence filled the van.

Tyler pulled the van into a convenience store parking lot to compare notes with her partner. Doctor Richard Fern and a female nurse were both found dead at the hospital moments earlier. They had been murdered. Witnesses indicated it was a huge black man posing as a detective from the New York City Police Department.

Wade slammed his fist into the dash. Then he cursed, and cursed some more. After he calmed down, they headed back to the station. The trip down under was no longer necessary.

Wade and Tyler were back to square one. The waiting game was back on. Hope existed that Detective John Lynch would soon gain the right people's attention.

UNDERCOVER GOODBYE

chapter fifteen

THE Board of Directors, using the Keeper's computer skills, scheduled another meeting. The time had come once again when the members would replenish their prized collection. The Gate Keeper set up the meeting exactly as he had so many times previously. He sent a message to the others, advising the coast was clear.

The last scheduled meeting for the Board of Directors had been deferred due to the sequence of events that had unfolded over the course of the last month. Thomas Hawkins wanted to ensure things had been straightened away before the party reunited.

The boardroom table was laid out with the same ritual materials that had adorned it for the last several years. The folders were stacked and ready to go. It was only a matter of minutes before the others arrived. The Gate Keeper left the boardroom and proceeded to the building's side entrance.

Cars appeared from various directions. They were familiar with the fact that much of the white stock from the cotton fields had died off.

Briefing notes to that effect had been circulated well in advance of tonight's meeting. All knew that emergency replacements were necessary.

The Gate Keeper greeted the arrivals eagerly, one after another, as their vehicles pulled up to the warehouse. He then ushered them back to the meeting room.

Once all the formalities were out of the way, Thomas Hawkins gave a brief summary of the events of the past month. He then directed them to begin reviewing the files before them. In total, twenty-two files were assembled for the One-Hundredth Anniversary meeting of the Board of Directors for Salvation's Chemical and Research Facility.

Hours passed and those present were still heavily preoccupied with reading the files in front of them. Gamba Kenya finished first. He had selected file number 466 belonging to a man named Henry Falkner.

Henry was a professional writer, whose claim to fame was his writings on the advantages of segregation of blacks and other minorities in the United States of America. He believed firmly that the economy was in such a sad shape due to the government's allowing various ethnic groups to populate and expand within its very boundaries.

Gamba tilted his candle and marked file 466. He then bid the others goodbye. Daren Yohance, Shebelle Jones, Skekwan Farrakhan, and Oprah Truville all selected the file numbered 666. This file belonged to Richard Pope. He was recently acquitted on a technicality of charges of murdering a number of innocent black children. These four board members had little hesitation in selecting this file, and would have done so sooner, except the file was on the bottom of the pile. Collectively, all four individuals left at roughly the same time.

Only Larsen Black, Thomas Hawkins and the Gate Keeper remained. Larsen was toying around with two files. One of the files, number 33, belonged to a young entrepreneur in Beverly Hills who specialized in ladies' fashions. He was known for providing less than ideal customer service and satisfaction to colored women. He never refused his services, for he knew this would result in harassment charges against him. He did, however, alter a percentage of his creations from the client's specifications. He also purposely sold articles of clothing to black woman that was not at all becoming to them.

The second file numbered 197, contained information about the director of a senior citizen's home in Cape Cod. This director was brought up on criminal charges on several occasions. The charges all pertained to elderly abuse, and in all cases the victims belonged to ethnic minorities. When complaints were lodged or court action taken, the charges were dismissed due to a lack of evidence.

This man knew how far he could push the system and get away with it. The rumor was that he only wanted whites as residents, but due to state law, he couldn't justify closing his doors to anyone. The only thing he could do was to mistreat those whom he felt never belonged in his establishment.

Larsen motioned for the Gate Keeper to pour him another drink. He sat back in his chair pondering, "Whom should I choose? Who should be removed from their place in society? Should it be Devan Udle, the fashion designer, or Blake Hiscock, the old folk's home director?"

It took three more drinks and a hellish amount of contemplating before he reached a conclusion. He placed file 33 back on the pile with the others. Ardently passionate about high fashion, he knew it should not be mocked, but worn with the respect it deserves. Therefore, despite how badly he wanted to punish the designer, the crimes outlined in this file were minor when compared to the other file. He picked up his candle and marked file 197 with the wax. He stood and raised his glass, then declared out loud, "Welcome aboard, Blake Hiscock!"

Thomas Hawkins had also made his selection. He had picked file 666, as the majority of the group had. Thomas bid farewell to the Gate Keeper, who as usual, remained behind to update Merlin's Poetic Website with the latest decisions stemming from the meeting:

"WELCOME BACK FROM THE LAND DOWN UNDER, THREE MORE PACKAGES FOR YOU TO PONDER. CONTENTS CAN BE FOUND AT THE USUAL PLACE, DELIVER THEM SOON AND MAKE IT A RACE.

IF PACKAGES ARE DELIVERED WITHIN A WEEK, A BONUS IS YOURS SO DON'T BE BLEAK. TRIPLE THE BOUNTY IS YOURS TO CLAIM. ONE OF THE PACKAGES WILL BRING YOU FAME."

Before the Gate Keeper reached his automobile, he was unexpectedly startled. Sounds not typical to this area dirtied this calm evening. His attention focused on two bums who were searching through the garbage dumpsters located to the rear of the warehouse. He moved closer to his car, sensing eyes glued to his every move.

Enough had transpired during the course of the last month to cause all members of the Black Alliance grave concern. As a consummate professional, the Gate Keeper did not take chances.

Sitting within the confines of his car, he picked up his cell phone and placed a call to the Black Dispatch, "We have a potential problem at my current location, the warehouse. Two white bums have been nosing around the board's meeting facility. Instructions: erase and dispose."

"Done."

The Gate Keeper flipped his phone shut and drove away. He was but a hundred yards from the warehouse when a black van came towards him with headlights turned off. It passed him, moving at high speed, heading in the direction from which he came.

The Keeper spoke aloud, "Now that's what I call service."

As the van pulled into the parking lot of the warehouse, the driver couldn't see anyone. The darkened vehicle came to a complete stop and the side door quietly opened. Four black men emerged and began to scout out the warehouse property.

Rather promptly, one of the black men had spotted a man looking through one of the side windows. The filthy man had crawled up over a stack of rusty oil drums and was doing some scouting of his own. He raised his arm and motioned to the others to advance.

The moment the bum noticed that several men were headed in his direction he threw his body flat onto the surface of the oil drums, hoping he wasn't seen. The four black men reached his position and surrounded the oil drums. One of them had called out to the bum, advising the man he was on private property and was required to come down from his location immediately. There was no response. They knew the bum was still there. His powerful smell gave him away.

The four men stepped back from the drums. One of them motioned for the van's driver to move forward. The driver accelerated the van rapidly towards the stacked oil drums. The bum had no time to react. Within seconds, the oil drums were sent in all directions.

Amongst the flying drums the old bum spun in the air. His body hit the side of the warehouse, bounced off, and smashed into several drums before it actually hit the ground. A few of the oil containers followed his path, striking different parts of his body while he lay on the ground. Although they were empty, the force of their hit broke several bones. In an attempt to escape the falling drums, the van reversed, the wheels crushing the bum's torso to pulp. He was dead.

The other bum had been sitting in the dumpster, peering at the action outside. The instant he witnessed the van roaring towards the oil drums, he jumped from the dumpster and ran into the dark fields located to the far left of the warehouse.

He no sooner had crawled through a series of broken links in the chain fence than he was spotted. Neither the van nor the men would have a chance of catching him at this point. They knew that this particular field eventually ran straight through to the pier. They also knew the pier was colonized with bums and vagrants.

Members of the Black Dispatch picked up the crushed man and placed his body in a thick plastic bag. Two of the men entered the van, carting the body with them. As soon as the door closed behind them, the driver sped off. The remaining two ran for the chain-linked fence, vanishing into the pitch-black fields. They would regroup on the other side.

Homer was the name of the vagrant who had escaped from the garbage dumpster and the clutches of the black hooligans. He and his friends made a habit of checking out all garbage bins and dumpsters within a two-mile radius. This was their livelihood.

The only thing on Homer's side that evening was the fact he was in such good shape. He didn't smoke, nor had he ever put a single drink to his lips for the greater part of his adult life. When he rummaged through garbage, often times he would carry heavy items back to his home camp over long distances. He'd usually carry anything that would fetch him a bounty from one of the local recycling plants. He bragged many times how he had carried an iron anchor, weighing two-hundred pounds, for two miles without resting. His strength allowed him to sprint through the dark without being captured.

Reaching the pier, he stopped and looked about, seeing if anyone had followed. The coast was clear. He ran from the edge of the field. Sliding down a loose gravel slope, he arrived home. He found himself before several rows of makeshift shelters, each constructed with an assortment of abandoned materials.

The shelters were built right under the pier itself. Even at high tide, they were back far enough from the water to remain dry and safe. Only a ferocious storm with waves of the highest magnitude could reach their living quarters. The probability of this was very unlikely.

Entering, he spotted several of his friends sitting around a small fire. Most of them were sharing bottles of cheap liquor or passing around cigarettes. This was a close-knit community, whose residents had little to nothing, but thoroughly enjoyed their existence just the same.

Homer started telling the others what had just happened to him and their pal, Boomer. They didn't have time to be upset over Boomer's death. Their main concern at this point was for their own personal safety. Especially when Homer told them he was seen and might have been followed.

Several of them took off. Others started gathering their belongings, grabbing whatever articles they needed during the night should they not be able to return. Those who had already left were greeted once they landed outside the boundaries of their community. Four black men, all bearing weapons, stood before them. The eight individuals who had had a head start on the others now stood out in the open. It took no time before each of them was savagely gunned down.

Ten other stragglers, including Homer, were safely hidden under the pier's wharf. Each knew it was only a matter of time before the black men would come in after them. One of them ran outside, shouting that the man they were looking for was still here and he would show them who it was.

He was drunk of course, which probably made this turncoat's death that much easier. No sooner was he in sight, than they shot him, ten times in the chest. They were not interested in survivors. All these bums were potential witnesses; none could be left alive.

Homer started to make his way towards the end of the pier, closest to the ocean. He noticed as he cautiously made his way back that two black men were walking opposite him along the outside of the wharf. He saw them plainly through the wooden pillars, which provided the support for the wharf.

Thinking quickly, Homer straddled both his hands and legs around one of the rough wood pillars and shimmied his way to the top. Upon reaching it, he squat his body between the pillar and the bracing used to secure the wharf upright. His timing couldn't have been better. No sooner had he concealed himself than some of the black men entered and began a killing rampage. A couple of his friends tried to run to the end of the wharf, but the two men Homer had spotted seconds earlier gunned them down.

Homer tried his hardest not to breathe too heavily. The splashing of the waves against the wharf muffled any chance of him being heard. He maintained his place in the beams for a long time, watching the black men moving about, killing everyone in sight.

Once they left the interior of the wharf, Homer's heart returned to its normal rhythm. He had all intentions of staying put, even if it meant hanging in the rafters for the entire night.

Every now and then another gun would fire. Either more of his friends were killed after returning from an evening of scavenging or those in hiding had been discovered.

Homer soon heard footsteps on the wharf directly above his head. Gasoline fumes filled the night air. He felt and saw the cool liquid now dripping down between the planks that lined the walkway above. The men who killed his friends were in the process of burning down the wharf and destroying the structures that housed the town's vagrants and bums.

Homer lowered his body from the rafters, gripping the beams with both hands. He fell to the ground below and landed on his feet. Without delay, he sprinted towards the ocean as fast as he could. His only thoughts were to get in the water. In the background, only yards away, he heard something that sounded like "woof." The sound started to move closer and a crackling noise followed. When he looked back over his shoulder, the entire wharf, above and below, was a moving, glowing inferno of rolling flames. Bright orange, red and yellow flames were moving progressively towards him with lightening speed.

His pace increased as he drew closer to the water. He was but inches from the security of the ocean, when in the background numerous explosions erupted. The last explosion he heard came at the same instant he had reached the water's edge. Its force was so powerful it sent the man soaring almost ten feet in the air before he actually made impact with the chilly water.

As he went under, he swallowed large amounts of water. Although slightly disoriented and still underwater, the glow from the fire guided him back to the surface. He noticed several of the black strangers standing around the beach, inspecting the site. Automatically, he assumed their intent was to ensure no one had survived. Using everything in his power, he did his utmost to stop from choking or gasping for breath. Homer lowered his mouth below water level to muffle the noise. Each time he spit out air it blended with the splashing of waves against the burning pier.

Homer treaded water for approximately ten minutes, remaining quiet the whole time. He was exhausted. He began to swim away from the pier to a more secure location. Reaching a section of shoreline, several yards away, he crawled swiftly out of the water and disappeared into the woods.

From a safe haven amid a hefty cluster of maple trees, Homer watched with pure anguish as his home and friends all went up in smoke. He waited in total darkness, in the daunting woods for three hours. He dared not move a muscle until the brutal murderers climbed aboard their van and drove off into the distance.

The pier was a great place for vagrants to congregate. This was especially true because it was so far from the town folks. No one had ever bothered these people until now. Once in a while, the local police visited the pier to ensure that nothing was out of the ordinary. Apart from this, the setup never posed a threat or disturbed the citizens of the nearby town.

. . .

The wheels of the Catcher's next three jobs were in motion. It was a gorgeous day and there was plenty to do. Driving down the highway, the Catcher picked up his cell and placed a call to Riverdale's Seniors Nursing Complex, located in Cape Cod, Massachusetts. When the operator answered, the Catcher asked to be connected to Blake Hiscock.

Following a brief wait, a man said, "Blake Hiscock, Director of Riverdale's Seniors Nursing Complex. How can I be of assistance?"

"Mr. Hiscock, Harvey Walters calling from New York City. I'm flying into Cape Cod this evening to scout out potential residences for my mother. I'm looking for an upscale private home for her to reside in."

"Well Mr. Walters, you've called the right place. We have only the best in living arrangements for our seniors. We have an inclusive package available, which meets our clientele's every need. It's costly, but it is the best!"

"Money's no object, Mr. Hiscock. I'm only interested in first class accommodations and the comfort of knowing that your home can provide, high quality, one on one nursing care for my ailing mother."

"What time will you be arriving this evening?"

"It will be sometime after 10:00 p.m. I have been provided with numerous references regarding the services you provide. I would like an appointment with you soon after I arrive. I realize this is last minute, but it will be worth your while. I'm sure that a generous charitable donation to your fine establishment would not be rejected?"

"Anything that will help in making our home a better place is never out of the question. I will drop back here for 10:00 p.m. and meet with you. We can go over the finer details then. I have plenty of information on our accommodations and the programs we offer our residents. Whether it's short, or long-term care, I know your mother will be happy here."

"See you around 10:00 p.m. I look forward to our doing business together."

Job number one was now in motion. The Catcher would have plenty of time to take care of the nursing home's director. He was already on his way to Cape Cod.

. . .

At 9:45 p.m., all was moderately quiet inside Riverdale's Seniors Nursing Complex. Minimum staff worked the late shift. Only one nurse, two orderlies and the night janitor were working on the first floor, which also housed the business offices. Most residents were settled for the night.

Blake Hiscock entered the premises and headed towards his posh office. Passing the Head Nurse, Lorianne Dysan, he said, "I'm expecting a potential client this evening who could prove very beneficial to Riverdale. He's flying in to check out the facilities and hopefully find a home for his mother. He is contemplating making a sizeable donation. Please ensure all staff are aware. There should be no doubt in his mind that we are the best. His name is Harvey Walters. When he arrives, bring him directly to my office."

"Yes, Mr. Hiscock."

He then entered his office. Once inside, he was startled at the presence of the colossal man admiring the artwork. The stranger approached him, his hand outstretched and said, "Mr. Hiscock, I presume. Harvey Walters. I love the artwork. Hope you don't mind. When I arrived, I couldn't find a staff member anywhere. Doesn't say too much about the security here. I trust this is not the norm?"

"I find that very strange, Mr. Walters. Someone is always at the main desk, unless an emergency came up with one of the residents and they had to attend to it. I'll check into that later."

The Catcher could sense that his presence put Blake Hiscock somewhat on edge. Blake gestured for his visitor to sit, his actions robotic in nature. The director promptly requested they get right down to business as he took his place behind the desk. He advised the Catcher that he was pressed for time. He pulled out a file folder, which contained pamphlets that advertised the nursing home and its services.

Before showing his client the contents of the file, he said, "Shall we start with your generous offer to make a donation to our home, Mr. Walters?"

"Afraid there's been some misunderstanding. Where I'm black, I won't be following through with a contribution at this point."

"I'm sorry, Mr. Walters, I'm confused. This meeting seems a little weird to me. Before we go on, I must advise the nursing supervisor you've arrived. I think it would be appropriate that she also join us. She's more familiar with our programs and the services we provide."

"That won't be necessary, you little bastard. I didn't come all this way to see your staff. I'm here for you. I hope you will find it in your heart to forgive me for my trickery, fool! You have been selected to attend White Man's Cotton. The details you will learn later, but for now you're leaving with me."

"I really don't think so. Leave my office now or I'll have you thrown out. Do you understand?"

"Let's see here. We have one big black motherfucker and one little white piece of shit. Now, unless you feed the seniors here steroids, I don't think you'll have much success in removing anyone, let alone me."

The director pushed the intercom button. The head nurse responded, "Yes, Mr. Hiscock."

"Send in Markus and James immediately!"

"That's a bad error in judgment on your part, Hiscock. Now I'll be forced to harm two innocent bystanders and I'm really pressed for time this week."

The Catcher stood and leaned inwards, about ready to punch the director in the face when the office door opened. In walked the two orderlies he'd called for. Blake looked at them and ordered, "Get rid of this black trash now!"

They each grabbed one of his arms and demanded he accompany them out of the building. The Catcher lifted his arms, taking both men off their feet. He then said, "Do you really want to do this?"

The orderlies knew what they were up against. A person this size would be hard to contend with and even harder to take down. Markus let go and stood in front of the Catcher. He appeared to be staring the black man down. Without blinking an eye, he drove his knee into the black man's testicles. The Catcher fell to one knee. Temporarily, he was incapable of breathing properly, although he showed no distress on his face. While still balanced on one knee, he was hit with a firm backhand across the face.

The orderly then said, "No one fucks with Mr. Hiscock."

James stood behind the Catcher and drove his knee into the man's back. It had no effect. The Catcher didn't even budge. Both men beat the Catcher for approximately thirty more seconds with minimal effect. The director watched from behind his desk.

What none of them knew was that the Catcher was blessed with a high tolerance to pain and even welcomed it. While the kick to his testicles hindered his ability to react swiftly, it was only a temporary setback. Once he recharged, he stood. Markus attempted to knee the man a second time, but was blocked. The Catcher grabbed hold of his knee and crushed his kneecap. Markus toppled over in agony.

James picked up a lamp from the coffee table and smashed it across the large man's arm. Splattered broken shards of glass went everywhere. Instantly, blood poured from his forearm.

The Catcher looked at James and said, "One thing I hate worse than blood is seeing mine flow. You will never live to regret what you've done."

He then reached over, wrapped his hand around James's neck. As he held the trembling man steady, his fist made contact with James's nose. The collision resulted in instant death. The Catcher turned his attention to the director and said, "I told you I have no time for this shit. You're coming with me now!"

The director reached out to activate the intercom, but his assailant reacted immediately. He had made his way to the side of the man's desk, stepping on the injured orderly as he passed. Each time he drew closer to the director, the man would dart to the opposite side of his desk. The Catcher's patience had grown thin. The Catcher pushed the desk towards the director and pinned the man to the wall. The Catcher then moved towards his prey, pulling the desk back as he drew nearer. Suddenly, he picked up the desk and held it over his head. Every muscle in his upper body bulged. The spineless director closed his eyes. At that very moment, he had concluded he was going to die. He heard a plea for help, which came from Markus, then a crash. He opened his eyes to discover his five thousand dollar desk had been dropped on Markus. The director went into shock.

The Catcher picked up Blake Hiscock, walked to the window and threw him through the glass panes. He then squeezed his enormous frame through the window, stepped onto the lawn, picked him up and carried the man over to his vehicle. He popped the trunk and pitched his captive inside.

Before closing the truck, he looked at the director's badly bruised body and said, "I now wish to make a charitable donation to the home asshole. It will be given to your replacement, a young black man who works for our organization. He'll find the money useful in getting rid of the trash you've got working here. When he restores the place, I'll have him send you some pictures."

He closed the trunk and was about to leave when he noticed several residents looking out the window. He lifted his arm and waved. He had one quick drop-off to make at the nearest airfield, prior to moving on with job number two.

. . .

The following morning was the start to another hot day. The Catcher drove his vehicle past the sign welcoming him to Hartford, Connecticut. His destination was a log cabin situated on the outskirts of town, the home of the famous and most controversial writer, Henry Falkner. He frequented the town on rare occasions, making this place his permanent residence. He was a private man and the only company he ever kept was that of his publicist, Lincoln Fry of Maximum Enterprises.

The Catcher admired the picturesque surroundings as he drove through the town. It was like going back in time. The buildings were old with an ominous Victorian style. He noticed the old general store, a post office, a couple of hunting and fishing outlets, and people moving about at a relaxed pace. The streets contained few vehicles and even fewer street signs and stoplights. The people living here were more than satisfied with their simplistic way of life.

As he left the town's perimeter, he drove onto a dust-filled road, which was full of potholes. It eventually led straight up a steep hill overlooking the town. He passed several cabins as he continued. At his destination, he stopped the vehicle next to a driveway with a sign that read:

> Falkner Residence
> Private Property
> Trespassers Will Be Prosecuted

He jumped from his car and walked towards the sign. Bending down, he gripped the post and pulled it from the ground. He then crossed over to the embankment on the opposite side of the road and threw the sign down the hillside into the woods below. He proceeded up the driveway as the heat from the sun beamed down. Sweat rolled off his forehead, down his neck and over his back. He loathed intense heat.

As he approached the log cabin, he noticed a man sitting out on the veranda. The man stood, leaned out over the veranda and held out a shotgun. He shouted, "This is private property. Go away now, or I'll call the local sheriff and have you locked up."

"My car broke down in front of your driveway, mister. I was wondering if you had a phone I could use to call a tow truck?"

"Listen carefully, you black bastard, you are not welcome on my property. Turn around now and go back to where you came from. Now get."

The Catcher pulled a handkerchief from his shirt pocket and wiped the sweat from his forehead. He then said, "I'm very hot and tired. I am only asking for the use of your phone for one minute. Will you please oblige me?"

"Fuck you and all your kind."

The Catcher gave the impression he was putting his handkerchief away. Instead, he used it to disguise the handgun he removed from his belt. He aimed and pulled the trigger. Henry Falkner had no time to react. The bullet struck the writer's shotgun and the impact sent it flying onto the deck. As Henry stood there shaking off the stinging sensation, the Catcher ran briskly towards him. The gap between them had closed.

Henry looked at him and said, "You're in deep trouble now mister. You think you can get away with this?"

The Catcher was just too hot to argue. He pulled back his right arm and with one swipe, he knocked the arrogant man unconscious. He pitched an oil lamp through the front door. He then lit a match and flicked it inside. The Catcher turned around and picked up Henry Falkner. He threw the man over his shoulders and started the walk down the driveway. By the time he made it to his vehicle, heavy gray smoke and orange flames poured from the log cabin. The Catcher threw the writer in the trunk and headed back down over the picturesque hillside.

As he approached the town below, he witnessed the local volunteer fire department in full motion. The lone fire truck headed towards the cabin. The Catcher smiled as he drove past the many frantic townspeople who were scurrying about. It was the most excitement this town had seen in years.

Package number two had been secured. It would soon be time to move on to the third and final assignment, the one most stimulating for him. It would also be the most challenging. He still had five days left to meet his week's deadline. The planning stage was complete and would soon be put into action. His next stop would bring him to Regal's Airstrip where he would unload his current human cargo.

As he was driving along, he came across an elderly man who had been walking along the road. The Catcher pulled his vehicle over to ask the old man for directions to Regal's Airstrip. The old man advised the Catcher to drive two miles down the road, make the first left by the Brown's Dairy Farm, and then drive an additional ten to twelve miles and he should see the sign.

The Catcher was about to pull back onto the road when the old man asked, "What's the racket coming from the trunk, buddy?"

The Catcher hadn't noticed the noise due to the roar of his engine. The old man suddenly became awkward and turned to leave. It was too late. The Catcher pulled out his gun and shot the old timer in the head, killing him instantly. His body dropped to the roadside and landed in a watery ditch.

The tires screeched as he drove off. When he arrived at the airstrip, he removed a wild Henry Falkner from the trunk of his vehicle. Growing tired of his captive's behavior he knocked him out again. He then bound the unconscious man's hands and feet and covered his mouth with duct tape prior to loading him into the Lear Jet. Blake Hiscock was already there from the previous night. The writer's body was dumped on the floor of the cargo hold and landed next to Blake's. He then left his captives in the hands of the pilot for delivery to White Man's Cotton.

. . .

At police headquarters, the team of four was busy reviewing the latest postings on Merlin's Poetic Website. They knew additional hits were ordered and were going to occur shortly. Security had been beefed up around Detective John Lynch, alias Richard Pope.

The objective at this point was not to snag the captor if and when he made an attempt to abduct Richard. They were hoping the surveillance equipment would lead them to the island. Richard was cautioned to watch his every move from here on in.

One thing Richard had been busy with over the past few weeks was establishing a routine, making regular appearances, setting up a schedule of places he'd visit consistently. He stayed at the mansion during the morning, leaving after lunch. His first visit was always to the local marina where he stayed on the water for three to four hours at a time. Upon returning from sailing, he visited the yacht club for a drink and dinner.

After dinner, he stood around chatting with socialites, throwing around gobs of money. It was easy to make friends in this environment. He usually stayed at the club until about eight-thirty p.m. or nine p.m. every evening.

After the yacht club, he headed to a lively entertainment lounge called, "Sparky's." The lounge was located in the heart of the downtown district, amongst several other hot nightspots. What made Sparky's so appealing was its atmosphere. It was reserved for members only, and membership was only available to the rich. An extremely large amount of cash was the one requirement you needed to be able to relax, wine and dine into the wee hours of the next day. Entertainment at Sparky's Lounge changed sporadically. Some nights there were high-class strippers, comedians and magicians. Other nights were casino night.

Without skipping a beat, Richard had gone through another day of his usual routine. He was pulling into the parking lot of Sparky's Lounge when the valet greeted him. Richard jumped from his car, advising the young fellow to ensure it wasn't scratched. He passed him a fifty-dollar bill for added insurance. He asked the attendant what form of entertainment was on the roster for the evening.

The valet replied, "It's optical illusion night, sir. We have two illusionists on hand to spin their trickery."

As he entered, he noticed it was a full house again this evening. The lounge only held about seventy-five patrons comfortably. Normally, at their prices, lineups were never an issue. Only regulars frequented the joint and if a few extras showed, flashing enough money, they would be squeezed in accordingly.

Richard headed for the main lounge, fighting his way past several drunken clients. Two gorgeous strippers just finishing up their routines, hurried past him en route to their dressing room.

No sooner had the female strippers left the stage, than a quarter of the clientele walked out the front door. Richard motioned the waiter over. He, as with most of the others here, was well known amongst the staff. They knew the needs of all their clients and bowed to their every whim. The tips were abundant for the staff and given in accordance with how well they served their customers.

As the waiter headed for Richard's table, a black man walked in front of him. He had almost knocked the perfectly balanced tray right out of the man's hand. Looking sincerely at the waiter, he offered humble apologies to the man and as a gesture of good faith he laid five twenty-dollar bills on his tray.

He said politely to the waiter, "Please excuse my clumsiness. The women tonight are hot. Not really keeping my mind on where it should be."

The waiter took the bills and placed them in his vest pocket. He looked around to thank the stranger for his generosity, but he had vanished.

Richard hadn't even taken notice of his waiter's encounter with the black man. He picked up the drink and with just three large gulps it had vanished. It was the undercover detective's own magical illusion. The waiter hadn't even left the table yet, when Richard requested another.

One of the attributes Richard's peers admired about him was that he was a master of disguise. When undercover, he could readily assume any character with ease and proficiency. He was the best of the best, and played this particular eccentricity to a tee. He spent the department's money like there was no tomorrow. He liked playing the part of a rich bastard who didn't give a shit about anyone or anything.

By the time he had consumed his fourth rum and coke, his attention was drawn to center stage. The illusionists had just stepped out and the audience erupted in cheers. Richard remained his usual calm self. Slowly scanning his surroundings, he thought to himself how the vast majority of the people here had little else to do to fill their time. It was as though liquor, food and expensive entertainment were their only interests in life.

The evening's show was slowly spiraling into an attention-grabbing affair. It was the first time that these particular illusionists had performed at the club. They hailed from South Africa and were scheduled to perform for a one-time only appearance.

Richard was beginning to feel the effects of the alcohol he had inhaled. Normally, he was able to consume twice the volume of liquor of the average man. His vision became markedly impaired. He wrote this off to several weeks of living it up, now finally catching up with him.

Two officers, who were there to provide backup for Richard, had been stationed outside the lounge. They'd been given strict orders to only interfere if Richard signaled them himself. He carried a beeper in his coat pocket with a direct alarm to the two officers.

Richard's detailed instructions from headquarters were also very explicit. He was to alert backup only in the event he felt his life was indeed in jeopardy, otherwise he was to stick to the established schedule.

The two officers were sitting in a car, conversing about how tiresome this assignment was. They both wished they were allowed in the club, but knew the risk. As it stood, they sat in a ghost car, supposedly unidentifiable to members of the general public.

They spotted a young black woman dressed like a high-classed hooker walk towards their car. She was exceptionally beautiful, with the body of a professional model.

When she approached the passenger window, one of the officers rolled his window down and said to the lady, "Not interested this evening, ma'am. I suggest you move along."

"Would one of you gentlemen have a light?"

The officer in the driver's seat reached across his partner and passed his lighter to the woman. She smiled as she took the lighter and lit her cigarette. She then thanked him. As she reached in to return the lighter, she sprayed the contents of an aerosol can into the car. Instantly, both officers fell fast asleep. She then tossed the can into the passenger's lap. As she walked away, she called the Catcher, who was at Sparky's Lounge, and advised him that all was clear. He, in turn, told her to prepare herself for the evening's finale.

The special effects being performed inside the lounge, impressed Richard and the other patrons. The illusionists created remarkable optical illusions, one after the other, which fixated all those in attendance. Even Richard was in awe.

For every trick performed, the men walked out into the crowd and asked for a volunteer . They would then escort the individual to the stage. When it came time for the finale, one of the illusionists walked from the stage towards Richard. He took the drunken man's arm and assisted him to his feet. By this time, Richard was wasted from the liquor he had consumed and didn't object.

Unbeknownst to the cop, his reduced inhibitions and lack of professionalism were a direct result of having been drugged earlier, accomplished as a result of the Catcher's initial encounter with his waiter. As the drugged man headed for the stage, he began to stumble. The illusionist helped keep the officer on his feet. On stage, he was told to enter a standing rectangular box. For the grand finale, the illusionists were going to turn Richard into a beautiful young lady.

He could barely stand. The door was shut behind him and he grew queasy as the box began to rotate. Both of the illusionists were outside rotating the box. Finally, the spinning stopped. As Richard leaned back, he fell through a false door that had been set up at the back of the box.

Richard was dragged from the box and slung over the shoulders of the big black man, the Catcher, who had just completed his three-man challenge for the week. Richard was too drunk to react. He noticed a beautiful woman take his place in the box. He also noticed she had his beeper in her hands and was pushing the alarm button.

After several rotations, the illusionists opened the panel on the box and out walked the same beautiful woman who had been on the parking lot no more than an hour earlier. She walked out, strutted around the stage and showed her stuff while the crowds cheered wildly.

Suddenly, smoke was billowing from the men's restrooms. The fire alarm sounded and the crowds started rushing towards the emergency exits. In the commotion, no one worried about the outcome of the final trick of the evening.

Richard Pope had been taken through the back exit on the Catcher's shoulders. As the Catcher rounded the corner, he passed the emergency back-up vehicle containing the two sleeping officers. He then dropped his latest catch into the trunk of his own vehicle.

As the Catcher left the parking lot, he could see his female friend toss the police department's beeper, which she had removed from the drunken undercover officer, into his passenger side window.

Detective John Lynch's abduction would soon impact the slaves of White Man's Cotton. Life in the underground mines was about to change.

HOPE AT LAST

chapter sixteen

THREE new citizens had arrived at White Man's Cotton: a racist writer, a child murderer and an abusive director of a senior's nursing home. After being processed, the three men were escorted to their new sleeping quarters in Section 34. The current occupants were all disappointed. They barely had room for themselves, without an additional three men.

Each time new recruits arrived in the underground, the ritual was the same. The men would sit around for hours and chat. All the new slaves would tell their stories and explain their eventual capture. Most ranted about the injustice of it all, while some acknowledged possible fault.

Of the newcomers, the slaves found Richard Pope most intriguing. They learned rather quickly that this was not his actual name. Although the masters denounced him as the murdering bastard, Richard Pope, Section 34 soon learned differently. His story was like music to their ears. He was Detective John Lynch, police officer, alias

Richard Pope. He was part of an undercover operation, which was set up to infiltrate White Man's Cotton. He instructed George to stand in the entryway to ensure he wouldn't be overheard. He then explained how he had become a resident.

After he finished his tale, the men just sat there mulling it over. He gave them hope of finally escaping the hell they lived in. There wasn't a man in the room who wasn't ecstatic. For the moment, everyone had forgotten about their surroundings and was caught up in the dream Richard represented. They were further astounded when he explained that he had two miniature transmitters planted on his person.

Once he began providing in-depth information about the transmitters, Robert interrupted the detective and said, "The tracking devices implanted on you are not guaranteed to work under solid granite."

John Lynch replied, "How would you know?"

"It's simple. You mentioned that the microprocessor chips in these devices have been equipped with Mac10 Sensors. Electronic tracking devices equipped with Mac10 Sensors cannot be picked up underground. In addition, the tracking devices are only good within certain ranges. The exact range, I am not completely sure about. Your peers, however, would have lost any signal the minute you began your descent into the underground."

Harry looked at Robert and said, "How would you know this?"

He responded, "Prior to becoming a police officer with Station 84, I worked as a computer technician for Largo's International Computer Works in New England. One of our pet projects was installing and testing computer chips for the Mac10 tracking devices. I have a fairly good idea of what I'm talking about."

George was completely and totally bewildered as he listened to Robert. He had been this man's partner on the police force for many years and had never heard his partner speak of such a thing before now.

John Lynch stood and paced, while scratching his chin. He stopped and said to the men, "There's still nothing to worry about. I would have been tracked to this very island at least. They would have followed the route we took right to the point I landed and that's where they'll start looking."

Robert responded, "I really hope you're right, my friend, but to my recollection, traversing large bodies of water messes with the tracking device. I seem to recall that it could be out by a radius of up to fifty miles. The only way it could be more accurate is if you were followed the whole time."

The detective looked at Robert and said, "They will find us. It's only a matter of time."

Robert responded, "Then I hope that when they come, they come with an army. No one is going to find us here, not unless they search every inch of this island, find the entrance and penetrate those damn hidden doors."

"You're a positive one, aren't you? You've obviously been here too long. I know that the police, the FBI, the CIA, and every other law enforcement agency in America are looking for us as we speak. My own team is well aware that what's going down is big. They'll send more than a couple of men in blue uniforms to look for us."

. . .

Back in New York, things weren't going well for Wade and Tyler. They were livid that the two officers at the nightclub had screwed up. Allowing the woman to pull one over on them as she had was inexcusable. Everyone involved knew that for this mission to be a true victory, the undercover detective had to be tracked at all times. All they could do now was wait and see what further suggestions the surveillance team would come up with. The entire group was to be briefed in a matter of minutes.

Lorne Vectra was the lead detective in charge of surveillance monitoring for the undercover detective. As he entered the squad room, silence prevailed. Each step he took echoed loudly against the floor.

Once he reached the front of the room he said, "The tracking device worked all night. The only problem is we lost the signal at 10:00 a.m. this morning. The last known signal placed Detective Lynch in the middle of the Indian Ocean. We are currently charting out all maps and landmasses in the area. We have surmised, taking into consideration a plane's fuel consumption and the traveling distance involved, that the plane used is no longer airborne. We know for certain there are a string of islands in the vicinity of the last known coordinates. We have good reason to believe he was dropped off on one of those islands. From what we can tell so far, there are a total of seventeen islands within a fifty-mile radius. We have a team of experts trying to narrow down some potential locations. Any questions?"

Tyler Collins, visibly upset, stood up to comment: "It was my understanding, Lorne, that those tracking devices were foolproof. How or what could have possibly gone wrong to lose the signal, and why is there such a large area of possibility?"

"There are two possibilities, Detective Collins. One, the people we're after located the tracking devices and disposed of them. Two is that the signal found its way under solid rock, concrete, metal, or any combination of these materials. Option two will prove to be a much bigger hindrance for us if the signal is blocked by at least a hundred feet of any one of these substances. In answer to your second question, land tracking within a couple of hundred miles can be pinpointed to within a couple of hundred yards. Our sensor equipment is designed to send out signals that bounce off the earth's crust. It isn't as accurate when we're dealing with water. It would have been much more accurate had we been alerted to the abduction when it actually occurred so that we could have tracked the signal as it moved. Any other questions?"

Wade Leaman asked, "What is the possibility that the perpetrators discovered the tracking devices?"

Lorne said, "The chances are slim. But even if one of the devices were found, the second would still be operational. The devices were fitted with deflectors, which block normal metal detection. The only way someone would know they existed is if they had been informed that they were there."

The only thing left to do was to see if the surveillance team could narrow down the search perimeter. Tyler knew that the specialists on this job were tops in their respective fields. If anyone was able to complete the job, they could.

Tyler and Wade were charged with setting up the search and rescue effort. With the possible exception of Lawrence and Marilyn, both recruited during the early stages of the investigation, no one else had the same knowledge of this case. Because of the loss of the tracking signal, the search was going to take a while longer than was anticipated originally. There were now more factors at stake in this mission. Various other agencies, including, CIA, FBI, and U.S. Coast Guard, and various Search, Rescue and Emergency Response teams were briefed on the case. A large amount of work had to be done in a shorter time span. Time was of the essence. The undercover detective was missing and the tracking system was out of commission. No one knew what possible danger now existed for the undercover detective.

. . .

In the very short period the new man had been there, Harry Barbour had become a good ally to Detective Lynch. They had little in common, but Harry had will, determination and was desperate to escape. To ensure his freedom Harry stayed close to the detective and volunteered his assistance.

At the cotton fields, Richard, Blake and Henry were quickly introduced to Avery's ways and their responsibilities. Henry experienced the hardest time adjusting to the work. He had colossal hands, and each time he reached between the barbed wiring, he tore away small pieces of skin and flesh from his hands. Blood dripped steadily from his wounds.

Just one week after Don Snow got back on his feet he was put back to work. Don made his way nearer and nearer to Detective John Lynch's workstation. He was pushing for information regarding the potential rescue efforts. He needed reassurance. He probed the officer for his best estimates on being rescued and who and how many were involved. Avery told him on several occasions to return to his station and to shut up. After being spoken to for the fourth and final time, Avery smacked him in the back of the head. Avery then grabbed the Klan member by the back of his neck and pulled him back from the work bins. After that, he dragged him from the cotton fields.

Several minutes had elapsed and no one was sure where Avery had taken Don. Finally, their attention was drawn to the ledges above them. Avery was standing at a lookout ledge, which typically held his armed cronies, who monitored the slaves below. Avery stood there holding Don by the back of the neck.

After he gained the attention of the men below, Avery spoke, "Listen up, white trash. I am sick and tired of passing out orders to you idiots and getting nowhere. Today we have several new workers in the field who have been with us for a very short period. They need to be shown the significance of the word 'obedient' and the consequences when orders are ignored."

Avery guided Don to the end of the ledge. He was about to throw him over when Don shouted, "No! My life for yours."

Avery hesitated, pulling him back just slightly. He looked at the shaken man and said, "Explain yourself!"

Don stalled briefly in his response, scanning his fellow slaves below. He contemplated what he would say next or whether he should say anything at all. Then he lost it. He knew of the consequences for being disruptive or disorderly, but it was as if he had snapped. He barked at Avery, "Never mind. Your days are numbered you black faggot. You will live to regret this day and every other day of your miserable fucking existence. It's down to the wire now and only a matter of time before it's all over for each of you black pricks."

Avery squeezed his neck harder and said, "You've got two seconds to speak or you'll not live to regret this moment."

"Fuck you, nigger, and all your stinking race."

Avery pulled him back and slammed his face into the rock wall. He called to the armed guard and told him to take Don to his underground chamber. He would be there shortly to deal with the man. He then looked down and said, "I don't know what he's muttering on about, but I will find out shortly. As for you pigs, back to work."

Avery stormed away, taking a direct path to one of his favorite places in the entire facility. It was his personal torture chamber in one of the smaller caverns where he had spent many pleasurable hours over the years. He had more tools there than one cared to imagine.

Don Snow was dragged into a room that resembled a mud-soaked dungeon. Its walls were adorned with evenly spaced instruments of torture. As he was dragged through the room, his legs and feet became tarred with the mixture of dirt and mud that covered the floor beneath him. His already grubby clothes looked like oil-soaked rags from the knees down.

The man who delivered Don to this chamber was one of the roughest and nastiest characters working the underground. He made Avery and his brothers look like choirboys in comparison. If what Avery had in mind for Don didn't cause enough damage, his escort was keen to finish the job.

He released his grip on Don, causing the Klansman to fall to the ground. He landed at the foot of an old timber table. His body sunk into the thick mud, which covered the floor. Still stunned from the blows to his head, Don was too weak to keep his head out of the muck. He started spitting, gasping and choking while trying to get up.

When Avery finally entered, he shouted at his subordinate to put Don on the table and strap him down. The guard picked Don up, held him high above the wooden table, and then dropped him several feet onto the hard surface.

Don had no strength remaining in him to resist. He lay motionless, allowing the black man to strap his body to the table.

Avery circled the table, watching the white man, as he turned green. Don Snow continued gagging on the dirt he'd inhaled, but didn't throw up. Avery finally took his place to the right of the table. Lifting his arm high, his elbow made direct contact with the pit of Don Snow's stomach.

Avery screamed, "Throw up now, you pathetic little white bastard. Go ahead, you weak piece..."

Avery never even had the words out. The blow had the desired effect. Dirt, mud and spit flew from Don's mouth as he desperately gasped for air. Avery provided a great service to the man. He had assisted in clearing out his lungs, enabling the man to breathe freely once again. Don may not have seen it that way.

Avery proceeded towards the far wall. In the center of the wall was a dark oak cabinet. It was six-feet wide with double doors covering its front. The height of the cabinet was not obvious, as the wooden bottom had sunk into the mud. The top of the cabinet almost touched off the ceiling. When he opened the double doors, he started to whistle. He reached inside, rummaging through the contents. When he found what he was looking for, he closed the doors and walked back to the table. The man lying there was utterly powerless.

Avery Hawkins had never showed signs of weakness. He didn't have a conscience and couldn't care less what he did to anyone, male or female. His philosophy in life was that all members of the white race were second-class citizens, dirt. He firmly believed that anything he did to them was exclusively their fault. He showed no pity or remorse for his cruelty. In his mind, nothing he could do would even the score for the pain and suffering his forefathers endured.

Standing next to the table, Avery lifted up one of his victim's hands and slid it into a white leather glove with no fingertips. He fixed the leather glove to a metal strip, which was then connected to the edge of the table using four-inch screws. Once Don's hand was locked in place, Avery looked at the pale man and said calmly, "I'm giving you a fair opportunity to speak. I want you to explain your earlier ramblings. If you cooperate and I'm fully satisfied with your response, you will not feel this pain!"

Avery, glaring at his victim, held a sharp knife against Don's face. Slowly he ran the blade down over the man's eyes and nose and finally, he traced out a pattern over his pale lips. The switchblade had a black marble handle that glistened when it moved. He removed the knife from the man's lips slowly and directed it towards Don's fingers.

As the tip of the blade rolled over the back of Don's hand, it began to itch. The rawhide material of the leather glove rubbed against his hand. Avery continued guiding the blade down over the little finger of Don's right hand. Suddenly, he stopped right at the tip of his little finger. Furiously, he took the sharp instrument and with one long drawn-out motion, he slit the Klansman's cuticle.

The noise within the small dungeon was deafening. When he screamed, Don Snow opened his mouth so wide, the corners of his lips cracked. Every muscle in his body tensed. The screaming continued, as did the slicing of each one of the man's cuticles.

Avery reached down to the tray of instruments he had retrieved from the oak cabinet. He picked up two sets of rubber earplugs and pitched one set to the guard. After inserting them, he looked down at Don, who was still screaming, and grinned. Although the plugs did not block all the noise, they did reduce it.

After slicing the fingers on his other hand, Avery shouted, "What did you mean when you said my days were numbered, you stupid pathetic white piece of horse shit?"

No response came. Snow just lay there, clenching his teeth. Beads of sweat flowed down his forehead. The only movement coming from any of his limbs was that of his bloody middle finger, grabbing the leg of his torturer's pants. As Avery looked down, he was greeted with a personalized gesture from the white man's middle finger.

This meager symbol of aggression infuriated Avery further. He reached down, pressing the offensive finger flat to the table. He then started rummaging around his tray until he had found a tool, which put the smile back on his face. It resembled a pair of needlenosed pliers, also with a black marble grip. In one swift tugging motion, his middle fingernail was ripped from its base, roots and all.

The poor man started trembling madly from head to toe. He was in mortifying pain. The louder he roared, the more he shook. Looking down on him once again, Avery leaned forward, until his face came to within inches of his slave. Smiling, Avery repeated his question without even allowing his white captive the opportunity of replying, "What did you mean, shit head? What did you mean, shit head? What did you mean, shit head?"

Spit flew from Avery's mouth with each word he spoke. Each time he repeated the question his voice grew louder and he grew angrier. He wanted answers and his tolerance level had bottomed out.

Avery used several more torture devices on the Klansman, but not one of them had worked. He was unsuccessful in getting any information, and as a result was totally pissed off. Don Snow had mustered enough willpower and psychological strength to resist. He had succeeded in wearing down the black master. Avery had grown tired with his failed attempts at prying information from the Klansman. His throat was hoarse from all the shouting he had done.

Avery walked from the table, pounding on his own throbbing forehead in anger and defeat. He even threatened his own guard, ordering him never to open his mouth about what had transpired. He paced the room for the longest time, not speaking a word. Sweat ran down his forehead.

Suddenly his pacing stopped. He returned to the table. With pure vengeance flowing in his veins, he repeatedly drove his fists onto his captive's body, from one end to the next. He continued his attack for quite a few minutes until he felt the stress leave him.

It had reached the point where Don no longer screamed. He was too weak, battered and bruised to utter another sound. His mouth opened, but nothing came forth.

Avery grabbed Don by his ears, lifting the man's head up until their eyes met. He looked at him and said, "I always get my way you dismal little sleaze. Let's see just how brave you really are once your daughters are brought on the scene."

Don tried to speak out, but couldn't. All he could do was listen as Avery picked up his radio and called the main house. Don lay there helplessly as he listened to the special request, "Bring the Snow girls from the main house pronto. I want them sent to separate posts overlooking Section 34's cotton fields!"

A male voice came back loud and clear, "As requested, Mr. Hawkins."

Following his radio communication, Avery returned his attention to the prisoner. He grabbed him by the hair, tilting his head up. Venomously, he spit directly in the Klansman's face. He then ordered the guard to return Snow to the same ledge he was recently perched on.

All the men from Section 34 were busy working and singing the same wretched song. At first, none of them noticed that anything had changed. Within a short time, fewer and fewer of the captives were belting out the underground chant until silence reigned. Two guards stationed on the ledges above the workstation were holding Isabel and Irene Snow. No one spoke. The girls' faces were distorted with worry. The slaves below just stood there and watched in silence. They could do nothing.

Avery entered a ledge from the opposing side, directly opposite the women. His guard, who was dragging a beaten Don by the back of his shirt, followed close behind.

Avery stood at the end of the ledge. Furious, he looked down at the slaves and said, "Welcome to today's entertainment, you worthless white souls. I want this to be a lesson to all. I get what I want, when I want and those who disobey me, or show disrespect, pay the consequences! Pay close attention."

He turned to Don Snow and said, "I assume you have a clear view of your two ugly daughters standing over there? They are what you might refer to as an insurance policy. I will ask you a question and you will of course answer it to my full satisfaction. If for some reason you choose to be disagreeable or stupid, then I'm going to see if your daughters can fly."

In a low pleading voice, the Klansman stuttered, begging Avery to leave his girls out of it. The master of all wouldn't even acknowledge the broken man's sudden burst of energy. Instead, he grabbed Don by the neck and raised him off his feet demanding, "What did you mean when you said my days are now numbered?"

Don knew the black man would do as he said. Before he had the chance to speak, a voice echoed from below. It was Detective John Lynch, alias Richard Pope. He shouted to Avery, "What he means, you stupid black bastard, is that your tropical paradise is about to be closed. The time has come when your entire retreat will be shoved up your fucking ass."

Several guards headed towards the crowd of white men gathered below. The detective continued, "As we speak, the Federal Bureau of Investigations, the Central Intelligence Agency, the American Coast Guard, and every other law enforcement agency in the United States are looking for us. Let me introduce myself. I am Detective John Lynch, Undercover Police Detective for the New York City Police Department."

Avery could have leaped from the very ledge he stood on. With his hands trembling, he motioned for his men to act.

The detective continued to shout for all to hear, "You're only half as stupid as you look, the other half of your brain must be dead. For the record, I have arrived here not as a result of your will, asshole, but of my own free will and as orchestrated by my department."

Every white man in attendance was absolutely astonished. Not only because of what John had just revealed, but because Avery was suddenly on the receiving end of the stick.

Three of Avery's men had managed to break through the group of whites clustered tightly together in the cotton field. They encircled the detective and began hitting him with their clubs until he fell to his knees. Avery shouted below, advising his men to bring the detective back to the main house. He then picked up his radio, contacted his father and filled him in on the latest chain of events.

Before he left, he took Don by the scruff of his neck and threw him over the edge. Don fell rapidly, rotated several times over the course of the seventy-five foot drop, and smashed into the rock surface below. The impact killed the man instantly.

Avery didn't bat an eye. He motioned to his men across the way to return the Snow girls to the main house. Both were carted off screaming, kicking and crying hysterically. They, like the rest of the slaves, went into a state of shock watching Don Snow fall to his death.

Robert and Harry were the first men to reach Don's lifeless body. The expression on their faces confirmed the inevitable. One side of his head had smashed in as it made contact with the solid rock. His skull and a portion of his brain were plainly visible.

His fellow slaves and comrades had all surrounded Don's body. They were nauseated. A pool of blood had formed from the streaming red liquid that flowed from his head. His left leg had also been crushed. Those who witnessed that day would always remember the horrible sensation and deathly silence that filled the musty stale air.

Lance was most affected with what he saw. As he walked over to Don's body, tears formed in his eyes. Choking back tears, he looked at Harry and said, "How much more pain and suffering do we have to endure at the hands of those bastards?"

Gently, the big man put his arm around Lance's shoulder, and said, "Don't worry Lance. It shouldn't be too much longer. The only thing we have to fear is how much shit we're in, now that the masters know about the undercover operation."

Two of the black henchmen had come to where the slaves were gathered. With rifles cocked they began to disperse the crowd. Robert, Harry and Lance were the closest ones to the body. They were also the ones chosen to dispose of it. The task was clear. They were to deliver the body to Rachel's watering hole. The minute Lance reached down to grasp one of Don's legs, he felt weak. Almost immediately, he lost full control of his stomach, throwing up all over the deceased.

He looked over at Harry and whispered, "I really don't think I can do this."

Harry looked back at him and said, "Come with us and don't say another word. Don't ask any questions. We have a plan. You'll find out soon enough."

Two of Avery's men moved in closer, telling the three men to shut the fuck up. Lance wished it were these two who had been killed. He then asked God to forgive him for the hatred he now felt building up inside him.

Harry was now standing directly across from Lance. The looks he threw his way actually frightened the young man. Robert and Harry picked up the corpse, pushing Lance aside, and began carrying it towards the exit. Harry then roared at Lance to go in front of them. He wanted him to lead the way towards Rachel's watering hole. Harry told the guards he needed someone ahead of them for when they reached the cliffs. They would need his eyes once they started to climb down. They all knew how easy it was to lose one's footing and fall, while descending such a steep slippery grade.

Harry started acting very peculiar. He started talking a mile a minute to the two black men who accompanied them. The guards ignored him. The one-sided conversation he was having wasn't making sense. It was as if Harry had gone crazy, babbling on with these foolhardy idiotic statements about completely insignificant things. Lance didn't realize until later that Harry was attempting to throw the men off. His intent was to distract them.

One of the guards had had enough and picked up his speed, quickly passing each of them, shaking his head in annoyance. The second man chose to stay behind and allowed Harry to continue with his mutterings. He was actually finding the apparently demented giant rather amusing.

The ground underneath them was very soggy and in most places slippery and treacherous. Their route had taken them down one of the main passages. Most of the dampness in the underground came from above, as water from the surface seeped slowly down. Once they left the main tunnel, they arrived at the top of the cliffs. This part of their expedition would be twice as dangerous as the previous part.

Harry was carrying the dead man by his chest. Suddenly, he picked up the pace. As the gap between him and Lance narrowed, Harry whispered, "Listen closely, Lance and don't say a word. When we arrive at the bridge, I am going to drop Don's body on the boardwalk. You must immediately drop to the ground too. Don't move a single muscle once you're laying flat unless I tell you otherwise."

The black man behind Harry and Robert called ahead, advising Harry to shut his trap. Harry slowed the pace, allowing the distance between him and Lance to increase.

The descent down the cliffs had begun. Lance felt his knees weaken and he started to feel dizzy. He really didn't think heights bothered him, but this particular pinnacle was something else. All he knew was that he had to keep going. He forced himself onwards. The path down was dreadfully narrow and it looked exceptionally dangerous. Several times he felt his feet slipping, but managed to regain his footing. He was stumped as to how his two friends were able to carry the lifeless man without falling.

When he arrived in safety at the bottom, he sighed with relief. The man who walked ahead of him stood still, sizing up his surroundings. He looked for sudden movement in or around the water. All of a sudden a splashing noise came from the opposite side of the underground lake. Rachel had slithered into the water. She was looking for her lunch.

The men were instructed to walk towards the bridge. Once there, they proceeded towards the middle. As they moved forward, Lance was alert.

Only feet from the middle, Lance heard Harry screaming out, "Now!"

Instinct and Harry's previous instruction had sent Lance falling to the wooden surface. Harry and Robert had hightailed it in opposite directions. The former wrestler and his law enforcement partner grappled a guard each. It only took Harry seconds to secure his foe on the walkway. Robert, on the other hand, was still struggling with his.

Harry called out and ordered Lance to assist Robert. Lance stood and looked at the two men fighting violently with one another. The only thing he saw nearby was a full pail of freshly gutted fish. He reached down and picked it up, then headed cautiously in Robert's direction. Without warning, Lance lifted up the pail and swung it around, picking up speed with each rotation. He ran onward and with perfect timing, the improvised weapon made direct contact with the back of the black man's head. The force of the blow compelled the man to his knees.

This allowed Robert enough time to tackle the man. He was quick to secure the dazed individual, face down on the landing. While Harry had used brute strength in the handling of his man, Robert had used his police officer training, along with Lance's valued assistance.

Lance looked from Robert to Harry and asked, "Now what? Do you realize we are all going to die for this?"

Harry, straining ever so slightly, looked up at him and replied, "Not to worry. We have a plan to get the hell out of here and you're included. The way things are going now, any one of us could end up just like Don. We need to take control of our destiny. No one knows when things will erupt for the worst and we all get taken down."

Lance's reply was simple, "What in the Christ are we going to be able to do underground?"

Harry's lips curled in a devilish grin as he replied, "Watch and learn the reality of a dog eat dog world."

He lifted his rival's body up, applying one knee to the lower back of the vulnerable black man. He then grabbed the man by both of his arms, applying sufficient pressure to force the man into an upright position. Only moments ago this man had been in control.

Using his feet, Harry kicked the weapons, sending them sliding towards Lance. Both weapons landed only inches from his feet.

Harry took the recently acquired captive and lifted him over his head. He then walked towards the bridge railing and threw the man into the water. The guard cried out for help as he flew over the railing. Just as he had been an accomplice to the death of so many whites in the past, he was feeling their terror. Lance stood stupefied, watching and listening to the black man's screams.

His cries for help intensified. He was barely inches from the water, when the calm liquid exploded. Out of the water rose the ferocious jaws of death. Rachel clamped her powerful jaws around the man's back with one massive, snapping motion. His pain lasted only seconds. The last thing Lance and the others saw was an array of reddish bubbles, hastily escaping from the watery depths.

Lance's legs went numb and he leaned against the railing to keep himself from falling. Harry immediately cautioned him to move away from the rails. Lance whispered, "Why did you have to kill him?"

"Because that could have been you, me or even Robert, this time tomorrow. If we don't move to save ourselves now, we could all be killed."

"You keep saying that."

"How long do you think it will be before the Hawkins family realizes it is no longer safe for them to continue with this set up? Our days are numbered. It will only take them a very short time. How do you think they clean house? They will get rid of all evidence, human or otherwise. Won't they, Robert?"

Robert nodded in agreement. Both men had been talking for days about making a break for it, in light of their newest visitor. Their plan didn't involve an escape from the underground, but merely an attempt to use its maze of tunnels to hide in until help eventually came. The detective had advised each of them that it was only a matter of time.

Since Don had let the secret slip out, it would only be minutes, hours or days before something drastic came down that would affect everyone.To ensure their future, Robert and Harry planned on using the master's own house of horrors against them. The underground, with its caverns and paths, provided the perfect hiding place. If they were to venture back to the cotton fields, they chanced death.

Harry went to Robert, who was still kneeling on the second guard's back. He had the man's arms secured behind his back, trapped by the weight of Robert's knees. Once they had taken the terrified man's possessions, Harry picked him up and threw him over the railing also.

When he hit the water, Rachel was nowhere to be seen. He immediately began to swim for the safety of the rocks, opposite from where Lance and the others stood. He was only successful in swimming half the distance. Rachel claimed the poor fellow front on, engulfing his body to the waist. She sank below the murky waters with the second man in her jaws.

Harry looked at the others saying, "The croc is not used to getting chocolate. It must be her lucky night."

Robert and Lance didn't really appreciate his humor. Neither of them said a word.

Harry picked up Don and gently dropped his body over the railing. In one sense, it was symbolic to the three men. While Rachel was preoccupied with one of the masters of the underground, the Klansman's body sunk peacefully to the bottom. It was as if, at that moment, his wife's spirit had wrapped itself around his body, guiding him home.

After picking up their newly acquired weapons from the boardwalk, Robert motioned for them to leave. He didn't head back to the bottom of the cliffs, but finished the journey across the bridge. The men entered the second half of Rachel's living quarters. As they proceeded, they kept their eyes peeled to every move the big crocodile made.

When they reached the other side, Robert showed them an opening in the rocks, which couldn't be seen from the bridge. Robert had discovered the opening during his last visit when he dumped the bodies of those who fell victim to the deadly virus. Robert had told Harry previously about the opening, which was the beginning of their escape plan.

Those same black men, now deceased, days earlier had forced Robert to keep watch for Rachel but she was nowhere in sight. Robert was ordered to make a more thorough search for her. After he had crossed the bridge and stepped off, he was still unable to find the ugly reptile. He guardedly roamed around for several more minutes. At last, he had spotted the beast in the mud, half concealed from view, resting comfortably.

It was then that Robert had noticed the opening in the rocks. Far enough away and out of view of the masters, he slipped inside. It was a very tight squeeze, but well worth the effort. Robert found several additional smaller tunnels and caverns inside. Not one of them looked as if they had been used before. Although he didn't have time to explore them, he had concluded rather quickly it was the perfect hiding place.

Robert entered through the opening in the rocks and Lance followed. Harry attempted to squeeze through, but encountered difficulty. The entrance was fine for an average sized man, but Harry was massive. As he pushed forward, forcing himself through, he ended up with multitudes of scrapes and cuts from his chest to his knees. Harry cursed as he plunged his mighty body forward. This was a small price to pay for possible freedom.

Inside they felt a refreshingly cool breeze. The area they entered was moderate in size. It smelled quite different from what they had been accustomed to. Fresh water rolled down portions of the rock walls, like miniature indoor fountains. As the water reached the floor, it ran along the base, exiting periodically beneath the walls in various places. The three men stood evaluating Robert's find. There were seven accessible openings leading from the main cavern. They spent the next few hours surveying all the openings for their safety and potential.

After exploring, Harry returned to Section 34 to obtain some food and any other essentials he could carry. He wanted to ensure that if the stand off dragged out, at least they would have a fighting chance at survival. He took a gun with him, leaving the remaining weapons behind.

Before departing, he warned Robert and Lance to play it safe and to not take any unnecessary chances. He left them with a flashlight that he had salvaged from the two dead black men. He then advised them that he would return with additional supplies soon. With that, he left the same way he had arrived. They heard him curse as he squirmed his way back through the small gap.

Robert and Lance continued to familiarize themselves with their surroundings. They scouted out all the viable openings, spending several minutes in each one to establish their potential. Most of the paths seemed to be never-ending, going on for what appeared to be miles. They met up with one another after having only investigated five of the entrances on their own. They examined the two remaining entrances together.

At first, they thought they had reached a dead end, but veering just to the right they discovered another long corridor. Vertical glimmers of sunlight shone down in tiny beams just ahead. They had discovered another opening with almost enough sunlight to light up the interior. In addition to the natural light, they found a medium-sized underground lagoon, which took up approximately one quarter of the actual space. It was breathtaking.

Looking at one other, without so much as a word, both men removed their beaten up sneakers and their dilapidated clothing, and ran out into the divine liquid. The water was icy cold, yet refreshing. After running through the water until it came up to their knees, they dove and began to swim to the opposite side where they rested against the rocks and caught their breath.

Taking a deep breath, they dove and discovered what they thought was an underground cave. Just ahead of them they could see light. The nearer they swam to it, the colder the water was. Unfortunately, they were running out of breath and retraced their path.

As they made it back to their original starting point, their heads shot out of the water, both men gasping desperately for air. Exhilarated, they raised their hands in a high five. It was very possible they may have discovered a way out of the caves. It could be their ticket to freedom, leading them to the waters of the outside world.

Things seemed to look up for them. If their hideaway were discovered, they had a place to run and hopefully have enough time to reach the outside world. There was just one problem left for them to solve. They had to find out how far the other side was. For this they would need someone who could easily swim the distance.

Robert and Lance returned to the main cavern where Harry was eagerly awaiting them. He managed to get his hands on some food, two empty tins, some nylon rope, a second lantern, and a few other odds and ends he figured would come in handy. Without delay, they updated Harry on their amazing discovery. He, in turn, had information to relay. He informed them of how the blacks were now scurrying throughout each section. Based on his personal observation he confirmed the inevitable, things were heating up. In his opinion, the masters were now clearly showing signs of panic and concern. Without giving the particulars, Harry also mentioned he had had two separate encounters with different masters. Both encounters had ended in palpable success as evident by the drops of blood now soiling the front of his shirt. Not one of the drops was his.

The three of them sat on the ground discussing their strategy. There was sufficient food and other supplies to last them at least a week. They could sense something bad was about to happen shortly. It could be as soon as Detective Lynch finished his visit with the Hawkins.

After a more lengthy discussion and much heated debate, the three men decided they would each select one additional person to bring with them into the safety of their hiding place. They knew this was very risky, but it was the right thing to do. Any more than one each would be taking too much of a chance. As things stood, once either of the men ventured out of the cave, they willingly accepted the liklihood of being caught. Once the decision was made to go back into the main population, it had to be done right away, as it would only be a matter of time before they or the guards they fed to Rachel were discovered missing.

Lance's choice was easy for him to make. He knew he had to help Joseph's mother, Mrs. Kieley. Her son was free and no longer in danger. He cherished the thought of one day being able to reunite the child with his mother.

Harry really didn't know too many men, with the exception of those in his section. For the most part, these individuals were not exactly his best friends. Everywhere Harry went usually meant trouble. Most of the males in the section had avoided him whenever possible. His only logical choice was Jean-Luc. He had been Harry's and the other's roommate for quite a while. In their view, he was a caring, sincere person. Harry thought that he too deserved an opportunity at possible freedom.

Robert, on the other hand, was deeply torn between choosing his police partner or Alana Normore, Melanie's mom. He couldn't shake the memory of that little girl's face, knowing how tragic the fragile child's life must be without her mom, but how could he turn his back on his long time partner?

Harry warned Robert to make up his mind on the way out of the cave for they had to leave immediately. Harry would travel to Section 34 to retrieve Jean-Luc. Lance's route would take him to the dump. It was a shorter route, which meant he would get there faster, and it led straight to the women's quarters. Robert went with Lance. He hoped he could make his mind up soon. Time was of the essence.

Each of the men took a weapon, for none of them knew what lay ahead. Harry had eagerly taken the stun gun. He was itching to stick it to one of the masters. Robert and Lance each took a handgun. They would take no chances on their journey.

Robert gave Lance a speedy lesson in proper gun handling just prior to them leaving. Harry had already left. Cautiously the two men passed Rachel's domain, climbed up the cliffs and started to close the gap between them and the women's quarters. Only minutes from reaching the dump, Robert still had not made up his mind. He advised Lance to go ahead as he stayed in one of the passageways to ponder his next move.

In a short time, Lance had finally reached the garbage dump, which was vacant and almost too quiet for comfort. No one was roaming about, not even the rats. As he moved through the dump, towards the entrance to the woman's quarters, the sound of footsteps approaching in the near distance startled him. Holding his breath against the stench, he leaned his body back against the garbage heap.

Voices soon followed the footsteps. Two females and the young boy, Adam, had made their way into the dump. Adam's parents had both died in the underground; Rachel consumed his father while he was attempting to rescue young Joseph and Melanie six months earlier. His mother, who also was fed to Rachel, had fallen victim to the infectious virus earlier that month.

Lance pushed himself up from the garbage. Walking in their direction he asked, "Do you know Grace Kieley? I need you to relay a message to her right away. It's very important."

At that point, a hand touched Lance's shoulder and startled him. He reached around pointing his gun. He came face to face with Robert, who swiftly blocked his arm and lifted it in the air.

Robert looked at Lance and said, "Be careful! You're liable to kill someone."

Lance was mortified! He could have shot him then and there. He hated having the gun in the first place. Lance looked at him still shaking and said, "What are you doing here?"

"After mucking about, I made my decision. The woman deserves a chance at freedom. If not for herself, for the girl."

This brought delight to Lance's soul. It wasn't because George didn't deserve the opportunity to escape, but his heart went out to the children. Young Joseph and Melanie were the ones who would need someone in their lives, to look after them during their recovery from the horrors they had endured.

Lance asked the women if one of them would fetch Alana Normore and Grace Kieley for them. They refused to take such a risk and told

Robert and Lance to get lost. The heightened tension in the air was causing the masters to beat and kill folks for no reason. The women feared if they were caught talking to Alana and Grace, the guards would retaliate.

Adam, surprisingly, turned to the two men and told them that he would get the women for them. In a flash, he was gone before the women could stop him.

Ten minutes passed. Robert and Lance remained hidden among one of the many mounds of garbage and on full alert. Suddenly, out of the blue, the women they had been waiting for ran into the dump followed by the young lad, Adam. When the two men showed themselves, the women came to them, demanding, "Have you heard any news about our kids?"

They told the ladies what they had heard, which wasn't more than they already knew themselves. Following this, they hastily briefed them on their current plan and answered each of the questions the cautious women asked. They were hesitant, to say the least, but seeing the men's weapons, and feeling a little reassured after hearing about the hiding place, they agreed to go. Lance asked, "Either of you strong swimmers?"

Both women shook their heads. One of them then said, "Adam was a junior diving champion. He was one of the best in his state. He competed nationally just weeks before his capture."

Dubiously, Lance looked to Robert and then Adam. The little boy displayed a huge smile, showing a noticeable gap in his front teeth. Adam bragged that he could swim better than a fish. He eagerly babbled on about his love for the water and how he could out swim his parents. Just then, he realized what he had said and his eyes swelled with tears. They felt this orphan's pain.

Robert pointed at Lance and said, "He's coming too."

There would be no quarrel from Lance on this one. All five of them headed speedily back towards their hiding place. As they moved onward, they repeatedly came across several masters but hid from view.

Robert and Lance held their weapons upright, ready to use them should the need arise. They were very fortunate, as a newly formed group, not to have been discovered. Along the way, they came across the remains of those not so lucky. The timing of their escape couldn't have been any better. It was obvious that trouble had reached the boiling point in the underground.

They reached the top of the underground cliffs without incident. One by one, they descended, all eyes peeled for any signs of the lurking crocodile. Everyone sighed a profound breath of relief as they made it to the concealed opening, past the opposite side of the bridge. The others had not yet arrived. They would have to wait patiently for Harry and Jean-Luc's return.

While waiting, Lance had Adam accompany him down the passage, which led to the clear blue water. With just a rope and a lantern, the two walked along the darkened path until they reached the opening. Lance secured the rope around Adam's waist and led the boy into the chilled water. Adam's teeth started chattering, but all he did was laugh and mock Lance for his teeth chattered also.

Once they swam across the water and had reached the other side, Lance said to Adam, "Now listen to me carefully young man! I need to see if you can swim underwater and out the other side. If you're under water for any more than sixty seconds, I'm pulling you back. If you have any trouble whatsoever, tug the rope and I'll pull you back or come get you. Are you perfectly clear in what I'm saying?"

Adam's teeth were still chattering. He was a daring lad, who continued to boast how he could stay under the water twice that long. He took a deep breath and went under.

As soon as he had gone under, Lance started to count out loud. Nearing the sixty-second mark, he could no longer feel tension from the rope. He panicked. He gripped the rope firmly and yanked it towards his chest. His heart skipped a beat the instant he realized there was no resistance.

Harry, Jean-Luc and Robert had just entered the cavern. Lance roared out, telling the others how Adam had been gone too long and the resistance on the rope had disappeared. Robert and Jean-Luc jumped frantically into the water, swimming flat out in his direction.

Taking a deep breath, Lance plunged below. No sooner had the others reached his position, than Adam emerged from the water. The little fish had passed Lance under water and had made his way back to the surface. He gasped for breath holding on to Robert's shoulders, trying to calm himself down. They all treaded water as Adam revealed that the ocean was on the other side, and that the subterranean underwater cave exited right at the bottom of gigantic cliffs.

The boy could barely contain himself. In the distance, he saw several beaches, which seemed far away, but they were there. He also saw several flat rocks that stuck out along the bottom of the cliff in different places. One or two people could possibly get out of the water and squeeze onto them if they needed to hide.

They all began to swim back. Adam broke free from them and was the first to make it out of the water. When the others left the water, Adam told Lance that the rope had slowed him down so he slipped it off. He also said it wouldn't take long to swim right through the cave if they all had to.

Next to Harry's massive body, Adam was like a mouse rummaging around an elephant's legs. Lance walked over to him and chastised the boy for letting go of the rope and giving him such a fright. Being a typical boy his age, he paid no attention. He was far too excited to listen.

As they walked back to the main cavern to join the others, Harry gave an account of his and Jean-Luc's latest encounter with another one of the masters. He laughed as he spoke, telling them that the poor man didn't know what hit him. He then proudly displayed an additional weapon he had confiscated from the unconscious man.

The group had established a safe new colony in their underground encampment. Even though it was temporary, it was a secure hiding place. With any luck and lots of hope, a promising future was within their grasp. Jean-Luc and Harry had gotten their hands on additional supplies, some blankets, food, and two water jugs. They were set up for the long haul.

This group's timing could not have been any better. For now they were safe and they had hope. Others in the underground would not be as lucky. Many more bad things were about to happen.

HOUSE CLEANING

chapter seventeen

THE male members of the Hawkins family had all gathered at the main house. They were expecting company to arrive very shortly. Detective John Lynch was, at that very moment, being escorted to the main dwelling. He was about to undergo an interrogation with the ruling members of the family.

Thomas was in a foul mood. He had already chastised every member of his family, one after the other, whether they had upset him or not.

Attitude was something each man in the family had inherited. It was also obvious that although the boys could dish it out, they couldn't take it, especially from their father, which was a completely different story. They behaved like scolded puppies that were disciplined for soiling the carpet.

Rita Hawkins had entered the main family room. She too was in a foul mood from fighting with her husband earlier in the day. His attitude didn't sit well with her and she'd let him know it. As she approached his side, she said firmly, "Are you ready for your visitor, Thomas?"

"Have the men bring him here!"

Minutes later, two men entered the room, dragging the undercover detective by his armpits. They walked him to an old wooden chair positioned in the middle of the room. He was then forced into the chair and secured. His vertebrae produced a thump as his body hit the solid wooden surface.

The old man rose from the couch and walked over to the captive. Standing inches from him, Thomas looked down and said, "I believe you may have some important information to share with me this evening, detective. If you don't cooperate then maybe I should call you an ambulance!"

"Call me what you like, it really doesn't matter at this point."

"For now, I will call you, 'white pig,' it suits your current position."

"As you please."

"Enough with the formalities, pig. I understand you have arrived at our little resort in an unwelcome capacity? Are you insane, or is there truth to the rumors and speculation floating around? Care to comment?"

"No."

"You are my prisoner. I can do to you whatever I please. I did some checking of my own. Even though someone has screwed up enormously, I leave nothing to chance. I have connections with every law enforcement agency in the world. A tiny white piss-off like yourself is no more than a cockroach under my foot."

"I'm not quite sure you actually understand the meaning of the word cockroach, old man."

With that, Thomas Hawkins slapped him across the face. Detective Lynch flinched slightly, looking back at the old man who was now grinning. Thomas Hawkins said, "Let's see, where was I before the pig interrupted? Oh yes, I know the rumors going around have some truth to them. However, I also know something else. There is something you are not aware of. Your peers have run into some minor difficulties with the tracking system. Our connections do go a long way, you know? The reason we have given you the privilege of our company is to locate your end of the tracking device. Surprised?"

Thomas calmly returned to the couch and sat down. He then picked up his cell phone and dialed. The only words he spoke were, "We're ready for you now."

Rita Hawkins knew what was about to occur and retreated to her bedroom. Entering, she headed over to the nightstand and turned on the radio. She lay on her bed and stared at the ceiling. Her mind wandered; she knew the walls around her would soon be crumbling down.

. . .

Tyler and Wade were busy working with the technicians charged with cleaning the bugs out of the tracking system. They managed to narrow the search down to within an estimated twenty square miles. This was based on whether Detective Lynch still had the implants on his person. At this point, it was the best they could come up with.

The only thing left was the set-up of a massive search and rescue detail. For this, they would need the cooperation of all law enforcement agencies available, including the Coast Guard. A search of this magnitude could take several days to initiate. Tyler had already made the necessary arrangements to put their plan into action. Four traditional teams had been established: two teams of air search whose main function would be to scan each of the remote islands in the region, and two teams who would conduct their searches by vessel in conjunction with the Australian Coast Guard. Wade and Tyler would lead the teams operating the water search, while Marilyn and Lawrence were assigned to coordinate the activities of the air search teams.

It was the first official day in which multiple law enforcement agencies had come together in what became known as "Operation Re-Coup." The New York Police Department, the FBI, the CIA, the Australian Coast Guard, and specialized tactical units from the United States Army and Navy, were now on board and ready to act.

Tyler and Wade had earned the right to lead the rescue operation. After all, they had come to within days of solving multitudes of unanswered files involving missing and abducted persons.

Tyler had opened the White Files and was updating the database when she noticed the mainframe was being tampered with. Someone had tapped into the application she had created for maintaining these files. She brought this to the others' attention immediately. They happened to be in the company of several qualified computer technicians. With a few flicks of the keyboard, they identified their hacker's location.

Someone in their own office had gained access and was somewhere on the third floor. He or she was currently reviewing the most recent information they had loaded into the White Files. This was clearly an unauthorized breach of security. The technician quickly surmised that the intruder, who had hacked into the files, was now in Human Resources on the third floor.

Tyler, Wade and several other cops all headed for the stairwell, which led to the third floor. Once they reached the top, they rushed through the main doors to the Human Resources Office. Inside they found a young black man sitting at a computer. Seeing them enter, he immediately shut down the system, and looked at them in shock and anger.

Tyler walked over to him and demanded, "Who are you and what gives you the right to access the White Files?"

The man looked at her and responded, "Fuck you!"

Wade's face reddened. Bending forward, he grabbed the man by his shirt and lifted him up. Violently, he slammed the man against a gray filing cabinet. Holding him firmly against the cabinet, he shouted to Marilyn and Lawrence, "Take this piece of shit back to the interrogation room. I'll deal with it shortly."

Heather Guest, the Human Resources Manager for the Department entered. She was abruptly questioned as to the employment status of the man. Heather advised them that he had transferred in recently. She went to her office, returning quickly with a blue file folder in her hand. Glancing briefly at the file's contents, she looked up and told Tyler and Wade that the man had transferred from Station 84 in Detroit, Michigan.

Because she'd memorized the White Files, Tyler knew this rookie had been previously assigned to the same department two white officers had gone missing from almost a year ago.

During their interrogation of Joseph Donnel, Tyler and Wade tried in vain to obtain any information they could. The tall male was stubborn. They finally ceased their questioning. Donnel was not about to divulge any information, and time was no longer a luxury they could afford. They held the hacker for twenty-four hours, pending a further analysis of the man's history. This was a temporary measure. Once they released him, he would be staked out. The officer assigned to this detail would report back on his every move.

. . .

Silence shrouded the living room of the Hawkins' residence. The occupants of the room sat just looking at one another. Mel Lucas entered the room. He walked over to Thomas Hawkins and shook his hand. He said, "Glad to be of service this evening, my friend. Very rough flight coming over indeed. Next time a little more notice would be appreciated."

"This is an emergency, Mel. I needed your services tonight. I will make it worth your troubles."

Mel carried with him a large brown leather attaché case. It was soft calf leather with expandable sides. Placing it on the coffee table, he tinkered with the combination until it clicked. The two brass latches snapped open. Reaching inside, he removed what resembled a miniature television set and a second gadget, which appeared to be a remote control.

He held the tiny gadget in his hand. Infrared lighting beamed out of the top of it. After the tiny monitor had been plugged in, Mel strolled over to the detective, pointing the device directly at the officer. Starting from the man's feet, he slowly moved the device upwards, covering every inch of the detective's body. As the gadget aligned with the man's hand the ten-inch screen lit up and the contraption beeped.

The men behind John Lynch had been instructed to hold the officer steady. The bigger of the two clamped down on the detective's hand, forcing it flat to the chair's armrest. Mel took the tiny device and placed it at the bottom of the man's hand. Slowly, he moved it down towards the captive's fingertips. When it found its target, the monitor practically danced. The beeping noise escalated in volume. Mel looked at Thomas and said, "A little creepy-crawler appears to have planted itself under his fingernail."

Thomas smiled and said, "I wish it removed, but not disabled."

Mel Lucas was extremely well prepared. He went to his case and withdrew a set of needlenosed pliers. Ensuring the detective's hand was still immobilized, he drove the pliers down behind the man's fingernail. Then, he clamped down on the handle and with one firm yank, tore the nail from its base, roots and all.

The officer's body twitched as if it had been electrocuted. Blood poured out from the tip of his finger. Sweat popped out on his brow and streamed down his face. John Lynch clenched his teeth together so hard you could hear a scraping noise. He sat up straight, looked at Thomas Hawkins and produced a painful grin.

Thomas said to Mel, "When you leave, take the device. I want it dropped from the plane, somewhere very far from here, in the middle of the Indian Ocean. I also want the device secured in a plastic container, one that floats. I wish to send the detective's associates on a wild goose chase, right across the Indian Ocean."

"Let's not be impatient, Thomas. I haven't finished checking out our little friend. I really don't think his associates are completely stupid. The receiving device they used is virtually untraceable. The only reason I was able to locate the receiver in the first place was due to our little connection at police headquarters. Without that advantage, I would never have known what to look for, nor would I have known what I would need to detect it."

Mel turned his attention back towards the bleeding prisoner. He knelt down, looking the man in the eyes and said, "You're the first! The first man I've ever removed a fingernail from and not so much as a word. Not a scream, nothing. Nothing worse than torturing a man who shows little to no emotion. Takes the fun right out of it, wouldn't you agree?"

Detective Lynch raised his head in the air and spit directly into the black man's face. Mel wiped it away with the back of his hand and then licked the white man's spit. He said to the defenseless detective, "They say every man should taste the fear of his enemy. You are a sour, sick little white man. On the other hand, being such a brave, stupid person, you deserve to spend your last days suffering. Strength, endurance and will power are something you seem to have acquired. You will have ample opportunity to develop these attributes in the days ahead."

With those soft-spoken words, Mel reached into his shirt pocket and removed a dirty silk handkerchief. He forced the material into his captive's mouth. Picking up his remote, he proceeded to run the sensor over the remaining parts of the injured man. As the device neared the detective's head, the monitor livened up once again. Slowly, he ran the device up one side of the white man's head and down the other. As it made contact with the cop's ear, Mel smiled. The beeping noise increased. He had located the second and final transmitter.

He turned about, facing Thomas and said grinning, "It pays to be thorough, Thomas."

"Where is the second device?"

"It's in his ear. It's disguised as a mini hearing aid. It appears to be attached just inside the eardrum. I believe this one may be somewhat more painful!"

Mel turned his attention to the detective, holding in his hand a tool that resembled a metal corkscrew. Mel motioned for his assistants to apply additional pressure to his foe and to hold him very steady. He wanted to ensure the detective's upper body did not move. Tilting the white man's head to one side, and without hesitation, he inserted the makeshift corkscrew right into the undercover cop's ear.

Desperately, he tried to move about, but the more energy he exerted, the faster the blood flowed, the greater the pain. His entire body felt as if it were on fire. The second device was now removed from his ear.

Mel returned to his briefcase and removed two plastic containers from within. He dumped the contents back into his briefcase and then placed a separate receiver in each one. After finishing, he walked to his victim and whispered in his good ear, "It's been a slice, so to speak!"

He then turned his attention back to Thomas and said, "Completed, as requested. I will dispose of the tracking devices exactly as you wish."

Thomas replied with a smirk, "Payment is in the mail!"

Thomas instructed the two men, who were still holding the detective in place, to return him to his work section. He then looked at his sons and said, "Unfortunately, we are in deep trouble. We are no longer able to remain on the island. I will be moving your mother and the majority of the staff off the island early tomorrow, just as soon as the boat arrives. I have specific instructions for each of you. Gather together ten men, ten women and all the children from each of the work sections. I want this done first thing in the morning. I've made some alternate arrangements regarding a temporary relocation."

Avery looked at his father and said, "And the rest?"

"As our new accommodations are much smaller than we are accustomed to, we can't take everyone. After you have completed your selections and the boat is loaded, the taps are to be opened. We cannot leave any witnesses."

Neither son questioned his father. Each of them was fully aware what was to happen should White Man's Cotton be jeopardized. The events this week only confirmed the inevitable. Years of planning and money were about to go down the drain. Tomorrow would be a busy day. For now, it was up to the Hawkins boys to determine which surviving white persons would be relocated.

As Thomas Hawkins was about to leave the room, he looked at Avery and said, "The Catcher has put in a special request. I also have one of my own. Please ensure Robert Lawlor and Lance Forrest are among the chosen ones from your work section."

Avery looked at his father, about to speak. Thomas raised his finger silencing his son, and that was that.

Detective John Lynch was being dragged back to Section 34. He was in severe pain. Reaching their intended destination, the guards noted the room was almost empty. The only one who remained was George Williams. The detective's body was dumped to the floor like a piece of trash. The men then looked at George, demanding to know the whereabouts of the others.

George replied, "They've gone on holidays and to where, I have no idea."

One of the men approached him and slammed a size twelve boot into his already badly injured arm. George let out a deep grunt. He too was in great pain, but nothing compared to the undercover cop. The black men turned and walked away, leaving George and the detective alone.

Despite his pain, the detective was relatively calm. Blood was still slowly running from his ear and finger. George gathered the tattered blankets lying on the floor. Using one good arm and his teeth, he managed to tear pieces from one of the mangy blankets, creating temporary bandages to cover the detective's wounds.

John asked him where the others had gone, but George honestly didn't know. The only information he could provide was that they had disappeared earlier in the day and he hadn't seen them since. Both were left wondering if their black masters were somehow responsible for their friends' absence.

That night was a trying one for both men. Neither was able to rest for any length of time. The night dragged on, with only brief periods of sleep. Avery Hawkins rudely awakened the injured males the next morning. He entered their quarters shouting, "You with the bum arm. Follow my men immediately."

Looking at the detective, he then said, "Where are the others?"

After several seconds of dead silence, Avery replied, "Nice day for a swim!"

Avery left the undercover detective alone while his goons escorted George Williams from the room. As Avery walked through Section 34, he started pointing at various men. No one knew what was happening. All feared for those now being singled out. None of them realized what was in store for the group of slaves now leaving the underground.

. . .

Harry, Jean-Luc, Robert, and Lance had spent the bulk of the night exploring possibilities, examining different scenarios and imagining stumbling blocks they could encounter over the next few days. One thing they all agreed upon and finalized was their escape plan. If their foes were to locate their hiding place, they would at once swim through the underwater cavern to the possible safety of the outside world. To set the stage, all of their supplies had been stored in a separate tunnel. This would provide them with a diversion, throwing off possible discovery.

Several other topics had been discussed during the night. Apart from the escape plan, a potential rescue and their safety, they also discussed the individuals who would be left behind. They were all feeling much guilt. They had put themselves in a difficult situation. The urge to assist the others was strong. It was just as powerful as the fear they felt. They knew that further attempts to help others could mean the group's demise. Morning was upon them and no resolution in this regard had been reached.

The women were the only ones with clear heads. They had pointed out to the men one important fact. If a rescue was in their future, it could be months just as easily as it could be happening at this very moment, and they would be none the wiser. The group needed to find out what was happening in White Man's Cotton.

The dangers lurking above were too great for all of them to face. They needed to send out a small scouting party. Their only issue was who would go. At this point, they were unable to come to an agreement as to who or how many should go. After more debate and no progress, they drew numbers. All agreed two people would be best for scouting. If something were to happen, the odds with two people working together were much better.

The women picked a number between one and ten. Each of the male adults shouted out a number, one after the other. Three and nine were the magic numbers and the eventual winners were Robert and Lance. Harry, acting as his guardian, insisted that he take Lance's place. For the first time since Lance's arrival in the underground, he felt the need to do for himself.

Looking at Harry with a slight smile on his face and speaking from the heart, he said, "Thanks for being my friend, Harry, but what's fair is fair. It's time I took the bull by the horns. Robert and I will take it from here!"

The two men then headed out. As they made their way through the narrow exit, they knew that the temporary safety of their secret hiding place lessened with each step they took. It was time for them to see exactly what was happening back at the cotton fields.

Avery, Eddie and Randle Hawkins had each selected ten people to be relocated. Several white men, women and all of the remaining children were now on the surface. They all stood directly in front of the main entrance to the underground world. Excluding the children, the slaves were chained together at the ankle. They were beginning their journey to *The Dark Side*, the same boat that provided so many of them with passage to the island in the first place.

The heat from the sun was unbearable. The weak and tired struggled along as their journey towards the boat continued. The adults were forced to walk quickly, while taking small steps to avoid tripping one another. Between the heat and the discomfort caused by the rubbing of metal against skin, they were drained. But the emotional strain was just as overwhelming for each adult. The sounds of children crying as they walked alongside the adults only intensified their pain.

Avery was not one to take defeat easily. He had positioned his men in numerous places throughout the underground with high hopes of living up to his father's expectations. His father's request was to have Robert Lawlor and Lance Forrest included with those being relocated. Once they had escorted and secured this group of slaves on the boat, Avery intended to return to the underground to complete a more thorough search.

The Hawkins brothers were enjoying their walk. They took great pleasure in using their whips every now and then to keep those who strayed in their proper place. The walk was a long one, and combined with the heat, many were affected negatively.

The chain gang had already reached the halfway point in their excursion when Avery received a radio transmission. "Avery, pick up. Your birthday present has come early this year. Your father's surprise package has been spotted heading towards Section 34 and you're not going to believe this, but you're getting two for the price of one."

"Apprehend them straight away and I'll meet you with my parcels up at the main entrance."

"Not going to be quite that easy. Looks like your packages are equipped for a fight. They've obtained weapons somewhere, which would account for the missing brothers. If you want them alive, I'll need back up quickly. Not too sure what their objective is or how long they'll be here."

"Follow them and keep me posted. I'm heading back now with re-enforcements."

Avery motioned for two of his comrades to follow. He then told his brothers to move ahead to the boat and have the slaves secured on board. He advised them that he would join up with them as soon as he could. He and his men ran to the underground.

Robert and Lance had cautiously made their way through several of the sections. With weapons in hand, they were just minutes from Section 34. Both of them were shocked not to have come across a single black man. Each fellow slave they had met told the two men that the masters were plentiful hours earlier, but as time passed, their numbers dwindled. They also learned that several white folks had been taken from the sections and no one knew the reason why.

. . .

Mel had already traveled half way across the Indian Ocean. The view of the water below was beautiful. For the most part, there wasn't so much as a ripple. Glistening speckles, like miniature diamonds, danced over the water. The only disturbance was a school of dolphins, periodically jumping from the water in perfect formation. Mel took a deep breath and released the stress from within.

This was the calm before the storm. Mel stood up. He grabbed a handle connected to a side hatch, specially installed on the Lear Jet for emergency situations. It had been used in the past for situations where white captives had to be disposed of mid flight. When he opened the hatch, a change in air pressure within the interior caused the jet to wrench about. Mel picked up one of the plastic containers and pitched it out of the plane. His eyes focused on the falling object until it vanished. Their scheduled flight would keep them in the air for two more hours before the second container would meet the same fate as its twin had.

. . .

Tyler Collins and her partner, Wade Leaman, had landed at Melbourne Airport. With only their carry-on luggage in hand, they were off and running. They proceeded directly to the next leg of their journey, the Coast Guard Vessel, *Angel White*.

They hailed a taxi and drove to the dockyard. After a few hours they arrived, and upon exiting their vehicle stood in front of the most remarkable ship they had ever seen. Wade pointed to the black and white plaque bearing the ship's name and said to Tyler, "Fitting, don't you think?"

Tyler made no response. Instead, she led the way as they boarded the vessel. When they reached the deck, the ship's captain, several senior Coast Guard officials and multiple other law enforcement agency personnel greeted them. This group had formed one of two teams about to officially launch the search and rescue operation.

Marilyn and Lawrence, accompanied by their team were already aboard one of the several army helicopters assigned to the mission. They had been airborne for several hours, heading out towards the Indian Ocean, completely energized and ready to participate in "Operation Re-coup."

The choppers flew closely together as they continued onwards. Within an hour, the tracking device signals were coming in clear and on the move. Readings had been picked up in two separate locations. In turn, they quickly relayed the information to the Coast Guard Vessel, *Angel White*.

Open discussions ensued with the various teams, as it related to this recent information and it was decided that the two helicopters would split up and each follow a separate tracking device. The remaining choppers and the *Angel White* would all perform different search patterns, covering an area within the two-hundred mile radius of the original signals. Their search would commence on the fringes of the perimeter and gradually work inwards to ensure maximum coverage.

Lance and Robert had made their way to Section 34. Entering their old sleeping quarters very slowly, they found Detective Lynch sitting in the center of the room. He had been gagged, tied up and looked as if he had been beaten severely. The two men ran over to untie the ropes.

The man struggled while Robert and Lance attempted to free him. But it was too late. Voices in the background set the hair on their necks on end. Turning around, they found Avery Hawkins and two of his companions blocking their path.

Robert lifted his gun and fired at them. The bullet missed the evil Hawkins by only centimeters. One of his associates was not as lucky. The man dropped to the ground. The bullet had struck him in the heart, killing the man instantly. Retaliating, the two remaining black men returned fire, not to kill, just to injure.

Robert's shoulder was struck, as was the detective's lower arm. Instinct guided Lance to shoot back. He fired off several rounds, missing his intended targets repeatedly. All of a sudden Lance's gun was empty. Avery stood before him, pressing his gun firmly against Lance's left temple. He muttered, "I could kill you bastards right now, but this is your lucky day. Someone wants you alive. There's been a special request for two of you anyway. I will do my part to keep you alive, however, that's the extent of it. Get to your feet now and drop those guns!"

As the three of them stood, they were ushered hastily from their sleeping quarters, forced to advance up towards the surface. As they reached ground level, the fresh air was both a treat and a shock to their systems. Hurriedly, they were directed down the path, which led to the pier. The heat was sweltering and sweat poured off of them. Lance's two friends, due to their injuries, found the walk brutal. The pace was too fast and Avery wouldn't let up for a second. Anytime one of them stumbled, all three would receive a harsh kick or crack from the whip.

As the journey neared the halfway mark, Avery stopped. He picked up his radio and said, "Have the men leave the cotton fields now. Once the coast is clear, open the valves and start the purification process."

Lance, Robert and the detective wouldn't find out for days what he actually meant by that statement. Their present situation had turned out to be their salvation. Following his radio communication, the three slaves were forced once again to move on. They did so in the scorching heat until the path branched. The section to their right led to the pier, while the one to their left led to the main house.

Avery stood at the fork, not uttering a word. He was deep in thought. After several minutes had passed, Avery reached out and grabbed Lance by the neck, shoving the young man to the left. Robert and John were forced to follow.

No one said a word. They could sense Avery was about to blow his fuse. He began beating and shoving them as they struggled along. In the near distance, they could see the main house and several town-houses.

Once again he stopped the men in their tracks. After delivering a few more blows, Avery had changed his mind. He diverted the three slaves to a small pathway some sixty yards from the main house. Moving quickly, their pace had increased from progressive marching to running. They were forced to maintain this pace all the way down the rough pathway until they entered a small clearing. Situated in the middle of the clearing lay five platforms, each one placed upright at a forty-five degree angle from the ground.

With weapons pointed directly at the three men, they were each ordered to strip down to their underpants. After this, they were forced to lay down, one to a platform, leaving an empty space between each man. Avery and his accomplice firmly secured their bodies to the wooden platforms. Once they had completed tying the men down, Avery stood back and shouted, "Fuck the special requests. You white bastards can slowly burn alive for all I care and if the sun doesn't kill you first, maybe the insects will!"

With this, he headed promptly towards the thick brush. From the corner of his eyes, Lance saw Avery enter an undersized shed. Avery returned carrying a large yellow bottle. Upon closer inspection, Lance noticed that the bottle was filled with a golden-colored liquid.

Avery opened the glass bottle, and removed handfuls of its sticky filling. One after the other, Avery and his men took turns smearing the slave's bodies from top to bottom with the substance. They continued until every single inch of the men's flesh was fully covered.

Once they finished, Avery's partner began licking his fingers clean. Avery's radio crackled, followed by a voice on the other end, "All's clear. Two of our men are still on the missing list. Radios were found at the swimming hole, but no weapons were found. Either Rachel had extra feed or some of our white foes grew brain cells."

"I have a good idea what happened to them and also where the weapons went. I'm looking after the situation now. Go ahead and open the taps. We're heading to the wharf now. I want you to join us there pronto."

"Done."

Just before he left, Avery said, "Not sure why the Catcher or my father wanted either of you bastards alive, but the penance for killing blacks is death. You will pay the price for your criminal actions."

Lance, Robert and John were then left abandoned and bound in the scorching heat. It didn't take long for the wrath of Avery's actions to reveal itself. Multitudes of insects began crawling all over the three men. Some of them were small, while others much larger. The majority of them delivered one hell of a bite.

Lance wasn't quite sure how his two friends were making out. Once those little bastards started walking, sliding and feeding on virtually every inch of his body, Lance's skin came alive and he started losing it. He could actually see his skin move in places from the crawling invaders. He felt as if he was slowly going insane. He was unable to distinguish the actual pain that he felt from the biting, from the itching sensation that came as a result of their movement. The sweetness of the sticky liquid, in combination with the sweat that flowed down their bodies provided a tasty feed for these unwelcome visitors.

SEASCAPE

chapter eighteen

THE commotion from the recent evacuation of specific individuals from the underground, combined with the events and rumors surrounding the undercover detective, and a possible end to the madness, left many restless. The abrupt removal of fellow captives and the absence of all masters eradicated any rules or direction in the underground. Two of the latest arrivals enjoyed their newfound freedom.

Blake Hiscock and Henry Falkner had spent several hours exploring the tunnels and pathways throughout the underground. While lurking quietly, they came across several other men doing the same thing. As they forged onwards, their numbers grew steadily. In total, seventeen people had joined forces with the pair and were each just as eager to fight for their lives if the opportunity presented itself. Too much had happened these past few days. The beatings, the whippings and various other acts, crueler than they'd endured previously had intensified the situation. Added to this fellow slaves actually abducted from their quarters without explanation, but fearing the worse, the underground inhabitants panicked.

The last two stragglers to join the scouting party were women. When the masters began their selection of the underground inhabitants, many, including these women, had scattered in fear of their lives. The unknown terrified them. Their fundamental goal was to find a way to freedom, which gave them a newfound strength.

Members of the group had gathered weapons as they traveled, which they carried with them. From the various work sections they had collected picks, shovels, broken-off wooden handles, rocks, broken glass, and a gun. These folks were determined to stay alive. They knew the time had come to take matters into their own hands.

For many, the time they spent living with fear, suffering, intimidation, and torture at the hands of their black masters was now fading. It had taken the detective's presence and the escape plan he spoke of to motivate them.

Survival had become vengeance. As they made their way around the caverns, they looked for any potential victims. They were entirely out of control.

In their single-mindedness, no one realized the significance of the increased number of rats scurrying about. In each passageway they embarked upon, these ugly creatures were running madly along the crevasses in the rock walls and on the ground.

Several of the men began stabbing or striking out at them. The number of rats had increased so much that the humans had to walk over them, crushing dozens of the vermin.

Each one of the passages they encountered were all beginning to fill with running water. One of the women in the group had slipped and fell face first in the newly acquired water supply. The final plan of the black masters became evident. Standing up hastily, she yelled to the others in a panicked state, "It's salt water! My God, they're flooding the underground!"

Her words terrified them. Men and women alike quickly scattered. The tunnel up ahead branched off into two separate directions and they had to chose which path they'd follow, with no time for consultation with the others.

Henry Falkner had followed one group of individuals into the tunnel, which led to the left. The others had retained enough sense to head in the same direction as the rats were running in. Of the original group of seventeen that had begun the journey, only nine followed the right path.

Henry Falkner's group ended up running until they could run no more and finally reached a dead end. The water quickly engulfed their confined surroundings. Their screams rang out until the water swiftly reached the ceiling, drowning all occupants in the cave.

The surviving members of the original group picked up the pace. They ran as fast as possible through the swiftly moving waters, which were rising higher and higher. The rats began climbing higher up the rock wall edges as they too moved forward. Blake Hiscock was among the men still running through the flowing waters. Unlike Henry, Blake's journey had taken him and the others to a familiar place.

The group had just reached the underground cliffs, which towered high above Rachel's swimming hole. Looking over, they all quickly came to the same conclusion—they had to go in. It was the only choice. The open cavern below had swelled to a monstrous size. It looked as if it could hold an ocean in its entirety.

One by one, the men began their descent. Water followed them. First in trickles, but within seconds, the cliff turned into a massive waterfall.

Jean-Luc and Harry heard the commotion from the safety of their hiding place. Standing up, they ordered the others to head for the escape route and wait there. Faint screams were heard nearby. Shortly thereafter, the thunderous sound of running water was bellowing throughout the safety of their secret hiding place.

Jean-Luc headed for the small opening and peered out. His mouth dropped open. He yelled for Harry to come see what was happening. Once through the entrance, the two were in complete awe.

Lifting their heads, they saw the torrential flow of water down various sections of the great towering cliffs. In sections along the cliff's facing, they also noticed the group of men fighting for their lives amid the flowing water. Jean-Luc and Harry ran out towards the bridge. Rachel was nowhere to be seen. When they reached the other side, the screams were more intense. One after another, the men started falling from the skies. Either they had slipped or fell due to the force of the rushing waters. Only one man was lucky enough to reach the bottom. Blake's feet touched the ground below.

Harry and Jean-Luc turned around to direct Blake towards them and potential safety. Rachel had been directly behind them, dragging a body into the water. In the excitement, neither Harry nor Jean-Luc saw her or even bothered to look for her.

The three men ran back over the bridge. By this time, the water level had increased tremendously and was already at the bridge. Within a minute, each of the men was fighting his way back through the opening.

Once inside, the men rapidly fought their way through the knee-high water towards the cavern, which led to the outside world. Alana, Grace and Adam had been waiting inside the cavern for Harry and Jean-Luc to return. They had no sooner entered the cavern than water gushed in directly behind them.

Harry ordered everyone into the water. Blake followed, not knowing what was next. All swam towards the opposite side of the cavern and when they arrived, they would balance themselves, and wait for the others. Given the fact the water level had already risen over three feet in only minutes, Harry directed them all to prepare for a swim.

One after the other, each person took hold of the safety rope, and then dove under. Harry had ordered the group to hold on to the rope for dear life and to kick their feet for all they were worth. Even though many of them were not very good swimmers, all six of them made it through.

Adam was the hero of the day. He was the courageous little person who led the entire pack through the underwater cave. The others drew on his courage and strength, following the little wonder, doing exactly as he did. As each one emerged from the water on the other side, they spit and choked while they caught their breath. Still holding the rope, they then swam directly to the base of the cliffs. Pulling themselves along the jagged edges, they began seeking a place to come aground.

The closest place they saw was a fair distance away. They knew that they would have to get out of the water as soon as possible. If the waves crashing their bodies against the base of the jagged cliffs didn't kill them first, then it was very likely that hungry sharks would. Gripping the serrated rocks, they continued to drag their way along the bottom of the rugged cliffs.

"Mega Two to *Angel White*, come in please. Mega Two to *Angel White*, come in please."

The Captain of the Coast Guard vessel responded, "*Angel White*, go ahead."

"We have located one of the tracking devices in the water. A member of our SEAL team has just retrieved a plastic container. The tracking device had been placed inside."

"Ten-four Mega Two."

Tyler and Wade had been standing at the Captain's side when the call came in. Both had suspected as much, nonetheless, the news was still devastating. Wade advised the Captain to instruct Mega Two to resume the search for the second device.

Tyler had been waiting impatiently for information pertaining to the various landmasses within their search perimeter. She was monitoring her laptop for plausible transmissions when an e-mail came through from headquarters. It read:

> *"Just received a report from child psychologist, Mary Freedmaine. It seems Melanie Normore and Joseph Kieley are on the mend. The report provides vivid descriptions of underground rooms, adults working hard, abuse, and a monster, a huge reptile that appears to eat people. The children have also stated that, 'a group of evil black men hurt them and their parents.'*
>
> *Headquarter's review of the islands within the search perimeter in general indicated most are uninhabited, however, some affluent socialites used some of the islands for vacation retreats, while fishermen used others. One of the islands in particular was most interesting.*
>
> *The locals in the area call the island, 'Locust.' Apparently it's off-limits and secured heavily. Headquarter's have also discovered it is currently being used to run Salvation's Chemical and Research Facility, which is owned and operated by Thomas Hawkins, a very rich and influential black man. There is currently no criminal activity associated with his name. An extremely interesting point is the island used to be a fully operational mining facility. The coordinates are being transmitted directly to 'Angel White'."*

Excited, Tyler turned to the others shouting, "Bingo! This is it. I feel it in my bones. A transmission is coming through now with the coordinates we need. How far is the island from here, Captain?"

The Captain walked to the monitor to view the coordinates. Standing straight at attention he ordered, "Set coordinates based on this transmission. Estimated time of arrival will be somewhere in the area of an hour and a half. Let's get this vessel moving now!"

The vessel had been moving full steam ahead for roughly an hour when an additional broadcast came in, "Mega Two to *Angel White*, come in please. Mega Two to *Angel White*, come in please."

Mega Two's SEAL Team had located the second tracking device, which had been disposed of in the same manner as the first one. It was now feared that Detective John Lynch was dead. Two of the helicopters were redirected to the island's coordinates. The remaining choppers were ordered to continue the search for any suspicious vessels in the area.

The estimated time of arrival for those traveling by boat and those in the air was approximately the same. They would cross paths on the way. When the distance between the vessel and island lessened, Wade and Tyler began scanning the horizon using a set of high power binoculars, compliments of the Australian Navy.

Suddenly, there was a clamor directly overhead. The roar from rotating helicopter blades had temporarily drowned out most of the sounds on deck. The choppers briefly stabilized themselves high above, acknowledging their presence. After a moment, they flew onwards, only minutes from Locust Island.

The deck crew was preparing to launch several rescue boats. Because of its size, the Coast Guard vessel couldn't successfully dock at the island's pier.

Several crewmembers, along with Wade and Tyler prepared to disembark the *Angel White*. Equipped with radio transmitters, weapons and emergency medical supplies, they led the rescue crafts that were heading towards the island.

Lawrence radioed Tyler. He said, "Send some boats around to the south side of the island immediately. You won't believe this. We have several people in the water who are clinging to the side of the cliffs. The waves are coming in high and they are being battered. Holy Christ, there are women, and, by the looks of it, at least one child in the midst of them. Get a move on, quickly."

Before the transmission had ended, several of the boats veered off to the south side of the island. Wade and Tyler stayed on course, headed for the dock. A second transmission then came in from Lawrence: "Several members of the SEAL team have taken position in the water to assist those stranded while we wait for the rescue boats to arrive. We are now proceeding to do a quick scan of the island itself. Over and out."

The instant the boats reached the wharf, Tyler and Wade led two of the five search teams of six. Each team set out in different directions, all relying on guidance from the helicopters overhead.

Tyler's team headed for the main house. All parties proceeded forward with guns drawn and ready. With the choppers guiding them through the camouflage, Wade led his team to the entrance of the mining shaft.

When Tyler and her team entered the main house it was vacant. Most of the contents of the house had been destroyed. Taking one room at a time, they made their way through the entire house. Another team had started their search through the adjacent row houses. Wade and his team were still making their way towards the mining shaft. All the remaining teams had gone to alternate sites.

One by one, radio reports started filtering in describing the areas and structures the different teams had encountered. The men and women who were involved in the search and rescue operation were totally astonished. From the elaborate set up, to the various torture rooms, to the concealed structures they came across, it was both amazing and terrifying.

One of the rescue teams still on the water radioed that the people in the water had all been pulled to safety. They were being transported back to the Coast Guard vessel for medical treatment and questioning. As their names came in, Tyler recounted the original White Files associated with each of the individuals.

During the return trip to the *Angel White* those rescued recounted much of what had happened to them. They spoke of those captives who had been viciously murdered over the years and others who were presumed dead. Unfortunately, the whereabouts of many more were unknown. It was also estimated that in excess of a hundred people had been trapped underground and were feared drowned. The more information the rescued provided, the grimmer the chance of anyone else turning up alive.

It didn't take long before the search teams realized that those referred to as, "the masters of the island" had fled by boat. This valuable information and a description of the vessel were immediately relayed to the helicopters of the Air Team Mega Force. Armed with a description and the name of the vessel they were seeking, they departed. Once the rescue team secured the survivors in the sick bay aboard the *Angel White,* the Captain radioed the land search team, advising them that they too were heading out to assist Mega Force. Other Coast Guard vessels had been dispatched and were on course for the island at that very moment.

Lawrence was scanning the island from inside the chopper when his mouth suddenly dropped open. He quickly radioed Tyler, "I'm not one-hundred percent sure, but it appears we have three bodies situated on some type of platform not to far from where you are. It's about a hundred yards to the east. There is a small clearing through some huge maple and spruce trees. You can't miss it. We are also going to attempt to set the chopper down in the same clearing. It doesn't look pretty!"

"We're on our way now, Lawrence," Tyler responded.

Suddenly, a cool breeze had replaced the scorching heat that Lance's body had endured for several hours. For a brief moment, it had taken what little breath he had away. He couldn't speak at all; his mouth had gone entirely dry and he felt as if his throat was on fire. Lance's eyes had also swelled completely shut. He could hear voices all around him, but couldn't make out a word of what was being said. He had completely forgotten about Robert and the detective.

The next thing he felt were several hands striking him, all over his body. Lance had thought that the masters had returned and were dishing out more punishment. The pain he felt was a result of the rescue team's efforts. They were attempting to restore life to Lance's mutilated body. They were also relentlessly attempting to remove the unwanted insects that were burrowing into his reddened flesh. Lance's body gave out and he drifted into unconsciousness.

The Captain of *The Dark Side* and his guests had been listening eagerly to the transmissions that were being broadcast during the last few hours. Thomas Hawkins knew that it was only a matter of time before they were captured. *The Dark Side* was a sitting target, somewhere in the middle of the Indian Ocean. Its current cargo was also a tremendously hazardous commodity.

After consulting with the Captain and his sons, Thomas Hawkins ordered, "Dump all the fish bait overboard. Ensure that for each bucket of fish bait thrown over, an equal share of cargo joins it. We cannot afford to have any witnesses. If there are survivors on the island, they will be dealt with later."

The cargo hatch was opened and one white occupant after another was plucked from the hole and thrown over the side of the boat. With each person that went over the railings, a fresh bucket of fish guts and blood followed.

As each person hit the water, two to three shark fins appeared. The slaves sparked a deadly feeding frenzy of the colossal great whites. Those in the water never stood a chance. Their screams went unheard. The lucky ones drowned before they were ripped viciously into pieces.

Only a few people remained in the cargo hold when the sound of chopper blades erupted overhead. Two of the choppers from Mega Force had found their target. Horrified, the chopper ordered, "Cease all activities now or we will open fire! Cease all activities immediately. Turn off your engines and have all hands show themselves on deck!"

Thomas Hawkins and the Captain had standing orders of their own. They told their men to break out the automatic weapons and to open fire on the choppers. The men obliged. Thomas then ordered Eddie to remove the last few white people from the cargo hold. He intended to use them as human shields, hopefully to evade a retaliation of gunfire against them.

When Eddie opened the hatch, he was delighted to find Isabel Snow as one of the white slaves who remained on *The Dark Side*. She looked up at him with revulsion. Pointing his gun at her, he demanded she and the others climb from the hole. She was the first on deck, promptly followed by her twin sister, Irene, and then George Williams. He was still badly injured and had a difficult time climbing up as the boat swayed back and forth.

The choppers withdrew to a safe distance once the gunfire erupted. When the three captives on deck were spotted, one of the choppers initiated a rescue attempt of those still struggling for survival in the lethal waters. The second chopper, while keeping a close watch on *The Dark Side,* called for backup from the Coast Guard and the remaining search and rescue teams.

Once the word was received that *The Dark Side* had been sighted, all available resources were redirected to move in fast.

From high above, two rope ladders were dropped to the sea, dangling from either side of the lone chopper. Mega Force attempted to get some of the people in the water to safety. The helicopter positioned itself directly above the individuals still struggling for their life. This was only partly successful. Of the seven people who managed to climb on to the ladder and out of the sea, three fell from the swaying rope, into the mouths of the sharks below.

Mega Force had received word that the E.T.A. of two Coast Guard vessels in the vicinity was less than an hour. A second warning was then issued to *The Dark Side,* advising them the two Coast Guard vessels would arrive shortly and there was nowhere to run.

Their time was running out. Thomas Hawkins decided it was time to finish up. He ordered his men to throw the remaining white captives into the sea with the others. He then ordered the Captain to move his vessel at full throttle. He was intent on making a run for it.

Eddie Hawkins had grabbed Isabel Snow by the hair and forcefully dragged the young woman to the side of the boat. Some of the other men on deck grabbed her sister, Irene, and George Williams. George was the first to be dumped over the side, then Irene.

Eddie Hawkins held on to Isabel's neck, forcing her head up. Looking at her, he planted a long wet kiss on her lips. She noticed her aggressor had a pocketknife strapped to his belt. She returned his attentions with feigned interest. Gently grabbing the man's genitals, she briskly rubbed him with her left hand. The man's penis grew. She pressed her lips to his, sticking her moist tongue into his mouth. Turning to nibble on his ear, she whispered softly to the black man, "I so enjoyed your passion in the past."

Eddie's fierce machismo ended up betraying him. Using her free hand, Isabel Snow removed the man's pocketknife from his belt. She tilted her neck back and looked Eddie in the eyes. She then said to him in a sweet tenderly voice, "It's time to say goodbye, you black bastard!"

His pupils widened. Isabel Snow stabbed the black man in the balls with all her strength. Holding on to his body securely, she forced herself backward over the side of the boat, hauling the bleeding man with her. No one on board had time to react. Most of them didn't even realize what had happened.

George Williams and Irene Snow were thrown overboard. They too were at the mercy of the ocean, praying help would make its way to them in time. Shark fins surrounded them. They witnessed from a distance the devastation that occurred to the others that were tossed into the ocean.

The instant Irene witnessed her sister falling to the water she swam towards her. George was unable to move. He was petrified, watching fins moving in all around him. He was so traumatized, he practically overlooked the rope ladder that suddenly appeared within feet of his head.

When Isabel and Eddie hit the water, they came to within inches of being chopped up from the rotating blades of the ship. By the time the guards had alerted the Captain and Thomas Hawkins as to what had happened, the vessel had moved too far away to provide immediate assistance.

Thomas Hawkins was outraged. The Captain was ordered to drop the motorized life raft into the water and retrieve Eddie without delay. He swore that if anything should happen to his son, there would be hell to pay. The men moved quickly, freeing the life raft from its secured position. Time was of the essence.

Motionless, Isabel Snow watched the chaos unfold. Her sister swam towards her, shark fins suddenly rose from the water and her tormentor was just a few feet away.

George Williams reached out with his one good arm in a frantic attempt to grip the rope ladder. A wave of water splashed into his eyes. Being temporarily blinded from the stinging salt water, he initially didn't feel anything as a shark attacked him. His arm was severed, cutting off any hope for the veteran officer's survival. Instantly, several other sharks had moved in to feed. One after another, slashing their massive bodies from side to side, they fought each other, hacking pieces of human flesh and bone from the man's body. It was over quickly.

Irene arrived at her sister's side as the rescue helicopter hovered above them. The wind from the chopper blades caused the rope ladders on either side to become entangled. The pilot was instructed to bring the helicopter down so that one ladder would touch the water. The lower the chopper went, the windier it became for the three people still besieged in the water.

Irene held her sister tightly with one arm as she reached for the ladder. Obtaining a firm grip, she began to pull herself up, still holding onto her sister. As soon as the bulk of her body was out of the water, she tugged on her sibling, pulling her along. Both girls could clearly see the sharks looming in the ocean below them. Irene was intent on getting them out alive, away from the jaws of the menacing sharks.

While dangling five-feet above the ocean, Isabel saw Eddie Hawkins, still in the water, waving to an approaching boat. *The Dark Side's* rescue boat was gaining ground on him and within seconds of pulling the man out. One of the men from the chopper had descended the rope to where the girls were. He was in the process of securing Irene to a cable so she could be hoisted up.

While Irene was preoccupied with her rescuer, Isabel anxiously watched the action below. It gradually appeared to her that although many sharks were zoning in on the black man, the rescue boat had almost reached him.

Sick to her stomach, she watched as one of the fierce sharks swam closer to Eddie. It was too close. The rescue boat was also within feet of its target.

In a last ditch effort for justice, Isabel Snow pulled herself away from her twin. She threw herself free from the rope ladder and dove towards the black man. The cable above her tightened and her sister's body moved upwards at the same instant hers flew down. Irene's chilling screams echoed across the ocean as she watched in horror as her twin landed with a solid clout on Eddie's head. The force of the hit rendered her unconscious and sent them both under water. Eddie Hawkins had gotten what Isabel Snow had deemed he so deserved.

Wildly hysterical, Irene twisted and kicked out as she continued to dangle from high above.

The rescuers from *The Dark Side* stood by, absolutely powerless. They had failed in their rescue attempt by mere seconds. They too helplessly watched as swarms of the deadly fish now arrived, finishing off Eddie and his murderess.

Thomas Hawkins and his family were devastated. He was distraught with his loss, but anger quickly took over. Thomas ordered all his men to resume firing, to take out the choppers, and to fight to the bitter end. He was out for revenge and had no intention of giving up.

Two of Australia's biggest Coast Guard vessels arrived, but *The Dark Side* was still not willing to surrender. The standoff lasted for hours. Flanked, out-manned, out-gunned, and with nowhere to escape to, *The Dark Side* was finally overtaken. Many of those who survived were seriously wounded; Thomas Hawkins, his wife, Rita, and his two surviving sons were airlifted to Melbourne for immediate medical treatment.

. . .

It was the longest running and ultimately the most devastating of court cases ever to hit the United States of America. Several years had elapsed since White Man's Cotton was closed, but the memories were as vivid for the survivors as if it were only days ago. Witness after witness kept disappearing, never to be seen again. Between the postponements, tainted jurors, appeals, riots, false confessions, falsified statements, and planted evidence, it seemed as if the guilty would never come to trial.

Each of the survivors provided extensive testimony for the prosecution. Each and every detail of their lives and their abduction to White Man's Cotton became public knowledge. In addition, they also endured an excruciating cross-examination process. Others also came forth to provide testimony on behalf of the prosecution, including the gardener, Oral Davis, and the vagrant, Homer. Oral provided many of the missing pieces the prosecutors needed. Homer verified the Board of Directors' meeting place and identified several of the Board Members. The prosecution had a solid case.

Thomas Hawkins and each member of his family refused to speak at their trials. Completely expressionless, they sat in the courtroom day after day. Their team of attorneys ensured their message was delivered loud and clear. They wanted the world to know that the time came for them to do what the law had failed to do, deliver their own sentences to those who continue to get away with injustices against members of the black race.

This trial had sparked one of the biggest news frenzies of the decade. The media used the tragic events that came to light during the trial not only to inform the public but also to bolster their stations' ratings. Special guests and various experts appeared in defense of both sides. The way in which the various news stations reported the events had a direct impact on how the global public perceived racial differences and crime itself. An overwhelming hatred was brewing, particularly in America.

Parents were extra cautious over whom their children could associate with and where they were permitted to go. Adults, not normally concerned with racial issues, were starting to think twice over the company they kept. Things were deteriorating rapidly.

Lance Forrest was the one survivor of White Man's Cotton who was recognized instantly and had become a household name. During the trial, he was repeatedly called to the witness stand for the prosecution, and had provided testimony against each member of the Hawkins family. The prosecution considered him to be their prize witness, and the media branded him a hero. Lance had been the only one from the days of White Man's Cotton who was sent to the island in error. He was seen as a non-partisan witness, someone without prejudice against blacks, a man of honor who had been victimized brutally at the hands of Thomas Hawkins and his brood.

In actuality, Lance felt like a man whose life had moved from island captivity to land incarceration. Harry, Robert, Jean-Luc, and several others were also in the same predicament. They had all been placed in witness protection. Daily, armed FBI officials escorted them to the court proceedings. Their lives were no longer their own. They had lost their true identities and lived each day in fear of reprisal. Their only contact with the outside world was through their protectors and the news media. The majority of the survivors watching the events unfold found it alarming.

Lance's main contact was Robert Lawlor. He and Lance had been roomed in one safe house while Harry and Jean-Luc had been segregated in another. Witnesses had been set up in various locations in groups of two, and no one party was privy to another's location. The rationale was obvious. If a pair was discovered and eliminated, it would be considered a slight blow to the prosecution's case. However, others would remain to testify. If the witnesses were all together and discovered, the case for the prosecution could be affected dramatically.

Robert and Lance had been watching the late night news and discussing its contents in comparison to the actual court hearing. The media's portrayal of the events was an exaggeration of how things really were. The media blamed White Man's Cotton for pretty much every cataclysm that occurred during the course of the trial. Expert panelists often substantiated their claims.

Lance was not very popular amongst the survivors of the island. They would not be satisfied with anything less than the death penalty for those charged. This, in Lance's opinion, would solve nothing.

The official court proceedings had finally ended. The full story had been told. Each member of the Hawkins family had been found guilty on varying counts of first-degree murder. Rita Hawkins was the one and only exception. She had been found guilty of being an accessory to the crimes.

The next few days were to be spent with the different parties making pleas to the judge, prior to final sentencing. Lance requested an opportunity to address the court, prior to sentencing. His closest acquaintances had all asked that he not speak to the court, but in his heart and soul he knew he had to.

As Lance was led to the front of the crowded courtroom, he could see several familiar faces, some with faint friendly smiles, others glaring.

Before speaking, he looked first at the accused and then at the remaining court occupants.

The judge instructed him to begin.

"This has been a very difficult journey for me. I have gone through countless days and nights feeling on the edge of insanity. The frightening thing is it has nothing to do with the days I spent in captivity. These feelings have evolved since being rescued. The physical scars I bear and the severe emotional trauma I experienced on the island, in my own mind, are minor to what I am currently living with. I have had several years to mull over what happened at White Man's Cotton and strongly feel the need to put closure to this part of my life. I want a fresh start, a brand new beginning. Thomas Hawkins and his family are not the only ones who have done an injustice against me. Society in general has failed. History has repeated itself, only this time the players have changed. We are all living in a world of hate. Hate only leads to more hate. It's like pouring gas on a fire. It spreads."

Lance gulped his water before proceeding, "The hate crimes that occurred on the island are a mirror of the days of slavery for blacks, the days when white people considered themselves superior. What transpired on the island is nothing more than retaliation against white people who still harbor hatred for the non-white members of our society. This is history repeating itself, and it will never stop until the human race takes a step back and has a long hard look at what is going on around them. This trial has fueled hate crimes all over the world. Friends have turned into enemies. The bottom line is, a stand has to be taken. I am here today before you all and I hope to use the media just as they have used us, as a means to get a message across. To tell it from my perspective, my words, and I hope it's telecast exactly as I say it. I am the only one still alive from our ordeal that fits into a separate category than the others, so you can be sure I don't harbor the same resentments as they do. I have always believed we were all put on this earth as equals. Sure, we all have differences, but we are all humans."

He paused a second time, taking a deep breath, and then looked at the judge and continued, "I implore you, think about what I have said. You have the power to determine whether or not the death penalty is the punishment to be meted out for the crimes committed against the victims of White Man's Cotton. I stand by what I say without hesitation. I also know in my heart that the guilty parties must be punished, but I plead the court to hand out consecutive life sentences without any possibility of parole. Look at what is happening around us. We have opposing members of our society calling for the death penalty. The crime rate has increased considerably all over the world. Everyone is watching the outcome of this trial. Racial crimes are also on the rise. If these individuals are put to death, it won't stop here. I fear society will regress even further. Punish the guilty parties by putting them away for life. Too many have died both on the island and since that time. The lives that have already been lost have drastically affected both races. Put a stop to it now. Send them away for good. Let them ponder over their ways and the life they have led. I am one of the victims here. I will never rest. My life will never be mine knowing I have their deaths on my conscience. I beg you to do the right thing and allow me to get on with my life and let the public at large to get on with theirs. Please don't add any more fuel to the rapidly burning flames. Thank you."

After the statement, Lance was ushered from the courtroom. As he left, the Hawkins' family members seemed to be in shock. The drive back to the safe house was very quiet. Lance's escorts didn't speak, nor did Robert. They would spend the next few days in protective custody awaiting the judge's final decision.

Days turned into weeks. It was obvious that the judge's decision was a difficult one. After all, the final ruling could have a strong influence on society's future direction.

Finally, one morning Lance and Robert were awoken to the sound of an agent shouting for them to get up, as the judge's decision had been made and they were due in court. Lance had no intention of going to the courthouse. He had chosen to keep his distance. Robert on the other hand had decided he wanted to be there.

Media had gathered at the courthouse to broadcast the judge's decision. His face was broadcast all over the globe as he read aloud his final decision to each male member of the Hawkins family, "Death by lethal injection."

Rita Hawkins was the one exception. She had been sentenced to consecutive life sentences for her role and indirect association in the criminal activities of White Man's Cotton.

Cheers of joy and happiness had erupted throughout the courthouse, while the picture outside was very different. Riot police were attempting to disperse clashes between protesters. The crowds were going crazy. It was not a safe place to be.

Later that day, Harry and Jean-Luc were permitted to visit Robert and Lance at their safe house. Now that the trial had finally ended, soon they would each be going their separate ways. This night would be a time for friendship and celebration. Although Lance's friends strongly disagreed with his viewpoint, they were still his friends. They had all made a pact to keep their friendship and had agreed to disagree to maintain that bond.

The four men drank one drink after another. Before they knew it, it was 3:00 a.m. and they were starving. One of the agents on duty had made arrangements to have pizza delivered. While waiting for the food to arrive, Lance and his friends continued to drink. A long time had passed and it seemed like it was taking forever for the pizza to arrive.

All of a sudden, there was a knock at the front door. After accepting the pizza, the agents returned to the living room and within minutes the pizza was devoured with everybody's help. The only evidence that remained was the two grease-stained boxes lying in the center of the coffee table.

The music was loud as the partying continued. Lance, who consumed more than his fair share of liquor, passed out shortly after eating.

Later that morning Lance awoke. His head was throbbing and as he tilted his head down, he noticed a small river of dried blood had formed on his upper chest. It startled him so much that he promptly jumped to his feet. At first, he was very dizzy and weak. He reached out and grabbed the side of a coffee table for balance. As he looked around the room, there were bodies lying everywhere. At first he thought he would have a heart attack, until his screams sent movement through each of the people lying on the floor.

One after another each of the men in the room stood up. They were desperately hung over, too much so for the amount of booze they'd drank. It didn't take them long to figure out that they had been drugged. In the confusion, Lance completely forgot about the dried blood. Robert, however, brought it to his attention. There was some sort of drawing on Lance's chest. Upon closer inspection, they discovered that he'd been tattooed. It was a black baby wearing a white diaper.

Someone had entered the room and completed the tattoo after they'd passed out. In the middle of the coffee table sat a black envelope with a white emblem as a seal. "Lance Forrest" was engraved on the front of the envelope in large, bold white letters. Lance reached down and picked up the envelope. He began to shake rapidly. It was at that point he realized that he could never disappear; they would always find him.

As Lance removed the letter from inside the envelope and opened it up, he was shocked. The words written inside had taken him completely off guard:

> "Mr. Forrest,
>
> You have taken a big chance in voicing your concerns to the outside world and you have upset many people. One of the many duties I have left to perform before my time comes is the granting of serenity to you. You have been given the symbol of freedom for my people. My followers will never see harm come to you. You are free to live your life out to its fullest. You are free to go."

One by one the others read the letter. No sooner had they finished, than Lance grabbed his jacket and proceeded to the front door.

One of the agents attempted to stop him, but Lance looked at him and the others and said, "I told you it would never end. It doesn't make a difference where we go and what identities we take on. Thomas Hawkins and his associates are powerful people. According to this letter, they will not bother me again, but even if it were a direct threat against me, there is nowhere to run. There is no safe house. There will be no place on the face of this earth where any of us can hide. I've had enough, folks. I intend to return to a normal life and whatever happens, happens. I wish you all the best and I hope things work out for each of you."

Lance left the safe house and went outside. Standing on the sidewalk he hailed the first cab that drove by. The minute he stepped inside the vehicle, he noticed Robert and the others running outside. Lance instructed the driver to move on. His friends in the background continued to grow smaller the further Lance went.

. . .

Six months have passed since the day Lance Forrest had left the others behind. Every now and then he hears from an FBI representative. They tell him that Harry Barbour, Robert Lawlor, Jean-Luc LeClaire, Alana Normore, Grace Kieley, and the children are all doing fine.

Less than one day remains before the execution of Thomas Hawkins and his sons is to take place. The latest reports indicate that the three men were currently on their way to a new destination pending the execution. Due to the ongoing riots and fighting that erupts in every city they end up in, the Hawkins men are moved regularly.

Lance picked up his coffee and went to the front door to grab the morning paper. It was a windy yet beautiful spring day. Multicolored leaves were blowing about everywhere. Mother Nature's colors blended so well together. It's such a shame the rest of the world didn't catch on.

As Lance looked at the morning paper, chills ran up and down his spine. The headline on the front page had been crossed out with a black marker. Thomas Hawkins and his sons had been the lead story. Next to a color picture, the original headline read:

"Death by Execution Has Finally Arrived."

Above the scribbled out words, written in that same black marker, were the words:

"Death by Execution Will Never Arrive."

Lance dropped his coffee mug and the morning paper and ran back into the house. The morning news was on. His mouth sagged. A reporter for CNN news was describing a collapsed bridge and the four vehicles that crashed into the river below. The vehicles contained Thomas Hawkins, his sons and their police escorts.

The female reporter closed her story by saying, "As of 10:00 a.m. Eastern Time, no bodies have yet been recovered. Divers have been brought in and the search continues. We will keep you posted as information becomes available on this latest development in the story of White Man's Cotton."